THE SIN OF ABI

ÉMILE ZOLA was born in Paris in 184
and his French wife. He grew up in Ai.
friends with Paul Cézanne. After an undistinguished school career
and a brief period of dire poverty in Paris, Zola joined the newly
founded publishing firm of Hachette, which he left in 1866 to live by
his pen. He had already published a novel and his first collection of
short stories. Other novels and stories followed, until in 1871 Zola
published the first volume of his Rougon-Macquart series, with the
subtitle *Histoire naturelle et sociale d'une famille sous le Second Empire*,
in which he sets out to illustrate the influence of heredity and environment on a wide range of characters and milieus. However, it was
not until 1877 that his novel *L'Assommoir*, a study of alcoholism in
the working classes, brought him wealth and fame. The last of the
Rougon-Macquart series appeared in 1893 and his subsequent writing was far less successful, although he achieved fame of a different
sort in his vigorous and influential intervention in the Dreyfus case.
His marriage in 1870 had remained childless, but his extremely happy
liaison in later life with Jeanne Rozerot, initially one of his domestic
servants, gave him a son and a daughter. He died in 1902.

VALERIE MINOGUE is an Emeritus Professor of French of the
University of Wales, Swansea. She is a co-founding editor, with Brian
Nelson, of *Romance Studies*, and edited the journal in various capaci-
ties from 1982 to 2004. She has published widely in nineteenth- and
twentieth-century French literature, including critical studies of
Proust's *Du côté de chez Swann*, Zola's *L'Assommoir*, and the novels of
Nathalie Sarraute; she co-edited the Pléiade edition of Sarraute's
works. She has been President of the London Émile Zola Society
since 2005. She co-edited with Patrick Pollard *Visages de la Provence*.
Zola, Cézanne, Giono: Études du colloque d'Aix 19–21 Oct 2007 (2008)
and *Rethinking the Real: Fiction, Art and Theatre in the time of Émile
Zola* (2014). She is co-editor of the *Émile Zola Society Bulletin* since
2014. She was made *Officier dans l'Ordre des Palmes Académiques*
in 2012.

OXFORD WORLD'S CLASSICS

*For over 100 years Oxford World's Classics have brought
readers closer to the world's great literature. Now with over 700
titles—from the 4,000-year-old myths of Mesopotamia to the
twentieth century's greatest novels—the series makes available
lesser-known as well as celebrated writing.*

*The pocket-sized hardbacks of the early years contained
introductions by Virginia Woolf, T. S. Eliot, Graham Greene,
and other literary figures which enriched the experience of reading.
Today the series is recognized for its fine scholarship and
reliability in texts that span world literature, drama and poetry,
religion, philosophy and politics. Each edition includes perceptive
commentary and essential background information to meet the
changing needs of readers.*

OXFORD WORLD'S CLASSICS

ÉMILE ZOLA

The Sin of Abbé Mouret

Translated with an Introduction and Notes by
VALERIE MINOGUE

OXFORD
UNIVERSITY PRESS

OXFORD

UNIVERSITY PRESS

Great Clarendon Street, Oxford, OX2 6DP
United Kingdom

Oxford University Press is a department of the University of Oxford.
It furthers the University's objective of excellence in research, scholarship,
and education by publishing worldwide. Oxford is a registered trade mark of
Oxford University Press in the UK and in certain other countries

Published in the United States of America by Oxford University Press
198 Madison Avenue, New York, NY 10016, United States of America

British Library Cataloguing in Publication Data

Data available

Library of Congress Control Number: 2016952430

ISBN 978-0-19-873663-9

Printed and bound in Great Britain by Clays Ltd, Elcograf S.p.A.

CONTENTS

INTRODUCTION

Readers who do not wish to learn details of the plot may prefer to read the Introduction as an Afterword

THE SIN OF ABBÉ MOURET is the fifth of Zola's twenty Rougon-Macquart novels. It is less tied in to the history of the time than the other nineteen, being focused on one individual, a priest in love, torn between the biddings of Nature and the forbiddings of the Church. Zola had the idea of writing a 'priest-novel', as he called it, even at the start of the Rougon-Macquart series, and this developed into two novels. One, *The Conquest of Plassans*, is the fourth and perhaps the most obviously anticlerical novel in the cycle. It exposes, through the machinations of the iniquitous Abbé Faujas, the political and social dimensions of the authority-charged role of the priest. The other was *The Sin of Abbé Mouret*, an almost direct, though free-standing, sequel to the previous novel.

The Sin of Abbé Mouret was published in Paris on 27 March 1875, and ran to four editions that same year—the first of Zola's novels to meet with such early success. Zola was no doubt becoming known to the public and the title had enough of a 'sensational' flavour to make it very saleable. The priest in love had been the subject of a number of popular novels, some of which Zola had reviewed.[1] Reception of this fifth novel was very mixed. The idyll in the park was frequently admired, but also censured for excessive quantities of description. Some regarded the entire novel as grossly immoral. A few, like Taine, Huysmans, Mallarmé, and Maupassant, recognized the poetic quality of the novel and saw it as a long and magnificent love poem.

Naturalism

The subtitle of the Rougon-Macquart cycle is *The Natural and Social History of a Family in the Second Empire*. Zola had dubbed his brand

---

[1] For instance, Abbé Jean-Hippolyte Michou, *Le Maudit* (1865); Alfred Assollant, *La Confession de l'Abbé Passereau* (1869); Ernest Daudet, *Le Missionnaire* (1869); Hector Malot, *Un curé de province* (1872).

of realism 'naturalism' and styled himself a 'naturalist'. As a naturalist, Zola would base his 'natural history' on genetic and physiological characteristics, while the 'social history', though focused on one family, would, like Balzac's *Comédie humaine*, encompass a vast range of French society. Starting in the fictional town of Plassans, based on Aix-en-Provence where Zola spent the early years of his life, the Rougon-Macquart novels follow the family from Louis-Napoleon's *coup d'état* in December 1851, which founded the Second Empire, right through to the ignominious end of the Empire at Sedan in 1870, related in *The Débacle*. Influenced by the work of the philosopher and critic Hippolyte Taine, whom he had dubbed 'the naturalist of the moral world', Zola based his treatment of the family on three factors emphasized by Taine: *race*, the genetic and cultural heritage; *milieu*, the political and social environment; and *moment*, the contemporary historical background.

The 1871 preface to *The Fortune of the Rougons* (*La Fortune des Rougons*), the first volume in the Rougon-Macquart cycle, effectively launched Zola's 'naturalism'. His interest in the scientific discoveries and theories of the age led him to stress the scientific character of his work, presenting the evolution of the Rougon-Macquart family in quasi-Darwinian terms, and emphasizing observation, scientific documentation, and realist representation. This led to a misleading image of the novelist as an unimaginative note-taker and compiler of documents. Later, *The Experimental Novel* (1880), in which Zola applied the experimental methodology of Claude Bernard's *Introduction to the Study of Experimental Medicine* (1865) to the novel, reinforced that image. Zola seemed to be endowing the novel with scientific authority. But Zola well knew and fully acknowledged that the 'results' of the 'experimental novelist' were not comparable to those obtained by the scientist in the laboratory. On the other hand, if the writer presented his characters accurately in carefully studied situations, it should be possible to create at least plausible 'results' not at variance with contemporary scientific knowledge. Zola so successfully imposed on the public perception the 'naturalist' brand name that for far too long it screened out much of the real range, character, and quality of his work, which frequently elbows its way through the constraints of naturalism, sometimes so thoroughly as to subvert the naturalist programme. *The Sin of Abbé Mouret* is perhaps particularly subversive.

Study of contemporary scientific work[2] had provided Zola not only with ideas but also with a discipline that he applied to his writing. His fiction must be securely grounded in observed reality, and it would respect and indeed draw on available scientific data—from the laws of heredity to recent work on psychopathology and physiology. Such studies indeed often provided a sort of repertoire of 'case studies' that could be used in the novels. Further, the environment, circumstances, and activities of the characters would be accurately represented, whether dealing with the political machinations that followed the *coup d'état* of 1851, as in *The Fortune of the Rougons*, or the property speculation accompanying the Haussmannization of Paris in *The Kill*. For his 'priest novel', Zola would provide the necessary grounding with a huge amount of preparation. He studied the Bible, the Catholic Missal, and the methods and teachings of the seminaries. He went to Mass and made detailed notes on clerical dress and accessories, and the whole complicated choreography of the ritual. He read *L'Imitation de Jésus-Christ*, the fifteenth-century Catholic devotional book generally attributed to Thomas à Kempis, and the accounts of saints and martyrs that were part of the education of would-be priests. He read the Spanish Jesuits on the cult of Mary, as well as general works on the Church and the priesthood. Besides, Zola had reviewed a number of novels on this subject, and could plunder them for useful details. For the illness of Serge Mouret, he drew on his own illness and convalescence, which he described in his *Journal d'un convalescent*.[3] For the plants of the Paradou, he studied horticultural catalogues and visited horticultural exhibitions to see for himself the flowers he would describe so vividly. For the park of the Paradou, he drew on memories of the domaine de Galice, west of Aix, where he had roamed in his youth with Baille and Cézanne.[4] He describes the domaine in an essay of 1869: a chateau built in the reign of Louis XV abandoned for over a century, its great empty rooms littered with plaster, broken statues in the park, and traces of the former garden's

[2] Darwin's *The Origin of Species* (published as *De l'origine des espèces*, in 1859), Prosper Lucas's *Traité philosophique et physiologique de l'hérédité naturelle* (1847–50), Letourneau's *Physiologie des passions* (1868), among others.

[3] Included in the dossier of Sophie Guermès's Livre de poche, *La Faute de l'abbé Mouret* (Paris, 1998).

[4] Jean-Baptistin Baille (1841–1918), friend of both Zola and Cézanne since their schooldays in Aix-en-Provence. He later became a professor of optics and acoustics at the École de Physique et de Chimie in Paris.

lanes and paths, fountains and lawns still faintly visible. It reads like
a preview of the Paradou.

Zola had always been aware that reality is subject to transformation
by the eye of the beholder, and that such transformations, as he wrote
to his friend Valabrègue in 1864, create the work of art. It is no
surprise then that thorough and detailed as Zola's observation and
research were, they are constantly overtaken by metaphor and ana-
logy even in his notebooks. In the very act of seeing, each detail
becomes expressive. Zola might well have said, along with Baudelaire:
'Tout pour moi devient allégorie' ('For me everything becomes alle-
gory').[5] The theorizing Zola is overtaken by the creator, and the
experimental scientist by an innovative, experimental novelist; the
note-taker yields to the poet, and the realist to the imaginative painter
of visions.

Science, after all, was not the only powerful factor in the shaping of
Zola's aesthetic; another was contemporary art, its theorizing and its
practices. Along with his childhood friend Cézanne, Zola was a frequent visitor to the studios of the painters Baudelaire termed 'the
painters of modern life', and he became closely associated with the
Impressionists. As a journalist and art critic, he vigorously defended
Manet, and supported other painters of the time, like Cézanne, Degas,
and Monet. He dubbed the Impressionists 'naturalists': naturalists in
their vigour, their discarding of the shackles of convention, and their
direct engagement with contemporary life in all its variety and modernity. Not only was their subject matter new, but so also was their style
of painting, and so it was with Zola, who not only dealt with modern
subjects like railways and department stores, but dealt with them in
a modern, indeed modernist, way. The subject matter of *The Sin of
Abbé Mouret*, the priest and the Catholic Church, is scarcely a modern subject, but the treatment of the subject, and Zola's use of physiological and psychological studies to depict hysteria and hallucination
in a manner that often seems to anticipate Freud, can be seen to be
modern.

Serge Mouret is not the only priest in the Rougon-Macquart series;
there are others, like the obstructive bishop Monseigneur Hautecœur
in *The Dream*, the grossly insensitive Abbé Ranvier in *Germinal*, and
the ruthless Faujas of *The Conquest of Plassans*. The priests in Zola's

---

[5] In the poem 'Le Cygne', in *Les Fleurs du mal*.

five *Portraits of Priests*⁶ written at roughly the time of *The Sin of Abbé Mouret*, are all devoted to their own worldly interests, with one exception, and that one finally abandons the Church to seek truth elsewhere. In the novels that followed the Rougon-Macquart cycle, the *Three Cities* and the *Four Gospels*, the best of Zola's priests turn away from the Church and become parents and reformers rather than priests.

Zola regarded the rule of celibacy as unnatural, and a cause of deep harm to the individual psychology in terms of neurosis and hysteria, and also to society at large. Celibacy was particularly undesirable at a time when there was serious concern in France about the declining birth rate, which was seen to be threatening the development of the nation, as is clear from parliamentary reports and sociological studies of the time. Zola addressed the subject himself in an article for the *Figaro* on *Dépopulation*, in which he condemns the exaltation of virginity when fertility is the preferable option, and deplores the fashionable notion that large families are socially undesirable. Zola's last novels glorify fecundity and propose a new religion of science and justice, freed from dogma.

Heredity, Characters, Milieu

The principal character of this novel, Serge Mouret, first appears in *The Conquest of Plassans* as a young man of 17. He is rather serious, gentle, kind to his mentally retarded sister, and of a religious disposition. He becomes a great favourite of the relentlessly manipulative Abbé Faujas, who is, disastrously, a lodger in the Mouret family home. Serge's mother, more and more obsessed with religion, becomes more and more obsessed with Faujas, who brutally rejects her in terms that anticipate the misogynistic tirades of Archangias in the novel that follows. Serge had decided to become a priest, and the novel ends with his being briefly called back from the seminary to his dying mother.

Serge links both sides of the Rougon-Macquart family: a Rougon through his mother Marthe Mouret (née Rougon), and a Macquart through his father François Mouret, son of Ursule Mouret (née Macquart). He is the great-grandson of Adélaïde Fouque ('Tante Dide'), the founding mother of the Rougons through her marriage to

---

⁶ The text of *Portraits de prêtres* was published in Russia in 1877. French version included in Roger Ripoll (ed.), *Émile Zola: Contes et nouvelles* (Paris: Gallimard, 1976), 982–1009.

the peasant gardener Rougon, by whom she had a son, Pierre, and the
Macquarts through her liaison with the drunkard smuggler Macquart,
by whom she had two children, Antoine and Ursule. She suffered from
nervous instability, and was prone to bouts of hysteria; she ends her
days in the asylum at Les Tulettes. The shadow of Les Tulettes, and
what Zola terms the *lésion* (flaw) or *fêlure* (defect) of Tante Dide hangs
over all the members of the family. Serge's parents are both said to be
very like Tante Dide. Marthe suffers hysterical fits, and her husband
will go mad. Serge's ambitious elder brother, Octave (*The Ladies'
Paradise* and *Pot Luck*), seems more Rougon than Macquart. Serge
and his sister Désirée belong to what Dr Pascal calls 'the tail-end of
the tribe, the final degeneration'. The physically frail Serge, with his
tendency to religious mysticism, takes after his mother, while Désirée,
physically strong and healthy, is mentally retarded. In Zola's preparatory notes Serge Mouret is described as a weakling, predestined to the
priesthood by his blood, his race, and the education that neuters him.
He will be the main protagonist in what Zola described as 'the great
struggle between nature and religion' in his 1896 list of projected
novels for the Rougon-Macquart cycle.

We meet the other characters in Book One in the remote village
of Les Artaud to which Abbé Mouret has, at his own request, been
appointed. We learn that after the death of his parents, he gave his
inheritance to his elder brother Octave, and took charge of his mentally retarded sister, Désirée. He chose to be in a place cut off from the
world, where nothing would distract him from his devotions. Book
Two is set in the Paradou, a quasi-Garden of Eden, in which Serge
and Albine will play—tragically—Adam and Eve. Book Three returns
to the church and Les Artaud. The three books are like the three acts
of a tragedy.

The people of Les Artaud are all one family, all called Artaud, and
distinguished only by nicknames. The whole tribe, much like the
Rougon-Macquart family, comes from one source. With incest and
promiscuity it has spread like the brambles that cover the rocky hillsides. Among the Artauds some individual figures, like Bambousse,
the ever-complaining Mother Brichet, or the Rosalie and Fortuné
couple, add lively interest to the novel, and at the same time shed light
on the life of the rural populace of France at that time: their poverty,
their hard life, and their attitude to the Church. Religion is largely
neglected, save for the traditional rituals of birth, marriage, and death,

and a few associated customs. The day's work is all-important and everything has to be fitted around it, so the marriage of Rosalie and Fortuné takes place before sun-up, much to the disgust of La Teuse, to avoid losing any of the day's pay.

There is little concern with morality. Rosalie's unmarried pregnancy does not bother her father, but the prospect of losing her in marriage to the penniless Fortuné certainly upsets him. She is a valuable commodity, as good a worker as any man, and if he has to part with her, he expects to be paid, as he would for a sack of corn. Each of the characters in this milieu has a specific role and La Teuse, the housekeeper in the presbytery, is the sensible, practical voice of rustic reasonableness. Against the background of mystical excesses, hallucinations, and an idealized landscape of love, she helps to maintain the solid 'reality' of the naturalist, that coexists and alternates with the imaginative exuberance of the poet. She not only does 'God's housework' in the church, but also, in her rough and ready way, looks after the abbé. She tries to curb the excesses of this young priest who denies all his physical needs to concentrate on his soul, and she shows a motherly affection for his sister, Désirée, the girl of 22 with the mind of a 10-year-old. La Teuse, like Zola, finds celibacy unnatural. Commenting on Abbé Caffin, the previous incumbent, sent to Les Artaud after breaking his vows, she remarks: 'I really don't understand how people can blame a priest so much, when he strays from the path' (p. 262), and although she has no liking for Albine, she will later tell a scandalized Archangias that if Albine 'represents the health of Monsieur le Curé... she can come whenever she likes, at any hour of the day or night. I'd lock them up together, if that's what they want' (p. 262).

Archangias, the other religious in Les Artaud, belongs to the order of the Lasallian Christian Brothers, who take vows of poverty, chastity, and obedience but are not ordained. Often derided for their lack of qualifications, they teach in the Christian Schools. Archangias's gross and violent nature is at once displayed in his bullying of the pupils at his school, and he shows a virulent hatred of women: 'they have damnation in their skirts. Creatures fit for throwing on the dungheap, with all their poisonous filth! It would be a good riddance if girls were all strangled at birth' (p. 25). He appoints himself 'God's policeman' in his zealous efforts to protect the abbé from sin. It is revealing of Zola's profound antagonism to Catholic dogma that this physically dirty priest, with his scabrous imagination, claims to speak 'in the name of God' to drive the lovers out of Eden.

Serge's sister, Désirée, makes a significant appearance as a symbol of Nature when she enters the church during the last phase of the Mass. Farmyard odours enter with her, making a lively intrusion into the ritual at the altar. In her childlike innocence, Désirée is at one with her farmyard of animals she loves. But she has no more qualms about the killing of a chicken or a pig than about taking her cow to be serviced by the bull. Such things are natural, therefore unquestioningly accepted. She is comfortable in her body, and totally in tune with Nature and Life. She is Nature: beautiful, powerful, and mindless, untroubled by perplexity or doubt. She accepts death as she accepts birth and procreation as necessary phases in the process of making way for the next generation in an endless life-cycle.

The caretaker of the Paradou, Jeanbernat, Albine's uncle and guardian, is a representative of sceptical rationalism. In Zola's early plans he is simply a 'ridiculous old atheist', but in the finished novel, he is an impressive and distinctive figure, still tall, upright, and strong in his eighties. He allows his niece to run wild, with no education, believing in a Romantic, Rousseauesque free 'development of the temperament'. Having thoroughly absorbed the work of the eighteenth-century philosophers from books left in the chateau, he has become a well-read rationalist and atheist, a formidable enemy of the Church and all its priests: 'You'll find I can more than hold my own, Monsieur le Curé', he warns. Pointing to 'the whole horizon, earth and sky', he solemnly declares that 'When the sun gets blown out, that will be the end' because 'There is nothing, nothing, nothing... (p. 36)—a cry he will repeat after the death of Albine. Jeanbernat spends most of his time quietly smoking his pipe and watching his lettuces growing, but he is goaded into using his stick on Archangias, and towards the end of the novel, the death of his niece provokes him to take dramatic revenge on the priest he despises and detests.

Dr Pascal, Serge's uncle, is not on stage a great deal, but has special importance for Zola, not only here but also in the first novel, *The Fortune of the Rougons*, and again in *Doctor Pascal*, the last of the series. Pascal frequently serves as narrator, as a connecting thread. Through him we learn the story of the Paradou: the lord who built the chateau in the time of Louis XV (like the chateau of the domaine de Galice) and his beautiful lady who died there. Through him we learn something of the past of Albine, and something of the past of Serge. Pascal keeps records of the life and actions of the entire Rougon-Macquart family: 'I have files on all of them at home', he tells Serge, and 'one day I'll be able to draw up a wonderfully interesting chart' (p. 33). That 'chart', which features prominently in *Doctor Pascal*, stands proxy for Zola's own notes on the Rougon-Macquart family, the notes that provide the material of the novels. It is Pascal who takes the abbé with him to visit the Paradou, and later takes the sick Serge to convalesce in the Paradou: he can be seen as the 'experimenter', an avatar of the novelist.

Albine is Jeanbernat's 16-year-old niece, a 'child of nature' scarcely touched by education since the age of 9—though she briefly attended Archangias's school, to the fury of Jeanbernat. She runs wild in the park of the Paradou, draping herself in wild flowers. The abbé's first view of Albine—in a blaze of light through a suddenly opened door—immediately conveys the startling effect of this vision on the self-contained and generally unresponsive priest, while the opening of a door suggests the unlocking of a door to new kinds of experience. Rather than analysing his characters' feelings, Zola shows them externalized in this way through symbols, physical gestures, movements, and emotionally charged descriptions. Gaudily dressed like a 'gypsy-girl in her Sunday best', Albine seems to the abbé 'the mysterious and disturbing daughter of that forest he had glimpsed in a patch of light' (p. 39). The disturbance she causes signals the awakening of the abbé's hitherto repressed sexuality, while Albine's response to the encounter is suggested by her throwing down leaves as 'farewell kisses' over the visitors when they leave. The only further insight into the abbé's feelings that Zola offers here is to remark that the abbé at first avoids any mention of his visit to the Paradou, because of 'a vague feeling of shame'. It is up to the reader to interpret that shame, but Zola has obliquely indicated the importance and impact of this first encounter between the abbé and the woman he will love.

Nature and the Church

From the first pages of the novel, Abbé Mouret is seen in the church, where life and death, light and dark, Nature and Church will do battle. The barn-like church is dilapidated and empty, but at the altar, the profoundly devout priest and the lad Vincent, the server, perform

ritual gestures and utter hallowed words in an ancient language. La
Teuse, meanwhile, obstinately rooted in the everyday here and now,
anxiously watches a candle, fearing its wax may be wasted. Description
of the interior of the church underlines the crude artificiality of its
ornaments: the painted lips of the Virgin and the ochre-stained body
of the Christ bedaubed with red paint, on the cross on which, we are
told, 'nature, damned, lay dying' (p. 11). But all around, Zola shows
nature vigorously thriving: the tree poking its branches through broken windows, sparrows flying in to hunt for crumbs, and then Désirée
entering with an apron full of newly hatched chicks. Finally the sun
enters, and takes possession of the whole church. The sun fills the empty
benches with the dust particles dancing in its beams, and everything
seems to partake of a life-giving sap, 'as if death had been conquered
by the eternal youth of the earth' (p. 13).

The abbé despises nature, 'damned as it was'; and with this accept-
ance of the view of nature as 'damned', he rejects life and denies his
own physical being. He has the serenity of 'a creature neutered and
marked by the tonsure as a ewe lamb of the Lord' (p. 21). Blind to
the beauties of nature, he sees in the surrounding countryside only
'a terrible landscape of dry moors'. But when Archangias has expati-
ated on the iniquities of Les Artaud and the shamelessness of the girls,
the same scene becomes a 'landscape of passion, dry and swooning in
the sun, sprawled out like an ardent and sterile woman' (p. 26). The
abbé's new awareness, and accompanying abhorrence, of ubiquitous
sexuality now colour and shape the landscape he sees.

As a priest, he cannot avoid contact with what he sees as the 'filthiness' of sexuality and procreation. Even at the seminary, he had
had to read a book about sex for the use of confessors, which had left
him feeling 'soiled forever'. Pastoral duty also obliges him to talk to
Bambousse about getting the pregnant Rosalie married to her lover,
and while he does so, Rosalie gazes at him boldly, trying to make him
blush. Everything seems to be testing or taunting 'the serenity that
allowed him to move without a tremor even through all the filthiness
of the flesh' (p. 31).

The Awakening Sexuality of Abbé Mouret

Believing himself still a child, a creature set apart, 'cleansed of his sex',
the abbé does not recognize the sensuality that drives his excessive

mysticism, but the sexual connotations of his adoration of the Virgin are clearly indicated. 'Where could he ever have found so desirable a mistress?' he ponders (p. 75), as if engaged in a love affair with Mary. The warning of Archangias—'Beware of your devotion to the Blessed Virgin'—seems well justified. The frenzy of his worship, the accompanying hysterical hallucinations, and his total neglect of his physical being lead to illness, which he sees as the result of multiple attacks on his senses: the heavy odours and overwhelming fecundity of Désirée's farmyard, 'the fetid warmth of the rabbits and fowls, the lubricious stink of the goat, the sickly fatness of the pig' (p. 54). Or perhaps it was 'the smell of humans' rising from the village, or Rosalie slyly laughing, or the girls of Les Artaud piling their branches on the altar, or maybe the girl of the Paradou. To shut out these intrusions, the abbé takes himself back in mind to the seminary, and Zola here retraces the whole process of the abbé's ordination, following step by step his preparation for the priesthood.

To exclude every troubling disturbance, the abbé fixes his thoughts and memories on the Virgin, but a vivid recollection of Albine bursts into his mind. 'She smelled of fresh air and grass and earth', which aligns her with Nature, but she also has the white skin and the blue eyes of the Virgin. 'And why,' he asks, 'why then did she laugh like that, as she gazed at him with her blue eyes?' (p. 91). That question offers an encoded message to the reader, mocking as it does, the abbé's intermingling of the Virgin and the flesh-and-blood woman in a confusion that will painfully torment him when he transfers his morbid worship of the Virgin to the woman, and later finds, to his horror, that he has sexualized the Virgin, endowing her with the attributes of Albine. The abbé struggles to escape the memory of Albine's laughter, numbing his senses, but 'Albine reappeared before him like a big flower that had sprung up and grown beautiful on this compost' (p. 91). The use of 'compost' here speaks revealingly of the characteristic conjunction in Zola of disgust of the sexual act and joyful celebration of life, a conjunction that may explain why so many young women die either as virgins or immmediately after losing their virginity,[7] in the works of such an advocate of fecundity. That conflict indeed accounts for a good deal of the ambivalence and ambiguity of

[7] Fleur-des-eaux in the story 'Simplice' dies in a kiss; Miette dies in *The Fortune of the Rougons*; Angélique in *The Dream* dies on the steps of the cathedral after her marriage; Catherine dies in the mine in *Germinal*.

Zola's presentation of love, in which sex may be filthy like compost, but is still creative of life. It is no accident that Zola has Désirée stand on the dungheap at the end of the novel to announce the birth of the calf, the triumphant continuation of life.

As Abbé Mouret grapples with the torments of his newly awakened sexuality, the whole countryside takes on a lubricious aspect, lying 'in a strange sprawl of passion. Asleep, dishevelled, displaying its hips, it lay contorted, with limbs outspread, heaving huge, hot sighs' (p. 89). In his fever and revulsion, the abbé turns to the statue of the Virgin, desperately begging her to restore his innocence, to make him a child again, to castrate him and thus preserve him from the filth of sex.

Love in the Paradou

Book One ends with the abbé collapsed on the floor of his bedroom in the presbytery and Book Two—with a bold and very modern disregard of literary convention—opens, with no explanatory connecting link, in a completely new space with no presbytery, no church, and no Abbé Mouret. The first paragraph is devoted to a detailed description of the Louis XV decoration of a room in which plaster cupids play on the walls. This is a 'faded paradise', which is 'still warm with a distant scent of sensual pleasure' (p. 97); the scent of the eighteenth-century love affair lingers in the room to disturb the innocence of the new occupants. Albine, no longer the gaudy 'gipsy-girl', is dressed completely in white with her hair bound in lace, like a new version of the Virgin, and sits at the bedside of a convalescent Serge, no longer 'Abbé Mouret'. In this new space, Albine and Serge will play the central roles in Zola's version of the Fall of Man, a version quite other than that given in Genesis.[8]

Serge has lost his memory, and it is as if he had been granted that return to infancy he prayed for. He imagines he has just been born in this room, and in a sense he is indeed reborn here. Innocence, either as noun or adjective, is constantly repeated through these pages. Zola's descriptions of the wonderful, wild garden of the Paradou show what Hannah Thompson has called a 'textual tension between the "explicit" message, that is the innocence of the protagonists [. . .] and the "implicit"

---

[8] 'Genesis' was the title of one of Zola's early poems, and the novel seems to continue the same poetic impulse.

message, the presence of erotic desire in even the most apparently pure of contexts'.[9] Zola describes with delicacy and tenderness the gradual awakening of love and desire, and descriptions of the garden provide markers for the progress of the love of the 'two children' (Albine is 16 and Serge 25) who become man and woman, Adam and Eve, in the Paradou which will become a paradise lost.

And it is a very beautiful, dreamlike paradise that is lost, with its own dreamlike time and space. Space in the Paradou seems limitless, yet is enclosed by high walls; and there are so many lanes, paths, and glades, and such a profusion of plants, trees, and flowers that the outlines blur in an increasingly fantastic landscape, like the landscape of a fairy tale. Time, too, moves erratically, seeming sometimes to stand still, then leaping forward. There are few temporal landmarks here of the sort found in Book One, where the abbé appears at a quarter past six in the morning, and does not eat the lunch prepared for eleven o'clock until half past two; there are no mealtimes here, no church services. It is often difficult to establish any clear chronology in the Paradou, the days seem to drift into each other: time simply flows. Serge's beard and the length of his hair are the only real indicators of the length of his illness.

The love story begins with the innocent friendship of the two 'children', who wander through the woods and fields of the Paradou, leap over streams, paddle in the rivers, and eat cherries off the trees. They are so innocent they can even play at being 'lovers', like the lord and lady of the chateau. They are surrounded by flowers and trees, sunlight and shade, blue sky and rippling streams, but in their wandering, they are also looking for a legendary tree, which is in a glade of such perfect bliss that one may die of it. They know the tree is forbidden, but the search continues. Gradually, new sensations creep in, and a new awareness of each other. The forbidden tree has become too disturbing, and they 'erase' it: 'The tree did not exist. It was just a fairy tale' (p. 151). Similarly, when the couple kiss and declare their love, their new situation is too disturbing, so the story is rewritten: 'They had not exchanged a kiss, they had not said they loved each other' (p. 159). They are tormented by frustrated sexual longings— longings they do not understand, and cannot satisfy. The landscape

---

[9] *Naturalism Redressed: Identity and Clothing in the Novels of Émile Zola* (Oxford: Legenda, 2004), 56.

becomes distorted and ugly: 'there was here a crawling-forth, an upsurge of nameless creatures glimpsed in nightmares', as if this was a description of their very desires.

This beautiful garden, Zola decreed in his preparatory notes, is Nature the Temptress. Zola the naturalist has studied his plants and describes real flowers, often with their botanical names, but in an unreal, implausible profusion that seems to undermine reality.[10] Alpine rock plants grow alongside tropical flowers and African shrubs. It is not surprising that Serge and Albine get lost in this exotic, surreal setting, where the senses are overloaded. This is both a garden of delights and a garden of temptation, where nature constantly provokes the senses. Flowers are sensualized and sexualized, transformed into tempting visions:

The living flowers opened out like naked flesh, like bodices revealing the treasures of the bosom. There were yellow roses like petals from the golden skin of barbarian maidens, roses the colour of straw, lemon-coloured roses, and some the colour of the sun, all the varying shades of skin bronzed by ardent skies. Then the bodies grew softer, the tea roses becoming delightfully moist and cool, revealing what modesty had hidden, parts of the body not normally shown, fine as silk and threaded with a blue network of veins. (p. 120)

Maupassant commented in a letter to Zola of the 'extraordinary power' of this novel, which plunged him into such an excitement of all the senses that at the end he felt 'utterly intoxicated'.[11] Zola makes of this garden a lyrical hymn to Nature:

Only the sun could enter here, sprawl in a sheet of gold over the fields, thread the paths with its runaway rays, hang its fine, flaming hair between the trees, and drink at the springs with golden lips that set the water trembling. (p. 108)

Zola the poet is a master of imagery, and shows an ever-changing, animate Nature, constantly transformed by metaphor. Grasses become a sea, with floods and waves and tides, through which the lovers wade. Flowers become dainty ladies with parasols, noisy harridans, blowsy prostitutes. The scents and colours of the plants are shrill or quiet, making loud or gentle music: 'Les couleurs, les parfums et les sons se

[10] See Sophie Guermès, 'Détruire le réel: "L'Outrance de sève" du Paradou', *Cahiers ERTA* 3 (2013), 69–82.

[11] The letter is included in Henri Mitterand (ed.), Émile Zola, *Les Rougon-Macquart* (Paris: Bibliothèque de la Pléiade, 1967), i. 1684–5.

répondent' ('Colours, scents, and sounds correspond') for Zola as for Baudelaire. Here in this magical garden, the lovers will at last find the forbidden tree, in whose shade they make love. There they briefly enjoy the 'perfect bliss' of consummation, before they are driven out of paradise for ever.

Adam and Eve

In the Genesis of the Bible, Eve, tempted by the serpent, gives Adam the apple from the forbidden tree of *knowledge*. Both eat, and are expelled from the Garden of Eden, to prevent them from eating the fruit of the tree of life. In Zola's version, however, it is the tree of *life* that is 'forbidden' and it is beneath the tree of life that Serge and Albine make love, with the connivance of the garden. That consummation was 'a victory for all the creatures, plants, and things that had willed the entry of these two children into the eternity of life'. God drove Adam and Eve out of Eden so that they should *not* 'take also of the tree of life, and eat, and live for ever' (Genesis 3:22). In Zola's version, Nature grants them entry into that endless life cycle which is the eternity of life.[12]

In his preparatory dossier, Zola wrote: 'Nature plays the role of the Satan of the Bible', and 'the woman helps Nature; she is the temptress, an Eve with no social nor moral sense, the human animal in love'. He unambiguously allocates the blame: 'it's the woman who brings down the man', and this has been seen as evidence of misogyny on Zola's part, but from dossier to novel is often a long jump, and Albine's role in the novel is not that simple. It is Albine who saves Serge's life and nurses him back to health, and she is allowed some confusion about Serge's priestly status. Albine takes Serge to the forbidden tree, and tells him it is not forbidden, but Zola, noting in his dossier that 'Eve pleads for the joys of the forbidden', at once adds: 'It's not true anyway, it's permitted.' Albine is perhaps only the temptress in so far as Nature is the temptress.

It has been argued that this replay of the Christian story reveals a Zola who is 'Christian in spite of himself',[13] but Zola's reworking of

[12] Naomi Schor observes that 'the concept of a great life-death-life cycle underlies the whole of the *Rougon-Macquart* series'. In 'Zola from Window to Window', *Yale French Studies*, 42 (1969), 38–51, at 50.

[13] See Henri Guillemin, *Zola légende et vérité* (Paris: Julliard, 1960).

the Genesis story and his views expressed elsewhere make a 'Christian Zola' a very dubious proposition. There can be little doubt that Zola's ideas, shaped in a Christian climate, are deeply marked by the Christian ethic, but this is adapted and used as the basis for a new mythology.

In *The Fortune of the Rougons*, a former cemetery scattered the streets of Plassans with bones when it was relocated. The bones serve as an extended, poetic imaging of the way the past dwells in the present, of how the paths of the living are strewn with relics of the dead, and the living are moulded by the history, the memories, and the heredity they carry within them. Throughout all the novels of the Rougon-Macquart series, the past is a constant presence,[14] and perhaps nowhere more so than in this novel.

The past hangs heavy over Serge and Albine, most obviously in the story of Adam and Eve; and the Paradou, unlike the garden of Genesis, is not newly created. It is already a place of love and death, still holding the scent of the previous love affair, which eventually becomes suffocating in the room where Serge convalesces. On the walls, faded erotic pictures reappear. The lady is said to be buried in the grove of the tree of life, where Serge and Albine make love, and the earlier love affair is echoed in the marble woman, lying in the pool, her face worn away by water, with a broken cupid standing nearby. Serge and Albine are in a haunted paradise. Behind the eighteenth-century love story lurks yet another potent background story, in which Adélaïde Fouque,[15] the founding mother of the Rougon-Macquart family, plays the Eve who stains the whole family with her 'sin', as well as her mental instability. Serge has to bear the full weight of his heredity and the education that has made a priest of him.

The Priest and the Church

After the sunlight and flowers of Book Two, Book Three is much darker, moving into the torments and hallucinations of the priest who has rejected Albine and returned to the Church. It begins with the marriage of Rosalie and Fortuné, with Abbé Mouret officiating and

---

[14] Naomi Schor comments perceptively on 'the prominent role played by the dead in Zola's fiction', in *Zola's Crowds* (Baltimore: Johns Hopkins Press, 1978), 120.

[15] The dead, in the Rougon-Macquart novels, refuse to remain dead, and Adélaïde Fouque refuses to die—both metaphorically and physically—she lives to the age of 105, dying only in the last novel.

repeating in his homilies the words that, as Serge, he used to Albine. This marriage makes a bitter comment on what has gone before. The abbé will be tormented and tortured, with grace descending on him to bring respite and serenity, then leaving him to sink back into the agonies of temptation. There is no serpent as such in this Eden, but at one moment the abbé recalls Albine with her 'bare arms, supple as snakes... It was she who led the way' (p. 250), as if blaming her as the temptress. She comes to the church to reclaim him, and he vividly recalls 'their love, the vast garden, the walks beneath the trees, the joy of their union' (p. 233). But that memory of love and happiness is damned and blackened when the man in Serge is vanquished by the priest, who condemns both Albine and the garden with a diatribe worthy of Archangias:

Where you live there is only darkness. Your trees distil a poison that turns men into beasts; your thickets are black with the venom of vipers; your rivers bear pestilence in their blue waters. (p. 242)

Zola dramatically conveys the twisting and turning, the illogicalities, the contradictions and tergiversations of a mind torn apart by the agonizing conflict of desire and renunciation. Albine's claim that he belongs to her is answered by 'I belong to God' (p. 234), and he drives her away quite brutally. Her image, however, remains tantalizingly vivid before him until at last, with no resistance left, 'he threw himself upon her breast, with no respect for the church; he seized hold of her limbs, and possessed her under a hail of kisses' (p. 245). That hallucinatory sexual act is followed by blasphemy, when he echoes Jeanbernat's cry of defiant atheism: 'There is nothing, nothing, nothing. God does not exist' (p. 254).

The abbé's earlier insistence to Albine that the church, though poor and small, 'will become so enormous, and cast such a shadow that all of nature will die' (p. 243), is mocked by a dramatic hallucination in which he sees the church destroyed by nature. Nature already invaded the church in the first scenes of the novel, but now it is 'Revolutionary Nature' attacking the Church that for centuries had overshadowed it. First the Artauds seem to break down the door, then animals batter the walls, and insects attack the foundations. Nature builds barricades with overturned altars and knocks down the walls. Nature tears the church apart piece by piece. The rowan tree that had earlier pushed its branches through the window, now enters the church as 'the tree

of life', and plants itself in the nave. There it grows and grows until it
bursts the heavens, reaching 'higher than the stars'. At this, 'Abbé
Mouret applauded furiously, like a damned soul [. . .] The church was
defeated. God no longer had a home. God would not bother him any
more' (p. 258). However, when he emerges from his hallucination, he
is amazed to find the church apparently unscathed. He is still caught,
as before, between 'the invincible church' and 'all-powerful Albine'
(p. 258).

'Revolutionary' Nature, and the reference to the traditional barricades of insurrection, suggest that Zola may here also have in mind
the revolution of the Commune in 1871, and the great push towards
secularization that followed. The radical socialist Commune was violently suppressed in the *semaine sanglante* (bloody week) of May 1871,
and the conservative moral order restored. The Church survived, and
the general situation in the Third Republic returned, to Zola's dis-
may, to much as it had been during the Second Empire. The continued dominance of the Church was further stamped on the Paris skyline
in the shape of the Sacré-Cœur, erected on the heights of Montmartre.
Building began the year this novel was published.

Throughout the novel there are swift and sudden changes of mood
and scene. The immensely dramatic invasion and destruction of the
church, for instance, is followed by a domestic scene in which Archangias
gallops round the table on a chair, and breaks plates with his nose!
Successive scenes comment on each other with striking contrasts and
parallels. The abbé drags Albine through all the stations of the Cross,
telling her of the sufferings of his God, but Albine can hardly bear to
look at 'the crudely coloured pictures on which scars of red paint cut
across the ochre of Jesus's body' (p. 239). She is recalling their walks
in the Paradou, and the paths that led to 'our love, to the joy of living
with our arms around each other' (p. 240). The abbé is absorbed by
the Cross, while Albine longs for life and love. A parallel scene shows
the same gulf between the two when Albine takes Serge through what
can be called 'the stations of the Paradou', reminding him of the happiness they had known there and telling him of the happy life they might
yet live together: 'We'll live with our little family all around us' (p. 273).
Serge does not even hear, he is thinking about stone saints and 'the
tranquil death of my flesh, the peace I enjoy through not living'
(p. 273). It was only with revulsion that he briefly imagined children,
and pushed them away—'no, he would not have children' (p. 265).

Albine's dream of life and love and children shows her as a natural, loving, mothering figure, while Serge rejects love, refuses children, and chooses death. With such alternations, contrasts, and parallels, Zola creates what Chantal Pierre-Gnassounou has called 'a harmonious ensemble, in which chapters echo each other across the text'.[16]

The church bell that opens the novel tolls again to call Serge back from the Paradou, and finally tolls for the funeral of Albine at the end of the novel. That last chapter exemplifies the rich texture of the narrative, as it interweaves the killing of the pig, the funeral procession, Jeanbernat's cutting off of Archangias's ear, and, just as the coffin is being lowered, an ironic last glance at 'the marble tomb of Abbé Caffin, that priest who had loved, and who lay there so peaceful beneath the wild flowers' (p. 291), before ending with the triumphant announcement of the birth of the calf. Such complex patterning is characteristic of what Henri Mitterand has called Zola's 'total mastery of a truly symphonic and choreographic composition'.[17]

The Sin of Abbé Mouret is a novel brimful of energy, audacity, and sheer lyical beauty. It boldly disturbs the reader's expectations and habits, and destabilizes the 'real'. The passage from immediate 'reality' into dream, memory, or hallucination is often blurred, creating a surreal effect; and the inclusion of so many 'stories' within the story of Serge and Albine shows the sort of reflexivity that is more usually associated with the *nouveau roman* (new novel) of the twentieth century than with a nineteenth-century novel: 'there is no garden. It's just a story I made up', says Albine (p. 110). The tree is after all not forbidden, indeed perhaps there is no tree. Zola's fictional paradise is riddled with fictions. Further, in reflecting through Pascal his own work within this work, Zola points obliquely to his own authorial activity, and in so doing, subverts the naturalist stance,[18] which stresses objective observation rather than authorship. *The Sin of Abbé Mouret* shows all the faces of this multifaceted writer—realist, poet, Impressionist, surrealist, and (almost) *nouveau romancier* (new novelist).

---

[16] 'Zola and the Art of Fiction' in B. Nelson (ed.), *The Cambridge Companion to Émile Zola* (Cambridge: Cambridge University Press, 2007), 93.

[17] In 'Popular Novel and Literary Novel: Zola at the Crossroads' (trans. Valerie Minogue), *Bulletin of the Émile Zola Society*, 49–50 (2014), 5–15, at 13.

[18] In the light of later literature and literary theory, French and English critics have reappraised Zola's work, finding in Zola, in the words of Susan Harrow, 'a more equivocal, more prospective writer than has traditionally been assumed' (in *Zola: The Body Modern: Pressures and Prospects of Representation* (London: Legenda, 2010), 207.

The Sin

And what, finally is the nature of the sin in this novel? For Abbé Mouret it is the sin of sex, the sin of breaking his priestly vow, while for Serge, it is the rejection of Albine. Albine is left seeking death and asking the fundamental question: 'What sin had she committed that the garden no longer kept the promises it had made her since she was a child?' (p. 277). Albine's challenge: 'Come on, answer me, accuse me, tell me it was I who came and tempted you. That will be the last straw' (p. 237) seems not only to challenge Serge but also to make an ironic and forceful protest for herself, and for Eve, against the biblically authorized condemnation. For Pascal, the sin is partly his, for not foreseeing the results of an 'experiment' intended to save his nephew and 'civilize' Albine. But it is Serge who, as Abbé Mouret, turns his back on love and life, and abandons Albine and her unborn child.

When Dr Pascal arrives with news of Albine's death, and learns the abbé is reading his breviary, he shouts angrily to La Teuse: 'No, don't call him, I'd strangle him, and there's no point... I only want to tell him that Albine is dead! Dead, do you hear? Tell him from me that she's dead!' Then he shouts once more: 'And also tell him from me that she was pregnant!' adding the bitterly ironic comment: 'He'll be pleased to hear that' (p. 283). He then goes to the Paradou where he sits by the bed where Albine lies dead among the flowers, and weeps, 'overwhelmed with grief'. In so far as Pascal stands in for the author, he here reflects the view of the author, who laments the terrible waste of life and condemns the Church that caused it. Zola gives the last word to life, as Nature emphatically resumes its sway, reasserting itself vigorously with the birth of the calf.

The novel has sometimes been regarded as pessimistic, but in its espousal of the cause of life and nature against repression and dogma, the novel seems to reaffirm what Anatole France commended at Zola's funeral: his 'real optimism, an obstinate faith in the progress of intelligence and justice'.

TRANSLATOR'S NOTE

THIS translation is based on the scrupulously annotated text in volume i of Henri Mitterand's Bibliothèque de la Pléiade edition of *Les Rougon-Macquart* (Paris, 1967). Other editions were also consulted, notably those of Colette Becker (Paris, 1972), Colette Becker with Gina Gourdin-Servenière and Véronique Lavielle in volume ii of *Les Rougon-Macquart* (Paris, 2002), and Sophie Guermès's Livre de poche edition (Paris, 1998). All include very helpful critical commentary and a dossier of relevant material.

The first English translation was made by Ernest Alfred Vizetelly and appeared under the title *Abbé Mouret's Transgression* (London, 1894); then an abridged version by M Smyth, *The Sin of the Abbé Mouret* (London, 1904), and in the second half of the twentieth century, Alec Brown's *The Abbé Mouret's Sin* (London, 1957; repr. 1970, also published as *The Sinful Priest*, 1960), and Sandy Petrey's *The Sin of Father Mouret* (Lincoln, Nebr., 1969).

The novel was adapted for the French film *La Faute de L'Abbé Mouret* (1970; English title, *The Demise of Father Mouret*), directed by Georges Franju. The Austrian composer Gerhard Wimberger based his opera *Paradou* (1981/5) on this novel. The vividly pictorial quality of the novel inspired the painting *Le Paradou* (1883, Museum of Fine Arts, Ghent) by Albin Joseph Édouard Dantan, and a painting by the British late Pre-Raphaelite painter John Collier, *La Mort d'Albine* (1898, Glasgow Museum Resource Centre).

It has been a privilege and a pleasure to make a new translation of this challenging and extraordinarily rich novel. I have tried to respect and preserve its verve and variety, its rich, poetic texture and powerful rhythms. While trying to make the language read easily for English readers, I have tried not to 'over-English' a work so deeply set in its rural French context. I have kept 'Abbé' rather than 'Father', and kept names—'Les Artaud', 'La Teuse', 'La Rousse'—in the form in which they are written and heard in the text. Similarly, while not wishing to write Victorian prose, I have tried to avoid language too obviously twenty-first-century in tone and mood.

I should like here to acknowledge my great debt to the scholarship and insights of other writers in this field, and I should like to thank

Nicholas Minogue for his untiring reading and helpful comments, Noonie Minogue for her patient support and advice, and Brian Nelson for long-standing support and encouragement. I should also like to express my gratitude to the immensely supportive team at Oxford World's Classics, and particularly to Rowena Anketell for her meticulous and sensitive copy-editing.

SELECT BIBLIOGRAPHY

Biographies of Zola in English

Brown, Frederick, *Zola, A Life* (London: Macmillan, 1996).

Hemmings, F. W. J., *The Life and Times of Émile Zola* (London: Elek Books, 1977; paperback, London: Bloomsbury Reader, 2013).

Horne, Eileen, *Zola and the Victorians* (London: Maclehose Press, 2015).

Schom, Alan, *Émile Zola: A Bourgeois Rebel* (London: Queen Anne Press, 1987).

Vizetelly, Ernest Alfred, *Émile Zola, Novelist and Reformer: An Account of His Life and Work* (London: John Lane, The Bodley Head, 1904).

Walker, Philip, *Zola* (London: Routledge & Kegan Paul, 1985).

Studies of Zola and Naturalism in English

Baguley, David, *Naturalist Fiction: The Entropic Vision* (Cambridge: Cambridge University Press, 1990).

Baguley, David (ed.), *Critical Essays on Émile Zola* (Boston: G. K. Hall & Co., 1986).

Berg, William J., and Martin, Laurey K., *Émile Zola Revisited* (New York: Twayne, 1992).

Bloom, Harold (ed.), *Émile Zola* (selected essays) (Philadelphia: Chelsea House, 2004).

Chessid, Ilona, *Thresholds of Desire: Authority and Transgression in the Rougon-Macquart* (Berne: Peter Lang, 1993).

Griffiths, Kate, *Émile Zola and the Artistry of Adaptation* (London: Legenda, Maney Publishing, 2009).

Harrow, Susan, *Zola, The Body Modern: Pressures and Prospects of Representation* (London: Legenda, 2010).

Hemmings, F. W. J., *Émile Zola* (2nd edn., Oxford: Clarendon Press, 1966).

Hemmings, F. W. J. (ed.), *The Age of Realism*, 'Pelican Guides to European Literature' (Brighton: Harvester Press, 1978) (a general study of European realism).

King, Graham, *Garden of Zola: Émile Zola and His Novels for English Readers* (London: Barrie & Jenkins, 1978).

Lethbridge, Robert, and Keefe, Terry (eds.), *Zola and the Craft of Fiction* (Leicester: Leicester University Press, 1990).

Levin, Harry, *The Gates of Horn: A Study of Five French Realists* (New York: Oxford University Press, 1963).

Mitterand, Henri, *Émile Zola: Fiction and Modernity*, selected essays, translated and edited by Monica Lebron and David Baguley (London: The Émile Zola Society, 2000).

Nelson, Brian, *Zola and the Bourgeoisie: A Study of Themes and Techniques in Les Rougon Macquart* (London: Macmillan Press, 1983).

Nelson, Brian (ed.), *Naturalism in the European Novel: New Critical Perspectives* (New York: Berg, 1992).

Nelson, Brian (ed.), *The Cambridge Companion to Émile Zola* (Cambridge: Cambridge University Press, 2007).

Nelson, Roy Jay, *Causality and Narrative in French Fiction: From Zola to Robbe-Grillet* (Columbus, Ohio: Ohio State University Press, 1990).

Pollard, Patrick (ed.), *Émile Zola Centenary Colloquium* (London: Émile Zola Society, 1995) (contains articles in both English and French).

Pollard, Patrick, and Minogue, Valerie (eds.), *Rethinking the Real: Fiction, Art and Theatre in the Time of Émile Zola*, papers from the London Colloquium 2013 (London: The Émile Zola Society, 2014) (contains articles in both English and French).

Schor, Naomi, *Zola's Crowds* (Baltimore: Johns Hopkins Press, 1978).

Snipes-Hoyt, Caroline, Armstrong, Marie-Sophie, and Rossi, Riika (eds.), *Rereading Zola and World-Wide Naturalism, Miscellanies in Honour of Anna Gural-Migdal* (Newcastle upon Tyne: Cambridge Scholars Publishing, 2013).

Thompson, Hannah (ed.), *New Approaches to Zola: Selected Papers from the 2002 Cambridge Centenary Colloquium* (London: The Émile Zola Society, 2003).

Thompson, Hannah, *Naturalism Redressed: Identity and Clothing in the Novels of Émile Zola* (Oxford: Legenda, 2004).

Wilson, Angus, *Émile Zola: An Introductory Study of His Novels* (London: Mercury Books, 1965).

Historical and Cultural Background

Baguley, David, *Napoleon III and His Regime: An Extravaganza* (Baton Rouge, La.: Louisiana State University Press, 2000).

Benjamin, Walter, *The Arcades Project*, trans. E. Jephcott and K. Shorter (London: Belknap Press, 1999).

Brown, Frederick, *For the Soul of France: Culture Wars in the Age of Dreyfus* (New York: Anchor Books, 2010).

Friedrich, Otto, *Olympia: Paris in the Time of Manet* (London: Aurum Press, 1992).

Green, Anne, *Changing France: Literature and Material Culture in the Second Empire* (London: Anthem Press, 2013).

Jones, Colin, *Paris: Biography of a City* (London: Penguin Books, 2004).

McAuliffe, Mary, *Dawn of the Belle Époque: The Paris of Monet, Zola, Bernhardt, Eiffel, Debussy, Clemenceau and their Friends* (Lanham, Md.: Rowman & Littlefield, 2011).

Articles and Chapters in English of Special Interest

Beizer, Janet, 'This Is Not a Source Study: Zola, Genesis, and *La Faute de l'Abbé Mouret*', *Nineteenth-Century French Studies*, 18/1–2 (1989–90), 186–95.

Campmas, Aude, 'The Priest and Narcissus: Sterility and Self-Love in Zola's Paradou', *Bulletin of the Émile Zola Society*, 51–2 (2015), 18–29.

Edwards, Wade, 'Straightening Out Serge Mouret: Confession and Conversion in Zola's *La Faute de l'Abbé Mouret*', *Nineteenth-Century Studies* (Fall–Winter, 2005), 75–88.

Grant, Richard B., 'Confusion of Meaning in Zola's *La Faute de l'Abbé Mouret*', in *Symposium*, 13/2 (Fall, 1959), 284–9.

Harder, Hollie Markland, 'The Woman Beneath: The *femme de marbre* in Zola's *La Faute de l'Abbé Mouret*', in Bloom (ed.), *Émile Zola*, 131–49.

Harrow, Susan, 'Zola's Paris and the Spaces of Proto-Modernism', *Bulletin of the Émile Zola Society*, 43–4 (April–October 2011), 40–51.

Minogue, Valerie, 'Zola's Mythology: That Forbidden Tree', *Forum for Modern Language Studies*, 14/3 (July 1978), 217–30.

Mitterand, Henri, 'Zola, "ce rêveur définitif"', *Australian Journal of French Studies*, 38/3 (September–December 2001), special issue: 'Zola: Modern Perspectives', 321–35; repr. in Bloom (ed.) *Émile Zola*, 243–58.

Mitterand, Henri, 'Popular Novel and Literary Novel: Zola at the Crossroads' (trans. Valerie Minogue), *Bulletin of the Émile Zola Society*, 49–50 (2014), 5–15.

Further Reading in Oxford World's Classics

Zola, Émile, *L'Assommoir*, trans. Margaret Mauldon, ed. Robert Lethbridge.

Zola, Émile, *The Belly of Paris*, trans. Brian Nelson.

Zola, Émile, *La Bête humaine*, trans. Roger Pearson.

Zola, Émile, *The Conquest of Plassans*, trans. Helen Constantine, ed. Patrick McGuinness.

Zola, Émile, *Earth*, trans. Brian Nelson and Julie Rose.

Zola, Émile, *The Fortune of the Rougons*, trans. Brian Nelson.

Zola, Émile, *Germinal*, trans. Peter Collier, ed. Robert Lethbridge.

Zola, Émile, *The Kill*, trans. Brian Nelson.

Zola, Émile, *The Ladies' Paradise*, trans. Brian Nelson.

Zola, Émile, *The Masterpiece*, trans. Thomas Walton, rev. Roger Pearson.

Zola, Émile, *Money*, trans. Valerie Minogue.
Zola, Émile, *Nana*, trans. Douglas Parmée.
Zola, Émile, *Pot Luck*, trans. Brian Nelson.
Zola, Émile, *Thérèse Raquin*, trans. Andrew Rothwell.

A CHRONOLOGY OF ÉMILE ZOLA

1840   (2 April) Born in Paris, the only child of Francesco Zola (b. 1795), an Italian engineer, and Émilie, née Aubert (b. 1819), the daughter of a glazier. The naturalist novelist was later proud that 'zolla' in Italian means 'clod of earth'.

1843   Family moves to Aix-en-Provence.

1847   (27 March) Death of father from pneumonia following a chill caught while supervising work on his scheme to supply Aix-en-Provence with drinking water.

1852–8   Boarder at the Collège Bourbon at Aix. Friendship with Baptistin Baille and Paul Cézanne. Zola, not Cézanne, wins the school prize for drawing.

1858   (February) Leaves Aix to settle in Paris with his mother (who had preceded him in December). Offered a place and bursary at the Lycée Saint-Louis. (November) Falls ill with 'brain fever' (typhoid) and convalescence is slow.

1859   Fails his *baccalauréat* twice.

1860   (Spring) Is found employment as a copy-clerk but abandons it after two months, preferring to eke out an existence as an impecunious writer in the Latin Quarter of Paris.

1861   Cézanne follows Zola to Paris, where he meets Camille Pissarro, fails the entrance examination to the École des Beaux-Arts, and returns to Aix in September.

1862   (February) Taken on by Hachette, the well-known publishing house, at first in the dispatch office and subsequently as head of the publicity department. (31 October) Naturalized as a French citizen. Cézanne returns to Paris and stays with Zola.

1863   (31 January) First literary article published. (1 May) Manet's *Déjeuner sur l'herbe* exhibited at the Salon des Refusés, which Zola visits with Cézanne.

1864   (October) *Tales for Ninon.*

1865   *Claude's Confession.* A *succès de scandale* thanks to its bedroom scenes. Meets future wife Alexandrine-Gabrielle Meley (b. 1839), the illegitimate daughter of teenage parents who soon separated; Alexandrine's mother died in September 1849.

1866 Resigns his position at Hachette (salary: 200 francs a month) and becomes a literary critic on the recently launched daily *L'Événement* (salary: 500 francs a month). Self-styled 'humble disciple' of Hippolyte Taine. Writes a series of provocative articles condemning the official Salon Selection Committee, expressing reservations about Courbet, and praising Manet and Monet. Begins to frequent the Café Guerbois in the Batignolles quarter of Paris, the meeting-place of the future Impressionists. Antoine Guillemet takes Zola to meet Manet. Summer months spent with Cézanne at Bennecourt on the Seine. (15 November) *L'Événement* suppressed by the authorities.

1867 (November) *Thérèse Raquin*.

1868 (April) Preface to second edition of *Thérèse Raquin*. (May) Manet's portrait of Zola exhibited at the Salon. (December) *Madeleine Férat*. Begins to plan for the Rougon-Macquart series of novels.

1868–70 Working as journalist for a number of different newspapers.

1870 (31 May) Marries Alexandrine in a registry office. (September) Moves temporarily to Marseilles because of the Franco-Prussian War.

1871 Political reporter for *La Cloche* (in Paris) and *Le Sémaphore de Marseille*. (March) Returns to Paris. (October) Publishes *The Fortune of the Rougons*, the first of the twenty novels making up the Rougon-Macquart series.

1872 *The Kill*.

1873 (April) *The Belly of Paris*.

1874 (May) *The Conquest of Plassans*. First independent Impressionist exhibition. (November) *Further Tales for Ninon*.

1875 Begins to contribute articles to the Russian newspaper *Vestnik Evropy* (*European Herald*). (April) *The Sin of Abbé Mouret*.

1876 (February) *His Excellency Eugène Rougon*. Second Impressionist exhibition.

1877 (February) *L'Assommoir*.

1878 Buys a house at Médan on the Seine, 40 kilometres west of Paris. (June) *A Page of Love*.

1880 (March) *Nana*. (May) *Les Soirées de Médan* (an anthology of short stories by Zola and some of his naturalist 'disciples', including Maupassant). (8 May) Death of Flaubert. (September) First of a series of articles for *Le Figaro*. (17 October) Death of his mother. (December) *The Experimental Novel*.

1882 (April) *Pot Luck* (*Pot-Bouille*). (3 September) Death of Turgenev.

1883 (13 February) Death of Wagner. (March) *The Ladies' Paradise (Au Bonheur des Dames)*. (30 April) Death of Manet.

1884 (March) *La Joie de vivre*. Preface to catalogue of Manet exhibition.

1885 (March) *Germinal*. (12 May) Begins writing *The Masterpiece (L'Œuvre)*. (22 May) Death of Victor Hugo. (23 December) First instalment of *The Masterpiece* appears in *Le Gil Blas*.

1886 (27 March) Final instalment of *The Masterpiece*, which is published in book form in April.

1887 (18 August) Denounced as an onanistic pornographer in the *Manifesto of the Five* in *Le Figaro*. (November) *Earth*.

1888 (October) *The Dream*. Jeanne Rozerot becomes his mistress.

1889 (20 September) Birth of Denise, daughter of Zola and Jeanne.

1890 (March) *The Beast in Man*.

1891 (March) *Money*. (April) Elected President of the Société des Gens de Lettres. (25 September) Birth of Jacques, son of Zola and Jeanne.

1892 (June) *La Débâcle*.

1893 (July) *Doctor Pascal*, the last of the Rougon-Macquart novels. Fêted on visit to London.

1894 (August) *Lourdes*, the first novel of the trilogy *Three Cities*. (22 December) Dreyfus found guilty by a court martial.

1896 (May) *Rome*.

1898 (13 January) 'J'accuse', his article in defence of Dreyfus, published in *L'Aurore*. (21 February) Found guilty of libelling the Minister of War and given the maximum sentence of one year's imprisonment and a fine of 3,000 francs. Appeal for retrial granted on a technicality. (March) *Paris*. (23 May) Retrial delayed. (18 July) Leaves for England instead of attending court.

1899 (4 June) Returns to France. (October) *Fecundity*, the first of his *Four Gospels*.

1901 (May) *Toil*, the second 'Gospel'.

1902 (29 September) Dies of fumes from his bedroom fire, the chimney having been capped either by accident or anti-Dreyfusard design. Wife survives. (5 October) Public funeral.

1903 (March) *Truth*, the third 'Gospel', published posthumously. *Justice* was to be the fourth.

1908 (4 June) Remains transferred to the Panthéon.

Adélaïde FOUQUE
(Tante DIDE)
1768–1873
m. ROUGON   Lover of MACQUART

Pierre ROUGON
1787–1870
m. Félicité PUECH

| Eugène ROUGON b. 1811 | Pascal ROUGON 1813–1873 | Aristide ROUGON (SACCARD) b. 1815 | Sidonie ROUGON b. 1818 | Marthe ROUGON 1820–1864 m. | François MOURET 1817–1864 |

| Maxime ROUGON (SACCARD) 1840–1873 | Clotilde ROUGON b. 1847 | Victor ROUGON (SACCARD) b. 1853 | Angélique ROUGON 1851–1869 | Octave MOURET b. 1840 | Serge MOURET b. 1841 |

Charles ROUGON (SACCARD) 1857–1873

Child born in 1874 to Clotilde and Pascal ROUGON

FAMILY TREE OF THE ROUGON-MACQUART

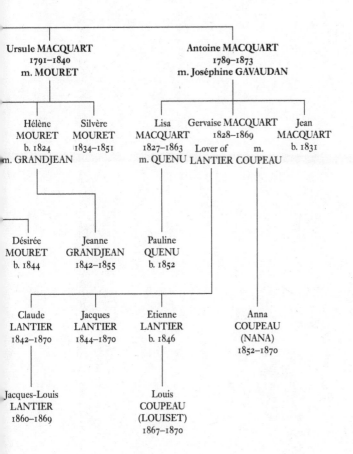

Ursule MACQUART
1791–1840
m. MOURET

Antoine MACQUART
1789–1873
m. Joséphine GAVAUDAN

Hélène
MOURET
b. 1824
m. GRANDJEAN

Silvère
MOURET
1834–1851

Lisa
MACQUART
1827–1863
m. QUENU

Gervaise MACQUART
1828–1869
Lover of   m.
LANTIER COUPEAU

Jean
MACQUART
b. 1831

Désirée
MOURET
b. 1844

Jeanne
GRANDJEAN
1842–1855

Pauline
QUENU
b. 1852

Claude
LANTIER
1842–1870

Jacques
LANTIER
1844–1870

Etienne
LANTIER
b. 1846

Anna
COUPEAU
(NANA)
1852–1870

Jacques-Louis
LANTIER
1860–1869

Louis
COUPEAU
(LOUISET)
1867–1870

THE SIN OF ABBÉ MOURET

BOOK ONE

CHAPTER I

LA TEUSE came in and propped her broom and her feather duster against the altar. She had spent too long setting about the six-monthly soap-making.* She made her way through the church to ring the *Angelus*, limping more than usual in her hurry and bumping against the benches. The bell rope, near the confessional, hung straight down from the ceiling, a plain, worn rope ending in a large knot, greasy from so much handling. She hung on to it with her whole bulk, pulling with regular strokes, then just let herself go with it, swinging around in her wide skirts, bonnet askew, with blood rushing into her broad face.

After setting her bonnet to rights with a little tap, La Teuse, now breathless, went back to sweeping in front of the altar. There was always dust there, every day, settling between the ill-fitting planks of the altar dais. The broom delved into the crevices with a growl of irritation. She then lifted the covering of the altar table and saw with annoyance that the large upper cloth, already darned twenty times or more, now had another hole worn through, right in the middle, so you could see the cloth underneath, folded in two; and that was so thin and transparent you could see through it to the consecrated stone embedded in the altar of painted wood. She dusted the cloths, yellow with use, and flicked her feather duster vigorously along the shelf before replacing the liturgy cards. Then, standing on a chair, she took the yellow cotton dust-covers off the cross and the two candlesticks. The brass was dotted with dull stains.

'Oh dear!' La Teuse muttered under her breath. 'They certainly are in need of a clean! I'll rub them over with tripoli.'*

Then, pegging along on one leg, and jolting enough to batter the flagstones into the ground, she went to the sacristy to find the Missal, which she placed without opening it on the lectern, on the side of the Epistle, with its edge turned towards the middle of the altar. And she lit the two candles. As she carried her broom away, she had a look round to make sure the good Lord's housekeeping was properly done.

The church seemed asleep; only the bell rope, near the confessional, was still swinging from the vault down to the floor with a long, lithe motion.

Abbé Mouret had just come down to the sacristy, a chilly little room with just a corridor separating it from the dining room.

'Good morning, Monsieur le Curé,' said La Teuse, putting her things down. 'You've had quite a lie-in this morning. It's a quarter past six, d'you know.'

And without giving the smiling young priest a chance to reply, she went on:

'I've a word or two to say to you. The altar cloth has a hole in it again. There's no sense in it! We only have one spare, and I've spent three days ruining my eyes to get that mended... you'll leave poor Jesus quite bare if you go on like this.'

Abbé Mouret was still smiling. He said gaily:

'Jesus doesn't need that much clothing, my good Teuse. He is always warm and always royally received so long as he is loved.'

Then moving towards a little water tap, he asked: 'Is my sister up? I haven't seen her.'

'Mademoiselle Désirée came down some time ago,' answered the servant, kneeling in front of an old kitchen dresser, in which the consecrated vestments were kept.

'She's already off with her chickens and rabbits... She was expecting chicks yesterday and they didn't get hatched. You can imagine the fuss!'

She paused, to say: 'The gold chasuble, isn't it?'

The priest, who had washed his hands, now rapt in his devotions, his lips murmuring a prayer, nodded his assent. The parish had only three chasubles: one purple, one black, and one gold. The last, which had to be used on the days when white, red, or green were prescribed,* was therefore specially important. La Teuse lifted it reverently from the shelf covered in blue paper, on which she laid it after every ceremony, and placed it on the dresser, carefully removing the flimsy strips of cloth protecting the embroidery, in which a golden lamb lay sleeping on a gold cross, surrounded by broad golden rays.* The material, worn along the folds, was shedding bits of fluff; the embossed embroidery was wearing thin and disappearing from sight. There was constant concern about this in the household, a tenderly anxious terror at seeing it vanishing like that, sequin by sequin. The priest had to put it on almost every day. And how were they to replace it, and how buy the three chasubles it stood in for, when the last threads of gold were worn away?

La Teuse spread the surplice on top of the chasuble, then the maniple, the cord, the alb, and the amice.* But she went on chatting, at the same time carefully crossing the maniple upon the stole, and arranging the cord like a garland, tracing out the hallowed initial of the sacred name of Mary.

'It's not much good any more, this cord,' she murmured. 'You'll have to make up your mind to buy another, Monsieur le Curé... it's not that hard, I'd weave you one myself if I had some hemp.'

Abbé Mouret made no response. He was preparing the chalice on a little table, a big, old, silver-gilt chalice with a bronze base, that he had just taken out of a deal cupboard in which were kept the sacred vessels and linen, the Holy Oils, the Missals, the candlesticks and crosses. He placed a clean purificator across the cup, and, on top of that, the silver-gilt paten containing a Host, and covered this with a linen pall.* As he was covering up the chalice, drawing together the two folds in the veil of gold cloth matching the chasuble, La Teuse shouted:

'Wait, there's no corporal in the burse...* Yesterday evening I took all the dirty purificators, palls, and corporals to launder them—separately of course, not in the ordinary washing... I haven't told you, Monsieur le Curé, I've just got the soap under way. It's really rich and foamy! It'll be better than the last lot.'

And while the priest was slipping a corporal into the burse, and placing the burse, with its gold cross on a gold background, on the chalice veil, she went on eagerly:

'By the way, I was forgetting! That rascal Vincent hasn't turned up. Do you want me to serve the Mass, Monsieur le Curé?'

The young priest looked at her sternly.

'Ah, it's not a sin,' she went on, with her amiable smile. 'I served the Mass once, in the time of Monsieur Caffin. I do it better than those naughty boys who laugh like heathens just at seeing a fly in the church... Come on, I may wear a bonnet, be sixty years old, and the size of a house, but I have more respect for the good Lord than those pesky children—I even saw them the other day playing leapfrog behind the altar.'

The priest went on looking at her and shaking his head.

'What a hole this village is,' she growled; 'with less than a hundred and fifty people... there are days, like today, when you wouldn't find a living soul in Les Artaud. Even babies in rompers go into the vines. Goodness knows what they can do among those vines! Vines that grow among stones, vines as dry as thistles! A land of savages this is, miles off the beaten track!... So unless an angel comes down to serve your Mass for you, Monsieur le Curé, you have no one but me, believe me! Or one of Mademoiselle Désirée's rabbits, with all due respect!'

But just then, Vincent, the youngest of the Brichet family, gently pushed open the door of the sacristy. With his red hair standing on end, and his little grey eyes gleaming, he really irritated La Teuse.

'Ah! the wretched boy!' she cried. 'I bet he's been up to some mischief!... Come on in, you naughty boy, since Monsieur le Curé is afraid I might soil the good Lord!'

On seeing the lad, Abbé Mouret had taken up the amice. He kissed the cross embroidered in the middle of it, placed the cloth for a moment on his head, then tucking it down on the collar of his cassock, crossed and fastened the cords, right over left. He then put on the alb, the symbol of purity, starting with the right sleeve. Vincent, crouching down, turned around him, adjusting the alb, making sure it fell evenly all round, just two inches off the ground. Then he presented the cord to the priest, who bound it tightly over his back in memory of the bonds borne by the Saviour during his Passion.

La Teuse remained standing, jealous and hurt, trying hard to keep silent, but her tongue so itched that she soon started up again:

'Brother Archangias called in... He won't have a single child in school today. He set off like a tornado to go and box the ears of those brats in the vines... You had better go and see him. I think he has something to say to you.'

Abbé Mouret silenced her with a wave of his hand. He had still not opened his mouth. He was reciting the appointed prayers, taking the maniple, which he kissed, then placed it on his left arm just below the elbow, as a sign indicating works of charity, then he also kissed the stole, and crossed it over his breast as a symbol of dignity and power. La Teuse had to help Vincent to fix the chasuble, which she tied with some fine strings, so that it would not slip backwards.

'Holy Virgin! I forgot the cruets!' she muttered, rushing towards the cupboard. 'Come on, you rascal, hurry up!'

Vincent filled the cruets, phials of crude glass, while she hastened to find a clean manuterge* in one of the drawers. Abbé Mouret, holding the chalice by the knot, in his left hand, with the fingers of his right hand placed upon the burse, bowed deeply without taking off his biretta, to the crucifix of black wood hanging over the dresser. The lad also bowed; then, leading the way and carrying the cruets, covered with the manuterge, he left the sacristy, followed by the priest, who walked with eyes lowered, deep in his devotions.

CHAPTER II

THE church, quite empty, was all white on this May morning. The bell rope hanging by the confessional was now still. The night light, in a coloured glass, was casting a patch of red on the wall to the right of the tabernacle.* Vincent, after carrying the cruets to the credenza, went back and knelt on the left, on the bottom step, while the priest, after a deep genuflexion to the Host, went up to the altar and spread out the corporal, in the centre of which he placed the chalice. Now, opening the Missal, he went back down. After another deep genuflexion, he made the sign of the cross, saying the words aloud, then joined his hands together on his breast, and began the great divine drama, his face pale with faith and love.

'*Introibo ad altare Dei.*'

'*Ad Deum qui laetificat juventutem meam,*'* muttered Vincent, who was mumbling the responses to the antiphon and the psalm while squatting on his heels, and watching La Teuse, who was roaming around the church.

The old servant was gazing rather anxiously at one of the candles. Her concern seemed to increase further when the priest, bending low, with his hands again joined together, recited the *Confiteor*. She stood still, and she too beat her breast, and with bowed head, went on watching the candle. The priest's grave voice and the stammering of the server continued to alternate for a moment or so:

'*Dominus vobiscum.*'

'*Et cum spiritu tuo.*'

And the priest, stretching out his hands, then clasping them together, said, in a voice of deeply felt contrition: '*Oremus...*'*

La Teuse could hold back no longer. She went behind the altar, and got to the candle, which she cleaned with the point of her scissors. The candle had been melting away. Two large drops of wax were already lost. When she came back, straightening the benches on her way, and checking that the holy water fonts were not empty, the priest was at the altar, praying quietly, his hands resting on the edge of the altar cloth. He kissed the altar.

Behind him, the little church looked wan in the pale morning light. The sun had not yet reached the tiles of the roof. The chants of *Kyrie Eleison* went quivering through the stable-like whitewashed building with its flat ceiling, on which the roughly painted beams were clearly visible. On each side, three tall windows of plain glass, mostly cracked or broken, opened up big patches of harsh, chalky light. The fresh air from outside blew in brutally, laying bare the dire poverty of the God of this desolate village. At the far end, over the main door that was never opened, its threshold blocked by weeds, a rough wooden gallery, reached by an open stair, stretched from one wall to the other, and creaked under the weight of clogs on festival days. Near the steps, the confessional, with its rickety panels, was painted lemon yellow. Opposite, beside the small door, stood the baptismal font, formerly a holy water stoup, mounted on a masonry base. Then, halfway down the church, one on the right and one on the left, stood two narrow altars, with wooden balustrades in front. On the left, the altar dedicated to the Holy Virgin had a large Madonna in gilded plaster, majestically bearing a gold crown upon her chestnut hair; and sitting on her right arm was a baby Jesus, naked and smiling, holding up the starry globe of the world in his little hand. She seemed to be walking with clouds all around her, and the heads of winged angels at her feet. The right-hand altar, where Masses for the dead were said, was surmounted by a Christ in painted pasteboard, making a pair with the figure of the Virgin. The Christ, about the height of a ten-year-old child, was shown dying in terrible agony, with head thrown back, ribs sticking out, hollowed belly, and limbs twisted and spattered with blood. There was also the pulpit, a sort of square platform reached by five steps, standing next to a pendulum clock in a walnut casing, whose dull strokes shook the whole church like the beating of an enormous heart hidden somewhere beneath the paving. Along the nave, the fourteen stations of the Cross, fourteen crudely coloured pictures, framed in black, stained the harsh whiteness of the walls with the yellow, blue, and red of the Passion.

'*Deo gratias*,'* stammered Vincent, at the end of the Epistle.

The mystery of love, the sacrifice of the Holy Victim, was about to begin. The server took the Missal, and carried it to the left side, the side of the Gospel, taking care not to touch the pages of the book. Every time he went across the tabernacle, he made a sideways genuflexion, which threw his figure quite askew. Once back on the righthand side, he stood upright, with arms crossed, during the reading of the Gospel. The priest, after making the sign of the cross upon the Missal, crossed himself as well; on his brow, to show that he would never blush at the word of God; on his mouth, to show he was always ready to confess his faith; and on his heart, as a sign that his heart belonged to God alone.

'*Dominus vobiscum*,' he said, and turned around, his eyes blank, as he faced the cold whiteness of the church.

'*Et cum spiritu tuo*,' came the response of Vincent, now on his knees once more.

After reciting the Offertory, the priest uncovered the chalice. For a moment he held up, in front of his chest, the paten containing the Host, which he offered to God for himself, for those present, and for all the faithful, living or dead. Then sliding it to the edge of the corporal, without touching it with his fingers, he took the chalice, which he carefully wiped with the purificator. Vincent had now gone to the credenza to find the cruets, which he presented, one after the other; wine first, then the water. The priest then offered, for the whole world, the half-full chalice, which he replaced in the centre of the corporal, then covered it with the pall. And after further prayers, he came back and had Vincent pour tiny streams of water on to the tips of the thumb and index finger of each of his hands, to cleanse himself from the slightest stain of sin. When he had dried himself with the manuterge, La Teuse, who was waiting there, emptied the tray of cruets into a zinc pail at the corner of the altar.

'*Orate fratres*,'* the priest continued, speaking aloud, and facing the empty benches with hands stretched out wide, then joined together, in a gesture of appeal to all men of goodwill.

And turning back to the altar, he went on with his prayers, in a quieter voice. Vincent muttered a long Latin sentence in which he got muddled. It was just then that flames of yellow burst in through the windows. The sun, answering the priest's appeal, had come to Mass. It spread great patches of golden light upon the left wall, the confessional, the altar of the Virgin, and the big clock. The confessional creaked loudly; the Holy Mother in a halo, in the brilliance of her crown and golden mantle, smiled tenderly at the Infant Jesus with her

painted lips, and the clock, now warmed up, struck the hour in a more
lively fashion. It was as if the sun was filling the benches with the
flecks of dust dancing in its beams. The little church, this whitewashed
stable, seemed now as if filled with a warm crowd. Outside could be
heard the tiny noises that mark the happy awakening of the countryside: grass sighing contentedly, leaves drying themselves in the warmth,
and birds preening their feathers and making a first flutter of their
wings. The countryside itself seemed to come in with the sun; at one
of the windows, a big rowan tree stretched upwards, thrusting its
branches through the broken panes, pushing out its buds, as if to have
a look inside; and through the cracks of the main door, one could see
the weeds on the threshold, threatening to invade the nave. Alone, in
the midst of this surge of life, the big Christ figure, still in shadow,
brought in death, and the agony of his ochre-smeared flesh, bespat-
tered with red paint. A sparrow came and perched at the edge of
a gap, looked about, then flew off, but came back almost instantly and
swooped silently down among the benches in front of the altar of the
Virgin. A second sparrow followed. Soon sparrows were coming down
from all the branches of the rowan tree, and calmly hopping about
along the paving.

'*Sanctus, Sanctus, Sanctus, Dominus, Deus, Sabaoth,*' said the priest
quietly, his shoulders leaning slightly forward.

Vincent rang the little bell three times. But the sparrows, startled
by the sudden clanging, flew off with such a noise from their wings
that La Teuse, who had just gone back to the sacristy, reappeared,
scolding:

'The little wretches! They're going to get everything dirty... I bet
Mademoiselle Désirée has gone and put crumbs down for them
again.'

The fateful moment drew near. The body and blood of a God were
about to come down upon the altar. The priest was kissing the altar
cloth, clasping his hands together, and making the sign of the cross
over and over on the Host and the chalice. The prayers of the Canon
of the Mass* now fell from his lips in an ecstasy of humility and
thankfulness. His attitudes and gestures and the inflections of his
voice all spoke of his littleness, and the emotion he felt at being chosen
for so great a task. Vincent went and knelt behind him and took the
chasuble in his left hand, lifting it gently, holding the bell ready in
his other hand. And the priest, his elbows resting on the edge of the

altar, and holding the Host between the thumb and forefinger of each hand, pronounced over it the words of consecration:

'*Hoc est corpus meum.*'*

Then, after a genuflexion, he slowly raised it as high as he could, keeping his eyes fixed on it, while the server, prostrate before the altar, rang the bell three times. The priest then consecrated the wine:

'*Hic est enim calix.*'*

The server rang three last times. The great mystery of Redemption had once again been renewed, and the adored Blood flowed once more.

'Just you wait, just you wait,' growled La Teuse, shaking her fist as she tried to scare away the sparrows.

But the sparrows had grown cheeky. They had come back, even during the ringing of the bell, boldly fluttering about the benches. The repeated ringing of the bell had indeed pleasurably excited them. They answered it with little twitters that cut across the Latin words like the rippling laughter of children at play. The sun was warming up their feathers, and they were delighted with the kindly poverty of the church. They felt quite at home, as if in a barn with a window left open, chirping and fluttering, fighting over the crumbs on the ground. One of them went and perched on the gold veil of the smiling Virgin; another flitted over to make an inspection of La Teuse's skirt, with an audacity that enraged her.

At the altar, the priest, lost in his devotions, his eyes fixed upon the sacred Host, with thumbs and forefingers joined together, did not even hear this invasion of the nave by the warm May morning, or the rising flood of sunshine, greenery, and birds, which overflowed even up to the foot of the Calvary, on which nature, damned, lay dying.

'*Per omnia saecula saeculorum,*'* said the priest.

'*Amen,*' Vincent responded.

When the *Pater** was over, the priest placed the Host on top of the chalice, and broke it in half. He then took, from one half, a tiny piece that he dropped into the precious Blood, to mark the intimate union into which he was about to enter with God through the Communion. He spoke aloud the words of the *Agnus Dei*,* quietly recited the three prescribed prayers, and made his act of unworthiness; then, his elbows resting on the altar, and the paten under his chin, he took Communion in both kinds* together. Next, after clasping his hands together in front of his face in a fervent meditation, using the paten, he gathered up on the corporal the sacred particles that had fallen from the Host, and placed them in the chalice. One particle which had stuck to his thumb he rubbed off with his forefinger. And crossing himself with the chalice, and placing the paten once more under his chin, he drank all the precious Blood in three draughts, never taking his lips off the rim of the cup, consuming the divine Sacrifice to the last drop.

Vincent had stood up to go and get the cruets on the credenza. But the door of the passage leading to the presbytery swung open, and fell back against the wall, letting in a beautiful girl of twenty-two with a childlike appearance, who had something hidden in her apron.

'There are thirteen of them,' she cried. 'All the eggs were good!'

And half-opening her apron, she revealed a batch of chicks, all squirming about, with sprouting feathers and beady black eyes:

'Just look! Aren't they sweet, the little darlings! Oh! Look at the little white one, climbing over the backs of the others! And that little speckled one, already flapping his wings... the eggs were wonderfully good. Not one sterile!'

La Teuse, who was helping with the Mass anyway, passing the cruets to Vincent for the ablutions, turned round and said loudly:

'Do be quiet now, Mademoiselle Désirée! You can see we haven't finished yet.'

A strong farmyard odour came in from the open door, blowing a sort of ferment of new life into the church with the warm sun now reaching the altar. Désirée just stood there for a moment, delighted with the little family she was carrying, watching Vincent pouring the wine of the purification, and seeing her brother drink that wine, so that no particle of the sacred Host could remain in his mouth. And she was still there when he came back, holding the chalice in both hands, to receive on his thumb and forefinger the wine and water of the ablution, which he also drank. But when the hen came clucking along in search of her little ones and seemed about to enter the church, Désirée went away, with motherly words of comfort for the chicks, just as the priest, after pressing the purificator to his lips, ran it along the rim of the chalice, then placed it inside.

This was the end, the act of thanksgiving to God. The server went one last time to get the Missal and bring it back to the right-hand side. The priest replaced the purificator, the paten, and the pall on the chalice; then once more he pinched together the two wide folds of the veil, and put down the burse, in which he had folded the corporal. His whole being expressed ardent thanksgiving. He was asking Heaven for the remission of his sins, for the grace of a holy life, and to be worthy of life everlasting. He remained lost in this miracle of love, this perpetual immolation which nourished him every day with the body and blood of his Saviour.

After reading the prayers, he turned around and said:

'*Ite, missa est.*'*

'*Deo gratias,*' came Vincent's response.

Then, after turning round to kiss the altar, the priest returned, his left hand below his breast, and right hand extended, to bless that church full of the joyfulness of sunshine and the noise of the sparrows.

'*Benedicat vos omnipotens Deus, Pater et Filius, et Spiritus Sanctus.*'*

'*Amen,*' said the server, crossing himself.

The sunshine had spread, and the sparrows were growing bolder. While the priest was reading, from the altar card on the left, the passage from the Gospel of Saint John telling of the eternal life of the Word, the sun was setting the altar aflame, bleaching the panels of imitation marble, and swallowing up the brightness of the two candles, whose short wicks now made only two dark patches. The triumphant sun gathered up, into its own glory, the cross, the candlesticks, the chasuble, the veil of the chalice, and all the gold that paled in the sun's rays. And when the priest took up the chalice with a genuflexion, and left the altar to return to the sacristy, his head covered, and the server going before him with the cruets and the manuterge, the sun was left sole master of the church. It was the sun that now lay upon the altar cloth, lighting up in splendour the door of the tabernacle, and celebrating the fecundity of May. Heat rose from the flagstones. The whitewashed walls, the big figures of the Virgin, and even the Christ, seemed to quiver with rising sap, as if death had been conquered by the eternal youth of the earth.

CHAPTER III

LA TEUSE rushed to douse the candles but paused for a moment, trying to chase the sparrows away. So when she carried the Missal back to the sacristy, Abbé Mouret was no longer there, having already washed his hands and put away the sacred vestments. He was by then in the dining room, standing up breakfasting on a cup of milk.

'You really should stop your sister scattering bread in the church,' said La Teuse as she came in. 'It was last winter she invented that little trick. She said the sparrows were cold, and the good Lord could well provide for them... You'll see, she'll end up making us go and sleep with her hens and her rabbits.'

'We'd be all the warmer for it,' said the young priest with a laugh. 'You're always scolding, La Teuse. Just let poor Désirée love her animals. She has no other pleasures, the dear innocent.'

The servant went and stood firmly in the middle of the room.

'Oh! You! You'd even let the magpies build their nests in the church. You just don't see, you find everything quite perfect... Your sister is really lucky you took charge of her when you came out of the seminary. No mother, no father. I can't think of anyone else who'd allow her to go squelching around in a farmyard as she does.'

Then, changing her tone, in a gentler voice:

'Well, of course, it would be a shame to stop her doing what she wants to do. There's no malice in her. She's really barely ten years old, for all that she's one of the strongest girls in the district... You know, I still put her to bed every night, and have to send her to sleep with stories, as if she were just a child.'

Abbé Mouret was still standing, finishing his cup of milk, his fingers a little reddened by the chill of the dining room, a large tiled room, with walls painted grey, and no furniture save a table and some chairs. La Teuse picked up a table napkin that she had spread ready for breakfast over one corner of the table.

'You hardly use any linen,' she murmured. 'Anyone would think you just can't sit down, that you're always about to leave. Ah! I wish you had known Monsieur Caffin, the poor curé who died, whom you replaced! Such a comfort-loving man! He wouldn't have managed to digest a thing if he had eaten standing up... He was a Norman. From Canteleu, like me. Oh! I don't thank him for bringing me to this land of savages! When we first arrived, Lord, how fed up we were! The poor curé had had some most unpleasant troubles back home... Oh dear! Monsieur Mouret, didn't you put any sugar in your milk? The two lumps are there on the table.'

The priest was putting his cup down.

'Yes, I think I forgot,' he said.

La Teuse looked him straight in the eye, shrugging her shoulders. She folded into the napkin a piece of brown bread which had also been left on the table. Then, as the curé was about to go out, she ran over to him and knelt down, shouting:

'Wait, your shoelaces are not even done up... I don't know how your feet survive in these peasant shoes. You, so delicate, looking as if you've always been thoroughly cosseted!... The bishop must have known a lot about you to give you the poorest living in the region.'

'Well no,' said the priest, smiling again, 'it was I who chose Les Artaud... You're in a really bad mood this morning, La Teuse. Aren't we happy here? We have everything we need, and we live in heavenly peace.'

At that she fell silent, then she also laughed as she replied:

'You're a saintly man, Monsieur le Curé... Come and see how rich my soap is! That will be much better than going on arguing.'

He had no option but to follow her, for she was likely to stop him going out altogether, if he didn't go and compliment her on her soap. He was just leaving the dining room when he stumbled over some rubble in the passage.

'What's that?' he asked.

'Nothing at all,' replied La Teuse in her most intimidating tone. 'It's just the presbytery falling to bits. But you're quite happy; you have everything you need... Lord! There are certainly plenty of holes! Just look at that ceiling. Is that cracked enough for you? If we don't get crushed by all this one of these days, we shall owe our guardian angel a very special candle. Still, if it suits you... It's just the same with the church. The broken panes should have been replaced two years ago. In winter, the good Lord gets frozen. Besides, it would stop those wretched sparrows getting in. I warn you, I'll end up pasting paper over those windows myself.'

'Ah! that's an idea,' murmured the priest, 'we could use paper... As for the walls, they're more solid than they look. In my room, the only bit of sagging in the floor is over by the window. The house will outlast us all.'

When he reached the little shed near the kitchen, wanting to please La Teuse, he enthused over the excellence of the soap; he even had to smell it, and dip his fingers in. Then the old woman, quite delighted, became quite maternal. She stopped scolding, and ran to get a brush, saying:

'You're surely not going out with yesterday's mud on your cassock! If you had left it on the stair-rail, it would be clean... It's still very serviceable, that cassock. But lift it up properly when you're going across a field. The thistles tear everything.'

And she made him turn around like a child, while making his whole frame shake from head to foot with her violent brushing.

'There now, that's enough,' he said, making his escape. 'Keep an eye on Désirée, will you? I'll go and tell her I'm going out.'

But just then, a clear voice rang out:

'Serge! Serge!'

Désirée ran up, flushed with pleasure, her head bare and her black hair tied tightly into a knot on the back of her neck, her hands and arms covered in manure up to the elbows. She had been cleaning her hens. When she saw her brother about to leave, with his breviary under his arm, she laughed more loudly, kissing him full on the mouth and throwing her hands behind her to avoid touching him.

'No, no,' she stammered, 'I'd get you dirty... Oh! I'm having such fun! You shall see the animals when you get back!'

And she ran off. Abbé Mouret said he'd be back about eleven for lunch. He was just leaving, when La Teuse, who had accompanied him to the doorstep, shouted out her last reminders:

'Don't forget to go and see Brother Archangias... Drop in on the Brichets too; the wife called in yesterday about that marriage again... Now listen, Monsieur le Curé! I've met that Rosalie. She'd like nothing better, for her part, than to marry big Fortuné. Have a word with old Bambousse, perhaps he'll listen to you now... And don't come back at twelve o'clock, as you did the other day. Eleven o'clock, remember, eleven o'clock, right?'

But the priest didn't turn round. She went back in, muttering under her breath:

'As if he'd be listening to me!... He's not yet even twenty-six, but does just as he pleases. Of course, in saintliness he could be a man of sixty; but he hasn't lived, he knows nothing of life, it's easy for him to be as good as a little cherub, the dear man!'

CHAPTER IV

ONCE Abbé Mouret felt La Teuse no longer just behind him he stopped, glad to be on his own at last. The church was built on a slight mound that sloped down to the village; it was a long building, like an abandoned sheep-barn, but with wide windows and brightened by the red tiles of the roof. The priest turned around, casting an eye over the presbytery, a poor, greyish building clinging to the side of the nave; then, as if he feared being caught up again in the endless chattering that had been buzzing in his ears the whole morning, he made his way up on the right-hand side, and felt safe only when he was at the main door of the church, and couldn't be seen from the presbytery. The façade of the church, utterly bare and eroded by years of sun and rain, was surmounted by a sort of stonework cage in which a bell showed its dark profile, and the end of the bell rope could be seen hanging down into the tiles. Six broken steps, half-buried at one end, led up to the high rounded door, cracked and pitted with dust, rust, and cobwebs, in such a wretched state on its torn hinges that it looked as if the wind would blow right through it at the first puff. Abbé Mouret, who was fond of this ruin, went and leaned back against one side of the door, on the front steps. From there he could see the whole region at a glance. Shading his eyes with his hands, he looked out and scanned the horizon.

In May a tremendous burst of vegetation broke through this stony soil. Huge lavender plants, bushes of juniper, and banks of rough weeds came right up to the steps, planting their bouquets of sombre greenery even on to the tiles. This first thrust of sap threatened to drag the church itself into the hard undergrowth of knotty plants. At this early hour, the work of growth was fully under way; there was a thrumming of heat, a long and silent, shuddering effort, pushing up the rocks. But the abbé was oblivious to the ardour of these difficult birth pangs: he simply felt the step wobbling, so went and leaned against the other side of the door.

The countryside stretched away for six miles or so, bounded by a wall of yellow hills, dappled with the black of pinewoods; a terrible landscape of dry moors with rocky outcrops thrusting through the ground. The few patches of arable land were like pools of blood, red fields with long lines of scraggy almond trees, olive trees with their grizzled heads, and fields of vines that streaked the ground with their dark stocks. It was as if a huge fire had passed that way, scattering the ashes of forests over the high ground, burning up the plains, and leaving its glare and blazing heat in the hollows. Only here and there, far off, did the pale green of a cornfield offer a gentler note. The horizon was totally inhospitable, with no trickle of water; it was dying of thirst, and flew into clouds of dust at the slightest breeze. And in the distance one could see, through a gap in the hills along the horizon, a distant prospect of well-watered greenery, a glimpse of the neighbouring valley, made fertile by the Viorne, a river flowing from the gorges of the Seine.

The priest now turned his dazzled eyes down to the village, with its few houses scattered haphazardly below the church. Wretched houses, made of drystone walls and planks, scattered along a narrow path with no indication of streets. There were about thirty of them, some piled up over a dungheap and black with poverty, others bigger and brighter with pink roof tiles. The bits of garden, won from the rock, showed plots of vegetables, divided by hedges. At this hour, Les Artaud was empty, with no woman at the windows, no child sprawling in the dust; just bands of chickens going around, fossicking through the straw, searching for food right up to the thresholds of the houses, whose open doors yawned pleasantly in the sun. A big black dog, sitting on its haunches at the entry to the village, seemed to be guarding it.

A feeling of laziness gradually crept over Abbé Mouret. The rising sun bathed him in such warmth that he let himself slide back against the door of the church, overcome by a feeling of happy peacefulness. He was thinking about this village, Les Artaud, which had sprung up here among the stones, like one of those knotty growths in the valley. All the inhabitants were related, all bore the same name, so they were given nicknames even from the cradle, in order to distinguish one from another. An ancestor, an Artaud, had come and installed himself in this moorland, like an outcast; and then his family had grown, with the savage vitality of the grasses sucking up life from the rocks; his family had ended up as a tribe, a community, in which relationships became confused and went back over centuries. They intermarried with shameless promiscuity; there was no mention of any Artaud bringing a wife from any neighbouring village; only the daughters, sometimes, went away. They were born and died, rooted in this bit of the world, multiplying on their dungheap, slowly, with the simplicity of trees growing again from their seed, with no idea at all of the vast world that lay beyond these yellowish rocks among which they vegetated. And yet they already had their rich and poor. Ever since the time some hens disappeared, the henhouses were locked at night with large padlocks; and one night, behind the mill, an Artaud had killed another Artaud. In the depths of this desolate band of hills, this was a race apart, a tribe born of the soil, a whole humanity of three hundred head, starting again as if at the beginning of time.

As for the priest, the dead shadow of the seminary still hung over him. For many years he had not seen the sun. Even now he was unaware of it, his eyes closed, turned inward on the soul, with nothing but scorn for nature, damned as it was. For a long time, during his hours of reflection, when he lay prostrated in reverent meditation, he had dreamed of a hermit's desert, some remote place in the mountains, where nothing living, no being, no plant, no water, could come to distract him from the contemplation of God. It was a surge of pure love, a horror of all physical sensation. There, dead to himself, turning his back on the light, he would have waited until he was no more, until he disappeared into the sovereign whiteness of the soul. Heaven seemed to him all white, a whiteness full of light, like a snowstorm of lilies, as if all purity, all innocence, all chastity blazed together. But his confessor reproved him when he told of his longings for solitude and his yearnings for Godlike innocence; he reminded him of the struggles of the Church and the duties of the priesthood. Later, after his ordination, the priest had come to Les Artaud at his own request, hoping to realize his dream of annihilating the human. In this wretched place, on this sterile ground, he would be able to close his ears to the sounds of the world and live in a saintly sleep. And for many months he had indeed been content; hardly any agitation from the village disturbed him; hardly had the sun's hot bite snapped at his neck as he walked the lanes, his mind solely on Heaven, oblivious to the prolific fecundity all around him.

The big black dog that guarded the entrance to Les Artaud had just decided to come and join Abbé Mouret, and now sat on his haunches at the priest's feet. But the priest remained lost in the softness of the morning. The day before, he had begun the exercises of the Rosary, and he attributed the great joy that came upon him to the intercession of the Virgin with her Divine Son. And how contemptible seemed to him the goods of the world! With what gratitude did he feel his own poverty! On entering holy orders, after losing his mother and father on the same day, as the result of a drama,* the full horror of which was still unknown to him, he had left his entire fortune to his elder brother.* His only link with the world now was through his sister. He had assumed responsibility for her, feeling a sort of religious affection for her poor weak mind. The dear innocent was so childish, so much a little girl, that she seemed to him to have the purity of the poor in spirit, to whom the Gospel grants the kingdom of Heaven.* But recently she had begun to worry him; she was becoming too strong, too healthy, too full of life. But this was little more than a slight unease. His days were spent in that inner life he had created for himself, abandoning everything in order to give himself entirely to it. He closed the door upon his senses and sought to free himself from all bodily needs, he was no more than a soul ravished by contemplation. Nature offered him nothing but snares and filth; he took special pride in doing violence to her, despising her, and freeing himself from the mud of his humanity. The just man is bound to be mad in the eyes of the world. So he regarded himself as an exile on earth, he imagined only heavenly benefits, and could not even imagine that anyone could give any weight to a few hours of transitory joy compared with an eternity of happiness. His reason deceived him, his desires lied. And if he made any progress in virtue, it was above all through his humility and obedience. He wanted to be the lowest of all and subject to all, so that the divine dew would fall on his heart as if upon dry sand; he saw himself as covered in shame and confusion, unworthy of ever being saved from sin. Being humble is believing, is loving. Blind and deaf, and his flesh dead, he no longer belonged to himself. He was but a thing in God's hand. And then, out of this self-abasement in which he was immersing himself, there rose a hosanna that carried him far above the prosperous and the mighty, into the splendour of everlasting bliss.

So, in Les Artaud, Abbé Mouret had found the raptures of the cloister that he had earlier so ardently longed for during each of his readings of the *Imitation*.* Nothing in him had resisted. From his first genuflexion, he had been perfect, with no struggle, no disturbance, as if struck to the heart by grace, in total oblivion of the flesh. An ecstasy at the approach of God, such as is sometimes experienced by young priests; the joyous moment when all is stilled, and all desires merge into the overwhelming need for purity. From no human creature had he sought comfort. When one believes that one thing is all things, one cannot be shaken, and he believed that God was all things, and that his humility, obedience, and chastity were everything. He remembered hearing about temptation as an abominable torture experienced by the most saintly. But he would simply smile, God had never abandoned him. He walked in his faith, as if in a suit of armour that protected him from the slightest breath of evil. He recalled that at the age of eight he used to tuck himself away and weep for love; he didn't know who it was he loved; he simply wept because he loved someone far away. He had always remained emotional in this way. Later, he had wanted to be a priest to satisfy that need for a superhuman love, which was his sole torment. He could not see any other way to love more. In the priesthood he satisfied his being, his inherited predispositions, his adolescent dreams and first desires as a man. If temptation should come, he awaited it with all the serenity of an ignorant seminarist. The man in him had been killed, he knew it, and was happy to see himself as one apart, a creature neutered and marked by the tonsure as a ewe lamb of the Lord.

CHAPTER V

MEANWHILE, the sun was warming the main door of the church. Golden flies were buzzing around a large flower growing between two of the steps in front of the door. Feeling a little dazed, Abbé Mouret was just deciding to move on when the big black dog rushed off, barking furiously, towards the gate of the little cemetery which lay alongside the church. At the same time, a harsh voice shouted:

'Ah! you rascal! You miss school, and this is where I find you—in the cemetery!... Don't deny it! I've been watching you for a quarter of an hour!'

The priest stepped forward and saw Vincent, whose ear was in the firm grip of one of the Christian Brothers.* The child was being dangled over a deep gully that ran alongside the cemetery, at the bottom of which flowed the Mascle, a torrent whose white waters hurled themselves into the Viorne some six miles away.

'Brother Archangias!' the abbé said gently, to persuade the terrible man to show some indulgence.

But the Brother did not let go of the ear.

'Ah! It's you, Monsieur le Curé,' he growled. 'This rascal, can you believe it, is always hanging about here. I don't know what mischief he can get up to here... I should just let go, so he can break his neck at the bottom down there. It would serve him right.'

The child did not utter a word, trying to cling to the bushes, and keeping his eyes craftily closed.

'Be careful, Brother Archangias,' the priest went on, 'he might slip.'

And the priest himself helped Vincent to get back up.

'Well now, my young friend, what were you doing here? Cemeteries are not meant for playing in.'

The lad had opened his eyes, and moved fearfully away from the Brother to place himself under the protection of Abbé Mouret.

'I'll tell you,' he murmured, raising his wily head towards the priest. 'There's a warblers' nest in the brambles just beneath this rock. I've been watching it for more than ten days... So, now the little ones are hatched, I came here this morning, after serving the Mass for you...'

'A nest of warblers!' said Brother Archangias. 'Wait just a moment, wait!'

He turned aside, reached for a clod of earth on one of the tombs and threw it into the brambles. But he missed the nest. A second clod, more skilfully thrown, shook the frail cradle and hurled the chicks into the torrent.

'Now,' he went on, rubbing his hands to get them clean, 'perhaps you'll stop prowling around here like a heathen... The dead will come and pull your toes in the night if you go on walking all over them.'

Vincent, who had laughed when he saw the nest hurtling down, looked around with the shrug of one not bothered by superstition.

'Oh! I'm not afraid,' he said. 'They don't move about when they're dead.'

There was indeed nothing frightening about the cemetery. It was a bleak patch of ground, on which narrow paths had disappeared under the invasion of weeds. Mounds here and there made humps in the ground. Just one tombstone, standing erect, quite new, the tomb of Abbé Caffin, made a splash of white in the centre. There was nothing more, save broken-off arms from crosses, dried-up twigs of box, and old slabs of stone, cracked and covered with moss. There weren't two burials in a year. Death seemed to have no habitation in this waste-land, where La Teuse came every evening to fill her apron with grass for Désirée's rabbits. Only one enormous cypress, standing at the cem-etery gate, cast its shade upon the empty field. This cypress, which could be seen nine miles away, was known to the whole countryside as the Lone Tree.

'It's full of lizards,' added Vincent, looking at the crevices in the church wall. 'It could be a lot of fun...'

But he leaped out of the way when he saw the Brother raising his foot. The Brother then pointed out to the priest the poor condition of the gate. It was eaten away with rust, had lost one of its hinges, and the lock was broken.

'That needs repairing,' he said.

Abbé Mouret smiled, without answering. And turning to Vincent, who was playing with the dog:

'Tell me, lad,' he asked, 'do you know where old Bambousse is working this morning?'

The boy glanced at the horizon.

'He must be in his field in the Olivettes,' he replied, pointing over to the left. 'Anyway, Voriau can take you there, Monsieur le Curé. He knows for sure where his master is.'

Then he clapped his hands, and shouted:

'Here, Voriau, Here!'

The big black dog paused a moment, wagging his tail, and trying to read the lad's eyes. Then barking joyfully, he ran down towards the village. Abbé Mouret and Brother Archangias followed him, chatting. A hundred yards further on, Vincent quietly slipped away, going back up towards the church, but keeping an eye on them, ready to duck behind a bush if they turned their heads. With snakelike suppleness, he slid once more into the cemetery, that paradise of nests, lizards, and flowers.

Meanwhile, as Voriau led them along the dusty road, Brother Archangias was saying irritably to the priest:

'Leave them alone, Monsieur le Curé, they belong with the damned, these toads! They need a good belting to make them pleasing to God! They grow up in godlessness like their fathers before them. I've been here fifteen years and I haven't managed to make a single Christian yet. As soon as they're out of my hands, that's it! They only care about their land, their vines, their olive trees. Not one of them sets foot in the church. They're just brutes, battling with their stony fields!... If you want to guide them, take a stick to them, Monsieur le Curé, take a stick to them!'

Then, getting his breath back, he added, with a terrible gesture:

'Look, these Artauds, they're like the brambles growing here on these rocks. Just one root stock was enough to infect the whole region! They cling on, they multiply, they survive, no matter what. It would take fire from Heaven—like Gomorrah*—to get rid of them.'

'We must never despair of sinners,' said Abbé Mouret, walking on slowly, wrapped in his inner peace.

'No, these people are the devil's own,' the Brother went on, even more vehemently. 'I was a peasant, just like them. Until I was eighteen, I worked with a spade. And later, at the Institute, I swept, I peeled vegetables, I did all the heavy work. It's not their hard labour I find fault with. The reverse, God prefers those who live in lowliness... But the Artauds behave like animals! They're just like their dogs that also don't go to Mass, and they couldn't care less about the commandments of God and the Church. They love their plots of earth so much, they would gladly fornicate with them!'

Voriau, his tail waving in the wind, kept stopping, then moving on again, after making sure the two men were still following him.

'There are, it's true, some deplorable failings,' said Abbé Mouret. 'My predecessor, Abbé Caffin...'

'A poor sort of man...' the Brother interrupted. 'He came to us from Normandy, as a result of some scandalous affair. Here, his only concern was living well; he just let everything go downhill...'

'No, Abbé Caffin certainly did all he could; but it must be admitted that his efforts didn't achieve anything much. My efforts too are mostly in vain.'

Brother Archangias shrugged his shoulders. He walked on for a moment in silence, swinging his rough-hewn, tall, and bony frame. The sun was beating down on the leathery skin of his neck, casting into shadow his hard, peasant face, sharp-edged as a sword.

'Now listen, Monsieur le Curé,' he began again, 'I am too lowly to offer you advice, but I am almost twice your age, and I know this part of the world, all of which gives me the right to tell you that you won't get anywhere with gentleness... Believe me, the catechism is enough. God has no mercy for the wicked. He burns them. Just hold on to that.'

And as Abbé Mouret, with bowed head, made no reply, he went on:

'Religion is leaving the countryside, because it's been made too motherly. It was respected when it spoke like an unforgiving schoolmistress... I don't know what they teach you in the seminaries. The new priests weep like little children with their parishioners. God seems to be quite different now... I'd be willing to swear, Monsieur le Curé, that you don't now even know your catechism off by heart?'

The priest, wounded by the obstinacy with which the Brother so roughly sought to impose his will on him, raised his head, and said with some asperity:

'Yes indeed, your zeal is commendable... But didn't you have something to say to me? You came to the presbytery this morning, didn't you?'

Brother Archangias brutally answered:

'What I had to say to you is what I've just said... The Artauds live like their own pigs. I learned yesterday that Rosalie, old Bambousse's eldest girl, is pregnant. They all wait for that to happen before they bother to marry. Over the last fifteen years, I haven't met one who didn't roll in the hay before rolling up to the church... And they just laugh and say it's the local custom!'

'Yes,' murmured Abbé Mouret, 'it's a real scandal... I'm just on my way to see old Bambousse, to talk to him about that. It would be best, now, for the marriage to take place as soon as possible... The father of the child, it seems, is Fortuné, that big son of the Brichets. Unfortunately, the Brichets are poor.'

'That Rosalie!' the Brother went on, 'she's just eighteen. Girls like her go wrong when they're still at school. Less than four years ago, I had her in school. She had already gone to the bad... now I have her sister Catherine, a girl of eleven, who looks like turning out even more shameless than her elder sister. You can find her all over the place with that wretched little Vincent... You see, it's no good pulling their ears till they bleed, the woman always comes out in them. They have damnation in their skirts. Creatures fit for throwing on the dungheap, with all their poisonous filth! It would be a good riddance if girls were all strangled at birth.'

Disgust and hatred of womankind made him swear like a trooper. Abbé Mouret listened with a calm face, and finally just smiled at his violence. He called back Voriau, who had gone off into a neighbouring field.

'And look!' shouted Brother Archangias, pointing to a group of children playing at the bottom of a gully, 'there are my good-for-nothings, missing school on the pretext of helping their parents in the vines!... You can be sure that baggage of a Catherine will be in the middle of them. She likes sliding down. You'll be able to see her skirts blowing over her head. There! What did I tell you!... Until this evening then, Monsieur le Curé... Just you wait, you wretches!'

And he ran off, with his dirty rabat* flying over his shoulder, his greasy cassock pulling up thistles as he went. Abbé Mouret watched him plunge into the midst of the band of children, who fled like startled sparrows. But he had managed to grab Catherine and another child by the ear. He led them back towards the village, holding them firmly with his thick, hairy fingers, hurling insults at them the while.

The priest went on with his walk. Brother Archangias sometimes provoked in him some strange scruples; in his vulgarity and coarseness, he seemed to him the real man of God, with no earthly attachments, simply doing the will of Heaven, humble, uncultivated, with filth in his mouth against sin. And the priest despaired at not being able to rid himself of his body, at not being ugly, revolting, or stinking of vermin like the saints. When the Brother had disgusted him with words too coarse, or a brutality too eager, he would reproach himself for his delicacy and innate fastidiousness, as if they were real sins. Wasn't he supposed to be dead to the weaknesses of this world? Once again he smiled sadly, remembering that he had almost been angry at the lesson delivered by the Brother. It was pride, he thought, that tried to lead him astray, making him despise the lowly. But, in spite of himself, he felt relieved to be alone, able to go and walk on slowly, reading his breviary, delivered from that harsh voice that so disturbed his dream of pure love.

CHAPTER VI

THE road wound on round fallen rocks, in the midst of which the peasants had here and there won four or five hard metres of chalky soil, planted with old olive trees. The dust in the deep ruts in the road crackled like snow under the abbé's feet. From time to time, when he felt a warmer breeze on his face, he raised his eyes from his book, looking around to find the source of that caress; but his eyes roamed vaguely, without really seeing it, over the burning horizon, and the twisted lines of this landscape of passion, dry and swooning in the sun, sprawled out like an ardent and sterile woman. He pushed his hat down over his brow to avoid the warm breeze, and went peacefully back to his reading, while his cassock stirred up behind him a little cloud of dust that rolled along the path.

'Good morning, Monsieur le Curé,' said a passing peasant.

The sound of digging, by the plots of earth, roused him again from his reflections. Turning his head, he could see, among the vines, tall and gnarled old men greeting him. The Artauds in the blazing sunshine, were, as Brother Archangias had put it, fornicating with the earth. There were sweaty brows appearing from behind the bushes, and heaving breasts slowly rising up again; it was an ardent effort of impregnation, in the midst of which he walked so calmly in his ignorance.

Nothing disturbing reached his flesh from these great labours of love that filled the whole splendid morning.

'Hey, Voriau, no need to eat me!' a strong voice cried out merrily, quieting the dog, who was barking furiously.

Abbé Mouret raised his head.

'Ah, it's you, Fortuné,' he said, moving up to the edge of the field where the young peasant was working. 'I was wanting to speak to you.'

Fortuné was the same age as the priest. He was a big lad, sturdy-looking, his skin already hardened. He was clearing a corner of rocky scrub.

'About what, Monsieur le Curé?' he asked.

'About what has happened between you and Rosalie,' the priest replied.

Fortuné began to laugh. He must have found it funny that a priest should concern himself with such a matter.

'Dammit, she was very willing. I didn't force her... So much the worse if old Bambousse refuses to give her to me! You saw how his dog tried to bite me just now. He sets him on me.'

Abbé Mouret was about to move on, when the old Artaud, known as Brichet, whom he hadn't seen at first, emerged from the shade of a bush, behind which he had been eating with his wife. He was small, dried up with age, and had a humble expression.

'Someone's been telling you stories, Monsieur le Curé,' he cried. 'The boy is very ready to marry Rosalie... The youngsters got together. It's nobody's fault. Lots of others have done just the same, and lived no worse a life for it... It's not up to us. You need to talk to Bambousse. He's the one who thinks we're not good enough, because of his money.'

'Yes, we're too poor for him,' moaned Mother Brichet, a tall, whining woman, who now also stood up. 'We only have this bit of field, on which the devil must be raining down stones. It doesn't even keep us fed... If it weren't for you, Monsieur le Curé, life would be impossible.'

Mother Brichet was the only religious devotee in the village. As soon as she had taken Communion, she hovered around the presbytery, knowing that La Teuse always kept a couple of loaves for her from the last bake. Sometimes she even went off with a rabbit or a hen from Désirée.

'There are too many scandals of this sort,' the priest went on. 'The marriage must take place as soon as possible.'

'Yes indeed, straight away, as soon as the others are willing,' said the old woman, very anxious about the gifts she received from the presbytery. 'Isn't that so, Brichet, we're not the ones who are such poor Christians as to go against Monsieur le Curé.'

Fortuné was sniggering.

'As for me, I'm very ready,' he declared, 'and so is Rosalie... I saw her yesterday, behind the mill. We haven't quarrelled, far from it. We stopped and had a laugh about it...'

Abbé Mouret broke in: 'Good. I'll go and talk to Bambousse. I think he's over there in the Olivettes.'

The priest was moving away when Mother Brichet asked him what had become of her youngest, Vincent, who had gone off that morning to serve the Mass. That young scamp really needed the guidance of Monsieur le Curé. And she accompanied the priest for a hundred yards or so, complaining about her poverty, the lack of potatoes, the cold weather that had frozen the olive trees, and the hot weather that threatened to burn their meagre harvests. At last she left, after assuring him that her son Fortuné said his prayers night and morning.

Voriau was now running ahead of Abbé Mouret. Suddenly, at a bend in the road, he set off into the fields. The abbé had to take a little path going up a hill. He was at the Olivettes, the most fertile part of the area, where the mayor of the community, Artaud, who went by the name of Bambousse, owned several fields of wheat, olives, and vines. Meantime the dog had hurled himself into the skirts of a tall, dark girl, who gave a loud laugh on seeing the priest.

'Is your father here, Rosalie?' the priest asked.

'Yes, just over there,' she said, stretching out an arm, still smiling.

Then, leaving the patch of ground she was hoeing, she walked over in front of the priest. Her pregnancy, still in its early days, showed only in a slight thickening of her hips. She had the powerful swinging gait of a hard-working woman, bareheaded in the sun, with her sunburned neck and her black hair like a mane. Her hands were stained green, and smelled of the weeds she was pulling up.

'Father,' she called out, 'here's Monsieur le Curé come to look for you.'

And she stayed where she was, bold as brass, and still with the sly laugh of a shameless creature. Bambousse, fat and sweating, with a round face, left his work to come cheerily to meet the priest.

'I'm willing to bet you've come to see me about repairs to the church,' he said, clapping his earth-covered hands together. 'Ah well, no, Monsieur le Curé, it can't be done. The village doesn't have a penny... If the Almighty provides the plaster and the tiles, we can provide the masons.'

This joke of his made the non-believer peasant burst out in a huge laugh. He slapped his sides, coughed, and almost choked.

'It's not the church I came to see you about,' the abbé replied. 'I came to talk to you about your daughter Rosalie...'

'Rosalie? What has she done to you?' asked Bambousse, narrowing his eyes.

The peasant girl was gazing boldly at the young priest, going from his white hands to his girlish neck with evident enjoyment, trying to make him blush. But he, with a calm face, and as if speaking of something quite indifferent, bluntly went on:

'You know what I mean, Bambousse. She is pregnant. She needs to be married.'

'Ah! so that's what it's about,' muttered the old man, with a slightly mocking air. 'Thanks for the message, Monsieur le Curé. The Brichets sent you, didn't they? Mother Brichet goes to Mass, and you're helping her out with getting her son settled; that's quite natural... But it's no concern of mine. It doesn't suit me, that's all.'

Surprised at this, the priest explained that the scandal must be brought to an end; he should forgive Fortuné, since the latter was very willing to right the wrong he had done, and a speedy marriage was needed for the honour of his daughter.

'Blah, blah, blah,' said Bambousse, shaking his head, 'such a lot of words! I'm not parting with my daughter. All that has nothing to do with me... Just a beggar, that Fortuné, with not so much as two half-pennies to rub together! A pretty situation it would be if the only thing needed to marry a girl was to go with her. Come on, with these youngsters, there would be weddings morning, noon, and night... Thank God! I don't have to worry about Rosalie. Everybody knows what's happened to her; that doesn't make her lame or hunchbacked, and she can marry anyone she likes in the region.'

'But what about her child?' the priest broke in.

'The child? It's not here yet, is it? Perhaps it never will be. If she does produce a child, we'll see.'

Rosalie, seeing which way the priest's intervention was going, decided to press her fists into her eyes, and moan. She even let herself fall to the ground, showing her blue stockings which went up even above her knees.

'You can just shut up, you little bitch!' shouted her father, suddenly furious.

And he went on, calling her everything, using crude language that made her laugh silently, behind her clenched hands.

'If I find you with your stud, I'll tie you together and drag you out just as you are in front of everybody. So you won't shut up? Then look out, you slut!'

And with that, he picked up a clod of earth and hurled it straight at her. The clod crashed on to her chignon and then down her neck, covering her with dust. Stunned, she got up and ran away, holding her head with her hands to protect herself. But Bambousse had time to hit her again with two more clods of earth: one merely glanced off her left shoulder; the other hit her so hard, full in the back, that she fell to her knees.

'Bambousse!' shouted the priest, snatching away from him the handful of stones he had just picked up.

'Leave it, Monsieur le Curé!' said the peasant. 'It was only soft earth. I should have thrown those stones... It's obvious you don't know anything about girls. They're as hard as nails. As for that one, I could douse her at the bottom of our well, or break her bones with a cudgel, and it wouldn't keep her from her filthy goings-on! But I have my eye on her, and if I catch her!... Anyway, they're all like that.'

He was getting over it now. He took a gulp of wine from a large flat bottle, encased in wicker, which was warming up on the burning earth. And with his former gross laughter, he added: 'If I had a glass, Monsieur le Curé, I'd happily share this with you.'

'So,' the priest asked once more, 'what about this marriage?'

'No, that just can't happen, people would laugh at me... Rosalie's a big strong girl. She's every bit as good as a man, you see. I'll have to hire a lad, the day she leaves... We can talk about all this after the grape harvest. The fact is I don't want to be robbed. Just giving, giving all the time, d'you see?'

The priest stayed there a good half-hour, preaching to Bambousse, talking to him about God, with all the arguments relevant to the situation. The old man had gone back to his work, now and again shrugging his shoulders, making jokes, growing more and more obstinate. At last he just shouted:

'Listen, if you were asking me for a sack of corn, you'd give me money for it... So why are you asking me to let my daughter go for nothing?'

Abbé Mouret went away, discouraged.

On his way down the path, he saw Rosalie rolling around under an olive tree with Voriau; the dog was licking her face and making her laugh. With her skirts whirling about, and her arms beating the ground, she was shouting at the dog:

'You're tickling me, you stupid creature. Stop it!'

Then when she saw the priest, she pretended to blush, tidied up her clothes, and once more pressed her fists into her eyes. The priest tried to comfort her, promising that he would make further efforts with her father. And he added that in the meantime, she should be obedient and not see Fortuné any more, to avoid making her sin any worse.

'Oh,' she said, with her brazen smile, 'there's no risk now, it's been done.'

He did not understand. He described for her the hell in which wicked women burn. Then he left her, having done his duty, wrapped once more in the serenity that allowed him to move without a tremor even through all the filthiness of the flesh.

CHAPTER VII

THE morning was becoming extremely hot. With the coming of the first fine weather, the sun made this vast, rocky amphitheatre into a flaming furnace. Abbé Mouret, judging by the height of the sun in the sky, realized he barely had time to get back to the presbytery if he was to get there by eleven o'clock and avoid the scoldings of La Teuse. His breviary read, and his mission to Bambousse completed, he started hurrying back, seeing in the distance the patch of grey which was his church, and the tall black outline of the great cypress, the Lone Tree, jutting out into the blue of the horizon. He was dreaming in the drowsy heat of how, that evening, he would decorate the chapel of the Virgin in the richest possible way, ready for the special services of May, the month of Mary. The path stretched out before his feet a soft carpet of dust, of pure and dazzling whiteness.

At the Croix-Verte, as he was about to cross the road that leads from Plassans to La Palud, a gig coming down the slope forced him to take refuge behind a pile of stones. He was just crossing to the other side, when a voice called out:

'Hey! Serge! Hello, Serge, my boy!'

The gig had pulled up, and a man was leaning out. Then the young priest recognized one of his uncles, Dr Pascal Rougon,* known simply as 'Monsieur Pascal' by the people of Plassans, where he treated the poor for nothing. Although he was barely over fifty, his large beard and abundant hair were already snowy white, and the regular features of his handsome face showed a delicacy full of kindness.

'What are you doing, scrambling about in the dust at this time of day?' he said jocularly, leaning out further to clasp the abbé's hands. 'Aren't you afraid of getting sunstroke?'

'No more than you are, Uncle,' replied the priest with a laugh.

'Oh, I have the hood of my carriage. Anyway, my boy, the sick don't wait. People die in all sorts of weather.'

And he explained that he was on his way to see old Jeanbernat, the caretaker of the Paradou, who had had an attack of apoplexy during the night. A neighbour, a peasant who was going to the market in Plassans, had come to fetch him.

'He must be dead by this time,' he went on. 'Still, it's always best to see... these old devils are amazingly tough.'

He was just raising his whip, when Abbé Mouret stopped him.

'Wait... What time do you make it, Uncle?'

'A quarter to eleven.'

The priest hesitated. He could already hear La Teuse's terrible voice in his ears, shouting that the lunch was going to be cold. But he decided to be brave and said:

'I'll come with you, Uncle... that poor wretch might want to make his peace with God, in his last hour.'

Dr Pascal could not restrain a burst of laughter.

'He? Jeanbernat! Ah, if you ever manage to convert him!... No matter, come anyway. Just the sight of you may be enough to cure him.'

The priest got in. The doctor, who seemed to regret his joke, chatted affectionately, while also clucking his tongue to spur the horse on. He observed his nephew closely out of the corner of his eye, with the keen attention of a scientist taking notes. With a series of short questions, he enquired in kindly fashion about his life, his habits, and the quiet happiness he enjoyed at Les Artaud. And at every satisfactory answer, seemingly reassured, he murmured, as if to himself:

'Good. So much the better. That's how it should be.'

He laid particular stress on the young priest's health. The latter, greatly surprised, assured him that he was in excellent health, had no fits of giddiness or nausea, and no headaches.

'Perfect, perfect,' Uncle Pascal went on repeating. 'In the spring-time, you know, the blood is very active. But you're solid enough, aren't you? By the way, I saw your brother Octave last month in Marseilles. He's going off to Paris; he'll have a good job there in a big business. Ah! what a lad, and what a life he leads...'

'What sort of life?' the priest naively asked.

To avoid answering, the doctor just clucked the horse on. Then he continued:

'In fact, everybody's well, your aunt Félicité, your uncle Rougon,* and the rest of them... That doesn't mean we're not in real need of your prayers. You are the saint of the family, my boy; I'm counting on you for the salvation of the whole lot.'

He was just laughing, but with so much affection that Serge him-self was able to take it as a joke.

'The trouble is,' the uncle went on, 'there are one or two in that lot who won't be very easy to take to Heaven. You'd hear some rich con-fessions, if they came to you one after the other... As for me, I don't need any confessions, I keep track of them from a distance, I have files on all of them at home, along with my plant collections and my med-ical records. One day I'll be able to draw up a wonderfully interesting chart...* We shall see, we shall see!'

He was getting quite carried away by his youthful enthusiasm for science. Then a glance at the cassock of his young nephew brought him up short.

'You, of course, you're a priest; you've done the right thing, it's a very happy state, being a priest. It's completely taken you over, hasn't it, so you're really turned towards the good. You'd never have been happy doing anything else. Your relatives, who started out like you, have committed their villainies without finding any consequent satisfaction... There's a logic to it all, my boy. A priest completes the family. It was inevitable anyway. Our blood was bound to go that way in the end... So much the better for you, you've been the luckiest.'

Then, with an odd smile, he corrected himself:

'No, it's your sister Désirée who's been luckiest of all.'

He whistled, cracked his whip, and changed the subject. After climbing a quite steep slope, the little carriage was now threading its way through desolate gorges. Then it reached some level ground, in a sunken lane bordered by an endless high wall. Les Artaud had disappeared; they were in a no man's land.

'We are getting near, aren't we?' asked the priest.

'This is the Paradou,' the doctor replied, pointing at the wall. 'Have you never come this way before? We're less than three miles from Les Artaud... A property that must have been splendid once, this Paradou. The wall of the park, on this side, is easily two kilometres long. But for more than a hundred years it's been left to run wild.'

'There are some lovely trees,' the abbé remarked, looking up in surprise at the masses of foliage spilling over the wall.

'Yes, this part is very fertile. Indeed, the park is a real forest, in the midst of the bare rocks that surround it on every side. Besides, this is where the Mascle rises. I think I was told there are three or maybe four springs.'

And disjointedly, with digressions into quite unrelated incidents, he told the story of the Paradou, which was a sort of local legend. In the time of Louis XV, a certain lord had built a splendid palace there, with vast gardens, fountains, flowing streams and statues, a real little Versailles, hidden away among the rocks, under the blazing sun of the Midi. But he had spent only one season there, with an adorably beautiful woman, who doubtless died there, for no one had ever seen her leave. The following year, the chateau burned down, the park gates were nailed up, and even the narrow slits in the wall filled up with earth, so ever since that distant era, no eye had penetrated the vast enclosure which occupied the whole of one of the high plateaux of the Garrigues.

'There must be no shortage of nettles,' said the abbé with a laugh. 'There's a smell of damp, the whole length of the wall, don't you think, Uncle?'

Then, after a silence:

'And to whom does it belong now, the Paradou?' he asked.

'As a matter of fact, nobody knows,' replied the doctor. 'The owner came on a visit, twenty or so years ago. But he was so alarmed by this nest of snakes that he never came back... The real master is the care-taker of the property, the eccentric old man, Jeanbernat, who has managed to make a home for himself in a lodge that still has walls... Look, you can see it, that dilapidated, grey building over there, with the big, ivy-covered windows.'

The gig went past a lordly gateway, ruddy with rust, boarded up with planks on the inside. The boundary ditches were black with brambles. A hundred or so yards away, the lodge where Jeanbernat lived was enclosed within the park, which it overlooked on one side. But on this side, the caretaker seemed to have barricaded his dwelling. He had cleared a little garden by the roadside; there he lived, facing south, turning his back on the Paradou, seemingly unaware of the vast expanse of greenery pouring out behind him.

The young priest jumped down, looking inquisitively around and questioning the doctor, who was hurriedly tethering the horse to a ring fixed in the wall.

'And does the old man live all alone in this remote spot?'

'Yes, quite alone,' his uncle replied.

But then he corrected himself:

'He has a niece with him, a niece he had to take into his care, an odd girl, quite wild... Hurry up. There's an air of death in the house.'

CHAPTER VIII

THE house seemed asleep in the midday sun, with its shutters closed, and the buzzing of the big flies climbing along the ivy up to the tiles of the roof. The sunlit ruin was bathed in happy peacefulness. The doctor pushed open the gate of the tiny garden, which was surrounded by a very high quickset hedge. And there, in the shade of a part of the wall, just straightening up his tall frame, was Jeanbernat, calmly smoking his pipe in the surrounding silence, and watching his vegetables growing.

'What on earth! So you're up, you joker!' cried the doctor in amazement.

'So, you were coming to bury me, were you!' the old man growled harshly. 'I've no need of anyone. I bled myself.'

He stopped short when he saw the priest, and made a gesture so threatening that Uncle Pascal hastened to intervene:

'He's my nephew,' he said, 'the new priest of Les Artaud—and a good lad... Devil take it! we didn't come all this way at this hour to eat you, Jeanbernat.'

The old man calmed down a bit.

'I don't want any Holy Joes round here,' he muttered. 'The sight of them is enough to kill people off. You hear, Doctor, no drugs and no priests when I depart, otherwise we'd fall out... But this one can come in anyway since he's your nephew.'

Abbé Mouret, quite astounded, could not find a word to say. He remained standing halfway up one of the paths, looking closely at this strange figure, this solitary, deeply wrinkled man, his face burned brick-red, his limbs withered and twisted like bundles of ropes, who yet seemed to carry his eighty years with an ironic disdain for life. When the doctor tried to take his pulse, he became angry again.

'Just leave me alone! I tell you I've already bled myself with my knife. It's all over now. What oaf of a peasant went and called you out? Doctor and priest, why not the undertakers?... Ah well, it can't be helped, people are stupid. That's not going to stop us from sharing a glass.'

He put out a bottle and three glasses on an old table that he pulled out into the shade. When the glasses were full to the brim, he wanted to clink glasses. His anger had melted away into a roguish jocularity.

'This won't poison you, Monsieur le Curé,' he said. 'A glass of good wine is not a sin... My word, it's the first time for me to clink glasses with a cassock, no offence to you. Your predecessor, that poor Abbé Caffin, refused to argue with me... He was afraid to.'

And he gave a loud laugh, before going on:

'Just imagine, he had made a pledge to prove to me that God exists... So every time I met him I would challenge him... He would rush off in confusion, I assure you.'

'What! God does not exist!' cried Abbé Mouret, at last breaking his silence.

'Oh, just as you wish,' Jeanbernat went on mockingly. 'We two can take it up all over again, if you like, but I warn you, I'm very good at it. Up there, in one of the rooms saved from the fire at the Paradou, are all the eighteenth-century philosophers, a heap of books on religion. I learned some great stuff from them. I've been reading those books for twenty years... Ah, my word! You'll find I can more than hold my own, Monsieur le Curé.'

He stood up. With a sweeping gesture, he pointed to the whole horizon, earth and sky, and solemnly repeated:

'There is nothing, nothing, nothing... When the sun gets blown out, that will be the end.'

Dr Pascal had given Abbé Mouret a gentle nudge. He narrowed his eyes, intently studying the old man, nodding agreement, to prod him into speaking further.

'So, Jeanbernat, you're a materialist?' he asked.

'Oh, I'm just a poor mortal,' the old man replied, as he relit his pipe. 'When the Count de Corbières, with whom I shared a wet nurse, died after falling off his horse, his children sent me here to look after this Sleeping Beauty park, to get rid of me. I was sixty, and thought I was finished. But death forgot me. I had to find myself somewhere to live... You see, when you live all alone, you end up seeing things in an odd sort of way. Trees are no longer trees, the earth comes to seem like a living person, stones tell you their stories. All sorts of silliness in fact. I know secrets that would bowl you over. Then what do you expect a person to do, in this devil of a desert? I read the books; it was more entertaining than hunting. The Count, who swore like a trooper, had always said to me: "Jeanbernat, my boy, I count on seeing you in hell, so you can serve me down there as you have served me up here."'

Again he made his sweeping gesture around the horizon, and went on:

'Understand me, there is nothing, nothing... all that stuff is just a big joke.'

Dr Pascal began to laugh.

'It's a good joke, anyway,' he said. 'Jeanbernat, you're a deceiver. I suspect you of being in love, for all your cynical airs. You spoke very tenderly of the trees and stones, a moment ago.'

'No, I assure you,' murmured the old man, 'I'm beyond all that. At one time, it's true, when I first met you and we went herb-gathering together, I was foolish enough to love all sorts of things in this great deceitful countryside. Fortunately, the books put paid to that... I would like my garden to be smaller; I don't go out to the road even twice in a year. You see this bench. I spend my days here, watching my lettuces grow.'

'And your tours of the park?' the doctor broke in.

'Tours of the park!' Jeanbernat repeated, looking extremely surprised, 'but it's more than twelve years since I set foot in the park. What would I be wanting to go there for, into that cemetery? It's too big. It's stupid, those trees that go on and on, with moss growing everywhere, broken statues, and holes you could break your neck on at every step. The last time I went in, it was so dark under the leaves, and stank so strongly of wild flowers, and such strange puffs of wind blew along the paths, that I was almost frightened. I barricaded myself in here so the park couldn't get in. A patch of sunshine, three feet of

lettuce to look at, a big hedge to blot out the horizon, that's already
more than enough for happiness. Nothing, that's what I'd like, nothing at all, something so small that the outside can't come in and disturb me. Six feet of earth, if you like, so I can lie down and die on
my back.'

He pounded the table with his fist, suddenly raising his voice, and
shouting at Abbé Mouret:

'Come on, another glass, Monsieur le Curé. You won't find the
devil at the bottom of the bottle, you know!'

The priest felt ill at ease. He didn't feel strong enough to bring
back to God this strange old man, whose mind seemed to him to be
strangely disordered. Now he began to recall some of La Teuse's gos-
sipings about the Philosopher, as the peasants of Les Artaud called
Jeanbernat. Vague scraps of scandalous stories lurked in his memory.
He stood up, with a sign to the doctor that he wanted to leave this
house in which he felt he was inhaling the odour of damnation. But
despite his confused fearfulness, a strange curiosity held him back.
He stayed on, going to the end of the little garden, intently scanning
the hallway, as if to see beyond it, behind the walls. Through the wide
open door, he could see only the dark of the staircase. And he went
back again, looking for some gap, some little glimpse on to that sea of
foliage that he knew to be very near from the great murmuring that
seemed to beat against the house with a sound like breaking waves.

'And is the little girl well?' asked the doctor, picking up his hat.

'Not bad,' Jeanbernat replied. 'She's never here. She often disap-
pears for the whole morning... But she might, after all, be in one of
the upstairs rooms.'

He raised his head and called out:

'Albine! Albine!'

Then, with a shrug of his shoulders:

'Oh well, you see, she's a real little baggage. Au revoir, Monsieur le
Curé. Always at your service.'

But Abbé Mouret didn't have time to reply to his challenge. A door
had just suddenly opened at the end of the hall, and a dazzle of light
had burst out in the darkness of the wall. It was like a vision of virgin
forest, a huge grove of tall trees, with the sun pouring down upon
them. In that flash of light, the priest made out, in the distance, some
precise details: a big yellow flower in the centre of a lawn, a sheet of
water falling from a high rock, a gigantic tree filled with a flock of

birds; and all of it drowned, lost, and blazing in such a chaos of green-ery, such an orgy of vegetation that the entire horizon seemed to have become one vast explosion of growth. The door slammed shut, and everything vanished.

'Ah! the wretched girl!' cried Jeanbernat, 'she's been in the Paradou again!'

Albine stood laughing at the entrance of the hallway. She was wear-ing an orange skirt, with a big red scarf tied round her waist, which made her look like a gypsy girl, in her Sunday best. She went on laugh-ing, with her head thrown back and her bosom heaving with mirth, delighting in her flowers, wild flowers, woven into her blonde hair, wound round her neck, on her breast, and round her thin, bare, suntanned arms. She was like a large, strongly perfumed bouquet.

'Oh, aren't you lovely!' growled the old man. 'You stink of green-ery... would anyone believe she was sixteen—this doll?'

Albine, quite unperturbed, only laughed louder. Dr Pascal, a great friend of hers, allowed himself to be kissed by her.

'So, you, then, don't feel afraid in the Paradou?' he asked.

'Afraid? Afraid of what?' she said, her eyes widened in astonish-ment. 'The walls are too high, no one can get in... there's only me. It's my garden, mine alone. It's splendidly big. I haven't yet found the end of it.'

'And the animals?' the doctor broke in.

'The animals? They're not harmful, and they all know me.'

'But it's so dark under the trees?'

'Of course! There's plenty of shade; without that, the sun would burn up my face... It's very nice and shady among the leaves.'

And she turned around, filling the narrow garden with the swirl of her skirts, and scattering that sharp scent of greenery that she carried with her. She had smiled at Abbé Mouret, with no embarrassment, undisturbed by the surprised look with which he gazed at her. The priest had moved away. This blonde child, with her long face, aflame with life, seemed to him to be the mysterious and disturbing daughter of that forest he had glimpsed in a patch of light.

'By the way, I've got a nest of blackbirds, do you want it?' Albine asked the doctor.

'No, thank you,' he replied with a laugh. 'You should give it to Monsieur le Curé's sister, who loves animals... Goodbye, Jeanbernat.'

But Albine had turned her attention to the priest:

'You're the curé of Les Artaud, aren't you? And you have a sister? I shall go and see her... Only, you mustn't talk to me about God. My uncle won't allow that.'

'You're bothering us, go away,' said Jeanbernat, with a shrug of his shoulders.

Then bounding away like a goat, she disappeared, leaving a shower of flowers behind her. The slam of a door was heard, then laughter from behind the house, resounding laughter that went off into the distance, like the gallop of some mad creature let loose in the grass.

'You'll see, she'll end up sleeping in the Paradou,' muttered the old man, seemingly quite indifferent.

And, as he saw his visitors out, he went on:

'Doctor, if you should find me dead one of these mornings, do me the favour of throwing me into the dungheap, over there, behind my lettuces... Good evening, gentlemen.'

He dropped back the wooden gate that closed off the hedge. The house resumed its air of happy peacefulness in the midday sun, with the buzzing of the big flies climbing up the ivy to the tiles of the roof.

CHAPTER IX

Now the gig was again running along the lane beside the seemingly interminable wall of the Paradou. Abbé Mouret was silent, gazing up at the massive branches that stretched out over the wall, like the arms of hidden giants. Noises came from the park, flutterings of wings, rustlings of leaves, branches giving way under furtive leapings, and huge sighs bending the tips of the young shoots, a huge breath of life rolling over the tops of a nation of trees. And sometimes the cry of a bird, sounding like human laughter, made the priest turn his head, as if troubled.

'Such an odd girl!' said Uncle Pascal, relaxing his grip on the reins.' She was nine years old when she landed on this pagan fellow. It was one of his brothers who lost all his money in something, I don't know what. The little girl was at boarding school somewhere when her father killed himself. She was quite an educated young lady already, reading and embroidering, chatting nicely and playing the piano a little. And such a coquette! I saw her when she arrived here, with lacy stockings, embroidered skirts, little lace blouses and cuffs, a heap of frills and flounces... Ah well, the frills and flounces didn't last very long!'

He laughed. A big stone almost upset the gig:

'It'll be a miracle if I don't end up leaving one of the wheels in this wretched road!' he muttered. 'Hold on tight, my boy!'

The wall still stretched on and on. The priest was listening.

'You see,' the doctor went on, 'the Paradou, with its sun, its stones and thistles, could devour an entire outfit in a day. The girl's beautiful dresses were gone in only three or four mouthfuls. She would come back quite stripped... Now she dresses like a savage. Today she was still passable; but there are times when she has nothing on save her shoes and petticoat... You saw how it was? The Paradou is hers. The day after she got here, she took possession. She lives there, jumping out of the window when Jeanbernat locks the door, still getting away, going who knows where, to secret places known only to her... She must have a fine time of it in this wilderness.'

'Just listen a moment, Uncle,' Abbé Mouret broke in. 'It sounds as if an animal is running along, behind this wall.'

Uncle Pascal listened.

'No,' he said, after a brief silence, 'it's the sound the gig makes on the stones... Well, the girl doesn't play the piano at all now. I think she's even forgotten how to read. Just imagine, a young lady returned to a state of uncivilized freedom, let loose to enjoy herself on a desert island. The one thing she has kept is her knowing, coquettish smile, when it suits her... Oh, my word! If ever you hear of a young girl who needs educating, I don't advise you to entrust her to Jeanbernat. He just lets nature take its course in a quite primitive way. When I dared to speak to him about Albine, he told me trees should not be prevented from growing however they like. He is all for the normal development of the temperament, he says... In any case, they are very interesting, both of them. I never come to these parts without calling on them.'

At last the gig was emerging from the lane. Here, there was a bend in the wall of the Paradou, which then stretched away as far as the eye could see, along the crest of the hills. Just as Abbé Mouret turned his head to cast one last glance at that grey barrier, whose impenetrable severity he had, in the end, begun to find strangely provoking, there was suddenly a noise of roughly shaken branches, and a grove of young birch trees seemed to wave a greeting to the passers-by from the top of the wall.

'I knew there was some animal running behind there,' said the priest.

But, although no person appeared, and nothing could be seen in the air save the birch trees, swaying ever more violently, a clear, laughing voice rang out, shouting:

'Au revoir, Doctor, Au revoir, Monsieur le Curé! I'm kissing the tree, and the tree is sending you my kisses.'

'Ah! It's Albine,' said Doctor Pascal. 'She must have run along beside our little carriage. She thinks nothing of going leaping over the bushes, that little sprite!'

Then he too shouted: '*Au revoir*, my dear!... You're a really tall girl to be waving to us like that!'

There was more laughter, and the birch trees bowed even lower, scattering leaves far and wide, even on to the hood of the gig.

'I'm as tall as the trees, and all the falling leaves are kisses,' the voice went on, changed by distance, and so musical, so merged into the breath rolling through the park that it made the young priest tremble.

The road was easier now. On the way down, Les Artaud came into view once more, at the far end of the scorched plain. When the gig reached the road to the village, Abbé Mouret absolutely refused to let his uncle drive him back to the presbytery. He jumped off, saying, 'No thanks, I'd rather walk, it will do me good.'

'As you please,' the doctor replied. Then, taking his hand:

'Well! if all your parishioners were like that brute Jeanbernat, you wouldn't have much to do. Still, it was you who chose to come here... And just keep well. At the slightest trouble, by day or by night, send for me. You know I look after the whole family for nothing... Goodbye, dear boy.'

CHAPTER X

WHEN Abbé Mouret was alone again, walking in the dust of the road, he felt more at ease. These stony fields brought back his dreams of severity, of an inner life lived in a desert. All along the lane the trees had dripped splashes of disturbing coolness on his neck, which were now being dried by the burning sun. The lean almond trees, the meagre corn, and the sickly vines on each side of the road seemed to calm him, drawing him out from the troubled state into which the too rich atmosphere of the Paradou had thrown him. And in the blinding light that flowed down from the sky upon this barren ground, the blasphemies of Jeanbernat no longer cast the slightest shadow. He felt a sudden surge of joy when, raising his head, he saw in the distance the motionless outline of the Lone Tree, and the patch of pink tiles on the church.

But as he went on, the abbé fell prey to another anxiety. La Teuse was going to give him quite a welcome with his cold lunch that must have been waiting for nearly two hours. He imagined the terrible face she would have, the flood of words with which she would greet him, the angry clatter of crockery he would hear the whole afternoon. When he had gone through Les Artaud, his fear became so intense that he hesitated, full of cowardice, wondering if it wouldn't be wiser to go round, and then get back through the church. But even as he pondered, La Teuse appeared in person, at the door of the presbytery, her bonnet askew, and her hands on her hips. With bent head, he had to climb the slope with that stormy gaze weighing down on his shoulders.

'I believe I'm rather late, my good Teuse,' he stammered, as he reached the last bend in the path.

La Teuse waited until he was right in front of her, up close. Then she glared at him furiously, and without a word, turned away and walked in front of him into the dining room, banging her heavy heels on the floor, so stiff with rage that she hardly limped at all.

'I've had such a lot to do!' began the priest, horrified by this silent reception. 'I've been running around the whole morning...'

But she cut him short with another look, so fixed and so cross that his legs seemed to give way. He sat down and began to eat. She served him with the brusque movements of an automaton, almost breaking the plates, so violently did she set them down. The silence became so intense that he was unable to swallow his third mouthful, quite choked with emotion.

'And my sister has already eaten?' he asked. 'She was quite right. Lunch must always go ahead, when I am held back elsewhere.'

No reply. La Teuse stood and waited for him to clear his plate, so she could remove it. Then, realizing he would not be able to eat with those unforgiving eyes watching him, crushing him, he pushed away his plate. This angry gesture was like a whiplash that drew La Teuse out of her obstinate implacability. She pounced.

'Ah, so that's how it is!' she cried. 'It's you who gets angry. Well, I'm leaving! You can pay for the journey so I can go back home. I've had enough of Les Artaud and your church, enough of everything.'

She was taking off her apron with trembling hands.

'You must have seen that I didn't want to say anything. What sort of a life is that? Only cheats behave like that, Monsieur le Curé! This is eleven o'clock, is it? Aren't you ashamed to be sitting down to eat at nearly two o'clock? It's not Christian! It's just not Christian!'

Then, standing firmly in front of him:

'Well then, where did you go? Who did you see? What business can have kept you?... If you were a child, you'd get a whipping. A priest is not meant to be out on the roads in the full sun, like some beggar with no home to go to... Oh, you're in such a state, your shoes are all white and your cassock smothered in dust! Who's going to brush that down for you? Who's going to buy you a new one?... Well, speak up! Tell me what you've been doing! My word, if people didn't know you, they might imagine you were up to all manner of things! And to be honest, I wouldn't want to take an oath on it. A person who eats at times like this is capable of anything.'

Relieved, Abbé Mouret just waited for the storm to subside. The old servant's angry words seemed to ease his nervous tension.

'Come on, my good Teuse,' he said, 'first, put your apron back on.'

'No, no,' she cried, 'it's all over. I'm leaving.'

But getting up, and with a laugh, he tied her apron back round her waist, as she struggled and stammered:

'No, I tell you... You're such a coaxer. I know what you're up to. I can see you're trying to put me off with your sweet talk... Where did you go? Tell me, then we'll see.'

He returned very happily to the table, like a man confident of victory.

'First of all,' he went on, 'you must let me eat. I'm dying of hunger.'

'Yes, you must be,' she murmured, with some sympathy. 'There's no sense in it... Shall I add a couple of fried eggs? It won't take long. Well, if you have enough... And everything is cold! And I'd prepared your aubergines with such care! A fine state they're in now! Like old shoe leather... Just as well you're not fussy about your food like poor old Monsieur Caffin... Oh! Well, you do have some good points, that I don't deny.'

While she chatted, she was serving him with motherly care. Then, when he had finished, she ran to the kitchen to see if the coffee was still hot. She was not making any effort now, and was limping quite outrageously in her delight at the reconciliation. Abbé Mouret usually shied away from coffee, since it upset his nerves; but in this instance, he accepted the cup she brought him. And as he paused for a moment at the table, she sat down opposite him, and like a woman tortured by curiosity, quietly repeated the question:

'Where did you go, Monsieur le Curé?'

'Well,' he answered with a smile, 'I went to see the Brichets, and I had a word with Bambousse...'

Then he had to tell her what the Brichets had said, and what Bambousse had said, and how they looked, and where they were working. When she heard the reply of Rosalie's father:

'Indeed,' she cried, 'if the babe were to die, the pregnancy wouldn't count.'

Then clasping her hands together with an expression of envious admiration:

'You must have had such a chat, Monsieur le Curé! More than half the day to achieve a result like that!... And you took your time getting back? It must have been devilish hot on the road?'

The abbé, who had got to his feet, made no reply. He was going to talk about the Paradou, and ask her some questions about it. But a fear of being too closely questioned, a vague feeling of shame that he didn't acknowledge even to himself, made him keep silent about his visit to Jeanbernat. He cut short any further questioning by asking:

'And where is my sister? I can't hear her.'

'Come with me, sir,' said La Teuse, starting to laugh and putting a finger to her lips.

They went into the next room, a rustic living room, with a wall-paper of large grey, faded flowers, and for furniture, four armchairs and a sofa covered in a horsehair material. On the sofa Désirée lay asleep, stretched out full length, with her head resting on her clenched fists. Her skirts were hanging down, leaving her knees bare, while her raised arms, bare to the elbows, emphasized the strong curve of her bosom. She was breathing quite heavily, through her red lips, which, slightly parted, showed her teeth.

'My word, she certainly can sleep!' muttered La Teuse.' She didn't even hear you shouting all those stupid things at me just now... Goodness, she must be quite worn out. Just think, she was cleaning out her animals until nearly midday. When she had done eating, she came in here and went off like a log. She hasn't stirred since.'

The priest gazed at her for a moment with great tenderness.

'We must let her rest as much as she likes,' he said.

'Of course... Isn't it a shame that she's such an innocent? Just look at that sturdy arm! When I'm dressing her, I always think of what a beautiful woman she would have become. Honestly, she would have given you some splendid nephews, Monsieur le Curé... Don't you think she looks rather like that stone statue of a fine lady in the corn market in Plassans?'

She was referring to the sculpture of a Cybele* stretched out on sheaves of corn, on the pediment of the market wall, the work of a student of Puget.* Without answering, Abbé Mouret gently pushed her out of the room, telling her to make as little noise as possible. And until the evening, total silence reigned in the presbytery. La Teuse was finishing off the washing soap out in the shed. The priest, at the bottom of the narrow garden, with his breviary fallen on his knees, was sunk in devout meditation, while pink petals rained down from the peach trees in bloom.

CHAPTER XI

At about six o'clock there was a sudden awakening. A noise of doors being opened and shut, accompanied by peals of laughter, shook the whole house, and Désirée appeared, with her hair hanging loose, and her arms still bare up to the elbows.

'Serge! Serge!' she shouted.

Then when she spotted her brother down in the garden, she ran to him, and sat on the ground for a moment at his feet, begging him:

'Come and see the animals!... You haven't seen the animals yet, have you! If you only knew how handsome they are now!'

He was hard to persuade. The farmyard rather frightened him. But when he saw tears in Désirée's eyes, he gave way. She then threw her arms around him, with the excited joy of a puppy, laughing even more, and not even trying to dry her cheeks.

'Ah, you're so good!' she stammered, as she dragged him off. 'You'll see the hens, the rabbits, the pigeons, and my ducks with their fresh water, and my goat whose room is now as clean as mine... I've got three geese and two turkeys, you know. Come on, hurry up. You shall see it all.'

Désirée was then twenty-two years old. Raised in the country with her wet nurse, a peasant from Saint-Eutrope, she had grown up in the muck of the farmyard. With an empty mind, no serious thoughts of any kind, she simply thrived on the rich soil and the open air of the country, developing only in the flesh, becoming a lovely animal, fresh and white, with pink cheeks and firm skin. She was rather like a pedigree she-ass, endowed with the gift of laughter. Despite squelching around from dawn to dusk, she still kept her delicate limbs, the supple curves of her hips, the bourgeois refinement of her virginal body; she was indeed a special creature, neither lady nor peasant, a girl nourished by the earth itself, with the broad shoulders and the narrow brow of a young goddess.

It was no doubt her lack of intelligence that drew her to the animals. It was only in their company that she was truly at ease, understanding their language better than human speech, and looking after them with maternal tenderness. In place of logical reasoning, she had a sort of instinct that put her on a level with them. At their first cry of pain, she knew what was wrong. She invented special meals for them that they fell upon greedily. With a wave of her hand she could settle their disputes, seemed to know at a glance their good or bad character, and could give immensely detailed and precise accounts of the life of the least little chick, to the profound astonishment of people for whom one little chicken is no different from any other. Her farmyard had become a veritable country, over which she reigned as absolute mistress; it was a country with a very complicated structure, disturbed by revolutions, and populated by very diverse beings, whose annals she alone knew. The sureness of her instinct was such that she could sense which ones in a clutch of eggs were sterile, and could tell in advance the number of baby rabbits there would be in a litter.

At the age of sixteen, with the arrival of puberty, Désirée had not had the fits of dizziness or nausea that afflicted other girls. She acquired the broad-shouldered look of a grown woman, became even more healthy, and stretched her dresses to the limit with the splendid blossoming of her body. From that time on, she had that well-rounded, freely swaying figure, the broad limbs of an ancient statue, and all the force of a vigorous animal. It was as if she had grown out of the soil of her farmyard, sucking up its sap through her sturdy white legs, as firm as young trees. And in this fullness of being, there was no whisper of carnal desire. She found constant satisfaction just feeling all around her a proliferation of life. From the heaps of manure, and the couplings of the animals, there rose a wave of generation, in which she tasted all the joys of fecundity. The laying of the hens satisfied something within her; she carried her female rabbits to the buck with the laughter of a beautiful girl, satisfied; she felt the joys of pregnancy as she milked her nanny goat. Nothing could have been healthier. She was filled, in all innocence, with the odour and heat of life. No depraved curiosity prompted her concern with reproduction, when she saw cockerels beating their wings, female animals in labour, or when the stink of the billy goat filled the little stable. She kept all the serenity of a splendid animal, with her clear gaze, devoid of thought, delighted to see her little world multiplying, feeling it as an enlargement of her own body, as if herself impregnated, and so identifying herself with all these mothers that she seemed the mother of them all, the natural mother, with a generative fluid falling from her fingertips without a tremor.

Ever since she had been at Les Artaud, Désirée's days had been spent in perfect bliss. At last she could fulfil the dream of her existence, the one desire that had ever tormented her in the infantile weakness of her mind. She had a farmyard of her own, a little place left entirely to her, where she could raise animals as she pleased. And so she buried herself in it, building with her own hands hutches for the rabbits, digging out a pond for the ducks, hammering nails in, carrying straw, allowing no one to help her. All La Teuse had to do was wash her afterwards. The farmyard was located behind the cemetery; indeed Désirée often had to go chasing among the tombs to catch some inquisitive hen who had jumped over the wall. At the far end was a shed, where the rabbit hutches were, and the henhouse; on the right, a little stable for the goat. In fact all the animals lived together, the rabbits running about among the hens, the goat paddling about among the ducks, the geese, turkeys, guinea fowl, and pigeons all intermingling along with three cats. As soon as Désirée showed up at the wooden gate that kept this whole population from getting into the church, she would be greeted by a deafening uproar.

'Ah! can you hear them?' she said to her brother, when they reached the dining-room door.

But when she had ushered him in, closing the gate behind her, she was fallen upon so fiercely that she almost disappeared. The ducks and the geese, clucking away, pulled at her skirts; the greedy hens leaped up and pecked vigorously at her hands, the rabbits huddled at her feet, and jumped up to her knees; and the three cats, meanwhile, were leaping on to her shoulders, and the goat, from the depths of the stable, was bleating at not being able to reach her.

'Leave me alone, you creatures!' she cried, her voice resonant with her lovely laughter, tickled by all these feathers and paws and beaks brushing against her.

And she didn't try at all to push them away. As she said herself, she would have let them eat her, she so enjoyed the feeling of all this life swooping upon her and wrapping her in its downy warmth. In the end, just one cat insisted on staying perched on her back.

'This is Moumou,' she said. 'His paws are like velvet.'

Then pointing to the farmyard, she added with pride 'Just see how clean it is!'

The yard had indeed been swept, washed, and raked over. But from the dirty water that had been disturbed, and the forked-up stable litter, rose an animal smell so rough and pungent that Abbé Mouret felt it catching in his throat. The dunghill was stacked up against the cemetery wall in a huge smoking heap.

'Ah! what a big pile!' Désirée went on, leading her brother into its acrid fumes. 'I got all of it there by myself, nobody helped me... Go on, it isn't dirty. It cleans. Look at my arms.'

She stretched out her arms, that she had simply plunged into a bucket of water, royal arms, superbly rounded, which had grown like rich white roses in that dunghill.

'Yes, yes,' murmured the priest, 'you have worked hard. It's all very nice now.'

He was moving towards the gate; but she stopped him.

'Wait a bit! You shall see it all. You can't imagine...'

She pulled him into the shed, by the rabbit hutches.

'There are little ones in every hutch,' she said, clapping her hands with enthusiasm.

Then, at some length, she told him all about the different litters. He had to squat down and press his nose against the wire netting, while she gave him the minute details. The mothers, with their big, anxious ears, looked askance at them, panting and rigid with fright. Then in one of the hutches, there was a sort of hollow, full of hair, at the bottom of which squirmed a living heap, an indistinct and blackish mass, whose strong breath seemed to come from one body. Alongside it, the little ones ventured to the edge of the hollow, with their enormous heads. Further along, they were already quite strong, looking like baby rats, ferreting and bounding about, with their rumps in the air, showing the white dot of their tails. These now had the playful grace of little children, racing around the hutches, the white ones with eyes of pale pink, and the black ones with eyes that gleamed like beads of jet. They were seized by sudden panics, leaping about, showing their thin paws, reddened by urine. Then they would settle down again in a heap, packed so closely together that only their heads were visible.

'It's you that's scaring them,' said Désirée. 'They're used to me.'

She called out to them, taking some bread out of her pocket. The little rabbits, reassured, came along, one by one, with their noses puckered up, and stood up against the wire netting. She left them like that for a moment or so, so her brother could see the pink down of their bellies. Then she gave the bread to the boldest one. At this, the whole lot rushed up, sliding forward, pressed together but without fighting; at times there were three little ones all nibbling on the same crust; others moved away, turning to the wall to be able to eat in peace; meanwhile their mothers stayed back, still huffing and puffing, distrustful and refusing the bread.

'Ah, the greedy things!' cried Désirée, 'they'd go on eating like that until tomorrow morning!... You can hear them in the night munching the leftover leaves.'

The priest had got to his feet, but she was not at all weary of watching her dear little ones.

'You see that one, over there, the white one with black ears... he just loves poppies. He's very good at picking them out among the other leaves... the other day he had a stomach ache. It hurt just under his back legs. So I picked him up and kept him warm in my pocket. Since then, he's been really frisky.'

She pushed her fingers in through the wire mesh to stroke their backs.

'It's like satin,' she said. 'They are dressed like princes. And very fussy about their appearance! Look, there's one who's always busy cleaning himself. He's wearing out his paws!... If you only knew how funny they are! Of course I don't say anything, but I'm perfectly aware of their little tricks. That grey one, for instance, the one who's looking at us, so hated one little female that I had to move her away. There were terrible scenes between them. It would take too long to tell you. But the last time he attacked her, and I arrived, furious, what did I see? That villain, huddled at the back, groaning as if at death's door. He was trying to make me think he was the victim...'

She broke off; then, addressing the rabbit, she said:

'Yes, I know you're listening to me, but you're nothing but a scoundrel.'

And turning to her brother, she whispered, with a wink:

'He understands everything I say.'

Abbé Mouret could stand it no longer, in the heat rising from the litters. The life swarming beneath the fur from the mothers' bellies had a powerful breath whose impact he could feel on his brow. Désirée, as if gradually intoxicated, was becoming more and more lively, more pink-cheeked, more firmly set in her flesh.

'But you don't have to go!' she cried, 'you always seem to want to get away... And my little chicks, look! They were born last night.'

She took some rice and threw a handful on the ground before her. The hen clucking to her brood, moved forward solemnly, followed by the whole band of chicks, who chirruped and scampered about as if demented. Then when they were in the midst of the grains of rice, the mother pecked at them furiously, and scattered the grains she had broken, while the little ones hastily picked at them in front of her. They were adorable in their infancy, half-naked, with their round heads, their eyes bright as steel spikes, their beaks so oddly placed, and their feathers ruffled in such a funny way, they looked like tuppenny toys. Désirée laughed delightedly at the sight.

'What little darlings they are!' she stammered.

She picked up two of them, one in each hand, and covered them with a frenzy of kisses. The priest had to examine them carefully, as she calmly added:

'It's not that easy to recognize the cocks, but I never get it wrong... That one is a hen, and this one, too, another hen.'

She put them back down. But now the other hens were coming along to eat the rice. A big red rooster, with dazzling plumage, came behind them, placing his broad feet with cautious majesty.

'Alexander is getting quite splendid,' said the priest, to please his sister.

Alexander was the rooster's name.

He was gazing at the girl with his fiery eyes, his head turned towards her, his tail outspread. Then he came and stood at the edge of her skirts.

'He's fond of me,' she said. 'I'm the only one who's allowed to touch him. He's a good cockerel. He has fourteen hens and I never find an unfertilized egg in the nests, do I, Alexander?'

She had bent down. The rooster didn't move away from her caresses. A surge of blood seemed to light up his crest. Beating his wings, and neck thrust forward, he crowed lengthily, with a sound as if blown from a brazen pipe. Four times he crowed, and all the cocks in Les Artaud responded from afar. Désirée was greatly entertained by the alarm on her brother's face.

'He's splitting your eardrums, isn't he?' she said. 'He has a really great voice, but I can assure you he's not nasty. The hens are the nasty ones... You remember the big speckled hen who laid yellow eggs? The day before yesterday, she hurt her foot. When the others saw the blood, they behaved like mad things. They all pursued her, pecking at her, drinking her blood, so by evening they had eaten her foot away... I found her with her head behind a rock, like an idiot, not making a sound, letting herself be eaten.'

The voraciousness of the hens left Désirée still laughing. She told of other cruelties with equanimity: little chicks with their tails torn to shreds, and their insides pulled out, all she had found of them was their neck and wings; a whole litter of kittens eaten in the stable in just a few hours.

'If you gave them a human being,' she went on, 'they would soon finish him off... And they're so hardy about pain! They carry on quite well, even with a broken limb. They may have wounds, holes in their bodies the size of your fist, but they gobble up their food just the same. That's what I love about them; their flesh grows back in two days, and their bodies are always warm, as if they had a store of sunshine under their feathers... When I want to give them a special treat, I cut up some raw meat for them. And as for worms! You shall see how fond they are of worms.'

She ran to the dungheap, and found a worm that she picked up with no sign of distaste. The hens rushed upon her hands. But she held the worm up high, amused by their greediness, until at last she opened her fingers. The hens then pushed and shoved each other; one of them got away with the worm in its beak, and the others in hot pursuit. The worm was caught, lost, and caught again, until one hen, with a great gulp, swallowed it. Then they all stopped dead, with their necks thrown back, their eyes eagerly waiting for another worm.

Désirée, delighted, called them by name, and spoke kindly to them, while Abbé Mouret took a few steps back from the intensity of this voracious life.

'No, I don't feel I can do that,' he said, when his sister tried to make him weigh a hen that she was fattening. 'It bothers me to touch a live animal.'

He tried to smile. But Désirée said he was a coward.

'Well, what about my ducks, my geese, and my turkeys! What would you do if you had to look after all that lot? What's really dirty is the ducks. You hear them clacking their beaks in the water? And when they dive, all you see is their tails, stuck straight up in the air like skittles... The geese and the turkeys aren't that easy to look after, either. Ah! Isn't it funny, when they walk along, some all white, and some all black, with their long necks. They're like grand ladies and gentlemen... And I wouldn't advise you to trust them with your finger. They'd swallow it up for you neatly, in one gulp... It's different for me, they kiss my fingers, as you can see!'

She was interrupted by a joyful bleat from the goat, who had at last managed to force open the ill-secured door of the stable. With two bounds, the animal was right beside her, bending its front legs to caress her with his horns. The priest felt it had a devilish grin, with its pointed beard and slanting eyes... But Désirée took hold of it by the neck, stroked its head, played at running with it, and talked of feeding on its milk. That often happened, she said, when she was thirsty in the stable, she would lie on the floor and suck.

'Look, they're full of milk,' she added, holding up the animal's enormous teats.

The abbé hastily closed his eyes, as if he had been shown something obscene. He recalled having seen on a gargoyle, in the cloister of Saint-Savournin in Plassans, a stone goat fornicating with a monk. Goats, stinking of sex, capricious and wayward as girls, offering their swinging udders to all comers, had remained for him hellish creatures, sweating with lewdness. His sister had only been given permission to keep one after weeks of entreaty. And when he came near, he avoided rubbing against the animal's long silky hair, and protected his cassock from the approach of its horns.

'It's all right, I'm going to let you go,' said Désirée, noticing his growing discomfort. 'But first there's something I must show you... You promise not to scold me? I haven't told you about it, because you wouldn't have been willing... But if you just knew how happy I am.'

She took on a pleading expression, clasping her hands, and leaning her head on her brother's shoulder.

'Some new bit of madness,' he muttered, but couldn't help smiling.

'You don't really mind, do you?' she went on, her eyes shining with joy. 'You won't be cross?... He's so pretty!'

She ran and opened a low door, under the shed. A little pig leapt out into the yard.

'Oh! the little cherub!' she said, looking utterly delighted, as she watched him scampering away.

The piglet was charming, all pink, with his snout washed in the greasy water, and a ring of dirt by his eyes, from his constant dipping into the trough. He trotted around, bumping into the hens, scurrying to eat the food thrown down for them, criss-crossing the small yard with his sudden twists and turns. His ears flopped over his eyes, his snout sniffed at the ground, and with his tiny paws he looked like a toy animal on wheels, and his tail, behind him, looked like the bit of string for hanging it up.

'I don't want that animal here,' cried the priest, very put out.

'Serge, my dear Serge,' Désirée pleaded once more: 'don't be mean... Look how innocent he is, the dear little thing. I'll wash him thoroughly, and keep him very clean. It was La Teuse who had him given to her for me. We can't send him back now... There now, he's looking at you, he's smelling you. Don't be alarmed, he won't eat you.'

She broke off in a fit of laughter. The little pig, in confusion, had run into the legs of the goat and knocked it over. He then went on running, squealing and rolling about, scaring the whole farmyard. To calm him down, Désirée had to give him a bowl of dishwater. Then he buried himself in the bowl right up to his ears; he gurgled and grunted, as shudders ran through his pink skin. His tail had lost its curl and hung down quite limp.

Abbé Mouret had a final surge of disgust at the noise of that stirred-up dirty water. Ever since he had been there, he had felt more and more that he was suffocating, his hands, his chest, and his face were burning with flushes of heat. Gradually he began to feel dizzy, as he smelled, in one pestilential breath, the fetid warmth of the rabbits and fowls, the lubricious stink of the goat, the sickly fatness of the pig. The air seemed loaded with fecundity, weighing down too heavily upon his virgin shoulders. It seemed to him that Désirée had grown, broadening at the hips, and waving enormous arms about, as she swept up from the ground with her skirts the powerful odour that was making him faint. He barely had time to open the wooden fence. His feet were sticking to the ground still wet with manure, so he felt as if he were being held in the grip of the earth. And the memory of the Paradou, though he tried hard to stop it, suddenly came back to him, the tall trees, the dark shadows, the powerful odours.

'You're all red now,' said Désirée, as she joined him on the other side of the fence. 'Aren't you glad to have seen all that?... Do you hear the noise they're making?'

The animals, seeing her leaving, had pressed themselves up against the netting, uttering piteous cries. The little pig, especially, was emitting a prolonged whining, like a saw being sharpened. But she, curtseying and blowing them kisses from her fingertips, was laughing at the sight of them huddled together there, as if in love with her. Then, pressing close to her brother as she accompanied him to the garden, she blushed and whispered in his ear:

'I'd like to have a cow.'

He looked at her, his hand already signalling his refusal.

'No, no, not now,' she went on eagerly. 'I'll talk to you about it later... There'd be enough room in the stable. A beautiful white cow, with brown patches. You'd see what lovely milk we'd have. A goat, in the end, is just too small... And when the cow had a calf!'

She was dancing about, clapping her hands, while for the priest she seemed really to be the farmyard she had carried with her in her skirts. So he left her at the bottom of the garden, sitting on the ground in the sun in front of a hive, while the bees, without stinging her, buzzed about like balls of gold on her neck, on her bare arms, and in her hair.

CHAPTER XII

BROTHER ARCHANGIAS dined at the presbytery every Thursday. He usually came early, to chat about the parish. It was he who, for the past three months, had been keeping the abbé informed, letting him know what was happening in the whole of the valley. That Thursday, while they waited for La Teuse to call them, they walked slowly round the church. When the priest related his interview with Bambousse, he was astonished to find the Brother thought the peasant's response was quite natural.

'He's quite right, that man,' said the Ignorantine.* 'You don't just give away what you have, like that. That Rosalie isn't worth that much, but it's always hard, to see your daughter throwing herself away on a beggar.'

'But still,' said Abbé Mouret, 'only marriage will put an end to the scandal.'

The Brother shrugged his massive shoulders and gave a disturbing laugh.

'If you really think you're going to bring health to this part of the world with this marriage!... In less than two years Catherine will be pregnant, then the others will go the same way, they'll all do it. And so long as they're to be married, they don't care what people think... These Artauds grow in bastardy as if in their natural compost. There's only one solution, I've told you, if you don't want the whole region poisoned, and that is: wring the neck of all the females... Not a husband, but a good beating, Monsieur le Curé, a good beating!'

Then calming down, he added:

'Let's allow everyone to dispose of his property as he thinks fit.'

Then he began to talk about arranging the hours for the catechism. But the abbé answered rather distractedly. He was gazing at the village that lay at his feet in the setting sun. The peasants were making their way home, silent men, walking slowly like weary oxen returning to the stable. The women standing outside the hovels called out to each other, gossiping loudly from door to door, while bands of children filled the road with the noise of their heavy clogs, pushing each other, rolling and sprawling around. A smell of humans arose from that heap of tumbledown houses. And the priest felt as if he were once more in Désirée's farmyard, looking at that proliferation of beasts incessantly multiplying. He felt the same heat of generation, the same endless births, the same sensation that had caused him to feel unwell. Caught up since that morning in the matter of Rosalie's pregnancy, he ended up thinking about that, the filth of existence, the urges of the flesh, and the unstoppable reproduction of the species, sowing men like grains of wheat. The Artauds were a herd, penned in between the four hills on the horizon, procreating and spreading themselves ever further across the land, with each new litter produced by the females.

'Look,' cried Brother Archangias, breaking off to point out a big girl being kissed by a lover behind a bush, 'there's another wretched hussy over there!'

He waved his long black arms about until he had driven the young couple away. In the distance, over the red earth and the barren rocks, the sun was dying with one last blaze of fire. Little by little, night fell. The warm scent of the lavender became fresher, carried by the light breezes now springing up. From time to time there was a great sigh, as if this terrible land, so burned by passions, had finally cooled down as the grey of twilight rained down upon it. Abbé Mouret, holding his hat in his hand, grateful for the coolness, felt the peace of the shade fall upon him once more.

'Monsieur le Curé! Brother Archangias!' La Teuse called out. 'Come quickly, the soup is on the table.'

It was a cabbage soup, and its strong aroma filled the presbytery dining room. The Brother sat down, and slowly emptied the enormous dish La Teuse had placed before him. He ate a lot, with such a gurgling of the gullet you could hear the food falling into his stomach. With his eyes fixed on the spoon, he did not speak.

'Is the soup not good, Monsieur le Curé?' asked the old servant. 'You're just poking it around your plate.'

'I'm just not hungry, my dear Teuse,' the priest replied with a smile.

'Well, that's not surprising when you mess things about as you do! You'd be hungry all right if you hadn't had lunch after two o'clock.'

Brother Archangias, after gathering into his spoon the few drops of soup left at the bottom of his dish, said gravely:

'You should keep regular meal times, Monsieur le Curé.'

Meanwhile, Désirée, who had also finished her soup quite solemnly, without uttering a word, had got up and followed La Teuse into the kitchen. The Brother, left alone with the abbé, was cutting himself some long slices of bread, which he ate while waiting for the main course.

'So you had a really long walk, then?'

The priest didn't have time to respond. A sound of footsteps, exclamations, and loud laughter arose from the end of the corridor on the farmyard side. There seemed to be a brief argument. A flute-like voice that disturbed the abbé seemed to grow angry, talking quickly, then dying away with a burst of merriment.

'What is it?' he asked, getting up from his chair.

Désirée bounded in. She was hiding something under her turned-up skirt. She kept repeating:

'Isn't she funny! She wouldn't come in. I got hold of her by her dress, but she's so strong, she got away from me.'

'Who's she talking about?' asked La Teuse, rushing in from the kitchen with a plate of potatoes, topped by a piece of bacon.

The girl had sat down. With infinite care, she drew out from under her skirt a blackbirds' nest, in which three baby birds lay asleep. She put it down on her plate. As soon as the little birds saw the light, they stretched out their frail necks, opening their blood-red beaks, demanding to be fed. Désirée clapped her hands, delighted, filled with extraordinary emotion on seeing these creatures that she didn't know at all.

'It's that girl from the Paradou!' cried the abbé, with a sudden realization.

La Teuse had gone to the window.

'It's true,' she said. 'I should have recognized her by her voice, piercing as a cicada. Ah! the Gypsy! Look, she has stopped just down there, to spy on us.'

Abbé Mouret moved forward. He did indeed seem to see, behind a juniper bush, the orange skirt of Albine. But Brother Archangias rose up angrily behind him, stretching out his fist, shaking his loutish head, and thundering:

'Devil take you, you brigand's child! I'll drag you round the church by your hair if I catch you coming here with your evil tricks!'

A burst of laughter, fresh as a breath of the night, rose from the path. Then came the sound of light footsteps running and the swish of a dress on the grass, like the slithering of a snake. Standing at the window, Abbé Mouret could just make out in the distance a patch of light colour sliding in and out of the pine trees, like a reflection of moonlight. The breezes from the countryside had that powerful scent of greenery, that perfume of wild flowers that Albine scattered from her bare arms, her unfettered figure, and her flowing hair.

'A damned soul, a child of perdition!' Brother Archangias growled, as he returned to the table.

He greedily ate up his bacon, swallowing the potatoes whole instead of bread. La Teuse was unable to persuade Désirée to return to her dinner. That great child was in a state of ecstasy over her nest of blackbirds, asking all sorts of questions, what they ate, whether they laid eggs, and how to tell which were cocks in these creatures.

But the old servant was struck by a suspicion. She stood firmly on her good leg, and looked the young priest straight in the eye:

'So you know the Paradou people?' she said.

Then he simply told her the truth, told her about his visit to old Jeanbernat. La Teuse exchanged scandalized looks with Brother Archangias. At first she made no response. She moved around the table, limping violently, bringing her heels down hard enough to crack the floor.

'You could very well have told me about these people during the last three months,' the priest said at last. 'I'd then at least have known what sort of people I was visiting.'

La Teuse stopped dead, as if her legs had suddenly given up.

'Don't lie, Monsieur le Curé,' she stammered; 'don't lie; that only makes your sin worse. How dare you say I didn't tell you about the Philosopher, that pagan, who is the scandal of the whole neighbourhood! The truth is that you just never listen when I'm talking to you. It goes in through one ear and out the other... Ah, if you'd only listen, you'd save yourself a lot of trouble.'

'I too have spoken to you about these abominations,' said the Brother.

Abbé Mouret gave a little shrug of his shoulders.

'Well, I didn't remember,' he went on. 'It was only at the Paradou that I thought I recalled certain stories... Besides, I would have gone anyway to see that poor man, since I thought he was dying.'

Brother Archangias, his mouth full, struck the table violently with his knife, shouting:

'Jeanbernat is a dog. He should die like a dog.'

Then seeing the priest shaking his head in protest, he cut him off, saying:

'No, no, there is no God for him, no penitence, no mercy, it would be better to throw the Host to the pigs than take it to that scoundrel.'

He helped himself to more potatoes, with his elbows on the table, and his chin in his plate, chewing furiously. La Teuse, with pursed lips, and white with anger, contented herself with saying starchily:

'Let be. Monsieur le Curé will do just as he pleases, Monsieur le Curé now has secrets from us.'

A heavy silence fell. For a while the only sound was the noise of the Brother's jaws, accompanied by the strange gurgling of his gullet. Désirée, with her arms wrapped round the blackbirds' nest, still on her plate, was smiling at the nestlings, with her face bent over them, while she went on talking quietly to them, in her own private twittering that they seemed to understand.

'People say what they're doing, when they've nothing to hide!' La Teuse suddenly burst out.

And silence fell once more. What exasperated the old servant was the mystery the priest seemed to have made of his visit to the Paradou. She saw herself as a woman shamefully deceived. Her curiosity was wounded. She walked round the table, not looking at the abbé, not talking to anyone, just relieving her feelings.

'I see now, that's why lunch was so late!... We go gadding about without a word to anyone, until two o'clock in the afternoon. We go visiting houses so ill-famed that we don't dare say where we've been. Then we tell lies, and deceive everybody.'

'But', Abbé Mouret gently interrupted, while making an effort to eat, to avoid further annoying La Teuse, 'nobody asked me if I had been to the Paradou, I didn't have to lie.'

La Teuse went on, as if she had not heard:

'We get dust all over our cassock and come back looking like a thief. And if some good person, taking an interest in you, questions you for your own good, she gets pushed around, treated as a woman of no account, someone not in your confidence. We hide like a sneak, we'd rather die than breathe a word, we don't even have the courtesy to amuse the household by telling what we've seen.'

She turned to face the priest.

'Yes, that's you, that is. You're secretive, you're a wicked man.'

Then she began to cry. The abbé had to comfort her.

'Monsieur Caffin used to tell me everything,' she cried.

But she was calming down now. Brother Archangias was finishing a big piece of cheese, seeming quite unperturbed by this scene. In his view, Abbé Mouret needed to be put straight, and La Teuse was quite right to pull him up. He emptied a last glass of wine and threw himself back in his chair to digest.

'So,' the old servant asked, 'what did you see at the Paradou? At least tell us about it.'

With a smile, Abbé Mouret related in a few words the odd way in which Jeanbernat had received him. La Teuse asked question after question, and gave vent to indignant exclamations. Brother Archangias clenched his fists and shook them.

'May Heaven strike him down!' he said, 'and burn them, him and that witch of his!'

Then the abbé in his turn tried to get some details about the people of the Paradou. He listened attentively as Brother Archangias told of monstrous doings.

'Yes, that devil-woman came along one morning and sat in the school. A long time ago. She would have been about ten. I let her be, thinking her uncle must have sent her for her first Communion. For two months she revolutionized the class. She made them all adore her, the hussy! She knew lots of games, and she made all sorts of pretty things with leaves from the trees and bits of rag. And she was so clever, like all such daughters of hell! She was the best at the cat-echism... Then one morning, the old man popped in, right in the middle of the lessons. He said he would smash everything, he said the priests had stolen his child. We had to get the local police to throw him out. The girl had got away. I could see her through the window, in a field opposite, laughing at her uncle's fury. She had been coming to school for two months, and he didn't have the slightest suspicion. Talk about stirring up trouble!'

'She's never taken her first Communion,' said La Teuse quietly, with a slight shudder.

'No, never,' Brother Archangias replied. 'She must be sixteen now. She's growing up like an animal. I saw her running on all fours in a thicket near La Palud.'

'On all fours,' the servant muttered, with an anxious glance at the window.

Abbé Mouret tried to express some doubt, but the Brother burst out in fury:

'Yes, on all fours! And she jumped like a wild cat, with her skirts tucked up, showing her thighs. If I'd had a gun, I could have shot her. Animals much more pleasing to God get shot... And besides, everyone knows she comes and wails every night around Les Artaud. Wailings like those of a bitch in heat. If a man ever fell into her clutches, she would surely skin him down to the bone.'

And all his hatred of womankind burst forth. He shook the table with a blow from his fist, and shouted his usual insults:

'They have the devil in their bodies. They stink of the devil, in their legs, in their arms, in their bellies, everywhere... that's what bewitches fools.'

The priest nodded in assent. The violence of Brother Archangias and the loquacious tyranny of La Teuse were like the lashes of a whip, whose sting he often felt on his shoulders. It was with a pious joy that he sank into these base depths, and these hands full of the grossest vulgarity. The peace of Heaven seemed to him to lie at the bottom of this contempt for the world, and this brutalization of his whole being. It was an insult he enjoyed inflicting on his body, a gutter into which it pleased him to drag his tender nature.

'There is nothing but filth,' he murmured as he folded his napkin.

La Teuse was clearing the table. She made to remove the plate on which Désirée had put the blackbirds' nest. 'You're not going to bed here, Mademoiselle,' she said. 'It's time to leave these nasty creatures.'

But Désirée defended the plate. She covered the nest with her bare arms, not laughing now, annoyed at being disturbed.

'I hope you're not going to keep those birds,' cried Brother Archangias. 'That would bring bad luck... You need to wring their necks.'

And he stretched out his big hands. The girl got up and moved away, trembling, holding the nest close against her chest. She was staring fixedly at the Brother, with swollen lips like a she-wolf about to bite.

'Don't touch the little ones,' she stammered. 'You are ugly!'

She emphasized this word with such strange contempt that Abbé Mouret shuddered, as if the ugliness of Brother Archangias had just struck him for the first time. The Brother merely growled. He had an unspoken hatred of Désirée, whose beautiful animal growth was offensive to him. When she had gone out, walking backwards, without taking her eyes off him, he shrugged his shoulders, muttering between his teeth an obscenity that nobody heard.

'She had better go to bed now,' said La Teuse. 'She'd be in the way later on in the church.'

'Have they come?' asked the abbé.

'The girls have been out there for some time, with armfuls of leaves... I'm going to light the lamps. We can begin whenever you like.'

A few seconds later, she could be heard swearing in the sacristy, because the matches were wet. Brother Archangias, now alone with the priest, asked in a surly voice:

'Is it for the month of Mary?'

'Yes,' Abbé Mouret replied. 'These last few days, the village girls had such a lot of work to do they were unable to come as usual to decorate the chapel of the Virgin. The ceremony had to be put off to this evening.'

'A nice custom indeed,' muttered the Brother. 'When I see them laying down their branches, I just feel like throwing them to the ground so they can at least confess their wickedness before touching the altar... It's shameful that women can parade their dresses so close to the holy relics.'

The abbé made a gesture of apology. He had only been at Les Artaud for a short time; he had to follow their customs.

'When you're ready, Monsieur le Curé?' La Teuse called out.

But Brother Archangias held him back for a moment:

'I'm going,' he said. 'Religion is not a whore, that it should be dressed up in flowers and lace.'

He was walking slowly to the door. He stopped again, pointing with one of his hairy fingers, to add:

'Beware of your devotion to the Blessed Virgin.'

CHAPTER XIII

INSIDE the church, Abbé Mouret found about ten girls holding branches of olive, laurel, and rosemary. As garden flowers rarely grew on the rocks of Les Artaud, it was the custom to decorate the altar of the Virgin with hardy greenery that lasted through the whole month of May. La Teuse added some wallflowers, with their stems stuck into old bottles.

'Will you leave it to me, Monsieur le Curé?' she asked. 'You're not used to it... Look, stand over there, in front of the altar. You can tell me if you like the decorations.'

He agreed, and it was she in fact who took charge of the ceremony. She had climbed on to a set of steps and she dealt roughly with the girls as they came up, one by one, with all their leaves.

'No, not so fast! Give me time to get the branches fixed. We can't have all these bundles falling down on Monsieur le Curé's head. Well! Babet, it's your turn. When you decide to look at me, with your big eyes! A fine bit of rosemary, yours is! It's as yellow as a thistle! All the donkeys in the country must have peed on it!... Now you, La Rousse.* Ah! well that, at least, is a lovely bit of laurel! Is it from your Croix-Verte field?'

The girls kissed the altar as they laid their branches upon it. They stayed for a moment beside the altar cloth, passing the branches to La Teuse, forgetting the look of piety they had slyly adopted to step up to the altar; they ended up laughing, butting each other with their knees, leaning their hips on the edge of the altar table, and thrusting their bosoms even on to the tabernacle. And above their heads, the big Virgin, in gilded plaster, bent her painted face and smiled with her pink lips at the naked little Jesus she carried on her left arm.

'That's it, Lisa!' cried La Teuse, 'you might as well sit on the altar while you're at it! Will you lower your skirts! Is it half decent to show your legs like that?... If one of you goes making an exhibition of herself, I'll be using her branches on her face! Can't you just pass these things to me without any fuss?'

And turning round, she asked:

'Does it look nice to you, Monsieur le Curé? Is it all right?'

She was creating, behind the Virgin, a niche of greenery, with the leafy tips hanging over to form a cradle, and falling back like fronds of palm. The priest uttered a word of approval, then risked a suggestion:

'I think', he murmured, 'that there should be a bouquet of softer leaves on top.'

'Yes, indeed,' growled La Teuse. 'They only bring me laurel and rosemary. Which one of you has brought an olive branch? Ah yes, not one! They're afraid they might lose two or three olives, these heathens!'

But Catherine stepped up with a huge olive branch that almost hid her from view.

'Ah! you have some, you minx,' the old servant went on.

'You bet she has!' said a voice, 'she stole it. I saw Vincent breaking off a branch for her, while she kept a lookout.'

Catherine, furious, swore that wasn't true. She had turned round without letting go of the branch, shaking her head free of the bush she was carrying; she lied with amazing ease, and invented a whole long story to prove the olive branch was really her own.

'And anyway,' she said in conclusion, 'all the trees belong to the Blessed Virgin.'

The abbé tried to intervene. But La Teuse asked what they thought they were doing, leaving her for so long with her arms up in the air. And she firmly attached the olive branch to the altar, while Catherine, who had climbed on to the steps behind her back, imitated the awkward way in which she used her good leg to manoeuvre her large bulk around; and the priest himself had to smile.

'There!' said La Teuse, coming down to stand beside him, to cast an eye over her work, 'that's the top part done... Now we're going to put some clumps between the candlesticks, unless you'd prefer a garland, running along the ledges.'

The priest opted for the large clumps.

'Come on then, let's get on,' said the servant, standing once more on top of the steps. 'We're not going to stay here all night... Will you just kiss the altar, Miette! Do you think you're in your stable?... Monsieur le Curé, can you see what they're doing, down there? I can hear them laughing like maniacs.'

When one of the two lamps was lifted up, the dark end of the church was lit up. Under the gallery, three big girls were playing at pushing each other; one of them had fallen with her head in the holy water stoup, and this made the other girls laugh so much they had collapsed on the floor to laugh at their ease. They came back now, with sidelong glances at the priest, looking quite happy to be scolded, with their hands dangling down, slapping against their thighs.

But what especially enraged La Teuse was suddenly catching sight of Rosalie going up to the altar with her bundle, along with the other girls.

'Will you come down from there!' cried La Teuse. 'It's not cheek you're short of, my girl!... Come on, hurry, and take your bundle away.'

'Why?' Rosalie boldly asked. 'I don't think anyone's going to accuse me of stealing it!'

The other girls drew closer, pretending to be stupid, and exchanging glances with gleaming eyes.

'Go away,' La Teuse repeated; 'this is no place for you, d'you hear!'

Then losing what little patience she had, she brutally let slip a really coarse word, which set off a giggle of delight among the peasant girls.

'Oh yes?' said Rosalie. 'And how do you know what others get up to? You haven't been watching, have you?'

Then she decided to burst into tears. She threw her branches away, and allowed herself to be led a few steps away by the abbé, who spoke to her very sternly. He had tried to silence La Teuse; he was beginning to feel very uncomfortable among these big shameless girls, filling the church with their armfuls of foliage. They were pushing right up to the altar steps, surrounding it with a patch of living forest, bringing in the strong scent of the aromatic woods, like an odour rising from the limbs of these hard-working girls.

'Let's get on, let's get on!' he said, gently clapping his hands together.

'Well, yes, I'd much rather be in my bed,' muttered La Teuse; 'do you think it's easy tying up all these bits of wood?'

She had now managed to tie some lofty plumes of foliage between the two candlesticks. She folded the set of steps and Catherine put it away behind the main altar. She now only had to plant two clumps of foliage, one on each side of the altar table. The last bunches of greenery were enough for that bit of the garden; there were even some branches left over, so the girls scattered them over the ground, up to the wooden railing. The altar of the Virgin had become a grove, a woodland coppice, with a green lawn in front.

La Teuse then agreed to make way for Abbé Mouret. He went up to the altar and once more lightly clapped his hands.

'Young ladies,' he said, 'we shall continue tomorrow with our devotions for the month of Mary. Those who are unable to come should at least say their Rosary at home.'

He knelt, while the peasant girls, with a great swishing of skirts, settled down on their heels, on the floor. They followed his prayer with a confused muttering, at times mingled with laughter. One of them, being pinched from behind, let out a yelp that she tried to smother with a fit of coughing, and that so amused the others that for a moment or so, after saying the Amen, they were doubled up with laughter, with their noses on the flagstones, unable to get up.

La Teuse sent these brazen girls away, while the priest, who had crossed himself, remained absorbed, in front of the altar, as if no longer hearing what was happening behind him.

'Come on now, clear off!' La Teuse was muttering. 'You're a bunch of good-for-nothings, who can't show respect even for God... It's shameful, it's unheard of, girls rolling about on the floor in a church, like beasts in a field... What are you doing over there, La Rousse? If I see you pinching somebody, you'll have me to deal with! Yes, yes, stick your tongue out at me, I'll tell Monsieur le Curé. Out, out, you hussies!'

She was driving them slowly to the door, hobbling round them, limping frantically. She had just succeeded in getting the last of them out through the door when she spied Catherine, sitting calmly in the confessional with Vincent; they were eating something with evident delight. She chased them out. And as she thrust her neck outside the church, before shutting the door, she saw Rosalie hanging on the shoulders of big Fortuné, who had been waiting for her; they disappeared into the darkness by the cemetery, with a faint noise of kisses.

'And that creature has the gall to present herself at the altar of the Virgin!' she stammered, as she shot the bolts. 'And I know the others are no better. They're all sluts, they came this evening with their branches just for a bit of fun, and to get kissed by the boys afterwards. Tomorrow not a single one of them will come; Monsieur le Curé can say his *Ave Marias* by himself... We shall only see the hussies who are meeting someone.'

She was bumping into the chairs, and straightening them up, then having a look around to see nothing unseemly was left behind, before going up to bed. In the confessional, she picked up a handful of apple peel that she threw behind the main altar. She also found a bit of ribbon torn from somebody's bonnet, with a lock of black hair; these she made into a little parcel for further investigation. Otherwise, the church appeared to be in good order. The night lamp had enough oil to keep it going, and the flagstones of the choir would last until Saturday without being washed.

'It's almost ten o'clock, Monsieur le Curé,' she said, as she drew near the priest, who was still on his knees: 'You should go to bed.'

He made no response, but merely bowed his head.

'Yes, I know what that means,' La Teuse went on. 'An hour from now, he'll still be there, on the cold stone, making himself ill... I'm going, because I'm annoying him. No matter, there's no sense in it: having lunch when others are having dinner, and going to bed when the hens are getting up!... I'm annoying you, aren't I, Monsieur le Curé? Goodnight! Go on with you, you're just not sensible!'

She had decided to leave; but she came back to put out one of the two lamps, muttering to herself that praying so late was 'murder on the oil'. At last she left, after using her sleeve to wipe the altar cloth, which she thought looked grey with dust. Abbé Mouret, with his eyes turned upward, and his arms pressed against his breast, was alone.

CHAPTER XIV

LIT by only one lamp, burning amid the greenery on the altar of the
Virgin, the church was filled at each end with big, floating shadows.
The pulpit cast a great patch of dark shadow up to the rafters of the
ceiling. The confessional was a large black shape, creating a strange
outline under the gallery, like a broken-down sentry box. All the light,
softened and tinged with green by the leaves, rested on the great gilded
Virgin, who seemed to descend, majestically, carried by the cloud on
which the heads of winged cherubs were playing. Seeing that round
lamp shining in the midst of the branches, one might have thought it
was a pale moon rising at the edge of a wood, lighting some regal
apparition, a heavenly princess crowned with gold, and dressed in
gold, walking, with the nakedness of her divine infant, into the depths
of mysterious paths. Between the leaves, along the high plumes of
foliage, in the wide cradle of the arch, and even on the branches
strewn on the ground, starry rays moved drowsily, like that milky rain
of light that shines through the bushes on clear nights. Slight noises
and creakings came from the two dark ends of the church; the big
clock to the left of the choir was ticking slowly, with the heavy breathing of a sleeping machine. And the radiant vision, the Mother with
her slender bands of chestnut hair, as if reassured by the nocturnal
peace of the nave, came down further, scarcely bending the grass in
the clearings under the gentle flight of her cloud.

Abbé Mouret gazed at her. This was the time when he loved the
church. He forgot the lamentable Christ, the tortured figure daubed
with ochre and crimson, agonizing behind him in the chapel of the
Dead. He no longer had the distraction of harsh daylight coming
through the windows, or the gaiety of morning coming in with the
sun, the life outside, the sparrows and the branches invading the nave
through the broken windowpanes. At this hour of the night, nature
was dead, shadows draped the whitewashed walls with black crêpe,
and the cold air made a salutary hairshirt for his shoulders; he could
dissolve into absolute love, without any play of light, caress of a breeze
or a scent, or beating of an insect's wing coming to draw him from the
joy of loving. His morning Mass had never given him such superhuman delights as his evening prayers.

Abbé Mouret gazed at the Virgin, with his lips moving in prayer.
He saw her coming towards him in ever increasing splendour from

the depths of her green niche. It was no longer moonlight flowing over the tops of the trees. She now seemed dressed in sunlight; she advanced majestically, glorious and colossal, so all-powerful that he was briefly tempted to throw himself face down on the ground, to avoid the blaze of this door opening on to Heaven. His whole being was rapt in adoration, the words died on his lips, and he then recalled Brother Archangias's final remark, which seemed a kind of blasphemy. The Brother often reproached him for this special devotion to the Virgin, which he saw as a real theft from the devotion due to God. According to him, it weakened the soul, put religion in petticoats, and created a sentimental type of piety, unworthy of the strong. He resented the Virgin for being a woman, for being beautiful, and for being a mother; he was always on his guard against her, he had a gnawing fear of finding himself tempted by her grace, and succumbing to her seductive charms. 'She will lead you astray,' he had one day cried to the young priest; he saw in her the seeds of human passion, a slide towards the delights of beautiful brown hair, large limpid eyes, and mysterious gowns that hung from the neck to the tip of the toes. His was the revolt of a saint, fiercely separating the Mother from the Son, and asking, as the latter had done: 'Woman, what have I to do with thee?'* But Abbé Mouret persisted, prostrating himself, and trying to forget the Brother's harsh words. He had nothing else save his ravished delight in the immaculate purity of Mary, to raise him out of the depths of self-humiliating baseness in which he was trying to drown himself. When alone, in front of the great, gilded Virgin, he hallucinated to the extent of seeing her lean towards him to give him the braids of her hair to kiss, and he once more felt very young, very good, very strong, very just, and brimming with a life made of love.

Abbé Mouret's devotion to the Virgin dated from his childhood. As a rather shy child, given to hiding away in corners, he liked to think that a beautiful lady was looking after him, that two very gentle blue eyes followed him with their smile wherever he went. Often at night, when he felt a light breath upon his hair, he would say that the Virgin had come to kiss him goodnight. He had grown up with this feminine caress, in an atmosphere full of the rustling of divine robes. From the age of seven, he satisfied his need for loving by spending all the money he was given on religious pictures* that he carefully hid, to enjoy them by himself. And he was never tempted by those of Jesus with the lamb, or Christ on the cross, or God the Father leaning over a cloud with his great beard; he always went for the tender images of Mary, with her small, laughing mouth and her delicate hands outstretched. Little by little, he had collected them all, Mary standing between a lily and a distaff, Mary carrying the Child as if she were an elder sister, Mary with a crown of roses, Mary with a crown of stars. For him they were a family of beautiful young girls, alike in their grace and their kindly expression, with the same sweet face, and so young beneath their veils, that in spite of their being called the Mother of God, he was not afraid of them as he usually was of grown-ups. They seemed to him to be his own age, to be little girls he would have liked to meet, little girls from Heaven, with whom little boys who died at the age of seven would forever play in some part of paradise. But he was already a serious child, and as he grew older, a prey to the delicate sensitivities of adolescence, he kept to himself the secret of his religious love. Mary grew older with him, always one or two years older than he, as is desirable in one's closest friend. She was twenty when he was eighteen. She no longer kissed his brow as he lay asleep; she stood a few paces away, with her arms folded, with her chaste and adorably sweet smile. He now spoke her name only under his breath, feeling a sort of fluttering at his heart each time the beloved name passed his lips in his prayers. He no longer dreamed of childish games in the garden of Heaven, but only of an everlasting contemplation in front of this white figure, so pure that he would not have dreamed of touching it with his breath. He hid even from his mother the intensity of his love for Mary.

Then a few years later when he was at the seminary, that beautiful love for Mary, so straightforward and natural, gave rise to an ill-defined uneasiness. Was the cult of Mary necessary for salvation? Wasn't he robbing God by giving part of his love, indeed the greater part, to Mary, his thoughts, his heart, his everything? Disturbing questions, an inner conflict that intensified his passion and bound him ever more tightly. So he buried himself in the subtleties of his feelings. He found amazing delights in arguing the legitimacy of his feelings. Books devoted to the cult of the Virgin seemed to excuse him, delighting him and filling him with arguments he could repeat with all the reverence of prayers. It was in these books that he learned how to be the slave of Jesus in Mary. He was going to Jesus by way of Mary. And he quoted all sorts of proofs, he noted distinctions, and drew conclusions: Mary, whom Jesus had obeyed on earth, was to be obeyed by all men; Mary still kept her maternal power in Heaven, where she was the great distributor of God's treasures; the only one who could beseech him, the only one who could allocate heavenly thrones. Mary, a humble creature in comparison with God, was raised up to him, to become the human link between Heaven and earth, the intermediary for every grace and mercy; and the conclusion was always the same, that she was to be loved above all else, in God himself. Then there were more arduous theological complexities, the marriage of the Heavenly Bridegroom, the Holy Spirit setting his seal on the Chosen Vessel, making the Virgin Mother into an everlasting miracle, giving her inviolable purity to the adoration of mankind; the Virgin victorious over all heresies, the irreconcilable foe of Satan, the new Eve prophesied as the one to crush the serpent's head, the august Portal of Grace, through which the Saviour had entered once and would do so again on the Last Day, a vague prophecy, announcing an even greater role for Mary, and leaving Serge in a dream of some immense expansion of love. This entry of woman into the jealous and cruel Heaven of the Old Testament, this figure of white purity, set at the feet of the awesome Trinity, was for him the very grace of religion, the consolation for the dread that accompanied faith, a refuge for him as a man lost in the mysteries of dogma. And when he had proved to himself, lengthily, point by point, that she was the easy, short, perfect, and certain pathway to Jesus, he abandoned himself to her once more, with no remorse; he strove to be her true devotee, to die to himself, losing himself in submission.

This was a time of divine voluptuousness. The books devoted to the cult of Mary burned in his hands. They spoke to him in a language of love that gave off a smoke like incense. Mary was no longer the adolescent girl veiled in white, standing with folded arms a few steps from his bed; she arrived now in a blaze of light, just as Saint John saw her,* dressed in the rays of the sun, crowned with twelve stars, with the moon at her feet; she perfumed him with her sweet scent, inflaming him with desire for Heaven, ravishing him even with the heat of the stars blazing upon her brow. He threw himself down before her, declaring himself her slave; and nothing was sweeter to him than this word slave, which he kept repeating, enjoying it all the more in his stammering mouth as he prostrated himself at her feet, to become her meanest possession, nothing more than the dust raised by the passing of her blue robe. He said, like David,* 'Mary is made for me.' And he added, like the Evangelist, 'I have taken her to be my sole wealth.' He called her 'my dear mistress', and bereft of words, descended into the babbling of a child or lover, in the breathless gasping of his passion. She was the Blessed among women, the Queen of Heaven, glorified by the nine choirs of angels, the Mother of purest love, the Treasure of the Lord. Vivid images spread out before him, comparing her to an earthly paradise of virgin land, with beds of flowers of virtue, green meadows of hope, impregnable towers of strength, and delightful dwellings of trust. She was also a fountain sealed by the Holy Spirit, a sanctuary on which the Holy Trinity rested, the throne of God, the city of God, the altar of God, the temple of God, the world of God. And he, walking in this garden, in the shade and in the sun, in the enchantment of this greenery, sighed for the water of that fountain, lived in the beautiful inmost being of Mary, leaning upon it, hiding within it, wholly losing himself in it, drinking the milk of infinite love that fell drop by drop from that virginal breast.

Every morning in the seminary, as soon as he got up, he would greet Mary, bowing reverently a hundred times, with his face turned towards the patch of the heavens he could see through his window; in the evening, he took his leave of her with the same number of inclinations, his eyes gazing at the stars. And often, when the night was clear and serene, and Venus shone golden and dreamy in the warm air, he would lose himself in contemplation and there would fall from his lips, in a sort of gentle singing, the *Ave Maris Stella*, the tender hymn that opened out for him distant blue shores and a calm sea, scarcely wrinkled by the quiver of a caress, and lit by a smiling star, the size of a sun. He would then recite the *Salve Regina*, the *Regina cœli*, the *O gloriosa Domina*,* and all the prayers, all the canticles. He would read the Office of the Virgin, the sacred books honouring her, and the little Psalter of Saint Bonaventure,* of such devout tenderness that tears made it difficult for him to turn the pages. He fasted and mortified himself to make her the offering of his wounded flesh. From the age of twelve he wore her livery, the holy scapular,* with the twofold image of Mary sewn on to the cloth, and he could feel the warmth of it on the bare skin of his back and chest, with shivers of delight. Later, he wore the chain* to show his enslavement to love. But his principal act of love was always the angelic salutation, the *Ave Maria*, the perfect prayer of his heart. 'Hail Mary', and he would see her coming towards him, full of grace, blessed among women; he would cast his

heart at her feet for her to walk upon, in her gentleness. That salutation he repeated over and over in a hundred different ways, always
inventing new ways to make it more efficacious. He would say twelve
Aves in honour of the crown of twelve stars that encircled Mary's
brow; he would say fourteen in memory of her fourteen joys;* or else
ten, seven times over, to mark the years she lived upon the earth. He
rolled the beads of his Rosary between his fingers for hours. Then on
certain days, assigned to special mystical meetings, he would lengthily
mutter all the endless prayers of the Rosary.

When he was alone in his cell, with time for his love, he would kneel
on the hard floor, and the entire garden of Mary would spring up around
him with its flowers of chastity blooming on high. The Rosary let its
garland of *Aves* and *Paters* flow between his fingers like a garland of
white roses, mingled with the lilies of the Annunciation, the blood-
red flowers of the Calvary, and the stars of the Coronation. He moved
slowly along the sweet-scented alleys, pausing at each one of the fifteen
decades of *Ave*, to dwell upon the mystery* to which it was related.
He would stay lost in joy, sorrow, and glory, according to the three sets:
the joyful, the sorrowful, and the glorious. The incomparable legend,
the story of Mary, was a complete human life, with all its smiles and
tears and triumph that he relived from beginning to end in an instant.
First he entered into the joy of the five happy mysteries,* bathed in
the serenity of dawn: the greeting of the Archangel, a ray of fecundity
slipping down from Heaven, bringing the adorable swooning of the
immaculate union; the visit to Elizabeth* on a bright morning full of
hope, when the fruit of Mary's womb made that first movement that
makes mothers grow pale; then the birth in a stable in Bethlehem,
with the long line of shepherds coming to greet the divine maternity;
the newborn child carried to the Temple, in the arms of the mother,
who, although still tired, is smiling, and already happy to offer her son
to the justice of God, to the embrace of Simeon,* and to the desires
of the world; then Jesus, later, revealing himself to the doctors of the
Temple, where his anxious mother finds him, proud of him and comforted. Then, after that morning of such gentle light, the sky seemed
suddenly to darken. The abbé walked now only among brambles,
scratching his fingers on the beads of the Rosary, bent under the horror of the five sorrowful mysteries:* Mary in agony with her son in the
garden of the Mount of Olives,* receiving with him the lashes of the
flagellation, feeling on her own brow the laceration of the crown of

thorns, carrying the dreadful weight of his cross , and dying at his feet
on the hill of Calvary.* These necessary sufferings, this atrocious
martyrdom of an adored Queen, for whom, like Jesus, he would have
given his own blood, created in him a revolt of horror that even ten
years of the same prayers and exercises had not been able to calm. But
the beads moved on, and a sudden opening appeared in the darkness
of the crucifixion, and the resplendent glory of the last five mysteries
burst forth with all the joy of a liberated star. Mary, transfigured, sang
the Alleluia of the resurrection, the victory over death, the eternity of
life; with arms outstretched, and head thrown back in admiration, she
watched the triumph of her son who ascended into Heaven among
gold clouds, edged with purple. She gathered the Apostles around her,
enjoying, as on the day of her conception, the burning of the spirit of
love descending from Heaven in ardent flames. She, in her turn, was
snatched up by a flight of angels, carried away on white wings like an
immaculate arch, and put down gently in all the splendour of the
celestial thrones; and there, as a final glory, in a light so dazzling that
it dimmed the sun, God crowned her with the stars of the firmament.
Passion has only one word, and saying one after the other, the hundred and fifty *Aves*, Serge had not repeated himself once. The monotonous murmuring of this word, always the same word, like the 'I love
you' of lovers, took on a deeper meaning each time; he went over it
slowly, conversing endlessly with the aid of that single Latin phrase,
and getting to know Mary thoroughly, until, as the last bead of the
Rosary slipped from his fingers, he felt faint at the thought of parting
from her.

The young man had so often spent his nights in this way, starting
again on the decades of *Aves* at least twenty times, always putting off
the moment when he had to take leave of his beloved mistress. Day
would break and he would still be whispering away. And to deceive
himself, he would say it was just the moon that was making the stars
grow pale. His superiors had to reprimand him about these vigils of
his, which left him languid, and so pale it was as if he had lost blood.
For a long time he had kept on the wall of his cell a coloured print of
the Sacred Heart of Mary,* smiling serenely, and pushing aside her
bodice to reveal the red hole in her bosom in which her heart was
burning, pierced by a sword,* and crowned with white roses. That
sword caused him great anguish, provoking in him such an intolerable horror of the suffering of the woman that the very thought of it

shattered his pious submissiveness. He erased the sword, keeping only the crowned and blazing heart, half torn from that exquisite flesh, and offered to him. And then he felt loved. Mary was giving him her heart, her living heart, even as it was beating in her breast, along with the rosy droplets of her blood. This was no longer an image of devout passion, but a material thing, a miracle of affection, which made him spread out his hands while he was praying, to receive in all reverence the heart leaping from that immaculate breast. He could see it, could hear it beating. He was loved, the heart was beating for him! His whole being was as if possessed with the need to kiss the heart, to melt into it, and lie with it deep in that open breast. She loved him actively, wanting him beside her in all eternity, hers forever. She loved him effectively, constantly concerned for him, following him everywhere, and avoiding even the slightest infidelities. She loved him tenderly, more than all other women put together, with a love that was as blue, as deep, as infinite as the sky. Where could he ever have found so desirable a mistress? What earthly caress was comparable to the breath of Mary in the air where he walked? What wretched coupling, what filthy pleasure could be weighed against this everlasting flower of desire, always growing without ever blossoming? Then the *Magnificat*,* like a cloud of incense, rose from his lips. He sang Mary's song of delight, her thrill of joy at the approach of the Divine Spouse. He glorified the Lord who put down the mighty from their thrones, and who had sent Mary to him, poor naked child, dying of love on the icy floor of his cell.

And when he had given everything to Mary, his body and soul, his worldly goods and spiritual goods, when he was left naked before her, with all his prayers done, the litanies of the Virgin would spring forth from his burning lips, with their repeated, obstinate, desperate appeals, in a supreme plea for heavenly succour. It seemed as if he were climbing a ladder of desire; with each bound of his heart he mounted one more step. First he called her Holy. Then he called her Mother, most pure, most chaste, kindly and admirable. And with renewed vigour he proclaimed her virginity, his mouth seemingly refreshed by each mention of the word 'virgin', to which he linked ideas of power, goodness, and fidelity. As his heart bore him ever higher up the steps of light, a strange voice, springing from his very blood, spoke within him, and blossomed into dazzling flowers. He would have liked to dissolve into a scent, to expand into light, or expire in a musical sigh. While he

was calling her Mirror of Justice, Temple of Wisdom, and Spring of
his Joy, he could see himself pale with ecstasy in that mirror, he knelt
on the warm flagstones of that temple, and drank long, intoxicating
draughts from that spring. And he went on transforming her, giving
free rein to the madness of his love, to be joined in ever closer union
with her. She became a Vessel of Honour chosen by God, a Bosom of
Election into which he longed to pour his whole being and sleep forever. She was the Mystic Rose,* a great flower blooming in paradise,
a flower made of the angels circulating around their Queen, so pure,
so fragrant that her scent reached him even in the depths of his
unworthiness, with such a surge of joy it almost made him burst. She
changed into a House of Gold, a Tower of David, an Ivory Tower
of immeasurable wealth, of a purity swans would envy, tall in stature,
a strong and rounded figure, upon which he would have liked to
stretch out his arms like a belt of submission. She stood erect on the
horizon, she was the Gate of Heaven, which he could see behind her
shoulders, when a breath of wind blew aside the folds of her veil. She
grew ever larger beyond the mountain, when night began to pale. She
was the Star of Morning, bringing aid to lost travellers, a dawn of
love. Then he, having reached these heights, breathless but not yet
satisfied, words no longer being equal to the pulses of his heart, could
only further glorify her with the title of Queen, which he bestowed
upon her nine times over, like nine swings of the censer. His canticle
seemed to be dying of joy in these cries of ultimate triumph: Queen
of virgins, Queen of all the saints, Queen conceived without sin! She,
rising ever higher, shone forth in splendour. He, on the final step, the
step reached only by Mary's intimates, paused there for a moment,
overcome by the rarefied atmosphere which made him dizzy, still too
far off to be able to kiss the hem of the blue robe, and already feeling
himself toppling, with the eternal desire to climb higher, to try to
reach that superhuman state of bliss.

How often, after the communal recital of the litanies of the Virgin
in the chapel, had the young man been left with crippled knees and
empty head, as if injured in a really bad fall. Since leaving the seminary, Abbé Mouret had learned to love the Virgin even more. He
devoted to her that passionate cult which, for Brother Archangias,
smacked of heresy. It was she, according to Abbé Mouret, who was to
save the Church by some amazing miracle, whose impending mani-
festation would delight the whole earth. She was the sole miracle of

our impious age, the lady in blue who appeared to simple shepherds,* the whiteness glimpsed at night between two clouds, with the hem of her veil trailing over the thatched roofs of the peasants' cottages. When Brother Archangias asked him brutally whether he had ever seen her, he merely smiled, with his lips tightly closed, as if to guard his secret. The truth was that he saw her every night. She appeared to him now, not as his joyful sister, nor as a beautiful, fervent girl: she wore a bridal robe, with white flowers in her hair, and from her partly lowered eyelids, her eyes, wet with hope, shed light upon her cheeks. And he understood that she was coming to him, that she was promising to delay no longer, that she was saying: 'Here I am, receive me.' Three times every day, when the *Angelus* rang out: at the awakening of dawn, in the maturity of noon, and in the gentle fall of twilight, he bared his head, and said an *Ave*, casting around him, looking to see if the bell were not at last announcing the coming of Mary. He was twenty-five. He was waiting for her.

In the month of May, the young priest's waiting was filled with a joyous hope. He didn't even worry any more about La Teuse's scoldings. If he stayed so late at prayer in the church it was with the mad idea that the tall gilded Virgin would finally step down to him. However, he also feared her, this Virgin who looked so like a princess. He did not love all Virgins in the same way. This one aroused in him a sovereign respect. She was the Mother of God; she had the fullness of fecundity, the august countenance, and the powerful arms of the Divine Spouse carrying Jesus. He imagined her in this way, in the courts of Heaven, letting the train of her royal robe float among the stars, too high for him, so mighty that he would crumble into dust if she deigned to lower her eyes to meet his. She was the Virgin of his days of weakness, the severe Virgin who, with the awesome vision of paradise, restored his inner peace.

That evening, Abbé Mouret stayed kneeling in the empty church for more than an hour. With hands clasped together, and eyes fixed on the gold Virgin, who rose like a star in the midst of the greenery, he sought to lull his ecstasy, and calm the strange disturbances he had felt that day. But he did not slide into the half-sleep of prayer with his usual happy ease. Mary's maternity, glorious and pure as it showed itself to be, that rounded figure of mature womanhood, and that naked child she bore on her arm, all worried him, seeming to continue in Heaven that overflowing thrust of generation, in the midst of

The Sin of Abbé Mouret

which he had been walking all that day. Like the vines of the stony hillsides, like the trees of the Paradou, like the human herd of the Artauds, Mary too was associated with birth, and the engendering of life. And his prayer faltered on his lips, he fell prey to distractions, seeing things he hadn't seen before, the soft curve of the light brown hair, the gentle swell of the pink painted chin. Then she had to become more severe and crush him with the blaze of her omnipotence, to return him to the words of the interrupted prayer. It was through her golden crown, her golden robe, and all the gold that transformed her into a tremendous princess that she at last succeeded in crushing him into a slavish submission, with prayer flowing smoothly from his lips, and his mind lost in the depths of one single adoration. Until eleven o'clock he stayed, half asleep, half awake, in an ecstatic trance, no longer conscious of his knees, feeling as if suspended in mid-air, rocked like a child being lulled to sleep, and yielding to this restfulness while still remaining aware of something heavy weighing on his heart. All around him, the church filled with shadows, the lamp grew smoky, and the greenery on high darkened the painted face of the tall Virgin.

When the church clock gave voice to a strangled creaking before striking the hour, Abbé Mouret shuddered. He had not felt the chill of the church falling upon his shoulders. Now he was shivering. As he made the sign of the cross, a rapid memory flickered through the torpor of his awakening; the chattering of his teeth reminded him of the nights spent on the cold stones of his cell in front of the Sacred Heart of Mary, his body shaking with fever. Painfully, he got to his feet, displeased with himself. In general, he left the altar with his body at peace, and the sweetness of Mary's breath upon his brow. That night, when he took the lamp to go to his room, it seemed as if his temples were bursting: his prayers had been in vain. He now felt once more, after his brief respite, the same heat that ever since the morning had been growing from his heart up to his head. Then, reaching the door of the sacristy, just as he was about to go out, he turned and mechanically raised the lamp for one last look at the tall Virgin. But she was drowned in the darkness falling from the rafters, engulfed in all the foliage, showing now only the gold cross of her crown.

CHAPTER XV

ABBÉ MOURET'S room, on one corner of the presbytery, was enormous, with two huge square windows, one on each side; one of the windows looked out on to Désirée's farmyard, and the other over the village of Les Artaud, with the valley in the distance, the hills, and the whole horizon. The bed with its yellow curtains, the walnut chest of drawers, and the three chairs with straw seats, seemed quite lost beneath the high ceiling with its whitewashed beams. A slightly acrid odour, that rather sour smell of old country buildings, rose from the red-polished tiles that shone like glass. On the chest of drawers a big statuette of the Immaculate Conception added a gentle, grey note between two earthenware pots that La Teuse had filled with white lilac.

Abbé Mouret put his lamp down in front of the Virgin, on the edge of the chest of drawers. He felt so unwell that he decided to light the fire of vine stumps which was already laid. And he stayed there, with the tongs in his hand, watching the twigs burning, his face lit by the flames. Beneath him he could hear the deep sleep of the house. The silence, buzzing in his ears, at length began to sound like whispering voices. Slowly, irresistibly, these voices took possession of him, redoubling the anxiety which already, during the day, had clutched at his throat. What could be the source of such anguish? What could it be, this strange discomfort, which had so quietly grown and become intolerable? He hadn't committed any sin after all. It seemed as if he had left the seminary just the day before, with all the ardour of his faith, and so fortified against the world that though he walked among men, he saw only God.

Then he believed himself to be back in his cell, at five o'clock one morning, about to get up. The deacon on duty went by, tapping on his door with a stick, uttering the regulation cry:

'*Benedicamus Domino.*'

'*Deo gratias!*' he replied, only half awake, and his eyes puffy with sleep.

Then he leaped on to his narrow mat, washed, made his bed, swept his room, and put fresh water in his jug. This bit of housework was a joy for him, with the chill of morning upon his skin. He could hear the sparrows in the plane trees in the yard outside getting up at the same time, with a noisy fluttering of wings and deafening chirping. It was their way of saying their prayers, he thought. He then went down to the Meditation room, where, after his prayers, he spent half an hour on his knees, considering this thought of Saint Ignatius:* 'What use is it for a man to conquer the universe if he loses his soul?'* This subject was a fertile source of good resolutions, which saw him renouncing all the goods of this world in favour of his long-cherished dream of a life in the desert, with a wide blue sky as his sole wealth. After ten minutes, his knees, bruised by the flagstones, hurt so much that he gradually felt his whole body fainting away into an ecstasy in which he saw himself as a great conqueror, master of a vast empire, throwing away his crown, breaking his sceptre, and trampling under his feet untold splendour, caskets full of gold, cascades of jewels, cloth studded with precious stones, to go and bury himself in some remote desert hut, clad in a rough shirt that scratched his spine. But Mass now dragged him out of these fantasies, from which he emerged as if from some lovely, real story, that he would have lived through in ancient times. He took Communion, sang ardently the psalm of the day, not hearing any other voice than his own, a voice of crystal purity, so clear that he could hear it soaring up to the ears of the Lord. And when he was going back up to his room, he mounted the stairs one step at a time, as directed by Saint Bonaventure and Saint Thomas Aquinas;* he walked slowly, deep in meditation, with slightly bowed head, finding an exquisite pleasure in following even the most minute recommendations. Then it was breakfast time. In the refectory, the hunks of bread, lined up alongside glasses of white wine, filled him with delight, for he had a good appetite and a merry disposition, saying, for instance, that the wine was a very Christian wine, in a bold allusion to the water the bursar was accused of adding to the bottles. This did not stop him resuming his air of gravity when entering the classroom. He took notes on his knees, while the teacher, with his wrists on the edge of the pulpit, spoke in his usual Latin, with the occasional French word, when he could think of nothing better. Discussions then arose; and the students debated in a strange jargon, without finding it funny. Then, at ten o'clock came twenty minutes of reading from Holy Scripture. He went to get the sacred book, which was richly bound, with gilt-edged pages. He kissed the book with special reverence, and read it with his head bared, bowing each time he came upon the names of Jesus, Mary, or Joseph. The second meditation found him fully ready to bear, for the love of God, another period of kneeling, even longer than the first. He was careful not to sit back on his heels even for a second; he enjoyed the examination of conscience which lasted three-quarters of an hour, striving to find sins he had committed, and managing to believe himself damned for having forgotten, the previous evening, to kiss the images of his scapular, or for having fallen asleep on his left side: abominable sins that he would gladly have expiated by wearing out his knees until evening, but happy sins too, that demanded his attention, and without which he would not have known how to occupy his guileless heart, lulled by the blameless life he was leading. He went to the refectory quite comforted, as if he had unburdened himself of some great crime. The seminarists on duty, with the sleeves of their cassocks rolled up and a blue twill apron tied round their waists, were bringing the vermicelli soup, the boiled meat cut into little squares, and servings of mutton with beans. There was a terrible noise of jaws at work, a gluttonous silence, a furious plying of forks, interrupted only by envious glances at the horseshoe table, where the staff of the seminary ate more delicate meats and drank redder wine; meantime, above the ravenous munching, the toneless voice of some peasant's son with sound lungs, and no respect for full stops or commas, stumbled through some pious reading-matter, missionaries' letters, pastoral letters from bishops, or articles from the religious press. Between mouthfuls, he listened. These scraps of polemic, these accounts of far-off journeys, surprised and even frightened him, revealing a welter of activities and a vast horizon outside the walls of the seminary such as he never imagined. They were still eating when the noise of a wooden clapper board announced it was time for recreation. The yard was sandy, and planted with eight big plane trees which in summer provided a cooling shade; on the south side of the yard stood a thick wall, five metres high, bristling with broken glass, above which all you could see of Plassans was the tip of the spire of Saint Mark, a short stone needle, piercing the blue sky. He walked slowly, from one end of the yard to the other, in a single line, with a group of fellow students; and each time he came back, facing the wall, he looked at the spire, which for him was the whole town, the whole earth, beneath the free-floating clouds. Some noisy groups started arguments beneath the plane trees; some friends went off in pairs into corners, watched over by a member of staff from behind his window curtains; some rowdy games of tennis and skittles were started, disturbing the quiet lotto-players, stretched out on the ground over their cards and numbers, which some reckless ball would often cover with sand. When the bell rang, the noise subsided, a cloud of sparrows would fly up from the trees, and the students, still out of breath, took themselves off to their plainchant lessons, with their arms folded and heads bowed. The rest of the day passed in the same peacefulness; he went back to the classroom, had tea at four o'clock, and set off once more on that everlasting walk facing the spire of Saint Mark; he had supper amid the same noise of champing jaws, while the same rough voice continued the reading of that morning; then he went up to the chapel to say his evening prayers, and went to bed at a quarter past eight, after sprinkling his bed with holy water to protect himself from bad dreams.

What lovely days like that he had spent in the old part of Plassans, in that ancient convent that smelled of centuries of piety. For five years the days had followed one after another, flowing along like the unchanging murmur of a limpid stream. He was remembering now all sorts of details that touched his feelings. He recalled going with his mother to buy his first priestly outfit: his two cassocks, two sashes, six neckbands, eight pairs of black stockings, and his three-cornered hat. And oh! the beating of his heart, that mild October evening when the doors of the seminary had closed behind him! He arrived, just twenty years old, after his years in school, full of a longing to believe and love. By the following day he had forgotten everything, as if he had fallen asleep in the depths of that large and silent house. He saw again in his mind's eye the narrow cell in which he had spent his two years of philosophy, a cubbyhole furnished with a bed, a table, and a chair, separated from the surrounding cubbyholes by ill-fitting planks in a huge hall that contained about fifty of these cubicles. He also revisited the cell in which he lived for three more years, studying theology, larger than the previous one, with an armchair, a washstand and a bookcase, a happy room filled with the dreams of his faith. At certain points, as he went along the endless corridors and stone stairways, he had had surprising revelations and received unexpected succour. From the high ceilings fell the voices of guardian angels. Not a flagstone in any hall, not a stone in any wall, not a branch of any tree but spoke to him of the happiness of his contemplative life, his stammerings of affection, his slow initiation, the marks of affection he received in return for the gift of his whole being, all the bliss of divine first love. One day, as he awoke, he had seen a bright light which had bathed him with joy; then one evening, as he was closing the door of his cell, he had felt warm hands taking hold of his neck with such tenderness that when he returned to consciousness, he found himself lying on the floor, weeping and sobbing. And sometimes, especially beneath the little archway leading to the chapel, he had abandoned himself to supple arms that carried him along. All of Heaven was looking after him, walking beside him, lending his slightest acts, and the satisfaction of even his most vulgar needs, a special significance and a surprising scent, whose faint odour seemed to linger forever in his clothes and in his very skin. And he still remembered the Thursday walks. They would set off at two o'clock for some pleasant, green spot two or three miles from Plassans. It was usually on the banks of the Viorne, in the corner of a meadow, where gnarled willows let their leaves go trailing along the water. He saw nothing, not the big yellow flowers in the meadows, nor the swallows, drinking as they flew, skimming the surface of the little river with their wings. Until six o'clock, sitting in groups under the willows, his fellow students and he recited in chorus the Office of the Virgin, or read aloud, in pairs, from 'Little Hours', the breviary recommended for young seminarists.*

Abbé Mouret smiled as he stirred the fire. He found in this past of his only a great purity, a perfect obedience. He was a lily whose sweet smell delighted his masters. He could not remember a single bad action. Never had he taken advantage of the absolute freedom of the walks, when the two supervising masters went off for a chat with a neighbouring priest, or a smoke behind a hedge, or to have a beer with some friend. Never had he hidden novels under his mattress, nor locked away bottles of anisette in his bedside table. For a long time indeed, he had remained unaware of all the sins being committed around him, chicken wings and cakes smuggled in during Lent, guilty letters brought in by servants, abominable conversations whispered in certain corners of the yard. He had wept salt tears the day he perceived that few of his fellows loved God for himself. Many were the sons of peasants who had entered holy orders only to avoid conscription; some were just lazy, and looking for a life of slothful ease; some were ambitious and already agitated by visions of the crozier and the mitre.* And finding the filth of the world even at the foot of the altar, he had withdrawn into himself even more, giving himself even more to God, to console him for being neglected by others.

However, the abbé remembered that one day he had crossed his legs in class. When the teacher rebuked him, he had turned very red, as if he had done something indecent. He was one of the best students, never arguing, and learning the texts by heart. He could prove the existence and the eternity of God by proofs drawn from Holy Writ, the views of the Church Fathers, or the universal consent of all peoples. Arguments of this sort filled him with unshakeable certainty. During his first year of philosophy, he worked so hard on his Logic course that his teacher had made him stop, reminding him that the most learned are not the most holy. So, in his second year, he restricted his study of metaphysics to just what was required of him, taking little part in the daily discussions. He was beginning to hold knowledge in contempt; he wanted to remain ignorant, in order to keep the humility of his faith. Later on, in theology, he only followed the course in the *Ecclesiastical History* of Rohrbacher* because it was required; he went as far as the ecclesiastical arguments of Gousset,* and on to the *Theological Instruction* of Bouvier,* but didn't dare touch on Bellarmin, Liguori, Suarez,* or Saint Thomas Aquinas. His sole passion was the Holy Scripture, in which he found all the knowledge he needed, a story of infinite love which should be quite sufficient instruction for men of goodwill. He simply accepted what his teachers said, discharging on to their shoulders any need for questioning; his love had no need of all that nonsense, he blamed books for taking time away from prayer. He had even succeeded in forgetting what he had learned in school. He was no longer a person of knowledge, he was simply an innocent, an infant, returned to the stammerings of the catechism.

In this way he had mounted step by step to the priesthood. And at this point, memories rushed at him, tender and still warm with celestial joy. Every year, he had moved nearer to God. He spent his holidays with an uncle, in a most devout manner, going to confession every day, and taking Mass twice a week. He imposed periods of fasting on himself, and concealed in the bottom of his trunk some boxes of coarse salt, on which he would kneel, with bare knees, for hours together. At recreation time, he stayed in the chapel, or went up to the room of one of the teachers, who told him extraordinary stories of piety. Then, on the feast of the Holy Trinity, he was rewarded beyond all measure, flooded with that emotion with which seminaries are always filled on the eve of ordination. This was the great feast-day, when Heaven opens to allow the chosen ones to climb one step higher. For a fortnight before the event, he had put himself on bread and water. And he closed the curtains of his window so as not even to see daylight, prostrating himself in the darkness, begging Jesus to accept his sacrifice. On the last four days, he was seized by terrible anguish, frightful scruples that got him out of bed in the middle of the night, to knock on the door of the foreign priest in charge of the retreat, some barefoot Carmelite,* perhaps a converted Protestant, about whom some wonderful story was going around. To him he made a full confession of his whole life, his voice often breaking into sobs. Absolution alone calmed and refreshed him, as if he had bathed in grace. On the morning of the great day, he was absolutely white; he was so aware of that whiteness that he felt as if he were spreading light around himself. And the seminary bell rang out with its clear voice, while the scents of June, of sweet-scented stock, mignonette, and heliotrope, drifted over the high wall of the yard. In the chapel, the relatives waited, all dressed up, and so moved that the women were sobbing behind their veils. Then came the procession: the deacons, who were about to become priests, in their gold chasubles, the subdeacons in their dalmatics;* the minor orders and the tonsured, with their surplices floating out from their shoulders, and their black birettas in their hands. The organ made itself heard, spreading flute-like notes with a hymn of joy. At the altar, the bishop officiated, crozier in hand, assisted by two canons. The whole chapter was there; the priests from all the parishes were crowded together in an unheard-of abundance of costumes, in a dazzle of gold, lit by the broad ray of sunlight falling from a window in the nave. After the Epistle, the ordination began.

Even now, Abbé Mouret could remember the cold chill of the scissors when he had been marked with the tonsure at the beginning of his first year of theology. It had given him a little shiver. But the tonsure then was very small, hardly the size of a twopenny piece. Later, it had grown bigger and bigger, with each new order, until he was crowned by a patch the size of a large Host.* The organ now grew softer, and the censers were swinging, their chains making a silvery sound, as they released a cloud of white smoke which unfurled in the air, like lace. He could see his newly tonsured self being brought to the altar by the master of ceremonies, then kneeling, with head bowed low, while the bishop, with gold scissors, cut off three strands of hair, one from his brow, and the two others close to his ears. He could see himself once more in the incense-filled chapel, a year later, receiving the four minor orders: led by an archdeacon, he went to the main door, which he closed with a bang, and then reopened, to show that he was entrusted with the guarding of churches; with his right hand he rang a little bell, thus declaring that he had the right to call the faithful to church; then back at the altar, the bishop conferred on him new privileges, that of chanting the lessons, of blessing the bread, catechizing children, exorcising the devil, serving the deacons, and lighting and extinguishing the candles. Then the memory of the following ordination returned to his mind, a more solemn and more frightening occasion, with the organ in full swing, and sounding like the very thunder of God; that day, he wore on his shoulders the dalmatic of a subdeacon, and he bound himself forever to the vow of chastity, and despite his faith, his whole body trembled at the bishop's terrible '*Accedite*',* which put to flight two of his comrades, who had turned pale at his side; his new duties included serving the priest at the altar, preparing the cruets, chanting the Epistle, wiping the chalice, and carrying the cross in processions. And now at last, he walked in procession one last time in the chapel, in the brilliance of the June sun; but this time he walked at the head of the procession, with the alb tied at his waist,* the stole across his breast, and the chasuble round his neck. Weak with extreme emotion, he could see the pale face of the bishop bestowing on him the priesthood in all its plenitude, with a triple laying-on of hands. After his vow of ecclesiastical obedience, he felt as if raised above the floor, when the resounding voice of the prelate spoke the Latin words: '*Accipe Spiritum Sanctum: quorum remiseris peccata, remittuntur eis, et quorum retineris, retenta sunt.*'*

CHAPTER XVI

THIS recalling of the great joys of his youth had given Abbé Mouret a touch of fever. He no longer felt the cold. He let go of the fire tongs, and went over to his bed as if he were going to lie down, then came back and leant his brow against a windowpane, looking with unseeing eyes into the night. Could he be ill, since he felt such lethargy in his limbs, and his blood seemed to burn in his veins? He had twice had a similar experience at the seminary, a sort of physical distress that made him very miserable; once he had even gone to bed, quite delirious. Then he thought about the young girl possessed of the devil that Brother Archangias claimed to have cured, simply with the sign of the cross, one day when she had fallen flat at his feet. That made him think of the spiritual exercises one of his masters had once recommended to him: prayer, general confession, frequent Communion, and choosing a wise mentor with real authority over the mind of the penitent. And with no transition, with a suddenness that astonished him, he saw deep in his memory the round face of one of his old friends, a peasant who had been a choirboy at the age of eight, and whose board in the seminary was paid by a lady who had taken him under her wing. He was always laughing, he looked forward in all naivety to the little benefits of the job: the stipend of twelve hundred francs, the presbytery with a garden, the gifts, the invitations to dinner, the little profits from marriages, baptisms, and burials. That friend must surely be happy in his parish.

The melancholy regret this memory brought with it greatly surprised the abbé. Was it that he was not happy? Until that day, he had had no regrets, no desires, no envy. And even now, in his questioning of himself, he could find no cause for bitterness. He was still, he thought, just as he had been in his first years as a deacon, when the required reading of his breviary at appointed times had filled his days with continuous prayer. Since that time, weeks, months, and years had rolled by, without his ever having had time for a single evil thought. He was not tormented by doubt; he simply prostrated himself before mysteries he could not understand, he found it easy to sacrifice his reason, which he despised. On emerging from the seminary, he had been delighted to find himself a stranger among men, not walking like other men, carrying his head in a different way, his gestures, words, and feelings those of a being apart. He felt feminized, brought nearer to the angels, cleansed of his sex, his odour of masculinity. It made him almost proud, this feeling of no longer being part of the species, of having been brought up for God, carefully purged of human filth by a rigorous education. He had the impression of having lived for years, bathed in a ritually prepared holy oil, which had entered into his flesh like a first step towards beatification. Some of his organs had disappeared, as if gradually dissolved; his limbs, his brain, had been drained of matter, in order to be filled with spirit, with a subtle lightness that sometimes intoxicated him, making him dizzy, as if the ground had suddenly given way beneath him. He had the fears, the ignorance, and the candour of a convent-educated girl. Sometimes he said with a smile that he was prolonging his childhood, imagining that he had remained a child, with the same sensations, ideas, and views; so, at the age of six he had known God just as well as when he was twenty-five, and in praying to him, he had the same inflections in his voice, and the same childish delight in putting his hands together just so. The world about him seemed the same as the world he saw long ago when his mother took him for walks, holding his hand. He had been born a priest, he had grown up a priest. When he betrayed, in front of La Teuse, some gross ignorance of life, she would look him straight in the eye, stupefied, commenting with an odd smile that 'he was indeed the brother of Mademoiselle Désirée'. In his whole existence, he could recall only one shameful shock. It was during his last six months at the seminary—at the stage between deacon and priest. He had been made to read the work of Abbé Craisson, the Father Superior of the great seminary of Valence: *De rebus venereis ad usum confessariorum.** He had emerged from that reading horrified and sobbing. This scholarly casuistry on the subject of vice, displaying the abominations of man, going into the most monstrous cases of unnatural passions, brutally violated his virginity of body and mind. He was left soiled forever, like a bride suddenly initiated into all the violence of love. And every time he heard confession, he was inevitably brought back to that questionnaire of shame. If the obscurities of dogma, the duties of the priesthood, the death of all free will, left him serene, and content to be no more than the child of God, he still felt, in spite of himself, the carnal disturbance of these filthy things he had to stir up; he was aware of a permanent stain somewhere deep inside him, which one day could spread and cover him with mud.

The moon was rising behind the Garrigues. Abbé Mouret, burning with fever even more, opened the window and leaned out, to feel the cool of the night on his face. He no longer knew just when he had begun to feel unwell. He remembered, however, that in the morning, when he was saying Mass, he was very calm and steady. It must have been later, during his long walk in the sun perhaps, or beneath the restless trees of the Paradou, or in Désirée's suffocating farmyard. And then he went back over the whole day.

The vast plain stretched out before him, looking more tragic under the slanting pallor of the moon. The scrawny trees, olive trees and almond trees, made patches of grey amid the chaos of the big rocks, right up to the dark line of the hills on the horizon. There were wide areas of shadow, uneven ridges, blood-red pools of earth in which the red stars seemed to be looking at themselves, and patches of chalky whiteness like women's clothes thrown off, uncovering bodies shrouded in darkness, slumped in the hollows of the ground. At night, this ardent landscape seemed to lie in a strange sprawl of passion. Asleep, dishevelled, displaying its hips, it lay contorted, with limbs outspread, heaving huge, hot sighs, and exuding the heady scent of a sweating, sleeping woman. It was as if some powerful Cybele* had fallen on her back, with her breasts exposed, her belly naked under the moon, drunk with the ardours of the sun and still dreaming of impregnation. In the distance, following the lines of that great body, Abbé Mouret's eyes moved along the road to the Olivettes, a thin, light-coloured ribbon, winding along like the loosened lacing of a corset. He could hear Brother Archangias lifting the skirts of the little girls, whipping them until he drew blood, and spitting in the faces of the older girls, while himself stinking with the odour of an insatiable billy goat. He could see Rosalie slyly laughing, and looking like some lewd animal, while old Bambousse threw clods of earth at her. And even then, he thought, he was still quite well, scarcely aware of the heat of the beautiful morning on the back of his neck. He had felt only a quivering behind his back, that confused hum of life that he had been hearing vaguely since the morning, in the middle of Mass, when the sun had come in through the shattered windows. Never before had the countryside so disturbed him as it did at this night hour, with its gigantic breast, soft shadows, and gleams of amber skin, all this Olympian nakedness, scarcely concealed by the silvery gauze of the moon.

The young priest lowered his gaze to look down at the village of Les Artaud. The village was sunk in the heavy sleep of weariness, the total oblivion of the sleep of peasants. Not a light to be seen. The hovels formed mounds of blackness, intersected by the white stripes of the lanes between them, threaded with moonlight. The dogs themselves must have been snoring outside the closed doors. Perhaps the Artauds had infected the presbytery with some abominable plague? At his back he was still hearing ever more loudly the breathing which filled him with anguish as it came nearer. Now he seemed to detect something like the trampling of a herd, and there came a sudden swirl of dust, laden with heavy animal exhalations. His morning thoughts returned to his mind, thoughts about this handful of men, starting again as if at the beginning of time, growing amongst the barren rocks like a handful of thistles sown by the wind: he felt as if he were present at the slow emergence of a race. When he was a child, nothing surprised or frightened him more than the myriads of insects he saw creeping out of a crack when he lifted up certain damp stones. Even asleep, exhausted, and deep in the darkness, the Artauds disturbed him with their sleep, as if he felt their breathing in the air around him. He would have liked to have nothing but rocks beneath his window. The village was not dead enough; the thatched roofs heaved as if breathing; from the cracks in the doors came sighs, faint creaking sounds, living silences, revealing the presence in this remote spot of a swarming litter in the night's black cradle. It was no doubt just this scent that was making him nauseous. But he had often smelled it before, just as strongly, without experiencing anything other than a need to refresh himself in prayer.

With sweating brow, he went and opened the other window, to try to cool himself. Down below, to the left, lay the cemetery, with the tall outline of the Lone Tree, its shadow undisturbed by any breeze. From the empty field rose the smell of newly cut grass. The big grey wall of the church, that wall full of lizards, with wallflowers growing all over it, was cooling in the moonlight, and one of the large windows was gleaming, its panes like plates of steel. At this hour of the night, the sleeping church could be alive only with the non-human life of the God of the Host, enclosed in the tabernacle. He thought of the patch of yellow made by the night light, swallowed up in the darkness, and was tempted to go back down, into that darkness free from all taint, to soothe his suffering head. But a strange terror held him back: his eyes fixed on the windows lit by the moon, he suddenly seemed to see the church lighting up from within, blazing like a furnace, with the splendour of some hellish festival, in which the month of May, the plants and animals, the girls of Les Artaud, all swirled about, wildly clasping trees in their bare arms. Then, leaning out, he saw beneath him Désirée's farmyard, all black and steamy. He could not clearly see the rabbit hutches, the hen roosts, or the shed for the ducks. It was just one single mass piled up in its stench, sleeping with the same pestiferous breath. The acrid smell of the goat came out from under the door of the stable; while the little pig, sprawled on its back, snorted loudly beside an empty bowl. From his brassy throat, Alexander, the big tawny rooster, uttered a cry that provoked, one after another, in the distance, the passionate calls of all the cocks of the village.

Suddenly, Abbé Mouret remembered. The fever he had seemed to hear pursuing him had caught up with him in Désirée's farmyard, when he was looking at the hens still warm from their laying, and the female rabbits tugging out the hair from their bellies. Then he had such a clear sensation of something breathing on his neck that he had turned round to see, finally, who was thus clutching at his neck. And he remembered Albine bounding out from the Paradou, and the door slamming on the glimpse of an enchanted garden; he remembered her galloping the length of that interminable wall, racing along behind the gig throwing birch leaves to the winds like so many kisses, and he remembered her again, in the twilight, laughing at the oaths of Brother Archangias, with her skirts flying along the path like a little cloud of dust, bowled along by the evening breeze. She was sixteen; she was strange, with her rather long face; she smelled of fresh air and grass and earth. And his memory of her was so precise that he could see again the scratch on one of her supple wrists, so pink on her white skin. And why then did she laugh like that, as she gazed at him with her blue eyes? He was caught in her laugh, as if in a sound wave that resonated through his whole body; he breathed it in, he could hear it vibrating within him. Yes, all his ills came from that laugh that he had absorbed.

He stood in the middle of the room, with both windows open, shivering, gripped by a fear that made him hide his head in his hands. So was the whole day then to end with this recalling of a girl with a rather long face, a girl with blonde hair and blue eyes? And the whole day came in through the two open windows. Far away were the heat of the red soil, the passion of the huge rocks and the olive trees growing up through the stones, and the vines twisting their arms at the edge of the roads; much nearer were the human sweat carried in the air from Les Artaud, the musty odour of the cemetery, the church's smell of incense, corrupted as it was by the smell of greasy-haired girls; and there were also the steamy smells of manure and the farmyard, the suffocating ferment of endless germination. And all these odours came in one burst, in one single asphyxiating gust, so strong, and bursting with such violence that it choked him. He shut down his senses, trying to make them numb. But Albine reappeared before him like a big flower that had sprung up and grown beautiful on this compost. She was the natural flower of this filthiness, delicate in the sunshine, opening the young bud of her white shoulders, so delighting in life that she leaped up from her stalk and flew on to his mouth, filling him with the scent of her rippling laughter.

The priest uttered a cry. He had felt a burning on his lips. It was like a stream of fire coursing through his veins. Then, seeking a refuge,

he threw himself down on his knees before the statue of the Immaculate
Conception, crying out, with his hands clasped together:

'Holy Virgin of all Virgins, pray for me!'

CHAPTER XVII

THE Immaculate Conception on the walnut chest of drawers smiled
down tenderly with her thin lips outlined in carmine. She was small
and entirely white. Her long white veil, which hung from her head to
her feet, had only an imperceptible thread of gold at its hem. Her
robe, draped in long straight folds upon a sexless figure, was tight at
the neckline, revealing only her supple neck. Not a single lock of her
chestnut hair could be seen. Her face was pink, and her light-coloured
eyes were turned heavenwards; her pink hands were clasped together,
childlike hands, with fingertips showing under the folds of her veil,
above the blue sash that seemed to be tying two loose ends of the firmament around her waist. As for her womanly attractions, not a single one was exposed, save her feet, feet that were adorably bare, treading
upon the mystic rose bush.* And from the nakedness of her feet grew
roses of gold, as if they were the natural flowering of her doubly pure
flesh.

'Faithful Virgin, pray for me!' cried the priest in a desperate plea.

This virgin had never troubled him. She was not yet a mother: her
arms did not hold out to him a little Jesus, her figure showed none of
the rounded outlines of pregnancy. She was not the Queen of Heaven,
descending in her gold crown and gold robes, like some earthly princess, borne along in triumph by a flight of cherubim. This virgin had
never taken on an intimidating aspect, had never spoken to him with
the severity of an all-powerful mistress, at the very sight of whom all
heads bow down to the dust. He could dare to look at her and love her,
without fearing to be too moved by the soft waves of her chestnut
hair; he experienced only a feeling of tenderness for her bare feet, her
feet of love, that flowered like a garden of chastity, in too miraculous
a fashion for him to satisfy his longing to cover them with kisses. She
filled the room with her scent of lilies. She was the silver lily set in
a vase of gold, she was purity, precious, eternal, impeccable purity.
In her white veil, so closely wrapped around her form, nothing human
remained, nothing but a virgin flame, burning with a steady light. In

the evening as he went to bed, and in the morning when he got up, he always found her there, with her very same smile of ecstasy. He took off his clothes in front of her with no embarrassment, as if he were facing only his own modesty.

'Mother so pure, Mother so chaste, Mother ever virginal, pray for me!' he stammered in fear, pressing himself against the feet of the Virgin, as if hearing at his back the sound of Albine's racing feet. 'You are my refuge, my source of joy, my temple of wisdom, the ivory tower in which I have locked my purity. I put myself in your spotless hands, I beg you to take me, cover me with a piece of your veil, hide me in your innocence, so no breath of carnality can reach me. I need you, without you I die, I feel I shall be parted from you forever if you do not take me in your kindly arms, and carry me far away from here into the ardent whiteness in which you live. Mary, conceived without sin, bury me deep in the immaculate snow that falls from your every limb. You are the miracle of eternal chastity. Your race has sprung from a ray of light like a wondrous tree, planted by no seed. Your son Jesus was born of the breath of God, and you were yourself born without any soiling of your mother's womb, and I want to believe that this virginity goes on in this way from age to age, in perpetual ignorance of the flesh. Oh, to live and grow outside the shame of the senses! Oh, to multiply, to procreate, without the abominable need for sex, at the mere touch of a kiss from Heaven!'

This desperate plea, this cry, purged of desire, had reassured the young priest. The Virgin, in her whiteness, with her eyes turned heavenwards, seemed to smile more sweetly with her thin rosy lips. He went on again in a softened voice:

'I should like to be still a child. I should like never to be other than a child, walking in the shadow of your robe. When I was little, I used to put my hands together to speak the name of Mary. My cradle was white, my body was white, all my thoughts were white. I could see you clearly, I heard you calling me, and I went to you in a smile, walking on rose petals. And that was all, I wasn't feeling or thinking, I was simply alive enough to be a flower at your feet. No one should ever grow up. Then you'd have around you only the blond heads of a race of children who would love you with pure hands, clean lips and gentle limbs, free of all stain, as if just emerging from a bath of milk. A kiss on the cheek of a child is a kiss on the soul. Only a child can speak your name without soiling it. Later, the mouth gets sullied and poisoned with passions. Even I, who love you so dearly, who have given myself to you, I do not dare always to call upon you, for fear of having you encounter the impurities of my manhood. I have prayed, I have punished my flesh, I have slept under your protection, I have lived in chastity; and now I am weeping, seeing that I am still not sufficiently dead to this world to be your betrothed. O Mary, adorable Virgin! If only I were just five years old, if only I were still the child who pressed his lips to pictures of you! I would gather you to my heart, lay you down beside me, and kiss you as a friend, a girl of my own age. I would have your slender robe, your childlike veil, your sash of blue, all the childlike things that make you my big sister. I would not try to kiss your hair, for hair itself is a nakedness that should not be seen; but I would kiss your bare feet, one after another, all night long, night after night, until my lips had stripped the petals from the gold roses, the mystic roses of your veins.'

He paused, waiting for the Virgin to lower her blue eyes upon him, and touch his brow with the hem of her veil. But she remained wrapped in muslin up to her neck, and down to her fingernails, down to her ankles, belonging totally to Heaven, with that upward thrust of her body that made her ethereal, as if already detached from the earth.

'Well then,' he continued, even more wildly, 'Virgin so good, so powerful, make me a child once more. Make me five years old. Take away my senses, take away my manhood. Let a miracle carry away everything of the man that has grown in me. You reign in Heaven, nothing is easier for you than to strike me down, wither away my organs, and leave me sexless, incapable of sin, and so drained of strength that I could not so much as raise my little finger without your consent. I want to be innocent with an innocence like yours, never disturbed by any quiver of human feeling. I want never more to feel my nerves, my muscles, the beating of my heart, or the agitation of my desires. I want to become a thing, a white stone at your feet, a stone on which you will leave only your scent, a stone that will not move from the spot where you have thrown it, with neither eyes nor ears, content to be under your heel, and incapable of thinking of filthy things with the other stones on the path. Oh then, what bliss for me! I shall reach, effortlessly, at my first attempt, the perfection of which I dream. I shall declare myself to be at last your true priest. I shall be what my studies, my prayers, my five years of slow initiation, were not able to make of me. Yes, I deny life, I say that the death of the human species is preferable to the abomination by which it is continued. Sin besmirches everything. It is a universal stench that spoils all love, infecting the bedchamber of husband and wife, the cradle of the newborn, the flowers swooning in the sun, and even the trees pushing forth their buds. The whole earth is soaked in this impurity, whose smallest drops spring forth in shameful growths. But so that I may be perfect, O Queen of the angels, Queen of virgins, hear my cry and grant what I ask. Make me one of those angels who have nothing more than two great wings behind their cheeks; I shall have no more trunk, no limbs; I shall fly to you, if you call me; I shall be no more than a mouth to sing your praises, or a pair of spotless wings to cradle your journeys in the heavens. Oh! death, death, revered Virgin, grant me the death of everything! I shall love you in the death of my body, in the death of everything that lives and multiplies. I shall consummate with you the only marriage that my heart desires. I shall go higher, ever higher, until I reach those fires where you shine in splendour. There, there is a huge star, an immense white rose, whose every petal burns like a moon, a silver throne on which you shine with such a blaze of innocence that the whole of paradise is lit simply by the light of your veil. Everything that is white, the dawn, the snow of inaccessible mountain tops, lilies not yet opened, the water of undiscovered springs, the sap of plants untouched by the sun, the smiles of virgins, the souls of infants who died in the cradle, all rain down on your white feet. Then I shall rise to your lips like a cunning flame; I shall enter into you through your half-open mouth, and the marriage will be consummated while the archangels tremble with our joy. To be virgin, to love virginally, and keep, even within the sweetest kisses, the same virginal whiteness! To have all of love, lying on the wings of swans, in a cloud of purity, in the arms of a mistress made of light, whose caresses are the raptures of the soul! Perfection, superhuman dream, desire that breaks my very bones, delights that take me to Heaven! O Mary, Chosen Vessel, castrate in me all humanity, make me a eunuch among men, so you may without fear grant me the treasure of your virginity!'

And Abbé Mouret, his teeth chattering, collapsed on the tiled floor, struck down by fever.

BOOK TWO

CHAPTER I

ACROSS the two wide windows, carefully drawn calico curtains filtered the white light of early dawn into the room. It was a very big room with a high ceiling, furnished with antique Louis XV furniture of painted white wood, and decorated with red flowers on a background of foliage. In the panels above the doors, on both sides of the alcove, paintings still showed the pink bellies and bottoms of little cupids flying about in groups, and playing games now impossible to make out. The woodwork on the walls with its oval panels, the double doors, and the rounded ceiling, once painted sky blue, and holding framed scrolls, medallions, and bows of flesh-coloured ribbon, had all paled into a very soft grey, a grey that preserved the tender melancholy of this faded paradise. Facing the windows, the large alcove opened out under banks of clouds that were being pulled aside by plaster cupids, leaning over and tumbling about, as if in a brazen effort to look at the bed; the alcove was closed, like the windows, by roughly sewn calico curtains of a surprising innocence in this room still warm with a distant scent of sensual pleasure.

Sitting beside a small table, on which a kettle was being heated over a spirit lamp, Albine was gazing attentively at the alcove curtains. She was dressed in white, her hair bound up in a scarf of old lace, her hands lying empty beside her, keeping watch with the serious look of a grown-up girl. A faint sound of breathing, like the breath of a sleeping child, could be heard in the deep silence. But she became anxious, and after a few minutes could not resist going over very quietly to lift up a bit of the curtain. Serge, on the edge of the big bed, seemed to be asleep, his head resting on one of his folded arms. During his illness, his hair had got longer, and he had grown a beard. He was very white, with bruised eyelids and pallid lips; he had the grace of a convalescent girl.

Albine, moved by this sight, was about to drop the bit of curtain.

'I'm not asleep,' said Serge in a very low voice.

And he stayed where he was, his head on his arm, without moving an inch, as if overcome by a pleasant weariness. Slowly his eyes opened and the breath from his lips blew softly on to one of his bare hands, stirring the downy hairs on his fair skin.

'I heard you,' he whispered. 'You were walking very quietly.'

Albine was delighted at his addressing her with the familiar *tu*.* She drew near and crouched beside the bed, to bring her face in line with his.

'How are you feeling?' she asked.

And she in turn enjoyed the pleasure of the *tu*, which she was pronouncing for the first time.

'You're much better now,' she went on. 'Do you know, I used to cry all the way home when I came back from over there with bad news. They told me you were delirious, and even if that awful fever spared your life, you would still lose your reason. Oh! how I hugged your uncle Pascal, when he brought you here to convalesce.'

She tucked in his bedclothes, in a motherly way.

'You see, all those scorched rocks over there were no good for you. You need trees, fresh air, and peace and quiet... The doctor hasn't even told anyone that he's hidden you here. It's a secret between him and those who love you. He thought you were done for... So nobody will disturb us. Uncle Jeanbernat smokes his pipe in front of his lettuces. The others will secretly get news of you. And the doctor himself won't come back any more, because I am now your doctor. It seems you have no more need of drugs. You just need to be loved, do you see?'

He seemed not to be hearing her, his mind still empty. As his eyes searched every corner of the room, though his head did not move, she thought he was worrying about where he might be.

'It's my room,' she said. 'I've given it to you. It's pretty, isn't it? I took the nicest pieces of furniture from the first floor; then I made these calico curtains, so you wouldn't be blinded by the light... And you're not putting me out at all. I'll sleep on the second floor. There are still three or four empty rooms.'

But he was still anxious.

'Are you alone?' he asked.

'Yes, why do you ask me that?' He did not reply, but muttered rather wearily:

'I've been dreaming, I'm always dreaming... I hear bells, and that's what's making me tired.'

After a silence, he went on:

'Go and shut the door, and put the bolt on. I want you to be alone, quite alone.'

When she came back, carrying a chair, and sat at his bedside, he showed a childlike joy, saying over and over:

'Now no one will come in. I shan't hear the bells any more... Now you, when you talk, it's restful.'

'Do you want something to drink?' she asked.

He made a gesture to show he was not thirsty. He was looking at Albine's hands, looking so surprised and so delighted to see them that she held out one of them and laid it on his pillow with a smile. Then he let his head slide over, and rested his cheek upon that small, cool hand. He gave a little laugh and said:

'Ah! it's as soft as silk. It seems as if it's blowing cool air into my hair... Please don't take it away.'

Then there was a long silence.

They were gazing at each other with great affection. Albine quietly looked at her reflection in the blank eyes of the invalid. Serge seemed to be listening to what that small, cool hand was telling him.

'It's so very kind, this hand of yours,' he went on. 'You can't imagine how much good it's doing me... it seems to enter right into me, to take away the aches I have in my limbs. It caresses me all over, it's comforting, healing.'

He gently rubbed his cheek against it, growing more animated, as if he were coming back to life.

'Tell me you won't give me anything nasty to drink, you won't torment me with all sorts of medicines? Your hand is quite enough for me, you see. I came here just so that you could put it there, under my head.'

'My dear Serge,' Albine murmured, 'you've suffered a lot, haven't you?'

'Suffered? Yes, yes, but a long time ago... I slept badly, I had dreadful dreams. If I could, I'd tell you all about it.'

He closed his eyes for a moment, and made a great effort to remember.

'I see only blackness,' he stammered. 'It's strange, I'm coming back from a long journey. I don't know now where I started from. I was feverish, a fever was galloping through my veins like a wild animal... That's it, I remember. Always the same nightmare that had me crawling along an endless underground tunnel. Then some severe pains would come, and the tunnel suddenly got walled in: a heap of stones fell from the vaulted roof, the walls on each side closed in, and I was left panting, overcome by rage, wanting to get past; and I went right into the obstacle, working with my feet, my fists, and my head, despairing of ever being able to get across that constantly growing rockfall... Then quite often, I only had to touch it with my finger and everything would disappear and I could walk freely in the now wide gallery, with nothing more than the fatigue of the struggle.'

Albine tried to lay a hand upon his lips.

'No, talking doesn't tire me. You see, I'm speaking in your ear. It seems that I just think, and you understand... The oddest thing is that in my tunnel, I never once thought of turning back; I was determined to go on, even while thinking it would take me thousands of years to clear away a single one of those rockfalls. It was an inescapable task that I had to accomplish on pain of even greater misfortunes. With bruised knees, and my brow battered by the rocks, I set my anguished mind on working with all my strength, in order to arrive as fast as possible. Arrive where?... I don't know... I don't know...'

He closed his eyes, dreaming and puzzling. Then, making a carefree face, he abandoned his head once more to Albine's hand, saying, with a laugh:

'Really, it's silly, I'm just a child.'

But the girl, to see if he was really hers, entirely hers, went on questioning him, taking him back to the confused memories he had been trying to capture. He remembered nothing, he really was in a happy state of childhood. He felt as if newly born.

'Oh, I'm not really strong yet. You see, as far back as I can remember, I was in a bed that burned my entire body; my head rolling around on the pillow as if on a brazier, and my feet wearing themselves out, rubbing against each other all the time... Oh, I really was very ill! It seemed as if I was having my body changed, as if every part was being taken out, and I was being repaired like a piece of broken machinery.'

The comparison made him laugh again. He went on:

'I'm going to be all new. It's really cleaned me up, being so ill... But what were you asking me? No. Nobody else was there. I was suffering all alone at the bottom of a black hole. Nobody. Nobody. And beyond that, there's nothing, I can see nothing. I am your child, may I be? You will teach me to walk. Now I can see only you. I don't care about anything that isn't you. I tell you, I really don't remember. I came along and you took hold of me, that's all.'

And then, comforted, he spoke again in an affectionate tone:

'Your hand is warm now; it's as good as sunshine... Let's stop talking now. I'm getting hot.'

In the big room, a tremulous silence seemed to fall from the blue ceiling. The spirit lamp had gone out, and the kettle gave off an ever thinner wisp of steam. Albine and Serge, each with their head on the same pillow, gazed at the long calico curtains drawn over the windows. Serge's eyes, especially, were drawn to them, to the white source of the light. He bathed in it, as in a dimmed daylight, adapted to his weakness as a convalescent. He could make out the sun behind one yellower bit of the curtain, and that was enough to make him better. In the distance he could hear a great rustling of foliage; and at the window on the right, the greenish shadow of a high branch, clearly outlined, brought him a disturbing imagining of that forest he felt to be so near.

'Do you want me to open the curtains?' asked Albine, misunderstanding his fixed stare.

'No, no,' he hastily replied.

'It's a fine day. You'd have the sun. You'd see the trees.'

'No, I implore you... I don't want anything that's outside. That branch there wearies me with its moving and growing, as if it were alive... Leave me your hand, I'm going to sleep now. Everything's white now... That's good.'

And he fell asleep like a child, watched over by Albine, who blew gently on his face to cool him in his sleep.

CHAPTER II

THE next day the fine weather had gone, and it was raining. Serge, whose fever had returned, spent a day of suffering, with his eyes fixed despairingly on the curtains, from which came only a sinister light, cavern-like and grey as ash. He could no longer find the sun, and he looked for that shadow which had previously alarmed him, that high branch which, drowned now in the steamy haze of the rain, seemed to him, in its disappearance, to have carried the forest away with it. Towards evening, he became rather delirious, and sobbing, cried out to Albine that the sun had died and he could hear the whole sky and the whole countryside mourning the death of the sun. She had to

comfort him like a child, promising him the sun, assuring him it would
come back, and she would give it to him. But he was also grieving for
the plants. The seeds must be suffering under the ground, waiting for
the light; they must be having his nightmares, dreaming they were
climbing along an underground tunnel, blocked by rockfalls, struggling madly to reach the sun. And he began to sob more quietly, saying that winter was an illness of the earth and he would die along with
it, unless spring came and cured them both.

For three more days, the weather remained dreadful. Torrents poured
down on the trees, with a distant clamour like a river that had burst its
banks. Gusts of wind rolled around and flung themselves at the windows with the cruel persistence of enormous waves. Serge had asked
Albine to bolt all the shutters. With the lamp lit, he no longer had the
funereal gloom of the colourless curtains, and he no longer felt the
grey of the sky stealing in through the tiniest cracks and flowing onto
him like a dust intent on burying him. He just lay there, with his arms
so thin and his pale face, growing all the weaker as the countryside's
illness got worse. At certain times of inky black clouds, when the
twisted trees cracked under the strain, and the earth let the grasses
trail out beneath the rain like the hair of a drowned girl, he almost
stopped breathing, seemed to die, as if himself beaten by the tempest.
Then, at the first break in the weather, at the tiniest trace of blue
between two clouds, he would breathe again, enjoying the peace of
the drying foliage, the whitening paths, and the fields drinking their
last draught of water. Albine too was now yearning for sunshine; doz-
ens of times a day she went to the window on the landing to examine
the horizon, delighted by the slightest patches of white, anxious on
seeing dark copper-coloured masses, laden with hail, and fearful that
some too dark cloud would kill off her dear patient. She talked of sending for Dr Pascal. But Serge didn't want anyone. He kept saying:

'Tomorrow, there will be sunlight on the curtains, and I'll be well
again.'

One evening, when he was at his lowest point, Albine gave him her
hand, so he could place it beneath his cheek. And when the hand
failed to comfort him, she wept at finding herself so helpless. Since he
had fallen back into the lethargy of winter, she no longer felt strong
enough to pull him out by herself from the nightmare in which he was
struggling. She needed the assistance of spring. She was herself wast-
ing away, with ice-cold arms, short of breath, and no longer able to

breathe life into him. For hours on end, she roamed around the big, sad room. When she went past a mirror, she saw an unpleasant image of herself, and thought herself ugly.

Then one morning, as she was plumping up the pillows, not daring to try again the broken magic of her hands, she fancied she saw once more the smile of that first day on Serge's lips, when she had just brushed his neck with her fingertips.

'Open the shutters,' he murmured.

She thought he was talking in a delirium, for but an hour before, she had seen from the landing window only a sky in deep gloom.

'Go back to sleep,' she replied sadly; 'I promised to wake you at the first ray of sunshine... Sleep on a while, the sun is not here yet.'

'Yes it is, I can feel it, the sun is here... Open the shutters.'

CHAPTER III

THE sun was indeed there. When Albine had opened the shutters behind the big curtains, that good yellow glow once more warmed up a bit of the white calico. But what made Serge sit up in bed was the sight of the shadow of that branch, the bough that announced the return to life. The whole of the resuscitated countryside, with its greenery, its rivers, its wide ring of hills, was, for him, contained in that greenish patch that quivered at the slightest breath. The branch no longer alarmed him. He followed its rocking movements eagerly, needing the strength of the sap it promised; and Albine, happily supporting him with her arms, said:

'Ah, my dear Serge, winter is over... We are saved.'

He lay back, his eyes already brighter, and his voice clearer.

'Tomorrow,' he said, 'I shall be very strong... You shall draw back the curtains. I want to see everything...'

But the next day he was seized by a childish fear. He would not allow the windows to be opened wide. 'In a while, later on,' he would murmur. He remained anxious, worried about the effect of the first impact of light on his eyes. Evening came, and he still had not been able to make the decision to face the sun again. He had stayed with his face turned towards the curtains, following, on the transparence of the cloth, the pale morning light, the blaze of noon, the mauve of twilight, all the colours, all the emotions of the heavens. Upon that screen were reflected even the quivering of the warm air when a bird flaps its wings, and the joyfulness of the scents throbbing within a sunbeam. Behind that veil, that softened dream of the powerful life outside, he could hear spring arriving. And at times he was even suffocated, when in spite of the barrier of the curtains the rush of the earth's new blood came at him too brutally.

The next morning, he was still asleep when Albine, trying to hurry his recovery, called out:

'Serge! Serge! Look, here's the sun!'

She swiftly drew back the curtains and threw the windows wide open. He raised himself up and knelt on the bed, suffocating, almost fainting, with his hands pressed tight against his breast to keep his heart from breaking. Before him he had the great wide sky, nothing but blue, an infinity of blue; in this he washed away his suffering, he sank into it, as if into a gentle cradle, and drank in its sweetness, its purity and youth. Only one thing, that branch whose shadow he had noticed jutting out over the window, splashed that sea of blue with its patch of lively greenery; and that was already too much for the convalescent's delicate sensibilities, which were hurt even by the smudge made by swallows flying on the horizon. He was being born. He uttered little involuntary cries, drowned in light, beaten by waves of warm air, and feeling engulfed by all the life flowing into him. With outstretched hands, he fell back and sank on to his pillow in a swoon.

What a happy and tender day this was! The sun came in on the right, far from the alcove. During the whole of the morning Serge watched it moving slowly forward, clipping the edges of the old furniture, frolicking in the corners, and sometimes sliding to the ground like an unrolled piece of cloth. It was a slow, confident progress, like that of a woman in love, stretching her blonde limbs, and moving up to the alcove with a rhythmic movement and a voluptuous languor that created a furious desire to possess her. At last, towards two o'clock, the pool of sunlight left the last armchair, climbed up the blankets, and spread over the bed like a woman's hair let down. Serge abandoned his thin, convalescent hands to this ardent caress, and with half-closed eyes, he could feel kisses of fire raining down on each of his fingers, he was bathed in light as if embraced by a star. And as Albine was still there, leaning over him with a smile, he stammered out, with his eyes quite closed:

'Leave me now, don't hold me so tight... How do you manage to hold me so completely in your arms, like that?'

Then the sun slipped down from the bed and went slowly away to the left. Then Serge watched it doing its rounds once again, sitting on one chair after another, sad that he had been unable to keep it with him, clutched to his breast. Albine had stayed there at the edge of the bedclothes. The two, with their arms around each other's neck, watched the sky getting slowly paler. Now and again a huge shudder seemed to make it blench with some sudden emotion. Serge, in his languor, could now let his eyes roam more comfortably over this expanse, discovering exquisite subtleties he had never suspected. It wasn't all entirely blue, there was pinkish blue, lilac blue, yellow blue, a living flesh, a vast, immaculate nakedness that heaved like a woman's breast at the slightest breath. With each new glance into the distance there were surprises, unknown regions of the air, secret smiles, some adorable roundness, and fine veils hiding, in the depths of barely glimpsed paradises, huge and magnificent bodies of goddesses. And he was flying away, his limbs made light by illness, into this shimmering silk, this innocent down of blue; his sensations seemed to float above his faltering being. The sun was getting lower in the sky, the blue was melting into pure gold, the living flesh of the sky grew ever more blond, and slowly sank into all the tints of evening. Not a cloud, just the self-effacement of a virgin at bedtime, a disrobing that left nothing more than a line of modesty on the horizon. The vast sky slept.

'Ah! the dear little child!' said Albine, looking at Serge, who had fallen asleep on her shoulder at the same time as the sky.

She laid him back down on the bed and closed all the windows. But the next day, even at dawn, they were open again. Serge could no longer live without the sun. He was gathering strength, and was becoming used to the great buffetings of air that sent the alcove curtains billowing. Even the blue, the everlasting blue, had begun to seem rather dull. He was growing weary of being a swan, a whiteness, forever swimming on the limpid lake of the sky. He even found himself wishing for a flight of black clouds, a tumbling down of clouds that would break the monotony of all that purity.

As his health improved, he felt the need for stronger sensations. He now spent hours looking at the green branch; he would have liked to see it grow, flourish, and thrust its boughs right up to his bed. It was no longer enough for him, it only aggravated his desires, speaking to him of other trees, those he could hear calling him, though he could not see their tops. There was an endless whispering of leaves, chattering of running water, and flappings of wings, making one high, long-drawn-out, and vibrant voice.

'When you're able to get up,' said Albine, 'you'll sit in front of the window... you'll see the lovely garden.'

He closed his eyes and murmured:

'Oh! I see it already, I hear it... I know where the trees are, where the water flows, where the violets grow.'

Then he went on:

'But I don't see it well, I see it without light... I need to be very strong to get to the window.'

At other times, when she thought he was asleep, Albine would disappear for a few hours. And when she got back she would find him burning with impatience, his eyes shining with curiosity.

'Where have you been?' he would cry.

And he would take her in his arms, sniffing at her skirts, her bodice, and her cheeks. 'You smell of all sorts of nice things. Ah! You've been walking on grass?'

Then she would laugh and show him her boots, all wet with dew.

'You've come from the garden! You've come from the garden!' he repeated in delight. 'I knew it! When you came in, you were like a big flower... You've brought me the whole garden in your dress!'

And he kept her with him, smelling her as if she were a bouquet of flowers. Sometimes she came back with brambles, leaves, and bits of twig caught in her clothes. Then he would pick these off and hide them under his pillow like sacred relics. One day she brought him a bunch of roses. He was so moved that it made him cry. He kissed the flowers, and laid them down in bed with him, wrapped in his arms. But when they faded, it caused him so much pain that he told Albine not to gather any more. He preferred her, herself, who was just as fresh and sweet-smelling, and didn't fade, didn't lose the scent of her hands, the scent of her hair, the scent of her cheeks. Later on, he would himself send her to the garden, telling her not to come back for at least an hour.

'You see, in that way, I have sunshine, I have fresh air, and I have roses to last until tomorrow.'

Often, when he saw her coming back quite breathless, he would question her. What path had she taken? Had she plunged into the trees, or had she gone along the edge of the fields? Had she seen any nests? Had she sat down behind a bush of wild roses, or under an oak tree, or in the shade of a clump of poplars? Then when she replied, and tried to describe the garden, he would put his hand on her lips and murmur:

'No, no, don't say any more. I was wrong. I don't want to know... I prefer to see for myself.'

He would fall back into his cherished dreaming of all this greenery he felt so near, just a step or two away. For several days he lived on that dream. At first, he explained, he had seen the garden more clearly. As he gained strength, his dream was disturbed by the rush of blood heating up his veins. He fell prey to more and more uncertainty. He no longer knew whether the trees were over to the right, whether the streams ran down to the bottom of the garden, even whether huge rocks might not be piling up under the windows. He talked to himself about it, very quietly. At the slightest indication, he would draw up marvellous plans of the garden, plans that the song of a bird, the cracking of a branch, or the scent of a flower would make him modify, and plant here a hedge of lilac, or there replace a lawn with flower beds. With each passing hour, he designed a new garden, to the great amusement of Albine who, finding him working on it, would exclaim with great bursts of laughter:

'That's not it at all, I assure you. You can't imagine. It's more beautiful than the most beautiful things you've ever seen... Don't go racking your brains over it. The garden is mine and I'll give it to you. Come on, it won't run away.'

Serge, who had already been afraid of the light, became very anxious when he found he was strong enough to go and lean on the windowsill. Once again, every evening he would say: 'Tomorrow.' He would turn towards the wall by his bed trembling, when Albine came back, and he would tell her she smelled of hawthorn, and that she had scratched her hands making a hole in the hedge, to bring all the scent back to him. One morning she suddenly grasped him in her arms, and almost carried him to the window, supporting him, then forced him to look out.

'What a coward you are!' she cried, with her lovely resonant laugh. And waving one hand at all points of the compass, she repeated, triumphantly:

'The Paradou! The Paradou!'

And Serge, speechless, looked out.

CHAPTER IV

A SEA of greenery in front, on the right, on the left, and everywhere.
A sea, rolling its great swell of leaves to the far horizon, with nothing
to interrupt it, no house, no stretch of wall or dusty road. A sea like
a desert, virginal and sacred, displaying its wild sweetness in the innocence of solitude. Only the sun could enter here, sprawl in a sheet of
gold over the fields, thread the paths with its runaway rays, hang its
fine, flaming hair between the trees, and drink at the springs with golden
lips that set the water trembling. Beneath this dusting of flames, the
big garden came alive with the extravagance of a happy animal let loose
at the ends of the earth, far from everything and free from everything.
There was such an orgy of foliage, so overwhelming a tide of grasses
that the garden seemed hidden from one end to the other, as if flooded
and drowned. Nothing but green slopes, stalks surging like jets from
a fountain, foaming masses, closely drawn curtains of forests, cloaks
of climbing plants trailing along the ground, and flights of gigantic
boughs swooping down on all sides.

Even looking carefully, one could hardly make out the original design
of the Paradou beneath this tremendous invasion of vegetation. In front,
in a sort of huge, semicircular enclosure, must have lain the parterre,
the main flower garden, with its sunken fountains, broken balustrades,
uneven steps, and fallen statues whose whiteness could be glimpsed
deep in the expanse of dark grass. Further on, behind the blue line
of a sheet of water, was a jumble of fruit trees; further still, a forest of
tall trees displayed its violet undergrowth streaked with light; now
returned to virgin forest, its treetops gently breasted the air one after
another, splashed with the lime green, pale green, and vivid green of
all the different species. On the right, the forest scaled the heights,
planting little pinewoods and fading out into meagre scrub, while
bare rocks piled up a huge wall like the debris of a fallen mountain
that barred the horizon; eager vegetation had thrust its way into the
soil, with monstrous plants that lay in the sun like sleepy reptiles.
A streak of silver, a splash that from afar looked like a cloud of pearls,
revealed a waterfall, the source of the quiet streams so lazily flowing
alongside the flower garden. Then on the left, the river flowed through
a vast meadow, where it split into four streams,* whose capricious
movements could be seen under the reeds, beneath the willows, and
behind the big trees. As far as the eye could see, stretches of pasture

added to the freshness of the low-lying ground, a landscape bathed in a bluish haze, a gleam of daylight melting gradually into the greenish blue of sunset. The Paradou, the flower garden and the forest, the rocks and streams and meadows, filled the whole expanse of the sky.

'The Paradou!' Serge stammered, opening his arms wide as if to clasp the whole garden to his bosom.

He staggered. Albine had to help him into an armchair. There he stayed for two hours without uttering a word. With his chin resting on his hands, he gazed into space. From time to time his eyelids fluttered, and a flush rose to his cheeks. He went on gazing slowly, with profound astonishment. It was all too huge, too complex, too overpowering.

'I can't see, I don't understand,' he cried, stretching out his hands to Albine in a gesture of utter weariness.

The girl then leant over the back of his chair, took his head in her hands, and forced him to look out again, as she quietly said:

'It's ours. No one will come in. When you're well again we shall go for walks. We'll have enough walks to last our lifetime. We can go wherever you like... where do you want to go?'

He smiled and murmured:

'Oh! not far. The first day, just a step or so outside the door. You see, I'd fall... Oh, I know, I'll go over there, under that tree near the window.'

She went on, softly:

'Do you want to go into the flower garden? You'll see the rose bushes, the big flowers that have swallowed up everything, even the old pathways, which they've covered with their bouquets... Or do you prefer the orchard, where I can only get in on hands and knees, since the branches are bent so low under their load of fruit... We'll go further still if you feel strong enough. We'll go to the forest, far into its hidey-holes of shade, so far that we'll sleep outside if night overtakes us... Or else, one morning, we'll climb right up there, on to those rocks. You'll see some plants that frighten me. You'll see springs, a real shower of water, and we'll enjoy feeling the spray on our faces... But if you prefer to walk along the hedges beside a stream, we'll go round by the meadows. It's very nice in the evening under the willows at sunset. You can lie down in the grass, and watch the little green frogs jumping around among the reeds.'

'No, no,' said Serge 'you're making me tired, I don't want to see that far... I shall walk two steps. That will already be a great deal.'

'And even I,' she continued, 'I've not yet managed to go everywhere. There are still places I don't know at all. For all the years I've been walking here, I still feel there are unknown places around me, places where the shade must be cooler, and the grass softer... Listen, I've always thought there was one special place, where I'd like to live forever. It's certainly there somewhere; I must have gone right past it, or perhaps it's hidden so far away that in all my roamings, I've never reached it... We'll look for it together, won't we, Serge, and we'll live there?'

'No, no, don't go on,' the young man stammered, 'I can't understand what you're saying. You're killing me.'

She let him weep in her arms for a while, worried and wretched at not being able to find the right words to comfort him.

'So the Paradou is not as lovely as you had imagined?' she then asked.

He hid his face, and said:

'I don't know any more. It was quite small, and now it's just getting bigger and bigger... Take me away, hide me.'

She took him back to his bed, soothing him once more like a child, lulling him with a lie.

'Oh well, no, it's not true, there is no garden. It's just a story I made up. Sleep in peace.'

CHAPTER V

EVERY day she made him sit at the window in the cool hours of the morning. He was beginning to try to walk a few steps, supporting himself on the furniture. His cheeks were now tinged with pink, and his hands had lost their waxy transparency. But in his convalescence he suffered from a torpor of the senses, which reduced him to the vegetative life of some poor creature born the day before. He was nothing more than a plant, aware only of the air around him. He remained withdrawn, with not enough blood in his veins to make any outward effort, a plant, holding on to the soil, and letting all the sap of his body drink from it. It was a second conception, a slow hatching in the warm egg of springtime. Albine, remembering one or two things Dr Pascal had said, felt greatly alarmed at seeing him like this, like a little boy, innocent, and as if dazed. She had heard that after recovery, some illnesses leave madness behind. She spent hours just looking at him, puzzling, the way mothers do, about how to smile at him and make him smile. He wasn't laughing at all yet. When she passed her hand before his eyes, he didn't see it, didn't follow its shadow with his eyes. When she spoke to him, he hardly turned his head towards the sound. She had but one consolation: he was growing superbly, he was a handsome child.

Then, for a week, he needed delicate care. She waited patiently, waiting for him to grow up again. She gradually noticed some signs of awakening, and began to feel reassured, thinking age would make a man of him. There were slight tremblings when she touched him. Then one evening he gave a little laugh. The next day, after seating him by the window, she went down to the garden and began to run about, calling out to him. She disappeared under the trees, scampered through patches of sunlight and came back, breathless, clapping her hands. With his wavering gaze, he did not at first see her. But when she started off again, playing the same game of hide-and-seek, leaping up from behind the bushes and calling out to him, he at last began to follow the white patch of her skirt with his eyes. And when she suddenly came and stood firmly beneath the window, looking up at him, he held out his arms, his face showing he wanted to join her. She went back up and embraced him with pride.

'Ah! you saw me, you saw me!' she cried. 'You want to come with me into the garden, don't you?... If you knew how sad you've made me these last few days, being like a dumb ox, not seeing or hearing me.'

He seemed to be listening, but with some slight pain that made him bend his neck in a rather frightened manner.

'But you're better,' she went on. 'You're strong enough to go down when you want to... Why aren't you saying anything now? Have you lost your tongue? Oh! What a brat! I suppose I shall just have to teach him how to talk!'

And in fact she then set about naming for him all the objects she touched. He was only able to stammer, saying each syllable twice, not pronouncing any words clearly. She was, however, beginning to walk him round the room. She supported him, leading him from the bed to the window. That was a great journey. He nearly fell over once or twice on the way, and that made her laugh. One day he sat down on the floor, and she had a very hard time of it getting him up again. Then she made him do a tour of the room which took a solid hour, sitting him down on the way on the sofa, on the armchairs, on the side chairs, the whole way round this little world. He was finally able to risk a few steps on his own. She stood in front of him, holding out her hands and calling to him as she walked backwards, so that he had to cross the room to reach the support of her arms. When he sulked and refused to walk, she took the comb from her hair and held it out to him like a plaything. Then he would come to get it; and sit quietly in a corner, playing with the comb for hours, gently scratching his hands with it.

At last, one morning, she found Serge standing up. He had already managed to open one of the shutters. He was trying to walk without leaning on the furniture.

'Well, now, what a strapping fellow!' she said gaily. 'Tomorrow he'll be jumping out of the window, if nobody stops him... So we're feeling pretty solid now, are we?'

Serge replied with an infantile laugh. His limbs had regained the health of adolescence, but without any awakening of his more conscious feelings. He stayed for whole afternoons at the window, facing the Paradou, with the face of a child who sees nothing but whiteness, and hears only the dull vibration of sounds. He still had all the ignorance of a little boy, and his sense of touch was still so primitive that it could not distinguish between Albine's dress and the material covering the old armchairs. There were still those astonished wide-open eyes that do not understand what they see, and the hesitant gestures that do not know how to go where they wish, still just the beginnings of a purely instinctive life, with no knowledge of the surroundings. The man in him was not yet born.

'All right, all right, go on being stupid,' Albine muttered. 'We shall see.'

She took out her comb and held it out to him.

'If you want my comb,' she said, 'come and get it.'

Then when she had got him out of the room, by going before him, backwards, she put an arm round his waist, supporting him over each step. She kept him amused, putting her comb back, and tickling his neck with the ends of her hair, and so preventing him from realizing that he was going down the stairs. But, once down below, even before she had opened the door, he took fright in the darkness of the corridor.

'Now look!' she cried.

And she pushed the door wide open.

It was a sudden dawn, a curtain of shade suddenly drawn back, to show the day in all the gaiety of the early morning. The park opened out, spread out before them in all its green clarity, fresh and deep as a well. Serge, delighted, enchanted, remained at the doorway, eager but hesitating to dip his foot into this lake of light.

'Anyone would think you were afraid of getting your feet wet,' said Albine. 'Come on, the ground is quite solid.'

He gingerly took a step forward, surprised at the gentle resistance of the sand. This first contact with the earth was a shock to his body, a renewal of life that for a moment brought him to his feet, taller now, and sighing.

'Come on, be brave,' Albine repeated. 'You know you promised me you'd walk five steps. We'll go as far as the mulberry tree, there beneath the window... There you shall have a rest.'

It took him a quarter of an hour to take the five steps. At each effort, he would stop, as if he had had to pull up roots that were holding him to the ground. The girl, who was pushing him along, said with a laugh:

'You look like a tree walking.'

She settled him with his back against the mulberry tree, in the shower of sunshine falling from its branches. Then she left him, bounding away and shouting to tell him not to move. Serge, with drooping hands, slowly turned his face towards the park. It was childhood everywhere. The pale greenery, steeped in the milk of youth, was bathed in a blond radiance. The trees were still in their infancy, the flowers had the soft skin of babies, the water was blue with the innocent blue of beautiful eyes wide open. There was a delightful awakening under every leaf.

Serge's gaze had paused at a big yellow gap created by a wide path, opening before him in the middle of a dense mass of foliage; at the end of it, to the east, some meadows bathed in gold seemed to be the field of light on which the sun would descend, and he waited for the morning to reach that path and flow towards him. He could feel it coming in a warm breeze, very faint at first, hardly perceptible on his skin, then gradually increasing, and becoming so lively it made his whole body tremble. He could taste it coming, with an ever clearer flavour, bringing him the healthy tang of fresh air, and touching his lips with the deliciously spicy sweetness of sharp fruits and milky tree-sap. He could smell it coming, in the scents that it gathered in its path, the smell of earth, the smell of shady trees, the smell of hot

plants, the smell of living animals, a whole bouquet of scents of diz-
zying intensity. He could hear it coming in the delicate flight of a bird,
skimming the grass, drawing the whole garden out of its silence, giving voices to everything it touched, and playing in his ears the music
of things and beings. He could see it coming from the end of the path,
from the meadows bathed in gold, the rosy air, so gay that it lit its way
with a smile, first just a small patch of daylight, then, in a few swift
bounds, all the splendour of the sun itself. And the morning came and
beat upon the mulberry tree, against which Serge was leaning. And
Serge was newborn in the childhood of the morning.

'Serge! Serge!' called the voice of Albine, hidden behind the high
bushes of the flower garden. 'Don't be afraid, I'm here!'

But Serge was no longer afraid. He was coming to life in the sun,
in that pure bath of light that flooded over him. He was being reborn at
the age of twenty-five, with his senses suddenly unlocked, enchanted
by the wide sky, the joyous earth, and the miracle of the horizon spread
around him. This garden, which the day before he did not know at all,
was now an amazing pleasure. Everything filled him with rapture,
down to the blades of grass and the stones on the paths, the breaths of
air he could not see but felt upon his cheeks. His whole body entered
into possession of this piece of nature, he embraced it with his limbs;
his lips drank it in, his nostrils breathed it in; he carried it away in his
ears, he hid it in the depths of his eyes. It was his. The roses in the
flower garden, the lofty branches of the tall trees, the rocks echoing
with the water falling from the springs, the meadows on which the
sun planted its spikes of light, they were all his. Then he closed his
eyes, and gave himself the pleasure of slowly reopening them, to be
dazzled by a second awakening.

'The birds have eaten all the strawberries,' said Albine, disconso-
lately, as she ran to him. 'Look, I've only been able to find these two.'

But she stopped a few steps away, looking at Serge with astonished
delight, struck to the heart.

'How handsome you are!' she cried. And she drew nearer, then
stopped, overwhelmed, and murmured:

'I had never seen you before.'

He had certainly grown taller. Dressed in loose clothing, he stood
erect, still rather thin, with his delicate limbs, broad chest, and rounded
shoulders. His white neck, tanned brown on the nape, moved freely
and tilted his head slightly backwards. Health, strength, and power

were on his face. He was not smiling; his face was in repose, with
a grave and gentle mouth, firm cheeks, a large nose, and grey eyes—very
clear, commanding eyes. His long hair, covering his entire skull, fell
to his shoulders in black curls, while a thin beard curled at his lips and
chin, showing the white of the skin beneath.

'You are handsome, you are handsome!' Albine slowly repeated,
crouching before him, and looking up with loving eyes.

'But why are you sulking with me now? Why aren't you speaking
to me?'

He, without answering, remained standing there. His eyes were
fixed far away, not seeing this child at his feet. He spoke to himself.
Standing in the sunshine, he said:

'How lovely the light is!'

It seemed as if those words were a vibration of the sun itself. They
fell into the air, little more than a murmur, like a breath of music,
a tremor of heat and life. It was already quite a few days since Albine
had heard Serge's voice. She found it different now, as he too was
different. It seemed to her to sound across the park more sweetly than
the voices of the birds, and more imperiously than the wind bending
the branches. It was majestic, it commanded. The whole garden heard
it, although it had seemed a mere breath, and the whole garden trembled with joy at it.

'Speak to me,' Albine implored him. 'You haven't ever spoken to
me like that. Up there, in the room, before you became dumb, you
used to prattle like a child... How is it then that I don't recognize your
voice now? A short while ago, I thought your voice was coming down
from the trees, that it was coming to me from the whole garden, that
it was one of those deep sighs that disturbed me during the night,
before you came here... Listen, everything is keeping quiet just to
hear you speak again.'

But he continued to be unconscious of her presence. She spoke
more tenderly:

'No, don't speak if it tires you. Sit down beside me. We'll stay here
on the grass until the sun moves away... And look, I've found two strawberries. And it took me quite a time! The birds eat everything. There's
one for you, or both of them if you like; or else we'll share them both,
so as to taste each one. You will say thank you, and I'll hear you.'

He did not want to sit down, and he refused the strawberries, which
Albine dejectedly threw away. She herself now remained silent. She

would have preferred him to be ill, as he was at first, when she gave him her hand as a pillow and felt him coming back to life when she puffed cool air on his face. She cursed this health that had him standing in the light like an indifferent young god. Was he going to stay like this, without a glance at her? Was he not going to get better, get well enough to see her and love her? And she dreamed of becoming once more his healer and, with the power of her own little hands, completing this treatment of new youth. She could see there was no flame in the depths of his grey eyes, and that his was a pale beauty, like that of the statues fallen among the nettles in the flower garden. Then she stood up, and tried to clasp him round the waist, while blowing on his neck to enliven him. But that morning, Serge did not even feel the breath stirring his silky beard. The sun had moved off, it was time to go in. Back in the room, Albine wept.

Every day, from that morning on, the convalescent took a short walk in the garden. He went beyond the mulberry tree, and on to the very end of the terrace, facing the wide stairway with the broken steps leading down to the flower garden. He was becoming accustomed to being in the open air, each bath of sunshine made him bloom anew. Even the young chestnut tree, sprung from a seed that had fallen between two stones of the balustrade, and now bursting open the resin of its buds and unfurling its fans of leaves, did not have as much vigour as Serge. One day he even tried to go down the steps; but his strength failed him and he sat down on one of the steps, among the stonecrop growing in the cracks between the paving stones. Down below, on the left, he could see a little arbour of rose trees. That was where he longed to go.

'Wait a while,' said Albine. 'The scent of the roses is too strong for you. I have never myself been able to sit beneath the rose trees without feeling weary and light-headed, and very sweetly wanting to cry... You'll see, I'll take you there under the rose trees and I'll cry, for you're making me very sad.'

CHAPTER VI

ONE morning she was at last able to support him to the bottom of the steps, trampling down the grass in front of him, and making a path through the wild rose bushes that barred the bottom steps with their supple arms. Then they went slowly on into the arbour of roses. It was indeed a wood, with a veritable forest of tall standard roses, spreading out leafy canopies as large as trees, and huge rose bushes, like impenetrable thickets of young oaks. In that spot, there had once been a most excellent collection of plant species. But since the abandonment of the formal flower garden, it had all gone wild, and virgin forest had established itself, a forest of roses invading the pathways in a tangle of wild offshoots, and mixing the different varieties to such an extent that roses of different scents and colours seemed to be blooming on the same stem. Rambling roses created mossy carpets, while climbing roses attached themselves to other rose trees like voracious ivy, shooting up like rockets of greenery, and at the slightest breath of wind, dropping showers of petals from their stripped flowers. New natural paths had formed in the midst of the woods, narrow alleys, and wide avenues, delightful covered passages where one could walk in the shade and the fragrance. These paths led to crossroads and clearings, went under arches of little red roses, and between walls covered with little yellow roses. Some sunny patches gleamed like swathes of green silk, patterned with bold splashes of colour; some shady parts had the seclusion of alcoves, the scents of love, and the warmth of a bouquet wilting on a woman's breast. The rose bushes had voices that whispered. The rose bushes were full of nests that sang.

'We must take care not to get lost,' said Albine, on entering the wood. 'I got lost once. The sun had already gone down before I managed to get away from the rose bushes clinging to my skirts at every step.'

But they had scarcely walked for more than a few minutes when Serge, overcome with fatigue, needed to sit down. He lay down and fell into a deep sleep. Albine stayed sitting pensively at his side. They were at the opening of a path, on the edge of a glade. The path plunged on afar, streaked with rays of sunshine, opening on to the sky at the far end, through a small, round blue gap. Other little paths led only into barriers of greenery. The glade was of big rose trees, rising one above the other in an orgy of branches, a tangle of thorny tendrils, like thick layers of foliage, clinging to each other in the air, and hanging there, stretching from bush to bush like parts of the roof of a flying tent. Through the holes in the lace-like patterning of the leaves, one could see only the tiniest dots of light—an azure screen, letting through light and an impalpable spray of sunshine. And from the vault, runaway

branches hung like chandeliers, thick tufts held by the green thread
of a stalk, and armfuls of flowers reaching to the ground from some
rip in the ceiling, hanging down like a piece of torn curtain.

Meanwhile, Albine was looking at Serge sleeping. She had never
before seen him with his limbs in such a state of total exhaustion, his
hands lying open on the grass, his face as if dead. He was indeed so
dead for her, she thought she could kiss him on the face without his
even feeling the kiss. And sadly, distractedly, she busied her hands
with stripping the petals off the roses that lay within her grasp. Above
her head drooped an enormous bunch, brushing against her hair, and
dropping roses on her chignon, on her ears, around her neck, and
casting a cloak of roses round her shoulders. Higher up, at the touch
of her fingers, roses showered down, their broad, soft petals having
the exquisite roundness and the scarcely blushing purity of a virgin's
breast. Like a fall of living snowflakes, roses had already hidden her
feet, which were lying in the grass. Roses climbed to her knees and
covered her skirt, enfolding her up to her waist, while three stray
petals, flying down on to her bodice, on to the opening of her breasts,
seemed to settle there like three end-marks of her adorable nudity.

'Oh! the lazy boy!' she murmured, suddenly feeling bored, and
gathering two handfuls of roses, she threw them on to Serge's face to
wake him up.

He remained weighed down with sleep, roses covering his eyes and
his mouth. This made Albine laugh. She leaned over. She kissed both
his eyes with all her heart, then she kissed his mouth, blowing her
kisses to make the roses fly off, but the roses remained on his lips, and
she laughed more deeply, greatly amused by this flowery caress.

Serge had slowly sat up. He was gazing at her, struck with astonish-
ment, and as if alarmed at finding her there.

'Who are you?' he asked. 'Where have you come from? What are
you doing here beside me?'

She just smiled, delighted at seeing him awake like this. Then he
seemed to remember; he went on with a gesture of happy reassurance:

'I know, you're my love, you have come from my flesh, and you are
waiting for me to take you in my arms so that we two can become one.
I was dreaming of you. You were in my chest and I gave you my blood,
my muscles, and my bones. I did not suffer. You took half of my heart,
so gently that for me it was an exquisite pleasure to share myself like
that. I sought out what was best in me, what was most beautiful, to

give to you. If you had taken everything, I would have thanked you...
You emerged from my eyes and from my mouth, I felt it. You were all
warm and sweet-scented, and so loving that it was the very quiver of
your body that made me sit up.'

Albine listened in ecstasy. At last he could see her; at last he was
really getting born, he was healing. With outstretched hands, she begged
him to go on:

'How could I ever have lived without you?' he murmured. 'But
I was not really alive, I was like some sleeping animal... And now you
are mine! and you are no other than myself! Listen, you must never
leave me, for you are my very breath, you would carry away my life.
We shall remain in ourselves. If ever I were to abandon you, may I be
cursed, and may my body shrivel like some useless weed.'

He took her hands, repeating, in a voice trembling with admiration:
'How beautiful you are!'

In the spray of sunshine that fell on her, Albine's skin was milky
white, slightly tinged with gold by a reflection of light. The shower of
roses around and upon her drowned her in rosy colour. Her blonde
hair, escaping from her comb, made a headdress like a setting star,
covering her shoulders with the riot of its last fiery tresses. She was
wearing a white dress, which seemed to leave her naked, so living
was it upon her, so bare did it leave her arms, her breast, her knees.
It showed her innocent skin, displayed with no shame, like a flower,
musky with its own perfume. She stretched out, not too tall, supple as
a snake, with softly rounded contours and curving voluptuous lines,
all the grace of a budding body, still bathed in infancy, yet already
swelling with puberty. Her long face, with its narrow brow and rather
strong mouth, laughed with all the tender life of her blue eyes. Yet she
remained grave, her cheeks smooth and her chin plump, a beauty as
natural as the beauty of the trees.

'Oh! how I love you!' said Serge, drawing her close to him.

They remained together, wrapped in each other's arms. They did
not kiss, but holding each other by the waist, the two lay cheek to
cheek, silently together, overjoyed at being one. All around them
the rose trees bloomed. It was a wild and loving flowering, full of
laughter—laughter red, rosy, and white. The living flowers opened
out like naked flesh, like bodices revealing the treasures of the bosom.
There were yellow roses like petals from the golden skin of barbarian
maidens, roses the colour of straw, lemon-coloured roses, and some

the colour of the sun, all the varying shades of skin bronzed by ardent
skies. Then the bodies grew softer, the tea roses becoming delightfully
moist and cool, revealing what modesty had hidden, parts of the body
not normally shown, fine as silk and threaded with a blue network of
veins. Then pink displayed its laughter-laden life; white pink, a white
scarcely tinged with colour, the snowy foot of a virgin dipping into the
water of a spring; then pale pink, more discreet than the warm whiteness of a half-glimpsed knee, or the glow of a youthful arm lighting
up a wide sleeve; then real pink, like blood under satin, bare shoulders, bare hips, all the nakedness of womanhood caressed by light;
then vivid pink, the budding flowers of the breast, the half-open flowers of the lips, exhaling warm and scented breath. And the climbing
roses, the high bushes, raining down their white flowers, clothed all
the different pinks, all the different bodies, with the lace of their flowery bunches and the innocence of their fine muslin; while here and
there, wine-dark roses, almost black, bleeding, pierced that bridal purity
with a wound of passion. It was the marriage of the scented woods,
bearing the virginities of May to the fertilities of July and August;
a first untutored kiss, gathered like a bouquet on the wedding morning.
Even down in the grass, moss roses in their long dresses of green wool
were waiting for love. Along the path dappled with sunbeams, flowers
were prowling, faces were thrust forward, calling up a breeze as they
passed. Beneath the outspread tent of the glade, all the smiles were
shining together. No flowering was like any other. The roses had their
own ways of loving. Some would do no more than half open their bud,
very timidly and with a blushing heart, while others, with unlaced
bodices, panting and fully open, looked quite crumpled, so madly in
love with their bodies as to be dying of it. Some were small, lively, and
gay, going along in a line with a cockade in their bonnets; some were
enormous, bursting with attractions, with the roundness of fattened
queens of the harem; some were brazen hussies, looking like prostitutes, in coquettish disarray, showing off petals whitened with face
powder; some were decent, like prim ladies with no more than a proper
décolletage; and some were aristocrats of smooth elegance and accept-
able originality, inventing their own revealing garments. Roses that
had opened like cups offered up their scent as if in precious crystal;
roses that had fallen over backwards in the shape of an urn let their
scent flow out drop by drop; and roses round as cabbages exhaled
their scent with the regular breathing of sleeping flowers; roses still in

bud drew their petals tightly together, releasing only the vague sigh of their virginity.

'I love you, I love you,' Serge was repeating in a low voice.

And Albine was a big rose, one of the pale roses that had opened that morning. A rose with white feet, pink knees and arms, blonde neck, and beautifully veined breast, pale and exquisitely moist. She smelled good and held out lips that offered their scent, faint as yet, in their coral cup. And Serge breathed in her scent, and laid her on his breast.

'Oh,' she laughed, 'you're not hurting me, you can take all of me.'

Serge was entranced by her laugh, so like the song of a bird in its rhythm.

'Only you have this song,' he said, 'I never heard anything so sweet... You are such a delight to me.'

And she laughed again, with even more resonance, with rippling scales of high flute-like notes, that sank slowly into deeper sounds. It was a laugh with no ending, a cooing of the throat, a sonorous, triumphant music, celebrating the joys of awakening. Everything laughed in this laugh of a woman newly born to love and beauty: the roses, the fragrant woods, the whole of the Paradou. Until now, the vast garden had been missing one charm, that of a graceful voice which would be the living gaiety of the trees, the streams, and the sun. Now the vast garden had been granted that charm of laughter.

'How old are you?' Albine asked, after closing her melody on a long note that died away.

'Nearly twenty-six,' Serge replied.

She was astonished. Good gracious! He was twenty-six! He too was very surprised at giving her that answer so easily. It seemed to him that he was less than a day, less than an hour old.

'And you, how old are you?' he in turn asked.

'Me? I'm sixteen.'

And she ran off again, full of life, repeating his age, and singing out her own age. She laughed at being sixteen, with a delicate laugh that flowed like a trickle of water with the tremulous rhythm of her voice. Serge looked at her closely, amazed at the liveliness of the laughter that made her face so radiant. He scarcely recognized her with her cheeks full of dimples, her lips curving to show the rosy moistness of her mouth, and her eyes like bits of blue sky, lit by the rising of a star. When she threw back her head, he felt the warmth of her chin, puffed out with laughter, as she rested it on his shoulder.

He stretched out his hand, unthinkingly, feeling the back of her neck.

'What do you want?' she asked. Then remembering, she cried:

'You want my comb! You want my comb!'

Then she gave him her comb, and let the heavy braids fall down from her chignon. It was like rolling out a cloth of gold. Her hair clothed her down to her waist. Some locks that fell upon her breast finished off that royal raiment. At this sudden flaming of light Serge gave a little cry. He then kissed each lock of hair, burning his lips on this blaze as of a setting sun.

But Albine was now making up for the long silence. She talked and asked questions, without stopping.

'Oh! how you made me suffer! I had become nothing to you, I spent my days, useless and helpless, in despair like someone of no worth at all... And yet, in those first days, I had comforted you. You saw me and spoke to me... Don't you remember when you were lying in bed, falling asleep against my shoulder, and saying that I was doing you good?'

'No,' said Serge, 'no, I don't remember. I have just seen you for the first time, beautiful, radiant, unforgettable.'

She clapped her hands impatiently, and protested:

'And my comb? You remember that I gave you my comb to pacify you when you had become a child again? You were looking for it again, a moment ago.'

'No, I don't remember... Your hair is like fine silk. I had never before kissed your hair.'

She became angry and spelled out some details, telling him of his convalescence in the room with the blue ceiling. But he, still laughing, simply laid his hand on her lips, saying with an uneasy weariness:

'No, be quiet, I don't know any more, and I don't want to know any more... I just woke up and found you there, full of roses. That is enough.'

He took her once more into his arms and held her a long time, dreaming aloud and murmuring:

'Perhaps I had a former life. It must have been long ago. I loved you in a painful dream. You already had your blue eyes, your rather long face, your childlike appearance. But you kept your hair carefully hidden under a cloth, and I didn't dare to push that cloth aside, because your hair was fearsome, and would have caused my death... Today your hair is the very essence of your sweetness. It's your hair that preserves your scent, takes all your beauty into its soft suppleness, and delivers it whole into my hands. When I kiss your hair, when I plunge my face into it, I drink up your life.'

He rolled the blonde curls in his hands, pressing them to his lips, as if to squeeze out of them all of Albine's blood. After a silence, he went on:

'It's strange, before being born, one dreams of being born... I was buried somewhere. I felt cold. I could hear, above my head, the movements of life outside. But I blocked my ears desperately, for I was used to my den of darkness, in which I tasted fearful joys, not even trying to rid myself of the pile of earth that lay so heavily on my chest... Where was I then? And who at last brought me to the light?'

He was making huge efforts of memory, and Albine grew anxious, fearing now that he would indeed remember. Smiling, she took a handful of her hair and tied it round the young man's neck, binding him to her. This playful act brought him out of his reverie.

'You're right,' he said, 'I am yours, what does anything else matter?... It was you, wasn't it, who pulled me out of the earth? I must have been under this garden. And what I heard was the sound of your feet disturbing the pebbles on the path. You were looking for me, you brought birdsong to me above my head, and the scent of carnations, and the warmth of the sun... And I felt sure you'd find me in the end. I had been waiting, you see, for a long time. But I hadn't even hoped that you would give yourself to me without your veil, with your hair let down, that fearsome hair that is now so soft.'

He drew her to him, and set her on his knees, putting his face alongside hers.

'Let us talk no more. We are alone forever. We love each other.'

They lay innocently in each other's arms. For a long time they remained so. The sun was rising higher, and the cloud of light falling from the high branches grew warmer. The yellow roses, the white roses, and the red roses were no more than a radiant emanation of their joy, one of their ways of smiling at each other. They had certainly opened up the buds around them. Roses crowned their heads and threw garlands over them. The perfume of the roses became so penetrating, so intense with loving tenderness, that it seemed the very scent of their breath.

Then it was Serge who set about rearranging Albine's hair. He took handfuls of hair with a charming clumsiness, and planted the comb askew into the huge chignon piled up on her head. As it turned out, this hairstyle suited her wonderfully well. He then stood up, held out his hands, and gripped her by the waist to raise her to her feet. Both were still smiling, and neither spoke. Quietly they went away down the path.

CHAPTER VII

ALBINE AND SERGE entered the flower garden. She was looking at him with anxious concern, fearing he might be getting overtired. But he reassured her with a little laugh. He felt strong enough to take her wherever she might want to go. When he found himself back in full sunlight, he gave a sigh of joy. At last he was living; no longer that plant subjected to the cruelties of winter. What tender gratitude he felt! He would have liked to spare Albine's little feet the harshness of the paths; he dreamed of having her clinging to his neck, like a baby being nursed to sleep by its mother. He was already protecting her like a zealous guardian, pushing away stones and brambles, and making sure the wind did not steal from those adored locks kisses that belonged only to him. She was pressed close against his shoulder, yielding to him, full of serenity.

Thus did Albine and Serge walk for the first time in the sun. The couple left a sweet scent in their wake, setting the path aquiver, while the sun unrolled a golden carpet beneath their feet. They walked like a moving rapture between the flowering bushes, so desirable that the distant paths they had not taken called out to them, greeting them with a murmur of admiration, like crowds greeting kings they have waited long to see. They were but one being, of sovereign beauty. The white skin of Albine was but the whiteness of the dark skin of Serge. They moved slowly, clothed in sunshine; they were the sun itself. Flowers bent forward to adore them.

In the flower garden, there was a long wave of emotion. The old formal garden became their escort, that vast field that had run wild for a century, that corner of paradise in which the wind had sowed the rarest flowers. The joyful peace of the Paradou, lying asleep in the full sun, had prevented any degeneration of the species. There was an even temperature and a soil that each plant had long nourished, to live in it thereafter in the silence of its strength. The vegetation was

enormous, superb, abounding in uncultivated vigour, randomly pro-
ducing monstrous flowerings that had never known gardener's spade
or watering can. Left to itself, free to grow shamelessly in the depths
of this solitude, protected by natural shelters, Nature had let herself
go more and more each spring, indulging in amazing frolics, and rel-
ishing the creation of strange bouquets in every season, bouquets no
hand was ever to gather. And she seemed to take a special, wild pleasure in upsetting everything the hand of man had done; she was in
rebellion, flinging masses of flowers into the middle of the paths, attacking the rockeries with an ever-rising tide of mosses, tying the necks of
marble statues that she then laid low, pulling on the flexible ropes of
her climbing plants; she broke the flagstones lining the fountains, the
steps and the terraces, thrusting shrubs deep into them; she crept over
everything until she was in possession of even the tiniest cultivated
spots, and moulded them to her will, planting her rebel flag upon them
in the form of some seed picked up on the way, some humble piece of
greenery she then converted into a gigantic mass of vegetation. The
flower garden, carefully tended for a master with a passion for flowers,
had once displayed a wonderful selection of plants in flower beds with
neatly trimmed borders. Now one could see the same plants, but per-
petuated and enlarged into such innumerable families, all gallivanting
to the four corners of the garden, that the whole garden was now just
a riot, an unruly shrubbery-school, beating against the walls, a suspect
area in which drunken nature hiccupped verbena and carnations.

Although she seemed to have yielded herself to him, weak and leaning on his shoulder, it was Albine who was guiding Serge. She took
him first to the grotto. Deep within a cluster of poplars and willows,
there spread out before them a sort of collapsed rockery, rocks that
had tumbled into the basin of a fountain, with water trickling over the
stones. The grotto had disappeared under the invasion of foliage. Below,
rows of hollyhocks seemed to bar the entrance with a fence of red, yellow, mauve, and white flowers, whose stems lay hidden among gigantic brownish-green nettles, quietly exuding the stinging fire of their
poison. Then came a prodigious leap, the vegetation climbing in a few
bounds: jasmines, starred with sweet-scented flowers; wisterias with
their leaves of delicate lace; dense ivy, serrated like varnished metal; lithe
honeysuckle, dotted with fine sprigs of pale coral; amorous clematis,
stretching out its arms in white-plumed finery. And other, more slender plants, winding around these, bound them more closely, weaving

them together with their fragrant twine. Nasturtiums, with bare and greenish bodies, opened their mouths of red and gold. Scarlet runners, strong as slender cords, here and there lit the blaze of their vivid sparks; convolvulus spread out the serrated heart of its leaves, and with its thousands of bells rang a silent carillon of exquisite colours. Sweet peas, like flights of butterflies just alighting, folded their tawny wings and their pink wings, ready to be carried far away by the first puff of wind. Altogether it was like a huge head of hair made of greenery, dotted with a scattering of flowers, its locks overflowing on all sides, escaping into wild disorder, suggesting some gigantic girl, lying on her back, swooning in the distance, throwing back her head in a spasm of passion, and sending her splendid hair streaming out and spreading like a pool of perfume.

'I've never dared to go into all this darkness,' Albine whispered to Serge.

He encouraged her, lifting her over the nettles, and as the entrance to the grotto was blocked by a boulder, he held her upright for a moment in his arms, so that she could lean over the hole that yawned a few feet from the ground.

'There's a marble woman', she murmured, 'who has fallen headlong into the flowing stream. The water has eaten away her face.'

Then he too wanted to see. He hoisted himself up by his wrists. A cool breath struck his cheeks. In among the reeds and the duckweed, in the ray of light sliding from the hole, the woman lay on her back, naked to the waist, with some drapery concealing her thighs. It was some woman drowned a hundred years ago, the slow suicide of a marble figure, toppled by sorrows into the bottom of the fountain. The clear water flowing over her had made her face into a smooth stone, a featureless patch of white, while her two breasts, as if lifted out of the water by the arching of her neck, remained intact, as if still living, and swelling with some former rapture.

'Look, she's not dead!' said Serge, getting back down. 'One day she will have to be got out from there.'

But Albine, who had shuddered, led him away. They returned to the sunshine, into the debauchery of the flower beds and borders. They walked freely across a meadow of flowers with no paths. Their feet found a carpet of delightful plants, dwarf plants that once made a border for the pathways, now simply spread out in endless layers. At times their feet disappeared up to the ankles in the spotted silk of

pink campions, the multicoloured satin of wild pinks, or the blue velvet of forget-me-nots, speckled with little melancholy eyes. Further
on, they went through huge banks of mignonette that came up to their
knees, like a scented bath; they cut through a field of lilies of the valley, in order to spare a neighbouring field of violets, so delicate that
they trembled at the thought of damaging the smallest tuft; then,
hemmed in on all sides, with nothing but violets all around them, they
were forced to walk gently upon that cool fragrance, in the very breath
of springtime. Beyond the violets, lobelias unfurled their leaves of green,
rather coarse wool, dotted with light mauve; the subtly shaded stars
of spikemoss, the blue cups of nemophila, the yellow crosses of saponaria,* and the pink and white crosses of wallflowers, all made patches
of rich tapestry, endlessly extending a royally luxurious carpet before
the couple so that they could go on without tiring, in the joy of their
first walk together. And violets kept on appearing, a sea of violets
flowing everywhere, pouring their precious perfume at their feet, and
accompanying them with the fragrant breath of their flowers hidden
under the leaves.

Albine and Serge were getting lost. Hundreds of much taller plants
created hedges and offered narrow paths that they enjoyed following.
The paths plunged on with sudden twists and turns, ran into each
other, and merged into inextricable thickets; ageratums with their sky-
blue tufts of flowers; sweet woodruffs with their delicate musky odour;
mimulus flowers with brazen throats, splashed with vermilion; scarlet
phlox and purple phlox, proudly holding aloft their distaffs of flowers
to be woven by the wind; red flax with sprigs as fine as hair; chrysan-
themums like full moons, moons of gold, giving off brief, dim rays of
white and purple and pink. The couple climbed over obstacles, and
pursued their joyous walk between the two hedges of greenery. On
their right rose slender fraxinellas and valerian, tumbling in heaps of
purest snow, and greyish hound's tongue,* holding a drop of dew in
each tiny cup of its flowers. On the left was a long line of every variety
of aquilegia, white, pale pink, and dark purple—the last almost black,
of funereal gloom, with petals creased and crinkled like crêpe, hanging down from a cluster of tall stems. As they moved further along,
the hedges changed, showing rows of huge larkspur, their flower-
covered stalks buried in a tangle of leaves, then the gaping jaws of wild
snapdragons, and now hoisting aloft the spindly foliage of schizanthus, full of butterfly flowers,* with wings of sulphur yellow, splashed

with delicate red. Campanulas ran wild, tossing their blue bells high, right up to the tall asphodels, whose golden stalks served as their bell towers. In one spot a giant fennel looked like a fine lace-clad lady opening her sunshade of sea-green satin. Then the couple found themselves in an impasse; they could go no further, a riot of flowers blocked the path, such a profusion of plants that it created something like a hayrick, with a triumphant plume on top. Down below, acanthus created a pedestal, from which sprang scarlet geum, rock roses whose dry petals were creased like wallpaper, and clarkia with elaborate big white crosses, like the crosses of some barbarian cult. Higher up were pink viscaria, yellow linanthus, white collinsia, and lagurus grass,* setting its greenish grey pompoms among all the bright colours. Higher still, red foxgloves and blue lupins rose in slender columns, supporting a Byzantine rotunda, vividly daubed in crimson and blue; while at the very top, a colossal castor-oil plant, with blood-red leaves, seemed to spread out a dome of burnished copper.

As Serge was already stretching out his hands to make a way through, Albine begged him not to hurt the flowers.

'You'd break the branches, you'd crush the leaves,' she said. 'In all the years I've lived here, I've always been careful not to kill any of them... Come, I'll show you my pansies.'

She made him retrace his steps, taking him away from the narrow paths to the centre of the flower garden, where large fountains had once stood. Their basins had filled up and were now just very large *jardinières*, edged with crumbling, broken marble. In one of the largest, a puff of wind had sown a marvellous basket of pansies. The velvet flowers seemed like living beings, with their braids of purple hair, their yellow eyes, their paler mouths, and chins of a delicate flesh colour.

'When I was younger, they used to frighten me,' Albine murmured. 'Just look at them, aren't they like thousands of little faces looking up at us from the ground? And they all turn their faces the same way. They're like buried dolls, sticking their heads out.'

She pulled him on again. They made a tour of the old fountains. In the next one, amaranths had grown, bristling with monstrous crests that Albine did not dare to touch, for they made her think of gigantic, bleeding caterpillars. Balsams, straw-coloured, the colour of peach-blossom, grey like flax, or pink-tinged white, filled up another basin, in which the seed-pods snapped with little cracking noises. Then, in the middle of the ruins of another fountain was a collection of superb carnations; white carnations poured over the edge of the mossy basin; multicoloured carnations planted a gaudy medley of flowers like ruffs of lacy muslin in the cracks of the stone, while deep in the jaw of the lion that once spat out water, a big red carnation was blooming with such vigour that the old, mutilated lion now seemed to be spitting out splashes of blood. And close by, the principal water feature, an old lake on which swans had once swum, had become a thicket of lilac, in whose shade stocks, verbenas, and day lilies protected their delicate complexions, all damp and fragrant, and half asleep.

'And we haven't even covered half of the flower garden yet!' said Albine with pride. 'Over there are some really big flowers, fields in which I totally disappear from sight, like a partridge in a wheatfield.'

They made their way there. They went down a wide flight of steps, whose toppled urns still blazed with the tall purple flames of irises. Along the steps flowed a stream of wallflowers like a carpet of liquid gold. On each side, thistles held up their spindly candelabra of green bronze, spiky and curved like the beaks of fantastic birds, products of some strange art, and elegant like Chinese incense-burners. Between the broken balustrades sedums let fall their blond tresses, their hair of river-green, stained with patches of mildew. Then at the bottom of the steps stretched yet another formal garden, set with box trees strong as oaks, box trees once carefully arranged and pruned into balls, pyramids, or octagonal towers, but now magnificently dishevelled, with holes in their big, dark, ragged greenery showing bits of blue sky.

Albine guided Serge to the right, into a field which seemed a sort of cemetery for the flower garden. Scabious were in mourning here. Funeral processions of poppies went along in a line, stinking of death, and displaying their heavy flowers with their feverish brilliance. Tragic anemones clustered in grieving crowds, with bruised complexions, grey from some passing epidemic. Squat daturas* spread out their purplish trumpets, in which insects weary of life came to drink their suicide poison. Marigolds buried their flowers beneath their congested leaves, flowers like the bodies of dying stars, already scenting the air with pestilent decomposition. There were yet other areas of sorrow: fleshy ranunculus, the dull colour of rusty metal, and hyacinths and tuberoses exhaling suffocation, and dying in their own perfume. But the cineraria dominated the scene, a whole invasion of cineraria, parading in their half-mourning robes of purple and white, some in striped velvet, some in a plain velvet of opulent severity. In the middle of this melancholy field a marble cupid still stood, though mutilated, his bow-holding arm fallen in the nettles, but still smiling under the lichens that made his naked infant body shiver.

Then Albine and Serge went up to their waists into a field of peonies. The white flowers were dying, making a shower of wide petals that cooled their hands, like the heavy raindrops of a storm. The red flowers had apoplectic faces, with broad, disturbing grins. On the left, they reached a field of fuchsias, a thicket of supple, slender shrubs, that delighted them like Japanese toys, laden with thousands of bells. They next went through fields of veronicas, with their purple clusters, then geraniums and pelargoniums, over which ardent little flames seemed to fly with the white, pink, and red incandescence of a brazier, constantly fanned into life by the slightest puffs of wind. They had to go round curtains of gladioli, tall as reeds, holding up their poles of flowers that burned in the light with the rich flame of blazing torches. They lost their way in a forest of sunflowers, with trunks the size of Albine's waist, a forest darkened by rough leaves, wide enough to cradle a baby, and peopled by giant faces, star-like faces, brilliant, like so many suns. And at last they reached a wood of rhododendrons, so densely packed with flowers that the branches and leaves were totally hidden, in a display of monstrous bunches, basketfuls, of soft flower heads, tumbling away to the horizon.

'Come on, we haven't reached the end!' cried Albine. 'Let's walk on, let's go on walking.'

But Serge held her back. They were just then in the centre of an old, ruined colonnade. Pieces of broken columns had created benches among clumps of primroses and periwinkles. Further on, among the columns still standing, lay other fields of flowers: tulips, with their vivid colours like painted pottery; calceolarias, light pouches of flesh, speckled with blood and gold; zinnias like big angry daisies; petunias with soft petals like a woman's fine batiste, showing the pink skin underneath; more and more fields, endless fields, with flowers no longer recognizable rolling out their carpets in the sunshine, with the confused, motley patterns of stridently bright clumps submerged in the gentle green of the grasses.

'We'll never be able to see it all,' said Serge, stretching out his hand, with a smile. 'This would be a good place to sit, with all this perfume around us.'

Beside them was a field of heliotropes, with such a sweet smell of vanilla that it made the wind feel like a soft caress. They sat down on one of the fallen columns, in the middle of a cluster of superb lilies which had sprung up there. They had been walking for more than an hour. They had moved from roses to lilies, after passing through all the flowers. The lilies offered a refuge of simplicity, after their lovers' walk among the ardent solicitations of silky honeysuckle, musky violets, verbena offering the cool scent of a kiss, and tuberoses whispering of a fatal swoon of ecstasy. The lilies with their tall and slender stalks became a white haven for them, under the snowy roof of flowers, brightened only by the delicate touch of gold on the pistils. There they remained, like two betrothed children, majestically modest, as if in the middle of a tower of purity, an unassailable ivory tower, in which they loved each other as yet only with all the charm of their innocence.

Albine and Serge stayed with the lilies until evening. They were happy there; they were completing the process of being born. There, Serge lost the last vestiges of fever from his hands. Albine became pure white, a milky white, not tinged with the pink of any blush. They no longer noticed that they had bare arms, bare necks, bare shoulders. Their hair no longer disturbed them as if it were a display of nakedness. Huddled close together, they laughed with innocent laughter, and their embrace seemed cool and refreshing. Their eyes retained the limpid calm of spring water, with nothing impure rising from their flesh to mar its crystal purity. Their cheeks were like scarcely ripe, velvety fruit, which they did not dream of biting into. When they left the lilies, they were less than ten years old; it seemed to them they had just met, alone in the depths of this large garden, to live and play there forever, in eternal friendship. And as they crossed the flower garden once more, returning home in the twilight, the flowers seemed more subdued, pleased to see them so young, and not wanting to corrupt these children. The groves of peonies, clusters of carnations, carpets of forget-me-nots, and hanging curtains of clematis no longer spread before them an alcove of love, but immersed now in the evening air, slept in a childhood as innocent as theirs. The pansies, with their honest little faces, gave them friendly looks. The languid mignonettes, when Albine's white skirt brushed against them, seemed full of compassion, avoiding any breath that might hasten their fever.

CHAPTER VIII

THE next day, at dawn, it was Serge who called Albine. She slept in
a room on the upper floor, and he didn't think of going up there. He
leaned out of the window and saw her opening the shutters after leaping out of bed. They both laughed merrily at catching sight of each
other like that.

'Today you won't be going out,' said Albine, when she came down.
'We must rest today... Tomorrow I want to take you a long way, very
far, somewhere really nice.'

'But we'll get bored,' Serge protested.

'Oh no, we shan't!... I shall tell you stories.'

They spent a delightful day. The windows were thrown wide open;
the Paradou came in and laughed with them in the room. Serge at last
took possession of that happy room, in which he believed he was
born. He wanted to see everything, and have everything explained
to him. The plaster cupids, tumbling round the edge of the alcove,
delighted him so much that he got up on a chair and tied Albine's
sash around the neck of the smallest one, just a little bit of a man,
upside down, with his bottom in the air, misbehaving. Albine clapped
her hands, and said he looked like a cockchafer on a string. Then,
pitying him:

'No, no, untie him... he can't fly like that.'

But it was the cupids painted above the doors that especially fascin-
ated Serge. It annoyed him that he couldn't see what games they
were playing, as the paintings had faded so much. With Albine's help,
he rolled up a table, and they both climbed on to it. Albine started
explaining:

'Look, these cupids are throwing flowers. Underneath the flowers,
all you can see is three bare legs. I seem to remember that when I first
arrived here, I was also able to make out a beautiful lady, lying there.
But she's long gone.'

They went round all the panels, without seeing anything impure in
the pretty bedroom indecencies. The paintings, which were flaking
like an over-rouged eighteenth-century face, were dead enough now
to reveal no more than the elbows and knees of bodies swooning in
pleasant voluptuousness. The excessively crude details, which probably delighted the one-time lovers whose distant scent still lingered in
the alcove, had disappeared, eroded by the fresh air; so the room, like

the park outside, had naturally returned to its virgin state under the tranquil glory of the sun.

'Oh!' said Serge, getting down from the table, 'it's just children playing. Do you know how to play hot cockles?'

Albine knew how to play every game. But you needed three to play hot cockles. This made them laugh. But Serge insisted it was too lovely being the two of them, and they swore to remain just two forever.

'We are really at home here, and we hear nothing from outside,' the young man went on, stretching out on the sofa. 'And the furniture has a nice smell of age... it's as comfortable as a nest. This is a room full of happiness.'

The girl shook her head gravely. 'If I had been a nervous person,' she murmured, 'I would have been quite frightened at first... That's the very story I want to tell you. I heard it from folk in the country round here. It may not be true, but it will keep us amused.'

She sat down beside Serge.

'Years and years ago... the Paradou belonged to a rich nobleman who shut himself up here with a very beautiful lady. The gates of the chateau were kept so tightly closed, and the walls of the garden were so high, that no one ever saw so much as the hem of the lady's skirt.'

'I know,' Serge interrupted, 'the lady has never been seen again.'

As Albine looked at him in surprise, irritated to find her story already known, he went on quietly, himself astonished:

'You already told me that story.'

She insisted she hadn't. Then she seemed to think better of it, and allowed herself to be persuaded. This didn't stop her from finishing the story with these words:

'When the lord left, he had white hair. He had all the entrances blocked, so that no one could disturb the lady... The lady had died in this room.'

'In this room!' exclaimed Serge. 'You hadn't told me that... Are you sure she died in this room?'

This irritated Albine. She was only repeating what everybody knew. The lord had had this lodge built for that unknown lady, who was like a princess. The people of the chateau later declared it was there that he spent his days and nights. Often, too, they would see him on one of the paths, guiding the little feet of the mysterious lady deep into the darkest thickets. But nothing would have persuaded them to dare spy on the couple who walked in the park for weeks on end.

'And this is where she died,' Serge repeated, much struck by this. 'You took her room, you use her furniture, and sleep in her bed.'

Albine smiled.

'You know I'm not a nervous person,' she said... 'Besides, all this, it's so old... The room seemed full of happiness to me.'

They fell silent, and looked for a moment at the alcove, its high ceiling, and the grey shadows in the corners. There was a sort of loving tenderness in the faded colours of the furniture. It was a gentle sigh from the past, so resigned that it still resembled the warm gratitude of an adored woman.

'Yes,' said Serge, 'you can't be frightened here. It's too peaceful.'

Albine went on, drawing closer to him:

'What few people know is that they had discovered in the garden a place of perfect happiness, where, in the end, they spent all their time. I learned that from a reliable person... A place of cool shade, hidden deep in impenetrable shrubbery, so wonderfully beautiful it makes you forget the world entirely. That's where the lady must have been buried.'

'Is it in the flower garden?' Serge asked curiously.

'Oh, I don't know, I don't know,' said the girl, with a hopeless gesture. 'I've looked everywhere, but I haven't yet been able to find that blissful glade... It's not among the roses, nor the lilies, nor on that carpet of violets.'

'Perhaps it's that place with the sad flowers, where you showed me a child still standing, with a broken arm.'

'No, no.'

'Perhaps in the depths of the grotto, near that clear stream, in which that tall, marble woman with no face lies drowned?'

'No, no.'

Looking thoughtful, Albine remained silent for a moment. Then she went on, as if talking to herself:

'As soon as I arrived here, I started searching. If I've spent day after day in the Paradou, and delved into every tiniest nook of greenery, it was only in order to sit for an hour within that glade. How many mornings I've wasted, sliding under the brambles, inspecting every remote corner of the park! Oh, I'd have recognized it at once, that enchanted retreat, with its enormous tree that must cover it with a roof of leaves, its grass as fine as softest silk, and its walls of green bushes that not even the birds can get through.'

She threw an arm round Serge's neck and raising her voice, she pleaded:

'What do you say? Now there are two us, we'll search together, and we'll find it... You, who are so strong, you'll push away the branches for me so that I can get right into the thickets. You'll carry me when I'm tired, and help me to leap over the streams, and you'll climb the trees if we happen to lose our way... And what joy it will be, when we can sit side by side under the leafy roof in the middle of that glade! I've heard that there you can live a whole lifetime in one minute. So, what do you say, my dear Serge? We shall set off tomorrow, we'll search the whole park, bush by bush, until we've found what we desire.'

Serge shrugged his shoulders with a smile.

'But why bother?' he said. 'Aren't we happy here in the flower garden? Better by far to stay here with the flowers, don't you think, than going so far to search for a greater happiness.'

'That's where she died, and where she's buried,' Albine said quietly, sinking back into her reverie. 'It was the joy of sitting there that killed her... The shade of the tree is of such delight that one dies of it... I would be quite willing to die like that. We would lie down together in each other's arms; we would die, and no one would ever find us again.'

Serge interrupted:

'No, enough of that, you're making me very unhappy, I want us to live in the sun, far from that deadly shade. Your words are upsetting me, as if they were pushing us towards some irreparable disaster. It should be forbidden to sit under a tree whose shade has such an effect.'

'Yes, it is forbidden,' Albine gravely declared. 'All the local folk told me it was forbidden.'

There was a silence. Serge got up from the sofa where he had been lying. He laughed, and said he didn't much like these stories. The sun was already lower in the sky when Albine at last agreed to go down to the garden for a moment. She took him over to the left, along the boundary wall, to an area of ruins, all bristling with brambles. It was the site of the old chateau, still black from the fire that had brought down its walls. Underneath the brambles, stones lay baked and cracked, and woodwork that had tumbled down was rotting. It looked like a place of arid rocks; it was furrowed, covered with mounds, and draped with coarse grass and creepers that slid into every crack like snakes. The two happily set about exploring every part of this stretch of ground, going down into the holes, examining the debris, seeing whether they could learn anything about this burnt-out past. They did not acknowledge their curiosity, they simply chased each other around, over broken flooring and fallen walls; but in fact, they were thinking only of the legends of these ruins, of that wondrously beautiful lady who had trailed her silken skirts over these steps, where now only lizards sauntered idly.

Serge at last climbed on to the highest pile of rubble to survey the park and its huge green expanses, searching among the trees for the grey outline of the lodge. Albine remained silent, standing beside him, serious once more.

'The lodge is over there, on the right,' she said, without his needing to ask. 'That's all that's left of the buildings... Can you see it, at the end of that line of lime trees?'

They fell silent again. And as if continuing aloud the thoughts they were both thinking, she went on:

'When he went to see her, he must have gone down that path; then he went round the big chestnut trees, and on under the lime trees... It took him barely a quarter of an hour.'

Serge did not say a word. When they went back, they too went down that path, round the big chestnut trees, and on under the lime trees. It was a path of love. As they walked on the grass, they seemed to be looking for footsteps, a bit of stray ribbon, a whiff of perfume from long ago, some sign that they were indeed on the path that led to the bliss of being together. Night was coming, and the park now had a mighty dying voice that called to them from the depths of the greenery.

'Wait,' said Albine, when they reached the front of the lodge. 'You can't come up for three minutes.'

She darted off gaily, and shut herself up in the room with the blue ceiling. Then, after letting Serge knock twice, she half-opened the door discreetly, and greeted him with an old-fashioned curtsey.

'Good day, my dear lord,' she said, embracing him.

This greatly amused them. They played at being lovers, with childish delight. They stammered out the passion that had once suffered and died in that room. They learned it like a lesson that they stumbled through in an adorable way, not knowing to kiss on the lips, but seeking out cheeks instead, and finally dancing up and down in front of each other, roaring with laughter, not knowing any other way of showing the pleasure they felt in loving each other.

CHAPTER IX

NEXT morning, Albine wanted to set out at sunrise for the great out-
ing she had had in mind since the previous day. She tapped her feet
merrily on the ground, saying they wouldn't get back home that day.

'Where are you taking me then?' asked Serge.

'You'll see, you'll see.'

But he took her wrist, and looked her in the eye.

'We must be sensible, mustn't we? I don't want you to go searching
for that glade of yours, that tree, and that grass where people die. You
know it's forbidden.'

She blushed faintly, protesting that she wasn't even thinking of such
things. Then she added:

'However, if we did happen to find it without looking for it, would
you not sit down?... Do you love me so little?'

They set out. They went straight across the flower garden, not
stopping to see the reawakening of the flowers, naked in their bath of
dew. The morning had a pink complexion, and the smile of a pretty
child opening its eyes among the whiteness of pillows.

'Where are you taking me?' Serge asked again.

Albine just laughed, and made no answer. But when they reached
the strip of water that cut across the park at the end of the flower
garden, she stopped in consternation. The river had swollen further
with the recent rains.

'We'll never be able to get past,' she murmured. 'Usually I take off
my shoes and lift my skirts. But today the water would be up to our
waists.'

They went along the bank for a while, looking for a place to cross.
Then the girl said it was useless, for she knew all the ins and outs of
that water. There had once been a bridge, and its collapse had littered
the river with big stones, over which the water now swirled with crests
of foam.

'Climb on to my back,' said Serge.

'No, no. I don't want to. If you were to slip, we'd both have no
end of a ducking... You don't know how treacherous those stones
can be.'

'Come on, get on my back.'

That finally persuaded her. She took a run-up and jumped like
a boy, so high that she ended up straddling Serge's neck. When she

felt him stagger, she shouted that he wasn't strong enough yet, so she would get down. Then she leaped up again, twice more. They greatly enjoyed that game.

'When you've finished!' cried the young man with a laugh. 'Now hold on tight. Here we go!'

And in three graceful bounds he crossed the river, scarcely wetting the tips of his toes. Halfway across, however, Albine thought she was slipping off. She gave a little cry and gripped his chin with both hands to steady herself. He was already carrying her over the fine sand of the further bank, galloping like a horse.

'Gee-up! Gee-up!' she cried, quite reassured now, and enjoying this new game.

He went on running like this for as long as she wanted, stamping his feet and imitating the sound of horse's hooves. She clucked her tongue at him, and taking two locks of his hair, pulled on them as if they were reins, to drive him to right or left.

'Well now, we're there!' she said, slapping him gently on the cheeks. She leaped down, while he, hot and sweating, leaned against a tree to get his breath back. Then she started scolding him, saying she wouldn't look after him if he fell ill again.

'Don't go on about it! It's done me good,' was his reply. 'When I've totally recovered my strength, I'll carry you on my back for whole mornings... Where are you taking me?'

'Right here,' she said, sitting down with him under an enormous pear tree.

They were in the former orchard of the park. A hawthorn hedge, a wall of greenery, with some gaps in it, cut it off from the rest of the garden. It was a forest of fruit trees that no scythe had trimmed for a century. Some, twisted out of shape, battered and bent by storms, were growing quite askew; while others, covered with enormous lumpy knots and deep holes, seemed only to hold to the ground by the huge remnants of their bark. The high branches, weighed down with fruit each season, spread out their vast sprays far and wide, while some, the most heavily laden, had even broken and now rested on the ground, while still continuing to bear fruit, sustained by their rich reserves of sap. The trees were propping each other up; they had become twisted pillars, holding up a vaulted roof of leaves that plunged into long arcades, soared suddenly into airy halls, and flattened out almost along the ground, like collapsed rafters. Around each of these giants, wild offshoots formed a thicket, adding the dense tangle of young stalks, whose berries had a delicious sharpness. In the greenish light that flowed like clear running water over the great silence of the moss, the only sound that could be heard was the thud of fruit being gathered by the wind.

There were patriarchal apricot trees, bearing their great age with fortitude, already paralysed on one side, with a forest of dead wood like the scaffolding of a cathedral, but so lively on the other side, so youthful, that tender shoots were everywhere breaking out through the rough bark. Some venerable plum trees, all hoary with moss, were still stretching up to drink in the blazing sun, without one leaf losing colour. Cherry trees were building whole townships with multistorey houses, flights of stairs, and floors made of branches, big enough to house ten families. Then there were broken-down apple trees like great invalids, their limbs twisted, their gnarled skin stained with patches of green rust; there were smooth pear trees, raising lofty masts of slender branches, like the opening of a port, cutting the horizon with dark stripes; and rosy peach trees, getting space made for them, even in the crush of their neighbours, with a friendly laugh and a gentle push, like pretty girls caught in a crowd. Some trees, formerly espaliered, had pushed through the low walls that supported them, and now were simply having the time of their life, free of the trellises, torn-off strips of which still hung on their arms; they grew just as they pleased, having kept of their former particular shape only the vague look of once well-brought-up trees now dragging the rags of their party clothes into a vagabond life. And vines ran everywhere with wild abandon, round every trunk and every branch from tree to tree. They climbed unstoppable, like fits of wild giggles, hooked themselves for a moment on to some lofty knot, then darted off again with a further outburst of even louder laughter, splashing all the greenery with the intoxicated jollity of their laden branches. It was a tender green, tipped with gold sunlight that lit up the ravaged heads of the grand old men of the orchard with a touch of drunkenness.

Then, on the left, more widely spaced trees, almond trees, with their sparse foliage, let the sun through to ripen the pumpkins lying on the ground like fallen moons. And alongside a stream that flowed through the orchard there were also melons, scarred with warts, lost in the midst of rampant foliage, and varnished watermelons, with the perfectly oval shape of ostrich eggs. At every step, redcurrant bushes barred the way to old paths, showing the timid bunches of their fruit like rubies, every currant glistening with a drop of light. Hedges of raspberry bushes spread out like wild brambles; the ground was simply a carpet of strawberry plants, the grass all strewn with ripe strawberries and their vanilla-tinged scent.

But the enchanted part of the orchard was yet further to the left, near the balustrade of rocks that began just there to climb to the horizon. Here, on burning ground, you entered a natural hothouse on which the sun poured directly down. First you had to pass gigantic, gawky fig trees, stretching their branches like greyish arms heavy with sleep, and so encumbered by hairy leathery leaves that in order to get through, you had to break off the young stalks growing out from their aged, desiccated feet. Then you walked through clumps of arbutus with foliage like giant box trees, and red berries making them look like May trees,* decorated with pompoms of scarlet silk. Next came a thicket of sorbs, azaroles, and jujube trees, and alongside these, pomegranate trees made a border of evergreen foliage; the pomegranates were scarcely set as yet, but large as a child's fist; the red flowers, sitting at the tip of the branches, seemed to flutter like the wings of hummingbirds, which do not even bend the grass when they alight on it. Last came a wood of orange and lemon trees growing vigorously on the uncultivated earth. Their straight trunks created row upon row of dark columns; their glistening leaves spread the gaiety of their bright colours upon the blue of the sky, and neatly cut the shade into thin pointed blades that sketched on the ground below the endless palm trees of a patterned Indian cloth. This was a very special shade, compared with which the shade of the European garden seemed very tame; this was a joyous glow of sunlight filtered into flying gold dust, the certainty of perpetual greenery, the strength of continuous fragrance, the intoxicating scent of flowers and the more sober scent of the fruit, all filling the limbs with the supple languor of hot climates.

'And now we shall eat!' cried Albine, clapping her hands. 'It must be at least nine o'clock. I'm really hungry!'

She had stood up. Serge admitted that he too would be glad to have something to eat.

'Silly man!' she went on. 'Didn't you realize I was taking you out for a meal? We are not going to die of hunger here, are we? Everything here is for us.'

They went in under the trees, pushing aside the branches, sliding in to the best of the fruit. Albine, who went in first, with her skirts gathered up between her legs, turned back to ask her companion, with her flute-like voice:

'What do you like best? Pears, apricots, cherries, redcurrants?... I warn you the pears are still green; but they're really very nice just the same.'

Serge decided on cherries. Albine said that would make a good start. But, as he was stupidly just going to climb the first cherry they came upon, she made him walk on for another good ten minutes, through an awful tangle of branches. That cherry tree there had nasty cherries, no good at all; the cherries on this tree were too sour; the cherries on the next tree would not be ripe for another week. She knew all the trees.

'Here now, climb this one,' she said at last, stopping at a cherry tree so laden with fruit that bunches of cherries hung down to the ground, like coral necklaces caught on the branches.

Serge seated himself comfortably beween two branches and began his meal. He could no longer hear Albine; he thought she was in another tree a few feet away, until looking down, he saw her, lying quietly on her back, just beneath him. She had slipped in there, and was eating without even using her hands, seizing with her lips the cherries the tree offered her mouth.

When she saw she had been spotted, she laughed long and loud, leaping on the grass like a white fish leaping on the water, turning over on her front, pushing herself along by the elbows, going round the tree, while continuing to capture the fattest cherries.

'Just imagine, they're tickling me!' she cried. 'It's just that they're so very fresh!... I've got them in my ears, in my eyes, on my nose, just everywhere! If I wanted to, I could squash one, and make myself a moustache... They're much sweeter down here than up there.'

'Come on!' said Serge, laughing. 'It's just that you don't dare to climb up.'

She fell silent with indignation.

'What, me? Me?' she stammered.

Then, pulling her skirt together and fastening it in front to her belt, never noticing that she was showing her thighs, she eagerly gripped the tree and hoisted herself on to the trunk, with one wristy effort. Then she ran along the branches, not even using her hands;

supple as a squirrel, she moved along, going around the knots, leaving her feet free, keeping her balance just by the curve of her body. When she was high up, at the end of a thin branch that shook furiously under her weight:

'Well now! So I don't dare to climb up, do I?'

'Will you please come down at once!' Serge implored, seriously alarmed. 'I beg you. You're going to hurt yourself.'

But in her triumph, she went even higher. She was at the very end of the branch, straddling it and edging herself slowly along above the sheer drop below, clutching handfuls of leaves with both hands.

'The branch is going to break,' said Serge, really frightened.

'Let it break then!' she replied with a great laugh. 'That will save me the bother of getting down.'

And the branch did indeed break, but slowly, with such a long tearing that it went down gradually, as if to return Albine to the ground in a very gentle manner. She was not the slightest bit frightened; she leaned back, shaking her half-naked thighs, repeating:

'It's so nice, it's like being in a carriage.'

Serge had leaped down from the tree to receive her in his arms. As he was still quite pale from the fright he had just had, she teased him:

'But falling out of trees is something that happens every day. One never gets hurt... Come on, laugh, you silly man! Look, put a bit of spit on my neck. I got scratched.'

He put a bit of spit on her neck with his fingertip.

'There, it's better!' she cried, bounding away like a little girl. 'Shall we play hide-and-seek?'

She went to hide first. She disappeared, calling out 'Cuckoo! Cuckoo!' from the depths of some green shrubbery that only she knew, and where Serge couldn't find her. But the game didn't go on without a terrible raiding of fruit. Their meal continued in the nooks and crannies into which these two big children chased each other. Albine, while darting along under the trees, would reach out a hand, munch a green pear, and fill her skirt with apricots. Then in some of her hiding places she found treasures that kept her sitting on the ground, forgetting about the game, totally occupied with the serious business of eating. At one point, unable to hear Serge at all, she had to look for him for a change. And it was a real surprise for her, almost an annoyance, to find him under a plum tree—a plum tree even she didn't know was there—with ripe plums that had a faint musky odour. She took him seriously to task. Did he want to gobble up everything then? Was that why he hadn't said a word? He pretended to be a ninny, but he had a keen sense of smell, and could sniff out the good things from afar. She was especially angry at the plum tree, a sneaky, underhand tree that one didn't even know about, that must have sprung up overnight, just to be annoying. Serge, refusing to eat a single plum while she was sulking, took it into his head to give the tree a violent shake. A shower, a veritable hail of plums fell. Under this shower Albine had plums in her arms, down her neck, and smack on her nose. Then she couldn't help laughing; she stayed there under the deluge, shouting 'More! More!', amused by the round balls bouncing off her, as she held out her hands and her mouth with her eyes closed, curling up in a little heap on the ground.

It was a morning of delightful childhood, with all the mischief of naughty little children let loose in the Paradou. Albine and Serge spent childish hours in that shrubbery school, running, shouting, and scuffling, with never a quiver in their innocent flesh. It was still simply the comradeship of two young rascals who might later thinking of kissing each other on the cheek when the trees had no more dessert to offer. And what a happy place it was for this first escapade! A den of leaves, full of excellent hiding places. Paths on which it was impossible to stay serious, with such gourmet laughter falling from the hedges. In this happy orchard, the park had the mischievous playfulness of bushes doing just as they liked, the cool shade for giving appetite, and the old age of kindly trees, like grandfathers laden with treats. Even in the depths of green and mossy hidey-holes, under broken trunks that forced them to crawl along one after the other, in corridors of leaves so narrow that Serge, laughing, held on to Albine's bare legs, they did not encounter any perilous reveries of silence. Nothing troubling came to them from this playtime of the woods.

When they were tired of the apricot trees, the plum trees and cherry trees, they ran beneath the spindly almond trees, eating green almonds, scarcely the size of peas, and searching for strawberries in the carpet of grass, annoyed that the melons and watermelons were not ripe. Albine at last ran off as fast as she could, followed by Serge who was unable to catch her. She went in among the fig trees, jumping over thick branches and tearing off leaves that she threw behind her into her companion's face. In a few bounds she went through the clumps of arbutus, tasting their red berries as she went by, and it was in the forest of sorbs, azaroles, and jujube trees that Serge lost her. At first he thought she was hiding behind a pomegranate tree; but what he had taken to be the two pink rosettes of her wrists were two flowers still in bud. He then searched the wood of orange trees, marvelling at how lovely it was in there, and thinking he was in the fairyland of the sun. In the middle of the wood he found Albine, who, not knowing he was so near, was vigorously rummaging and peering into the green depths.

'What are you looking for there?' he cried. 'You know perfectly well that it's forbidden.'

She started, and slightly blushed for the first time that day. And sitting down beside Serge, she talked about the happy times when the oranges were ripe. The woods then were all golden, lit by those round stars that pierced the vault of greenery with their yellow eyes.

Then, when at last they moved on, she stopped at every wild off-shoot, filling her pockets with little sour pears and bitter little plums, saying they would serve for eating on the way. It was a hundred times better than what they had tasted before. Serge had to eat some, in spite of making grimaces at every bite. They returned home exhausted but happy, having laughed so much that their ribs ached. And that evening indeed, Albine did not have the strength to go up to her room; she fell asleep lying across the bed at Serge's feet, dreaming she was climbing trees, and still munching in her sleep the fruit of the wild trees that she had hidden beside her under the blanket.

CHAPTER X

A WEEK later there was another great journey into the park. This time they were to go over to the left beyond the orchard, where there were vast meadows, with four streams flowing through them. They would go several miles over the open grass; if they should happen to get lost, they would live on whatever fish they could catch.

'I'm bringing my knife,' said Albine, bringing out a rustic knife with a thick blade.

She put all sorts of things into her pockets: string, bread, matches, a little bottle of wine, some rags, a comb, and some needles. Serge had to carry a blanket; but at the end of the lime tree grove, when they arrived at the ruins of the chateau, the blanket had already become such a nuisance that he hid it under the debris of a fallen wall.

The sun was stronger now. Albine had spent too long over her preparations. In the morning heat they set off, side by side, behaving almost sensibly. They were managing twenty paces or more without pushing each other for fun. They chatted:

'I just never wake up in the night,' said Albine. 'I slept well last night, what about you?'

'I did too,' Serge replied.

She went on: 'What does it mean if you dream that a bird is talking to you?'

'I don't know... And what did he say, your bird?'

'Oh! I've forgotten. He said very nice things, and a lot of things that I thought rather funny... Oh, look at that great big poppy over there. You shan't have it, you shan't have it!'

She set off with a bound; but Serge, thanks to his longer legs, overtook her, picked the poppy, and brandished it triumphantly. At this, she remained silent, with puckered lips, on the edge of bursting into tears. The only thing he could think of was to throw the flower away. Then, to make peace, he suggested:

'Would you like to get on my back? I'll carry you, as I did the other day.'

'No, no.'

She was sulking. But she had not gone more than thirty paces or so when she turned around, laughing. A bramble was holding her fast by her skirt.

'Gracious! I thought it was you, deliberately treading on my dress... How determined this bramble is not to let me go! Get me loose, please!'

When she was freed, they walked on once more, side by side, very properly. Albine declared it was more fun walking like this, like serious grown-up people. They had just got into the meadows. Long swathes of grass stretched endlessly before them, interrupted at distant intervals by the softer green of a curtain of willows. The expanses of grass were downy, like lengths of velvet; they were a rich green, getting gradually paler in the distance, sinking into bright yellow on the edge of the horizon, in the blaze of the sun. The groves of willow, over there, seemed to be pure gold in the vibrant sunlight. Dancing flecks of sun-dust laid gleams of brightness on the tips of the grasses, and occasional puffs of wind, blowing freely over this bare solitude, made the grass shimmer like plants quivering beneath caresses. All over the nearest fields, crowds of little white daisies, heaped up, scattered about, or else in groups, like throngs of people crowding the streets for some public festival, filled the dark grass with their widespread joyfulness. Buttercups had all the gaiety of their little bells of polished brass, ready to tinkle at the touch of a fly's wing: some large poppies, standing alone, burst into explosions of red or, drifting further away in clusters, made cheerful pools like empty wine vats still stained red with wine; tall cornflowers waved their light, blue-ruched country bonnets, almost sending them flying at each breath of wind. Then there were carpets of woolly feather-grass, honey-scented meadowsweet, hairy birdsfoot, fescue grass, crested dogtail, bentgrass, and meadow grass. Sainfoin reared its long, slender locks, and clover showed its patterned leaves, plantain brandished forests of lances, lucerne created soft beds with eiderdowns of sea-green satin, edged with purplish flowers. Everywhere, to right and left and straight ahead, it all stretched away, rolling over the flat ground, softening the mossy surface of a stagnant sea, slumbering beneath a sky that seemed ever more vast. In this immensity of grass, here and there were grasses of limpid blue, as if reflecting the blue of the sky.

All the while, Albine and Serge were walking through the meadows with grass up to their knees. It felt as if they were wading through a stream of fresh water that slapped against their calves. At times they found themselves moving through real currents of grass, with tall, bowed stalks streaming by, and rushing past their legs with a sound they could hear. Then came calm and sleepy lakes, basins of short grass that scarcely came over their ankles. They played as they walked along, no longer at breaking everything, as in the orchard, but on the contrary, pausing, with their feet bound by the plants' supple fingers, to enjoy the purity, the caress of a stream that tempered their youthful brutality. Albine moved away and went into a patch of gigantic grass that came up to her chin. Only her head was visible. For a moment she kept quite still, calling Serge:

'Come here! It's like being in a bath, with green water all around.'

Then she bounded off, without even waiting for him, and they walked alongside the first river that barred their way. The water was calm and shallow, flowing between two banks of wild cress. It moved very gently, slowly meandering along, so clean and so clear that it reflected like a mirror even the smallest reed along the banks. For quite a long time, Albine and Serge had to follow the current, which moved less quickly than they, until they found a tree that cast its shadow into that idle water. As far as their eyes could reach, they saw only the bare stream on its grassy bed, stretching out its pure limbs and sleeping in the full sun with the suppleness of a half-uncoiled, bluish snake. At last they reached a grove of three willows: two had their feet in the water, while the other stood a little further back; their shattered trunks, crumbling with age, were crowned with a mass of blond and youthful hair. Their shadow was so pale that it scarcely striped the sunlit bank with their faint outlines. However, the stream, so tranquil both upstream and down, here gave a little shiver, disturbing its limpid surface, expressing surprise at feeling the end of this veil trailing in its water. Between the three willows, the corner of a field sloped almost imperceptibly down to the water, placing poppies even in the cracks of these old and broken trunks. It was like a tent made of greenery, raised on three poles at the edge of the stream in the rolling desert of grasses.

'This is the place! This is the place!' cried Albine, sliding under the willows.

Serge sat down at her side, with his feet almost in the water. He looked around, and murmured:

'You really know everything, you know all the best places... This is like an island ten feet square, sitting in the middle of the sea.'

'Yes, here we are at home,' she went on, so full of delight that she pummelled the grass with her fist. 'This is our house... we shall do everything ourselves.'

Then, as if struck by a glorious idea, she threw herself at him, and close up to his face said, with an explosion of joy:

'Will you be my husband? I'll be your wife.'

He was delighted with this invention; he replied that he would gladly be her husband, laughing even more loudly than Albine. Then she suddenly became serious, and took on the expression of a busy housewife.

'You realize, of course,' she said, 'that I am in command... We shall eat only when you have set the table.'

She issued her orders imperiously. He had to put away, in a hollow in one of the willows, which she designated 'the cupboard', everything she took out of her pockets. The rags were the table linen, the comb was the dressing table, the string and the needles were for mending the clothes of the explorers. As for provisions for eating, they consisted of the little bottle of wine and the few crusts left over from the day before. Indeed, there were also matches, for cooking the fish they were to catch.

As he was finishing laying the table, with the bottle in the middle and the three crusts around it, he risked remarking that the feast would be rather meagre. But she shrugged her shoulders, with an air of superior womanhood. Putting her feet in the water, she said sternly:

'I shall do the fishing. You can watch.'

For half an hour she made enormous efforts to catch some tiny fish in her hands. She had pulled up her skirts and tied them with a bit of string. She moved forward cautiously, taking great care not to disturb the water; then, when she was very near the little fish hiding between two stones, she stretched out her bare arm, creating a terrible splashing, and caught only a handful of gravel. Serge burst out laughing, and this brought her back to the bank in a rage, telling him he had no right to laugh.

'But what are you going to cook it with, this fish of yours?' he finally asked. 'There isn't any wood.'

That thoroughly discouraged her. Anyway, this fish didn't strike her as all that marvellous. She came out of the water, not bothering to put her stockings back on. She ran about in the grass with bare legs to get herself dry. And her laughter returned, because some of the grasses were tickling the soles of her feet.

'Oh, here's some burnet!' she suddenly cried, throwing herself on to her knees. 'Burnet is really nice. We shall have a feast.'

Serge now had to put a heap of burnet leaves on the table. They ate the burnet with their bread. Albine insisted that it was nicer than hazelnuts. She served the food, as lady of the house, and cut up Serge's bread for him, never letting him have the knife.

'I'm the wife,' she replied sternly to his various efforts to rebel.

Then she had him carry back to the 'cupboard' the few drops of wine still left in the bottle. And he even had to sweep the grass, before they could move from the dining room to the bedroom. Albine lay down first, stretching out full length, and said:

'You understand, now we are going to sleep... You must lie down beside me, close to me.'

He stretched out, just as she commanded. They both lay very stiff, touching from shoulders to feet, with their empty hands thrown back above their heads. It was their hands that specially bothered them. They both maintained a settled gravity. They gazed up into the air with their eyes wide open, declaring that they were asleep and very comfortable.

'You see,' Albine murmured, 'you're warm when you're married... Can't you feel how warm I am?'

'Yes I can, you're like an eiderdown... But we mustn't talk, because we're sleeping. It's better not to talk.'

They remained silent for quite a while, still very serious. They had turned their heads, imperceptibly moving away from each other, as if the warmth of their breath had disturbed them. Then into the great silence Serge dropped just these few words:

'I like you very much.'

This was love before sexuality, the instinctive love that sets little boys of ten waiting for little girls in white dresses to go by. Around them the wide open grasslands helped to soothe their slight fear of one another. They knew they were seen by all the grasses, seen by the sky gazing down at them through the light foliage; and this in no way disturbed them. The willow tent above their heads was simply a piece of transparent cloth, as if Albine had hung a bit of her dress up there. The shade was still so light that it did not bring them the languors of deep thickets, nor the incitements of remote nooks or green alcoves. From the far horizon came a flow of air, a healthy breeze, carrying all the freshness of that sea of greenery, in which it created a swell of flowers; at their feet the river was yet another form of childhood, an innocence with a light, fresh voice that sounded to them like a friend laughing in the distance. Such a happy solitude, full of serenity, displaying its nudity with the adorable boldness of ignorance! So vast a field, in which the small patch of grass that provided their first bedroom took on the naive simplicity of a cradle.

'There, that's it,' said Albine, getting to her feet. 'We've had our sleep.'

Serge was rather surprised that it was over so quickly. He stretched out his arm and pulled her by her skirt, to bring her back to him. And she dropped on to her knees, laughing, and repeating: 'What was that for? What was that for?'

He didn't really know. He looked at her, taking her by the elbows. For a moment he grasped her by her hair, which made her cry out. Then, when she rose to her feet once more, he buried his face in the grass which still held the warmth of her body.

'There, that's it,' he said, as he also got up.

They ran about in the grasslands until the evening. They kept going on just to have a look round. They were inspecting their garden. Albine led the way, with the inquisitive nose of a young dog, saying nothing, but still searching for that blissful glade, although there was no sign of those tall trees of which she dreamed. Serge was full of all sorts of gallantry; he threw himself so energetically into pushing away the tall grasses that he almost knocked her over, and when he tried to help her over the streams, he lifted her bodily with a quite bruising grip. It was a great joy to them to discover three more rivers. The first flowed over a bed of pebbles between two continuous lines of willow, so they had to slide their way along through the branches, at the risk of falling into some deep hole in the water; but Serge, who was the first to slip, with water only up to his knees, took Albine in his arms, and carried her to the opposite bank to save her from a wetting. The other river was very dark, shaded by a line of tall, leafy trees, through which it moved languidly, with the slight rustling and the white creases of a satin skirt trailing behind some lady dreaming in the woodland; it was a deep, ice-cold, alarming expanse that they were luckily able to cross on a tree that had fallen across the stream, straddling the trunk and playfully disturbing that mirror of burnished steel with their feet, but then hurrying on, frightened by the strange eyes that even the tiniest drops of water seemed to open in the sleeping stream. It was the last river that especially held their attention. It was as playful as they were, slowing down for some bends, then setting off with bubbly laughter through some really big stones, and calming down, breathless and still aquiver, in the shelter of a clump of shrubbery; it displayed every possible mood, with its bed being by turns fine sand, flat rocks, limpid gravel, and rich soil on which frogs leaped about, sending up little clouds of yellow. Albine and Serge paddled around delightedly. They made their way home, going barefoot through the river, preferring the watery path to the grassy path, and pausing at every island that barred their way. There, they made a landing, conquering barbarous countries, and rested among the tall reeds that seemed placed there expressly to serve as shelters for the shipwrecked. It made a charming return journey, with the entertainment provided by the banks displaying their spectacle and the cheerful good humour of the lively water.

But as they left the river, Serge realized that Albine was still looking for something, along the banks, on the islands, and even among the plants sleeping in the flow of the current. He had to go and pull her out of the middle of a patch of water lilies, whose wide leaves grandly adorned her legs with their large ruffs. He did not say a word, but waved a threatening finger at her, and at last they went home arm in arm, filled with the delights of their day, like a young married couple returning after a jaunt. They looked at each other and found themselves to be more beautiful as well as stronger; their laughter, certainly, was somehow different from their laughter of that morning.

CHAPTER XI

'ARE we not going out any more?' asked Serge, a few days later. And on seeing her wearily shrugging her shoulders, he added, just to tease her:

'So you've given up trying to find your tree?'

They joked about this for the rest of the day. The tree did not exist. It was just a fairy tale. Yet they spoke of it with a slight shiver. And the next day they decided they would take a walk to the far end of the park, into the woods of tall trees that Serge had not yet seen. On the morning they set out, Albine decided not to take anything with her; she seemed thoughtful, even a little sad, though with a very sweet smile. They breakfasted and did not go down until quite late. The sun, already quite hot, made them feel rather languid and inclined to walk slowly, looking for patches of shade. They did not pause in the flower garden, nor in the orchard, though they had to go through both. When they reached the cool shade of the tall trees they slowed down even more; they plunged into the gentle quietness of the forest without a word, but with a heavy sigh, as if with relief at escaping from the full sun. Then once they had nothing but leaves around them, and no gap in the foliage to show the sunlit parts of the park in the distance, they looked at each other, smiling, but slightly uneasy.

'How nice it is here!' Serge murmured.

Albine nodded, her throat too choked to reply. They were not holding each other round the waist as they usually did. With arms dangling down and empty hands, they were walking without touching each other, their heads slightly lowered.

But Serge came to a stop when he saw tears rolling down Albine's cheeks, and disappearing into her smile.

'What's wrong?' he cried. 'Are you not well? Have you hurt yourself?'

'No, I'm just laughing, I promise you. I don't know really, it's the scent of all these trees that's making me cry.'

She looked at him, and went on:

'You're crying too. You see, it's nothing really.'

'Yes,' came his quiet reply, 'all this shade, it takes you by surprise. It feels, don't you think, as if you were going into something so extraordinarily sweet that it hurts... But you must tell me if you're unhappy about something. I haven't offended you? You're not angry with me?'

She swore she was not angry. She was very happy.

'So why aren't you enjoying yourself?... Would you like to play racing?'

'Oh! No, not racing,' she replied, with the pout of a grown-up girl.

And when he spoke of other games, like climbing trees to find birds' nests, or searching for strawberries or violets, she ended up saying rather impatiently:

'We're too old for all that. It's silly to be playing all the time. Wouldn't you rather just walk quietly beside me, like this?'

She was indeed walking so nicely that it was a great pleasure to hear the tapping of her little boots on the hard ground of the path. He had never before noticed the swaying of her waist, or the lively way her skirt swung behind her, with a snake-like movement. He was discovering such new charms in the slightest supple movement of her limbs that it was an inexhaustible joy for him to see her walking so sedately beside him.

'You're right,' he cried. 'It's nicer than anything. I'd walk with you to the ends of the earth if you wished.'

However, a few steps further on, he asked her whether she was feeling tired. Then he indicated that he would quite like a rest himself.

'We could sit down,' he stammered.

'No,' she said, 'I don't want to!'

'You know, we could lie down as we did the other day in the grasslands. We'd be warm and comfortable.'

'I don't want to! I don't want to!'

She had leaped away, horrified at these male arms reaching out to her. But he had scarcely touched her with his fingertips than she let out so desperate a cry that he stopped, trembling all over.

'Did I hurt you?'

She didn't reply at once, astonished herself at her cry, and already smiling about her fear.

'No, let me be, stop tormenting me... What would we do, if we sat down? I'd rather go on walking.'

And she added gravely, but pretending it was just a joke:

'You know very well that I'm looking for my tree.'

Then he began to laugh, offering to help her in the search. He tried to be very gentle, so as not to frighten her again, for he could see she was still trembling, although she had resumed her slow walk beside him. It was forbidden, what they were going to do there, it would not bring them any luck, and he felt moved, like her, by a delicious terror that made him shudder at each distant sigh from the forest. The scent of the trees, the greenish light that fell from the high branches, and the whispering silence of the bushes filled them both with a sort of anguish, as if the next bend in the path would take them into a perilous happiness.

For hours they walked on through the trees. They walked in their usual way; they scarcely spoke to each other, but never separated even for a moment, following each other even into the darkest holes in the foliage. At first they went into thickets in which the young trunks were not as thick as a child's arm. These they had to push aside to open up a path through the tender shoots that blocked their view with the fluttering lace of their leaves. Behind them, all trace of their passage vanished, the paths they opened closed up again after them; and they went on haphazardly, lost and confused, leaving no trace of their passage, save the swaying of the high branches. Albine, tired of not being able to see three paces ahead, was delighted when she was able to leap out of this vast tangle of bushes, from which they had long been wanting to escape. They were in the middle of an opening-out of little paths; on every side were narrow pathways running between hedges, turning back on themselves, criss-crossing each other, twisting and stretching out quite capriciously. They stood on tiptoe to look over the hedges. But they were not in any great hurry; they would gladly have gone on wandering through the endless detours, enjoying the pleasure of just walking without ever getting anywhere but for the fact that constantly before them they had the proud outline of the forest of tall trees. At last they went into the forest, reverently, with a sort of sacred awe, as if they were under the vaulted roof of a church. The tree trunks, straight, and whitened by a pale grey lichen the colour of ancient stone, reached up amazingly high, in lines like endless rows of columns. In the distance, naves were hollowed out in the greenery, with side aisles more densely packed; naves that were bizarrely bold, supported by very slender, serrated pillars, and so elaborately fretted and finely wrought that they everywhere let in the blue of the sky. A religious silence descended from the gigantic arches; an austere bareness gave the earth the worn look of flagstones, seeming to make it harder, with no grass at all, scattered only with the reddish dust of dead leaves. And they listened, as they walked, to the echoing of their footsteps, struck by the grandiose solitude of this temple.

This, surely, was the place where the sought-after tree must be, the tree whose shade provided perfect bliss. They felt it to be near, by the delight that flowed into them, along with the half-light of the high arches. The trees seemed to be kindly beings, full of strength, full of silence, full of a happy stillness. They looked at them one by one, loving them all, and expecting their majestic tranquillity to reveal some secret that would make them grow like them, in all the joy of a powerful life. The maples, ash trees, hornbeams, and dogwoods were a race of giants, a throng of proud gentleness, kindly heroes who lived in peace, though the fall of just one of them would have been enough to wound and kill a considerable part of the wood. The elms had enormous bodies, with swollen limbs, engorged with sap, scarcely hidden by the light clusters of their little leaves. The birches and alders, in their maidenly whiteness, arched their slim bodies, and cast their hair to the wind, like great goddesses already half changed into trees. The plane trees stood up straight with their smooth torsos, and their sleek skin with its red tattoos seemed to drop off flakes of dried paint. The larches, like a band of savages, made their way down a slope, draped in their tunics of woven greenery, scented with a balm of resin and incense. And the oaks were kings, huge oaks, firmly set on their stocky bodies, sending out conquering arms to occupy all the space in the sun, trees like Titans struck by lightning, thrown back in the postures of unbeaten wrestlers, whose scattered limbs alone sufficed to plant an entire forest.

Wasn't it one of these gigantic oaks? Or was it one of these beautiful plane trees, one of these girlish white birches, or one of these elms, with their creaking muscles? Albine and Serge plunged onwards, not knowing at all any more, just lost in this throng. For a moment they thought they had found it; they were in the middle of a patch of walnut trees, in a shade so cool it made them shiver. Further on, they had another moment of excitement on entering a little wood of chestnut trees green with moss, with an expanse of strange, very long branches, vast enough for whole villages to be built on top. Further still, Albine discovered a glade to which they both rushed, panting with eagerness. At the centre of a carpet of fine grass, a carob tree created what seemed an avalanche of greenery, a Babel* of foliage, whose ruins were covered with extraordinary plants of all sorts. Stones, torn out of the soil by the upward thrust of the sap, lay trapped in the wood of the trunk. The lofty branches were bending over to root themselves elsewhere, surrounding the trunk with deep arches and a new population of young, endlessly multiplying trees. And on the torn and bleeding bark, carob-pods were ripening. Even the fruiting of this monster was an effort that ruptured its skin. Slowly they walked around it, then went in under the branches spread in all directions like the streets of a city, and explored with their eyes the gaping cracks in the bare roots. Then they went on, not having found in that place the superhuman happiness they sought.

'Where are we?' Serge asked.

Albine didn't know. She had never before been to this side of the park. They now found themselves in a grove of laburnum and acacia, whose clusters of flowers exuded a very sweet, almost sugary scent.

'We're quite lost,' she murmured, with a laugh. 'I certainly don't know these trees.'

'But', he went on, 'the garden does have an end. You do know the end of the garden?'

She made an expansive gesture.

'No,' she said.

They remained silent, never before having had so vivid a sense of the immensity of the park. They were delighted at being alone in the midst of a domain so huge that they had themselves to give up trying to find its limits.

'Oh well, we're lost,' Serge repeated cheerily. 'It's better when we don't know where we're going.'

He drew closer to her, shyly.

'You're not afraid?'

'Oh no! There's only you and me in the garden. Who is there to be afraid of? The walls are too high. We can't see them, but they're protecting us, you know.'

He was very close to her now. He whispered:

'A little while ago, you were afraid of me.'

But she looked him in the eye, quite serene, not batting an eyelid.

'You were hurting me,' she said. 'Now you seem nice again. So why should I be afraid of you?'

'Well then, may I hold you like this? We'll go back under the trees.'

'Yes. You can hold me tight, I like it. And let's walk slowly, shall we? So we don't find our way too quickly.'

He had put an arm around her waist. And it was in this fashion that they went back into the tall forest, where the majesty of the vaulted roof slowed down even more the walk of these two big children, just awakening to love. Albine said she felt a little tired, and leant her head on Serge's shoulder. Yet neither of them suggested sitting down. They didn't want that. It would only have disturbed them. What joy could they get from resting on the grass, compared to the joy they already had, walking along side by side? The legendary tree was forgotten. The only thing they sought now was to bring their faces closer together to bring their smiles nearer each other. And it was the trees, the maples, elms, and oaks that whispered the first tender words in their gentle shade.

'I love you,' said Serge in a soft voice that ruffled the little golden hairs on Albine's temples.

He wanted to find some other word, but simply repeated:

'I love you! I love you!'

Albine listened, with a beautiful smile. She was learning this music.

'I love you! I love you!' she sighed, more delightfully, with her rippling girlish voice.

Then, raising her blue eyes, in which a dawn of light was breaking, she asked:

'How do you love me?'

Serge thought for a moment. The forest trees had a solemn sweetness, and the deep naves still quivered with the soft footfalls of the couple.

'I love you more than anything,' he replied. 'You are more beautiful than everything I see when I open my window in the morning. When I look at you, you are all I need. If I had nothing at all but you, I'd be perfectly happy.'

She lowered her eyelids, letting her head loll back, as if being rocked to sleep.

'I love you,' he went on. 'I don't know you, I don't know who you are, I don't know where you come from; you are neither my mother nor my sister; and I love you with my whole heart, keeping no part of it for anyone else... Listen to me, I love your cheeks smooth as satin, I love your lips with their scent of roses, I love your eyes in which I can see myself and my love, I love you down to your eyelashes and the little veins that add a tinge of blue to the whiteness of your temples... All that is just to tell you I love you, I love you, Albine.'

'Yes, and I love you,' she said again. 'You have a very soft beard which doesn't hurt me when I lean my brow on your neck. You are strong, and tall, and handsome. I love you, Serge.'

For a moment they were silent, in rapture. It seemed as if the sound of a flute went before them, and that their words came to them from a sweetly playing orchestra they could not see. They walked on now only with tiny steps, leaning towards each other and endlessly going round and round through the gigantic trees. In the distance, along the colonnades, there were glimpses of the setting sun, like a procession of girls in white dresses going to church for a betrothal, accompanied by the dull roar of the organ.

'And why do you love me?' Albine now asked. Serge smiled and did not answer at once. Then he said:

'I love you because you came to me. That says it all... Now we are together, and we love each other. I believe I'd stop living, if I didn't love you. You are my very breath.'

He lowered his voice, speaking as if in a dream.

'It's not something you know straight away. It grows in you, along with your heart. You have to grow and get strong... You remember how we already loved each other! but we didn't speak of it. When one is a child one is stupid. Then one fine day, it all becomes clear, and it bursts out. Anyway, we have no other concern, we love each other because loving each other is our life.'

Albine, with her head thrown back, and eyelids completely closed, was holding her breath. She was savouring the silence still warmed by this caress of words.

'Do you love me? Do you love me?' she stammered, without opening her eyes.

He was silent, very unhappy at not finding anything more to say, to show he loved her. His eyes travelled slowly over her rosy face, which lay back as if asleep; her eyelids had the delicacy of living silk; her moist lips were adorably folded in a smile; her brow was a purity that merged into a line of gold at the roots of her hair. And he wanted to put his entire being into the words that he felt on the tip of his tongue, but could not speak. He leant over her once more, as if deciding on which exquisite point on that face he would lay the supreme word. Then he said nothing, but merely gave a little sigh. He kissed Albine on her lips.

'Albine, I love you!'

'I love you, Serge!'

And they stopped, trembling with that first kiss. She had opened her eyes wide. He remained with his mouth slightly pushed forward. They looked at each other without a blush. Something powerful, something imperious seemed to possess them; it was like a long-awaited meeting, in which they rediscovered themselves grown-up and made for each other, bound together forever. For a moment they were simply astonished, raising their eyes to the religious vaulting of the foliage, seeming to question the tranquil populace of trees, to find some echo of their kiss. But in the face of the serene acquiescence of the forest, they felt all the joyous impunity of lovers, a long-lasting, resonant joy, full of the garrulous eloquence of their newborn love.

'Oh! tell me about the days when you loved me. Tell me everything... Did you love me when you fell asleep, resting on my hand? Did you love me that time when I fell out of the cherry tree, and you stood underneath, so pale, with your arms outstretched? Did you love me in the grasslands, when you held me round the waist to help me to jump across the streams?'

'Stop talking, and let me tell you. I have always loved you... And you, did you love me? Did you love me?'

Until nightfall, they lived on that word, love, which ceaselessly returned with a constantly new sweetness. They sought it out, brought it into every sentence, uttering it without any real cause, merely for the joy of saying it. Serge did not think of planting a second kiss upon Albine's lips. Ignorant as they were, it was quite enough for them simply to keep the fragrance of that first one. They had now found their way, without paying the slightest attention to where they were going. As they came out from the forest, twilight had fallen and the moon was rising, yellow between the dark of the leaves. It was a delightful return journey, through the middle of the park with that discreet star watching them through the gaps in the tall trees. Albine said the moon was following them. The night seemed very soft, and warm with stars. In the distance, the forests made a great murmuring sound, to which Serge listened, and thought: 'They're talking about us.'

When they went through the flower garden, they walked in a marvellously sweet scent, the scent that flowers have at night, more languid and caressing, and which seems the very breath of their sleep.

'Goodnight, Serge.'

'Goodnight, Albine.'

They were holding hands on the first-floor landing without going into the bedroom where they usually said goodnight. They did not kiss. When he was alone, sitting on the edge of the bed, Serge listened for a long time to the sounds of Albine going to bed upstairs, above his head. He was weary with a happiness that made his limbs grow sleepy.

CHAPTER XII

FOR the next few days, however, Albine and Serge were not at ease with one another. They avoided any reference to their walk in the trees. They had not exchanged a kiss, they had not said they loved each other. It was not shame that prevented them from speaking, but fear, a fear of spoiling their happiness. And when they were not together, they lived on their lovely memories; they plunged into them, reliving the hours they had spent with their arms around each other's waists, caressing each other's faces with their breath. In the end, this made them feverish. They looked at each other with bruised and very sad eyes, and talked about things of no interest. Then after many long silences, Serge anxiously asked Albine:

'Are you not well?'

But she shook her head, and replied:

'No, no, you're the one who's not well. Your hands are burning.'

The park now filled them with a vague anxiety they could not explain. There was danger round every turn in the path, something dangerous that would seize them by the neck, throw them to the ground, and do them harm. They never mentioned these things; but certain cowardly looks told of the anguish that made them strange to each other, as if they were enemies. But one morning, after much hesitation, Albine ventured:

'You're wrong to stay indoors all the time. You'll fall ill again.'

Serge gave an embarrassed laugh.

'Bah!' he muttered, 'we've been everywhere, we already know the whole garden.'

Albine shook her head in denial; then she repeated quietly:

'No, no... We don't know the rocks, and we haven't been to the springs. That's where I used to warm myself in the winter. There are some places where the very stones seem alive.'

The next day, without any further word on the subject, they went out. They went up on the left, behind the grotto where the marble woman lay sleeping. As they set foot upon the first stones, Serge said:

'Yes, I think that was worrying us. We must see everywhere, then perhaps we'll be at peace.'

The day was stifling, with the sultry heat of impending storm. They had not dared to clasp each other by the waist. They walked one behind the other, burning in the sun. Albine took advantage of a widening in the path to let Serge get in front of her, for she was troubled by his breath, did not like feeling him behind her, so close to her skirts. All around them, the rocks rose up in broad layers; gentle slopes lay between expanses of huge flagstones, bristling with rough vegetation. First they came upon golden gorse, beds of thyme, of sage and lavender, all sorts of balsamic plants, then junipers and bitter rosemary, with an aroma so strong it went to their heads. On both sides of the path, holly occasionally formed hedges that looked like the delicate work of locksmiths, like railings of black bronze, wrought iron, and polished copper, with very elaborate ornamentation, all very florid, with thorny rosettes. Then they had to go through a pinewood to reach the springs; its meagre shade fell on their shoulders like lead; the dry needles crackled beneath their feet, creating a slight resinous dust, which further burned their lips.

'Your garden's not that friendly round here,' said Serge, turning towards Albine.

They both smiled. They were at the edge of the springs. The clear waters were comforting. These springs did not hide under greenery like the springs in the plains that plant thick foliage all round them, so that they can sleep lazily in the shade. These leaped into life in bright sunlight from a hole in the rock, without a blade of grass to bring a touch of green to their blue water. Drenched in light, they seemed made of silver. In their depths, the sun lay on the sand, in a dust of living, breathing light. The streams darted on from the first basin, reaching out with arms of purest white and bouncing around like naked children at play, then they suddenly toppled over into a waterfall, whose soft curve was like the outline of a woman's fair-skinned body, leaning backwards.

'Dip your hands in,' cried Albine. 'At the bottom, the water is icy.'

They were indeed able to cool their hands. They splashed water on their faces, and stayed a while in the shower of spray that rose from the tumbling water. Even the sun seemed wet with it.

'Oh, look!' Albine cried. 'There's the flower garden, and the grass-lands, and the forest.'

For a moment they stood there, looking at the Paradou stretched out at their feet.

'And you see, there's no sign of the slightest bit of wall. The whole country is ours, right up to the edge of the sky.'

They had at last, without noticing, put their arms around each other's waist, with a sure and confident gesture. The springs calmed their fever. But as they moved off, Albine seemed to be caught by a memory, and led Serge back, saying:

'Down there, below the rocks, I saw the wall once, a long time ago.'

'But there's nothing to be seen,' Serge murmured, looking a little pale.

'Yes, yes, there is... It must be behind the avenue of chestnut trees, beyond those bushes.'

Then, feeling Serge's arm nervously tightening his grip, she added:

'Perhaps I'm mistaken... Yet I remember finding it suddenly in front of me when I came out from the path. It blocked my way, and it was so high it frightened me... And a few steps further on, I had another surprise. It was broken, there was an enormous hole, through which you could see the whole of the nearby countryside.'

Serge looked at her with an anxious plea in his eyes. She shrugged her shoulders reassuringly.

'Oh, I filled up the hole! Come on, I told you, we really are alone... I filled it up at once. I had my knife with me and I cut some brambles and rolled up some big stones. I defy even a sparrow to get through... If you like, we'll go and have a look one of these days. That will set your mind at rest.'

He shook his head. Then they went on, clasping each other by the waist, but they had grown anxious again. Serge darted a sidelong glance at Albine's face, and she, blinking unhappily, didn't like being looked at like that. They would both like to have gone back down, to avoid the uneasiness of a longer walk. And yet, in spite of themselves, as if yielding to some imperious force driving them on, they went around a rock and reached flat ground, on which they were met once

more by the bright, intoxicating sun. It was not now the happy languor of aromatic plants, the musky scent of thyme, or the incense of
lavender. It was foul-smelling plants they were now treading underfoot: absinthe with its drunken bitterness, rue with its aroma of mal-
odorous flesh, fierce valerian soaked in its aphrodisiac sweat. From
the mandrakes, hemlocks, and hellebores rose an odour that made them
dizzy and drowsy, so that they fell unsteadily into each other's arms,
with their hearts on their lips.

'Would you like me to carry you?' Serge asked Albine, feeling her
body yielding to his.

He already held her tight in his arms. But she pulled herself free,
breathing heavily.

'No, no, you're suffocating me,' she said. 'Let me go. I don't know
what's the matter with me. The earth is moving beneath my feet...
Look, this is where it hurts.'

She took his hand and placed it on her breast. He then went white
and was nearer to collapsing than she was. Both had tears in their
eyes, seeing each other in this state, without finding any remedy for
their plight. Were they going to die of this unknown illness?

'Come into the shade, come and sit down,' said Serge. 'It's those
plants that are killing us with their scent.'

He guided her by the fingertips, for she trembled if he so much as
touched her wrist. The wood of green trees, where she sat down, was
made up of a lovely cedar that spread out the flat roofs of its branches
more than ten feet. Then further back were some unusual varieties of
conifers; cypress with its soft, flat foliage, like a thick band of lace; fir
trees, straight and solemn, like ancient sacred stones still black with
the blood of sacrificial victims; yews, whose sombre robes were fringed
with silver; and all the evergreen trees, with their thickset foliage,
their dark leaves of polished leather, leaves splashed with yellow and
red, and so strong that the sun slid over them without ever softening
them. A monkey-puzzle tree was especially strange, with its wide regular arms like an architectural construction made of reptiles grafted
one on another, with overlapping leaves bristling like the scales of angry
serpents. Here, under the heavy shade, the heat seemed to sleep
voluptuously. The very air was asleep, without the slightest breeze, in
the warm closeness of an alcove. An Oriental love perfume, the perfume of the painted lips of the Shulamite,* was exhaled by the odorous woods.

'Aren't you going to sit down?' asked Albine.

She moved over a bit, to make room for him. But he drew back, and remained standing. Then when she asked him again, he sank on to his knees a few steps away from her, and said quietly:

'No, I'm more feverish than you, I'd burn you. Listen, if I weren't afraid of hurting you, I would take you in my arms and hold you so tight, so tight that we'd no longer feel all this suffering.'

He dragged himself a little nearer, on his knees.

'Oh! to hold you in my arms, in my flesh... that's all I think of. At night I wake up, hugging the air, hugging a dream of you. I wish I could first hold you just by the tip of your little finger, then, slowly, I'd take all of you, until nothing remains of you, until you've become entirely mine, from your feet to the last eyelash. I would keep you forever. It must be a wonderful thing to possess the one you love like that. My heart would melt into your heart.'

He drew still nearer. He had only to stretch out his hands to touch the hem of her skirt.

'I don't know what it is, but I feel far away from you... There is a sort of wall between us, that even my fists can't knock down. Yet I'm strong now; I could bind you with my arms, throw you over my shoulder, and carry you off as if I owned you. And that would not be enough. I still wouldn't have enough of you. When my hands take hold of you, I hold only a tiny scrap of your being. Tell me where you are, the whole of you, so that I can come and find you?'

He had fallen forward on his elbows, prostrate in an attitude of total adoration. He placed a kiss on the hem of Albine's skirt. At once, as if she had received that kiss upon her skin, she leaped to her feet. She clasped her brow with her hands, panic-stricken and stammering.

'No, I beg you, let's walk on.'

She didn't run away. Slowly, wildly, she allowed herself to be followed by Serge, her feet bumping against the roots, and still holding her head in her hands to stifle the clamour rising within her. When they emerged from the little wood, they took a few steps over some ledges of rock on which a whole population of ardent succulents had settled itself. There was here a crawling-forth, an upsurge of nameless creatures glimpsed in nightmares, monsters like spiders, caterpillars, and woodlice, fantastically enlarged, some with bare and glaucous skin, some tufted with filthy down, dragging diseased limbs, stumps for legs, and broken arms, some hugely swollen like obscene bellies, others with spines covered by a teeming mass of huge lumps, yet others gawky and falling to bits like dislocated skeletons. The nipple cacti piled up their living pustules, like a swarm of greenish turtles, hideously bearded with long hairs, harder than spikes of steel. Golden-barrel cacti, revealing more skin, were like nests of writhing young vipers. Hedgehog cacti were a sort of brush, an excrescence of red hair, rather like giant insects rolled up into a ball. The prickly pears held out their fleshy leaves like trees, leaves scattered with reddened needles, like swarms of microscopic bees, or purses of vermin, bursting at the seams. Ox tongues spread out their paws like upside-down harvestman spiders, with blackish, speckled, striped, and patterned limbs. Torch cactus displayed disgusting vegetation, enormous polyps, diseases of this overheated soil, the debauchery of a poisoned sap. But the aloes, especially, displayed abundantly their swooning plants' hearts; they were in every shade of green, some pale, some vivid, yellowish or greyish, brown splashed with rusty red, or dark green fringed with pale gold; and they were of every shape, some with wide heart-shaped leaves, some with narrow leaves like sword-blades, some jagged and thorny, others with neatly hemmed edges; some were enormous, carrying to one side the high stalk of their flowers, from which dangled necklaces of pink coral; there were small ones, all sprung together from one stem, as well as fleshy blooms, darting their long snake-like tongues in every direction.

'Let's get back in the shade,' Serge pleaded. 'You'll be able to sit down, just as you did a little while ago, and I'll kneel down and talk to you.'

It was raining down huge splashes of sun. The orb was all-conquering, it took the naked earth and pressed it to its blazing breast. Dizzy with the heat, Albine staggered, and turned to Serge.

'Hold me,' she said, in a dying voice.

As soon as they touched, they fell down, with lips on lips, without a cry. They seemed to be falling forever, as if the rock had sunk down endlessly beneath them. Their hands were now searching over their faces, their necks, and all over their clothes. But this was an approach so full of anguish that they got up again almost immediately, exasperated, unable to move any further towards the satisfaction of their desires. And they fled away, each in different directions. Serge ran to the house, and threw himself on his bed, with his head on fire, and his heart in despair. Albine did not get back until nightfall, after crying her eyes out in a sheltered spot of the garden. This was the first time they had not come back together, weary with the joy of their rambles. For three days, they sulked with each other. They were dreadfully unhappy.

CHAPTER XIII

Now, however, the entire park was theirs. They had taken sovereign possession of it. There was not one bit of ground that did not belong to them. It was for them that the roses bloomed, for them that the flower garden produced the sweet and languorous perfumes that blew in through the open windows at night, and lulled them to sleep. The orchard kept them fed, filling Albine's skirts with fruit, and offering them the refreshing musky shade of its branches, beneath which it was so pleasant to breakfast after sunrise. In the grasslands, they owned both the grass and the streams: the grass that extended their kingdom, endlessly rolling out its silky carpets before them; the streams of water which were like the best of their joys, their great purity and innocence, and the cool flow in which they loved to bathe their youth. They possessed the forest, from the huge oaks, too wide for ten men to clasp in their arms, to the slender birches that a child could easily break; the forest with all its different trees, all its shade, avenues, glades, and hideaways of greenery that even the birds did not know. The forest they could use as they wished, as if it were a gigantic tent, to shelter at midday their love born in the morning. They reigned over everything, even the rocks and the springs, and that dreadful ground, covered with monstrous plants, that had quivered beneath the weight of their bodies, and which they loved more than the other, softer couches of the garden, for the strange thrill they had felt in that place. So, now, in every direction, straight ahead, to left or right, they were the masters, they had conquered their domain, they walked in a natural landscape which was their friend, which knew them and greeted them with a laugh as they went by, offering itself up for their pleasure, like a submissive servant. And they also enjoyed the sky, that wide expanse of blue, spread out above their heads; walls could not enclose it, yet it belonged to their eyes, it was part of their joy in living, by day with its all-conquering sun, and by night with its warm shower of stars. It delighted them at every minute of the day, changing like a living being, whiter in the morning than a young girl just rising from her

bed, golden at noon with a desire for fecundity, and swooning in the
evening in the happy weariness that follows love. Never was its face
the same. Every evening it especially amazed them at the hour of farewell. The sun slipping down to the horizon always found a new smile.
Sometimes he departed in serene peacefulness without a cloud, just
sinking gradually into a bath of gold. At other times, he burst into
streaks of crimson, broke through a robe of mists, and poured out
in surging flames, striping the sky with gigantic comets' tails, whose
tresses set aflame the tops of the lofty forest trees. Then there would
be a tender sunset on stretches of red sand and long banks of rosy
coral, with the sun blowing his rays out one by one; or going to his
rest modestly draped behind some large cloud, like the grey silk curtain of an alcove, showing only a glow like that of a night light, deep
in the growing darkness; or yet again, there would be a passionate sunset, with all whiteness overthrown, soon bleeding under the bite of that
burning disc, then finally rolling away with him beyond the horizon
in a chaos of twisted limbs that crumbled away in the light.

Only the plants had refused submission. Albine and Serge walked
majestically among the host of animals making their obeisance. When
they went through the flower garden, flights of butterflies rose up to
delight their eyes, and fanned them with the flapping of their wings;
they followed them like the very quivering of the sunlight, like flowers
flying through the air, scattering their perfume. In the orchard, high
in the trees, they encountered the greedy birds; sparrows, chaffinches,
orioles, and bullfinches pointed out the ripest fruit, all scarred by
their pecking beaks; it was like the noisy clamour of schoolchildren in
the playground, the riotous merriment of marauding and shameless
gangs that came and stole cherries at their very feet, while they sat
astride the branches, breakfasting. In the grasslands, Albine enjoyed
even more catching the little green frogs squatting among the reeds,
with their golden eyes and the gentleness of contemplative creatures;
while Serge poked crickets out of their holes with a straw, tickled the
bellies of cicadas to make them sing, and collected blue insects, pink
insects, and yellow insects, which he then spread out on his sleeve like
buttons of sapphire, ruby, and topaz. Here too was the mysterious life
of the rivers, the dark-backed fish flitting through the half-light of the
water, eels only revealed by a slight disturbance of the grass, tiny tid-
dlers that scattered at the slightest sound like a cloud of blackish sand,
and flies, mounted on their high skates, wrinkling the still surface with

wide silvery rings; all that silent, teeming life that drew them to the riverbanks, and often made them want to stand midstream with bare legs, just to feel those millions of living things endlessly sliding past. On other days, days of tender languor, it was to the sonorous shade of the forest trees that they went, to hear their musicians serenading them, the crystal flute of the nightingales, the little silvery trumpet of the blue tits, and the distant accompaniment of the cuckoos; they marvelled at the sudden upward flight of the pheasants, whose tails seemed to create a ray of sunlight among the branches. They would stop, with a smile, to let a playful band of young roebucks go by, a few steps away, or pairs of solemn stags that slowed down to take a look at them. On yet other days, when the sky was afire, they would climb up on the rocks, delighted at the clouds of grasshoppers that their feet sent up from the banks of thyme, with the crackling sound of a flickering brazier; snakes, that lay uncoiled beside the russet bushes, and lizards, stretched out on the white-hot stones, followed them with a friendly eye; pink flamingos, dabbling their feet in the water of the springs, did not fly away at their approach, and their confident gravity reassured the moorhens dozing in the middle of the pool.

Albine and Serge had only become aware of all this life growing around them in the park since the day when they had felt themselves come to life, in a kiss. Now it sometimes deafened them, speaking to them in a language they did not understand, and making demands on them to which they had no idea how to respond. It was all that life, all those voices, and all that animal heat, the odours and shadows of plants, that disturbed them to the point of setting them at odds with each other. And yet they found in the park only an affectionate familiarity. Every blade of grass, every creature became their friends. The Paradou was just one huge caress. Before their arrival, for more than a hundred years, only the sun had reigned here as undisputed master, hanging his splendour from every branch. Back then, the garden knew only him. It saw him every morning, jumping over the boundary wall with his slanting rays, sitting straight down at midday on the swooning earth, and going away in the evening to the other end of the garden with a farewell kiss that touched on every leaf. So the garden felt no embarrassment, it welcomed Albine and Serge as, for so long, it had welcomed the sun, as pleasant companions who needed no fuss made. The animals, the trees, the streams and stones remained delightfully extravagant, speaking aloud, living quite nakedly with no secrets, displaying the boldness of innocence and the beautiful tenderness of the first days of the world. This piece of nature chuckled quietly at the fears of Albine and Serge; it became gentler, unrolling softer beds of grass beneath their feet, and pressing the bushes together to create narrow paths for them. If it had not yet thrown them into each other's arms, it was because it enjoyed displaying their desires, and laughing at their clumsy kisses, that sounded, from under the shade of the trees, like the cries of angry birds. But Serge and Albine, suffering from the great voluptuous atmosphere all around them, were beginning to curse the garden. On the afternoon when Albine had wept so bitterly after their walk on the rocks, she had cried out to the Paradou, feeling it so alive and ardent around her:

'If you are our friend, why are you making us so miserable?'

CHAPTER XIV

THE very next morning, Serge shut himself up in his room. The smell of the flower garden was really irritating him. He drew the calico curtains across, to avoid seeing the park and to prevent it coming in. Perhaps here he would be able to recover the peace of childhood, far from all the greenery, whose very shadow seemed palpably to brush against his skin. Then in the long hours they spent together, Albine and he no longer talked about the rocks, the streams, the trees, and the sky. The Paradou no longer existed. They tried to forget it. And yet they could feel it, all-powerful and enormous behind the flimsy curtains; the scent of grass came in through cracks in the woodwork; echoing voices rattled the windowpanes; all that life outside seemed to be laughing and whispering, lurking beneath the windows. Then, turning pale, Serge and Albine spoke more loudly, and looked for some distraction to stop them hearing it.

'Haven't you noticed?' asked Serge, one morning, in one of these uneasy moments. 'Up there, over the door, there's a painting of a woman who looks like you.'

He laughed noisily. And they went back to the paintings; once more they dragged the table along the walls, eager for something to do.

'Oh no!' Albine murmured, 'she's much fatter than me. But then you can't really tell, she's lying in such an odd position with her head thrown back!'

They fell silent. Out of that faded, time-worn painting, arose a scene they had not before noticed. It was like a resurrection of tender flesh emerging from the grey of the walls, a picture brought back to life, its details appearing one by one in the warmth of the summer. The woman was lying back in the embrace of a faun with the feet of a goat. You could now make out clearly the arms thrown back, the surrendered body, the rolling contours of this big naked girl, who had been taken by surprise on great bunches of flowers cut by little cupids, who, sickle in hand, kept adding more and more handfuls of roses to her bed. You could also see the effort of the faun, with his panting chest bearing down. Then, at the other end, there was nothing but the woman's two feet, thrown high in the air, flying off like two pink doves.

'No,' Albine repeated, 'she's not like me... She's ugly.'

Serge said nothing. He looked at the woman and looked at Albine, as if comparing them. Albine pushed back one of her sleeves right up to the shoulder, to show that her arm was whiter. And they fell silent a second time, returning to the painting with questions trembling on their lips, questions they did not want to ask each other. The wide blue eyes of Albine rested for a moment on Serge's eyes of grey, in which a flame was glowing.

'Have you been repainting the whole room?' she cried, leaping down from the table. 'It looks as if all those people are coming back to life.'

They began to laugh, but it was an uneasy laughter, with many glances at the frolicking cupids and the great display of almost entirely naked bodies. They decided, out of bravado, to look at it all again, exclaiming at each new panel, and calling out to each other to point out various limbs of persons who had definitely not been there a month ago. There were supple backs, arched over muscular arms, legs outlined right up to the hips, women reappearing in the embrace of men whose outstretched arms formerly clutched nothing but air. Even the plaster cupids in the alcove seemed to tumble about more brazenly than before. And Albine no longer spoke of children playing, and Serge no longer ventured any explanations. They grew serious, they lingered over certain scenes, wishing the paint could suddenly recover its former brilliance, feeling languid and troubled all the more by the last veils still hiding the crudities of the pictures. These voluptuous ghosts were completing their education in the science of love.

But Albine was frightened. She moved away from Serge, whose now warmer breath she could feel on her neck. She went and sat down on one end of the sofa and murmured:

'They frighten me. The men look like bandits, and the women have the dying eyes of people being murdered.'

Serge installed himself in an armchair a few feet away and began to talk about other things. They were both very tired, as if they had walked a very long way. And they were uneasy, feeling the pictures were looking at them. The clusters of cupids seemed to roll out of the panelling with a clamour of amorous bodies, a stampede of shameless little boys throwing their flowers at them, and threatening to tie them together with the blue ribbons they were using to bind two lovers together in one corner of the ceiling. The couples were springing to life, unfolding the story of the naked girl and her faun lover, a story they could reconstruct, from the faun spying on her from behind a rose bush to the girl's surrender among the rose petals. Were they all going to come down on them? Were they not there already, sighing, and with their breath filling the room with the odour of the lusts of long ago?

'It's quite suffocating, isn't it?' said Albine. 'No matter how many times I've aired it, this room has always smelled old and stuffy.'

'The other night,' said Serge, 'I was awakened by a scent so strong that I called out to you, thinking you had just come into the room. It was like the warm scent of your hair when you decorate it with sprigs of heliotrope... On my first days here, it came from afar, like a memory of a scent. But now I can't sleep, the odour grows stronger and stronger until it becomes suffocating. In the evening especially, the alcove is so warm I shall end up sleeping on the sofa.'

Albine put a finger to her lips, and said quietly:

'It's the dead woman, you know, the one who once lived here.'

They went round the alcove, sniffing, and joked about it, but deep down they were very serious. Certainly, the alcove had never before had such a disturbing smell. The walls seemed to be still trembling from the touch of a musky skirt. The floor had kept the sweet fragrance of two satin slippers dropped beside the bed. And on the bed itself, on the wood of the headboard, Serge thought he could see the imprint of a small hand that had left behind it a persistent scent of violets. From all the furniture now, there rose the scented phantom of the dead woman.

'Look! this is the armchair where she must have sat,' cried Albine. 'You can still smell her shoulders on the back of it.'

She sat down in it herself, and told Serge to get down on his knees and kiss her hand.

'Do you remember the day I welcomed you and greeted you with "Good morning, my dear lord"... But that wasn't all, was it? He kissed her hands, after they had closed the door... Here they are, my hands! They're yours.'

Then they began to play their old games, in order to forget the Paradou which they could hear laughing ever more loudly, to stop seeing the pictures, and succumb no more to the languors of the alcove. Albine simpered, threw herself back in her chair, and laughed at how silly Serge looked at her feet.

'You big ninny, put your arm around my waist and say nice things to me, since you're supposed to be my lover... Don't you have any idea how to love me?'

But as soon as he took hold of her, and began to lift her up, quite roughly, she fought him off, and escaped angrily from his grasp.

'No, let me be, I don't want that... This room is killing me.'

From that day forward they were afraid of that room, just as they were afraid of the garden. Their last refuge had become a fearsome place, in which they could not be together without watching each other furtively. Albine scarcely went in at all now; she stayed in the doorway with the door wide open behind her, as if to allow herself a swift escape. Serge lived there on his own, in a state of painful anxiety, suffocating even more, and sleeping on the sofa to try to avoid the sighs rising from the park and the odours of the old furniture. At night the naked figures in the paintings gave him mad dreams, of which all that remained when he awoke was a nervous uneasiness. He decided he had fallen ill again; his health needed one more thing to be fully recovered; that need was for a supreme fullness of being, an absolute satisfaction, and he did not know where it might be sought. So he spent the days in silence, with dark-ringed eyes, only coming awake with a slight start when Albine came to see him. They would stand, facing each other, with just a few tender words that made them even more unhappy. Albine's eyes were even darker than Serge's, and seemed to beseech him.

Then after a week, Albine would only stay for a few minutes. She seemed to be avoiding him. She would arrive with a worried expression, would not sit down, and was in a hurry to leave. When he questioned her, reproaching her for seeming no longer to be his friend, she would turn her head away to avoid answering him. She never told him anything about how she spent her mornings apart from him. She just shook her head with an embarrassed air and said she was lazy. If he insisted, she would rush away, with nothing more than a quick goodbye from the doorway. He, however, could see perfectly well that she must be crying a good deal. He followed, on her face, the different phases of a hope constantly disappointed, and the continual rebellion of a desire determined to find satisfaction. Some days she was mortally sad, with her face full of despair and her step slow, as if reluctant now even to attempt any joy in life. On other days, she was full of suppressed laughter, her face radiant, as if thinking of a triumph she did not yet want to explain, and her feet restless, unable to stay in one place, in a hurry to rush to some final certainty. And the next day she would fall back into her desolation, only to return to hopefulness the day after. But what it soon became impossible to hide was her terrible tiredness, a weariness that seemed to crush her body. Even in her confident moods, she would falter, and fall asleep with her eyes open.

Realizing that she was unwilling to answer, Serge had stopped questioning her. Now, as soon as she came in, he looked at her anxiously, fearing that one evening she wouldn't even have the strength to come back. Where could she be getting herself so very tired? What continual struggle could be bringing her such despair and such happiness? One morning he was startled by the sound of a light step beneath his windows. It couldn't be a deer, daring to come so close. He well knew those rhythmic steps that touched the grass so lightly. Albine was roaming the Paradou without him. It was from the Paradou that she brought back her discouragement, that she brought her hopefulness, and all that struggle, all that weariness that was killing her. And he could easily guess what she was looking for on her own, without a word, in the depths of all that foliage, with the dumb obstinacy of a woman who has sworn she will succeed in her search. After that he listened for her footsteps. He didn't dare lift the curtain to follow her movement through the branches, but he felt a strange, almost painful emotion, knowing from her steps whether she was going to left or right, whether she was plunging into the flower garden, and how far she was going in her search. Even amid the noisy life of the park, the restless voice of the trees, the flowing of the streams, the

perpetual noise of all the creatures, he could distinguish the sound of
her little boots so clearly that he could tell if she was walking on the
gravel by the rivers, the crumbling soil of the forest, or the flat stones
of the bare rocks. Eventually he could even tell whether Albine was
happy or sad from the sound of her heels as she made her way back.
As soon as she started to climb the stair, he left the window, he did not
confess he had been following her in this way everywhere she went.
But she must have guessed, for thereafter, at a glance, she told him
about her searches.

'Stay here, don't go out any more,' he begged her with clasped hands
one morning, when he saw how breathless she still was from the day
before. 'You're driving me to despair.'

She rushed away in annoyance. And he now began to suffer all the
more from that garden constantly echoing with Albine's footsteps.
The sound of her little boots was one more voice calling out to him,
a dominant voice, whose resonance grew ever louder within him. He
closed his ears and tried to stop hearing it, but still the footsteps in the
distance kept echoing in the very beating of his heart. Then in the
evening when she came back, it seemed the whole park came back
with her, with all the memories of their walks, and the slow awakening
of their love, attended by the complicity of nature. Albine seemed to
have grown taller and more serious, as if matured by her solitary rambles. Nothing remained in her now of the playful child, so much so
indeed that it sometimes made his teeth chatter, when he looked at
her, and saw how desirable she was.

It was towards noon, one day, that Serge heard Albine come racing
back. He had not allowed himself to listen when she set out. She usually did not get back until late. He was surprised to see what leaps she
had to make to keep going straight ahead, breaking the branches that
blocked the paths.

Down below, beneath the windows, she was laughing. When she
reached the stairs, she was panting so much he thought he could feel
the heat of her breath on his face. She opened the door wide, and
shouted:

'I've found it!'

She sat down, and quietly, in a voice choked with emotion, she
repeated:

'I've found it! I've found it!'

But Serge put a hand to her lips, stammering in confusion:

'I beg you, don't tell me. I don't want to know. If you told me, it would kill me.'

Then she fell silent, her eyes burning, and her lips tightly pressed together to stop the words bursting out in spite of her. And she stayed in the room until evening, trying to catch Serge's eye, and confiding a little of what she knew when she succeeded in doing so. She seemed to have a sort of light on her face. She smelled so nice, and was so resonant with life that he was breathing her in, and she was getting inside him as much through his hearing as his sight. All his senses were drinking her in. And he tried desperately to defend himself against this slow possession of his whole being.

The next day, as soon as she was up, she installed herself in the same way in the room.

'Aren't you going out?' he asked, feeling he would be defeated if she stayed.

She answered that no, she would not be going out any more. As she recovered from her fatigue, he felt her growing stronger and more triumphant. Soon she would be able to lead him by his little finger to that grassy bed of whose sweetness her silence spoke so loudly. That day she still didn't speak, but merely pulled him over to sit on a cushion at her feet.

Only on the following day did she dare to say:

'Why are you staying shut up in here? It's so nice under the trees.'

He stood up, with arms outstretched, imploring her. But she laughed.

'No, no, we won't go out since you don't want to. It's just that this room has such a funny smell! We'd be much better off in the garden, more at ease, more sheltered. You're quite wrong to be angry with the garden.'

He had set himself down at her feet again, silent, with lowered eyelids and trembling face.

'We won't go out, so don't get upset about it. But don't you prefer the grass in the park to these paintings? You remember everything we saw together... It's these paintings that make us sad. It's annoying the way they're always watching us.'

And as he gradually leaned closer to her, she put an arm round his neck, and laid his head back against her knees, still murmuring, more quietly:

'This is how we could be really happy, in a place I know. There, nothing would bother us, and the fresh air would cure your fever.'

Then she stopped, feeling him trembling. She feared a wrong word might awaken his old terrors. Slowly, she was conquering him, merely by letting the blue caress of her eyes play over his face. He had raised his eyelids, and was resting now with no nervous tremors, all hers.

'Ah, if you only knew!' she breathed softly in his ear.

She grew bolder, seeing that he still continued to smile.

'It's a lie, it's not forbidden,' she murmured. 'You're a man, you shouldn't be afraid... If we went there, and I was threatened by some danger, you'd defend me, wouldn't you? You'd be able to carry me away on your shoulders, wouldn't you? I feel quite safe when I'm with you. Look how strong your arms are! How can one be afraid of anything when one has arms as strong as yours!'

With one hand she slowly stroked his hair, his neck and shoulders.

'No, it's not forbidden,' she went on again. 'All that is just a pack of nonsense. Those who invented that story long ago were just wanting to stop people disturbing them in the most delightful part of the garden. Just say to yourself that as soon as you're sitting on that grassy carpet, you'll be perfectly happy. Then at last we shall know everything, we shall really be the masters... Listen to me, come with me.'

He refused, shaking his head, but without any anger, like someone quite enjoying this game. Then, after a silence, sad to see her sulking, and wanting her to caress him again, he at last opened his mouth and asked:

'Where is it?'

She didn't answer at once. She seemed to be gazing into the distance.

'It's over there,' she murmured. 'I can't tell you exactly. You have to go down the long pathway, then turn to the left, and left again. We must have gone past it a score of times. Anyway, you'd look in vain, you'd never find it if I didn't take you there myself. I could go straight to it even though I can't explain to you how to get there.'

'And who took you there?'

'I don't know... The plants that morning all seemed to be pushing me in that direction. The long branches behind me whipped me on, the grass seemed to slope towards it, and paths seemed to offer themselves to me. And I think the forest creatures also took part, for I saw a deer galloping along in front of me, as if inviting me to follow, while a flight of bullfinches flew from branch to branch, uttering little cries to warn me when I was tempted to take the wrong path.'

'And it's very beautiful?'

Once more, she did not reply. Her eyes seemed lost in an intense ecstasy. And when she was able to speak:

'More beautiful than I could possibly tell you... I was so enchanted that I was conscious only of an indescribable joy falling down from the leaves, and sleeping on the grass. And I ran all the way back because I didn't want to enjoy the happiness of sitting there in that shade without you.'

She wrapped her arms once more around his neck, ardently pleading with him, so close to him that her lips were almost on his.

'Oh! you will come,' she stammered. 'Just think how terribly sad I would be if you didn't come... This longing I have, it's a need I've had for so long, and which has grown every day, and now really hurts... You surely can't want me to suffer?... And even if you were to die of it, even if that shade were to kill us both, would you hesitate? Would you have the slightest regret? We'd remain lying together at the foot of that tree, and sleep forever in each other's arms. That would be lovely, wouldn't it?'

'Yes, yes,' he stammered, overwhelmed by the frenzy of this passion, throbbing with desire.

'But we shan't die,' she went on, speaking more loudly, with the laugh of a woman who has won the day; 'we shall live to love each other... It's a tree of life, and under that tree we'll be stronger, healthier, more perfect. You'll see, everything will become simple. You'll be able to hold me as you dreamed of doing, hold me so tight that not one bit of my body will be beyond your grasp. Then I think something heavenly will come down into us... So will you?'

He grew pale and blinked, as if his eyes were dazzled by a bright light.

'Will you? will you?' she repeated, even more ardently, already half rising to her feet.

He stood up and followed her, very shakily at first, then holding on to her waist, as if he could not bear to be separated from her. He went where she went, drawn along by the warm air flowing from her hair. And as he was a little behind her, she kept turning around, her face glowing with love, and her mouth and eyes full of temptation, calling him on so imperiously that he would have gone with her anywhere at all, like a faithful dog.

CHAPTER XV

THEY went down and walked into the garden; Serge was still smiling. He saw the greenery only as reflected in the clear mirrors of Albine's eyes. The garden, on seeing the couple, had seemed to give a long laugh and a murmur of satisfaction that flew from leaf to leaf, down to the very end of the longest avenues. It must have been waiting for days to see them like this, arms around each other, reconciled with the trees, and looking for their lost love on the grassy banks. A solemn hush ran through the branches. The afternoon sky was drowsy with heat. Plants raised their heads to watch them pass.

'Can you hear them?' Albine asked very quietly. 'They stop talking when we get near. But further on, they're waiting for us, and they tell each other the way they must show us... I told you we wouldn't have to bother about paths. The trees are pointing out the way with their outstretched arms.'

Indeed, the whole park was pushing them gently along. It seemed as if a barrier of bushes sprang up behind them to stop them going back, while the carpet of grass unrolled before them so smoothly they no longer looked where they were going, but simply surrendered to the gentle slopes of the terrain.

'And the birds are coming with us,' Albine went on. 'This time it's blue tits. Can you see them? They're flying along the hedges, stopping at every bend to make sure we don't wander off the track. Ah! if only we understood their song, we'd know they're telling us to hurry.'

Then she added:

'All the creatures in the park are with us. Can't you hear them? There's such a rustling behind us: it's the birds in the trees, the insects in the grass, the roe deer and the stags in the thickets, and even the fish, whose fins are stirring the silent water... Don't look back, that would frighten them, but I'm sure we have a splendid procession behind us.'

Meanwhile, they walked on tirelessly. Albine was talking merely to charm Serge with the music of her voice. Serge was obedient to the slightest pressure of Albine's hand. Neither of them knew where they were going, but knew they were going straight to where they wanted to go. And as they advanced, the garden grew more discreet, suppressing the sighing of its shady nooks, the chattering of its streams, the ardent life of its animals. There was now only a great quivering silence, a religious anticipation.

Then, instinctively, Albine and Serge raised their heads. Facing them was an immense mass of foliage. And, when they hesitated, a roe deer, gazing at them with its lovely, gentle eyes, leaped into the thicket.

'It's here,' said Albine. She went in first, her head once more turned towards Serge, drawing him on; then they disappeared behind the disturbed and quivering leaves, and everything became calm. They were going into a delightful peace.

In the centre was a tree, surrounded by a shade so dense it was impossible even to make out what species it was. It was a tree of huge stature, with a trunk that seemed to breathe in and out like a human breast, and branches that stretched out like protective arms. It seemed good, strong, powerful, and fruitful; it was the patriarch of the garden, the father of the forest, the pride of all the grass, and the friend of the sun which every day rose and set upon its crest. From its green vault poured all the joy of creation: the fragrance of flowers, the songs of the birds, gleams of light, dawn's cool awakenings, and the drowsy warmth of dusk. Its sap was so powerful it flowed out from the bark, and bathed it in a mist of fecundity, which made it seem to be the virility of the earth itself. And that was enough to create the enchantment of the glade. The other trees built up around it the impenetrable wall that isolated it in a tabernacle of silence and half-light; within, there was only greenery, no patch of sky, no glimpse of the horizon, only a rotunda everywhere draped in the tender silk of the leaves, and carpeted on the ground with the silky velvet of moss. It was like going in to the crystal of a spring, surrounded by a greenish limpidity, a silvery surface slumbering under reflected reeds. Colours, scents, sounds, and quiverings—everything was vague, transparent, nameless, and swooning with such happiness that all material things seemed to fade away. The languor of a boudoir, the glimmer of a summer night dying away on the bare shoulder of a loving woman, indistinct murmurings of love suddenly falling into a great mute spasm, all hung in the stillness of the branches, unruffled by any breath of wind. The solitude of a wedding night made for embracing beings, an empty bedroom, in which one could sense, somewhere behind the drawn curtains, nature being satisfied in an ardent coupling in the arms of the sun. Sometimes there was a creaking in the loins of the tree; a stiffening of its limbs, like those of a woman in labour; and the sweat of life that flowed from the bark rained down more abundantly upon the grass around, exuding the softness of desire, filling the air with surrender, and making the glade pale with pleasure. Then the tree seemed to faint away with its shade and its grassy carpets, its girdle of thick shrubbery. It was now nothing but voluptuous delight.

Albine and Serge stood there in rapture. As soon as the tree had taken them into the sweetness of its branches, they felt cured of the intolerable anxiety they had been enduring. They were no longer subject to the fear that had made them avoid each other, the hot and desperate struggles in which they hurt each other without knowing what enemy they were resisting with such fury. Now, on the contrary, they were filled with an absolute confidence, a supreme serenity; they gave themselves freely to each other, slipping slowly into the pleasure of being together, far away, deep inside a miraculously hidden hideaway. Not knowing yet what the garden was asking of them, they left it free to dispose of their love as it would; they waited, untroubled, for the tree to speak to them. The tree held them in such a blindness of love that the glade, immense and royal, disappeared, leaving nothing but a cradling of fragrance.

They had stopped, with a faint sigh, struck by the musky scent.

'The air smells like a fruit,' Albine murmured.

Serge then said very quietly:

'The grass feels so alive that I keep thinking I'm treading on the hem of your dress.'

They lowered their voices with a feeling of religious awe. They did not even have the curiosity to look up in the air to see the tree. They were too aware of its majesty, weighing on their shoulders. With a questioning look, Albine was asking whether she had exaggerated the enchantment of this greenery. Serge answered with two bright tears that rolled down his cheeks.

Their joy at being there at last was simply indescribable.

'Come,' she said in his ear, in a voice softer than a whisper.

And she went first, and lay down at the very foot of the tree. She held out her hands to him, smiling, while he, still standing, smiled too, and gave her his hands. When she held them, she slowly pulled him to her. He sank down at her side. He straight away pressed her to his breast. That embrace filled them both with pleasure.

'Ah!' he said. 'You remember that wall that seemed to keep us apart... Now, I can feel you, and there is nothing between us any more... I'm not hurting you?'

'No, no,' she replied, 'it's all good.'

They fell silent, without letting go of each other. They were filled with a delightful, untroubled emotion, gentle as a spreading pool of milk. Then Serge ran his hands over Albine's body. He was repeating:

'Your face belongs to me, your eyes, your mouth, your cheeks. Your arms belong to me, from your fingernails to your shoulders... Your feet belong to me, your knees belong to me, your whole being belongs to me.'

And he kissed her face, kissed her eyes, her mouth, her cheeks. He kissed her arms, with rapid little kisses moving up from her fingers to her shoulders. He kissed her feet, he kissed her knees. He was showering her with a hail of kisses that fell in large drops, everywhere, warm as the raindrops of a summer shower, upon her neck, her breasts, her hips, her sides. It was an act of possession, calm and continuous, conquering even the tiniest blue veins beneath her roseate skin.

'I am taking you only to give myself to you,' he went on. 'I want to give myself to you entirely and forever; for I know now that you are my mistress, my sovereign, the one I must worship on my knees. I am here only to obey you, to lie at your feet, awaiting your wishes, protecting you with my outstretched arms, and blowing away the flying leaves that might disturb your peace... Oh, please allow me to disappear, to be absorbed into your being, to become the water you drink, the bread you eat. You are my be-all and end-all. Ever since I awoke in this garden, I've moved towards you, I've grown tall for you. Always, as my aim and my reward, I've seen your grace. You went by in the sunshine, with your golden hair; you were a promise, telling me that one day you would explain to me the reason for this creation, this earth, these trees and streams, this sky, whose ultimate meaning still eludes me... I belong to you. I am a slave, I shall hear and obey you, with my lips upon your feet.'

He spoke these words, bending to the ground, worshipping the woman. Albine, full of pride, allowed herself to be worshipped. She held out her hands, her breasts, her lips to Serge's devout kisses. She felt she was indeed a queen, when she saw Serge so strong and so humble before her. She had conquered him, she had him at her mercy, she could dispose of him with but a word. And what made her omnipotent was that all around them, she could hear the garden rejoicing at her triumph, and helping her with an ever louder clamour.

Serge was reduced to stammerings. His kisses went astray. He still murmured:

'Ah! I wish I knew... I'd like to take you, keep you, die perhaps, or fly away with you, I can't tell...'

Both, lying back, remained silent and breathless, their heads spinning. Albine found strength enough to raise one finger, as if asking Serge to listen.

It was the garden that had willed their sin. For weeks it had devoted itself to the long apprenticeship of their love. Then, on that last day, it had guided them to this green alcove. Now it was the tempter, with all its voices teaching love. From the flower garden came the scent of swooning flowers, and a long whispering, telling of the wedding nights of roses, the voluptuous pleasures of violets; and never had the heliotropes emitted so sensual and ardent an appeal. From the orchard the wind blew whiffs of ripe fruit, a rich smell of fertility, the vanilla scent of apricots, the musky odour of oranges. The grasslands struck a deeper note, composed of the sighs of the millions of grasses kissed by the sun, the widespread plaint of countless creatures on heat, stirred by the cool caresses of the rivers, the nakedness of the flowing streams, on whose banks the willows dreamed aloud of their desire. The forest told of the giant passion of the oaks and the organ notes of the woods of tall trees—a solemn music, accompanying the marriage of the ash trees, birches, hornbeams, and plane trees in leafy sanctuaries; while the bushes, the young thickets, were full of delectable mischief, the noise of lovers chasing each other, throwing themselves down on the edge of ditches, and stealing their pleasure amid a great rustling of branches. And in this coupling of the whole park, the crudest embraces could be heard far off, on the rocks where the heat made the stones split open, swollen with passion, and where spiny plants made love in tragic fashion, with the neighbouring streams unable to offer them any comfort, being themselves aflame with the sun coming down into their bed.

'What are they saying?' murmured Serge, bewildered. 'What do they want from us, that they entreat us in this way?'

Albine, without answering, pressed him close to her.

The voices had become more distinct. The creatures of the garden, in their turn, now cried out to them to love each other. Cicadas sang of love as if to die of it. Butterflies scattered kisses as they flapped their wings. Sparrows had brief dalliances, like the rapid caresses of sultans moving quickly through the harem. In the clear waters, fish were swooning as they laid their eggs in the sunlight, frogs made their ardent and melancholy appeals, a whole mysterious passion was being monstrously satisfied in the glaucous dimness of the reeds. Deep in the woods, nightingales cast into the air their rippling, voluptuous laughter, stags were belling, drunk with such lust that they were dying of fatigue beside females they had almost eviscerated. And on the flat stones of the rocks, near the spindly bushes, snakes, coiled up together two by two, were softly hissing, and big lizards, their backs quivering, sat on their eggs with a little groan of ecstasy. From the most distant corners of the park, from stretches of sunlight, as from patches of shade, rose an animal odour, hot with universal rut. All of this swarming life was aquiver with birth. Under every leaf an insect was conceiving; in each tuft of grass a family was growing; flies fastened one upon another in the air, not waiting to land to get impregnated. The invisible particles of life that inhabit all matter, and the very atoms of matter itself, were loving, coupling, giving the earth a voluptuous stirring, making the park one huge fornication.

Then Albine and Serge understood. He said nothing, but clasped her in his arms even more closely. They were surrounded by the fatality of procreation. They yielded to the demands of the garden. It was the tree that whispered in Albine's ear what mothers tell brides on their wedding night.

Albine surrendered. Serge possessed her.

And the whole garden sank, with the couple, into a last cry of passion. Tree trunks swayed as if in a great wind; grasses uttered a sob of intoxication; flowers, swooning, with lips apart, breathed out their souls; the sky itself, aflame in the setting sun, held unmoving clouds, clouds that had fainted away, and from which fell a superhuman ravishment. And it was a victory for all the creatures, plants, and things that had willed the entry of these two children into the eternity of life. The park applauded with fervour.

CHAPTER XVI

WHEN Albine and Serge awoke from their trance of bliss, they smiled at each other. They were returning from a land of light. They were coming down from a great height. Then they pressed each other's hands in gratitude. There was a mutual recognition, and they each said in turn:

'I love you, Albine.'

'I love you, Serge.'

Never had the words 'I love you' carried so supreme a meaning for them. They meant everything, explained everything. For some time, they could not tell how long, they remained there, in a state of delicious rest, still embracing each other. They were experiencing an absolute perfection of being. They were bathed in the joy of creation, which made them equal to the mothering powers of the world, made them the very forces of the earth. And in their happiness there was also the certainty of a law obeyed, and the serenity of a goal logically discovered, step by step.

Serge, clasping her once more in his strong arms, said:

'See, I'm cured; you've given me all your health.'

Albine, yielding herself to him, replied:

'Take me, all of me, take my life.'

A plenitude of being filled them to the very lips with life. Serge, in possessing Albine, had at last discovered his sex as a man, the energy of his muscles, the courage of his heart, the final health that his long adolescence had lacked. Now he felt complete. His senses were keener, his intelligence broader. It was as if he had suddenly awakened as a lion, a king of the plains, gazing at the open sky. When he stood up, his feet planted themselves firmly on the ground, and his body grew stronger, with pride in his limbs. He took Albine's hands, and drew her up beside him. She tottered a little and he had to support her.

'Don't be afraid,' he said. 'You are the woman I love.'

Now it was she who was the servant. She threw back her head on to his shoulder, looking at him with an expression of anxious gratitude. Would he never blame her for having brought him here? Would he not one day reproach her for that hour of adoration, in which he had declared himself her slave?

'You're not angry?' she asked, humbly.

He smiled, tidying her hair, and stroked her with his fingertips as if she were a child. She went on:

'Oh, you'll see, I shan't be a nuisance. You'll hardly know I'm there. But you'll let me stay like this, won't you, in your arms? For I need you to teach me to walk... I think I've forgotten how to walk.'

Then she became more serious.

'You must love me for always, and I'll be obedient, I'll do my best to please you, and give you everything—even down to my most secret desires.'

Serge felt a redoubling of his power, on seeing her so submissive and loving.

'Why are you trembling?' he asked. 'Why would I be reproaching you?'

She didn't answer, but gazed almost sadly at the tree, the greenery, and the grass they had crushed.

'Silly girl!' he went on, with a laugh. 'Are you afraid I'll bear you a grudge for the gift you have made me? Come on, this cannot be a sin. We have loved each other as we were meant to love each other... I'd like to kiss the prints made by your feet as you brought me here, just as I kiss your lips that tempted me, and as I kiss your breasts which have just completed the cure begun—do you remember?—by your little, cool hands.'

She shook her head. And turning her eyes away, to avoid seeing the tree any more, she quietly said:

'Take me away.'

Serge slowly led her away. He gave one long, last look at the tree. He was thanking it. The shade was growing darker in the glade; a shudder like that of a woman surprised at her bedside ran through the greenery. When they emerged from the foliage and saw the sun again, its splendour still filling part of the horizon, they were reassured, especially Serge, who was finding a new meaning in every living creature and every plant. Around him, everything bowed, everything paid homage to his love. The garden was no more than an offshoot of the beauty of Albine, and it seemed to have grown and become more beautiful through the embracing of its masters. But Albine remained uneasy in her joy. She would break off her laughter to stop and listen, suddenly shivering.

'What's the matter?' Serge asked.

'Nothing,' she replied, casting furtive glances behind her.

They didn't know in what remote part of the park they were. Ordinarily, it amused them not to know where their fancy was leading them. This time, they felt worried, and strangely disturbed. They gradually quickened their pace. They were plunging ever more deeply into a labyrinth of bushes.

'Didn't you hear that?' Albine asked nervously, coming to a halt, out of breath.

And as he listened, he too now was gripped by the anxiety she could no longer hide.

'The thickets are full of voices,' she went on. 'They sound like people mocking us... Listen, wasn't that a laugh coming from that tree? And down there, didn't those grasses mutter something when I touched them with my dress?'

'No, no,' he said, trying to reassure her. 'The garden loves us. If it spoke, it wouldn't be to frighten you. Don't you remember all the nice things it whispered to us in the leaves?... You're on edge, you're imagining things.'

'I know the garden is our friend... So someone must have got in. I assure you I can hear someone. I'm trembling too much. Oh! I beg you, take me away, hide me.'

They started walking again, looking carefully into the thickets, thinking they saw faces appearing behind every trunk. Albine swore that footsteps in the distance were searching for them.

'Let's hide, let's hide,' she repeated, imploring him.

She had become quite flushed. It was a nascent modesty, a shame that gripped her like an illness, staining the whiteness of her skin, which had never before shown any disturbance of the blood. Serge was alarmed, seeing her thus, her face all pink, with burning cheeks, and her eyes full of tears. He wanted to embrace her again, and calm her with a caress; but she drew away, and indicated with a despairing gesture that they were no longer alone. Blushing even more, she was looking at her dress which was undone and showed her naked flesh, her arms, her neck, her breast. Stray locks of her hair touching her shoulders made her shiver. She tried to repin her chignon; then she feared she was leaving her neck exposed. Now the rustling of a branch, the slight noise of an insect's wing, or the slightest breath of wind made her shudder, as if at the indecent touch of an invisible hand.

'Calm down,' Serge begged her. 'There's no one... You're quite red and feverish. Let's rest for a moment, I beg you...'

She did not have a fever, she wanted to go home straight away, so that nobody could look at her and laugh at her. And walking faster and faster, she was gathering bits of greenery from the hedges, to cover her nakedness. She knotted her hair round a mulberry twig; she wrapped her arms in convolvulus that she fastened to her wrists; she hung round her neck a necklace of clematis stems, so long that they covered her breast with a veil of leaves.

'Are you off to a costume ball?' asked Serge, trying to make her laugh.

But she threw him some of the foliage she was still collecting, and looking really alarmed, she quietly said:

'Can't you see that we're naked?'

And he, in turn, was filled with shame, and fastened the foliage on to his own dishevelled clothes. However, they could not get out of the bushes. Suddenly, at the end of one path, they found themselves facing an obstacle, a high, grim, grey mass. It was the boundary wall.

'Come, come!' cried Albine.

She tried to pull him away. But they had gone less than twenty paces before they were again facing the wall. Then they ran alongside it, in a panic. It was unremittingly sombre, with no crack in it to show what lay outside. Then, on the edge of a meadow, it suddenly seemed to crumble. A breach in the wall opened a window of light on to the nearby valley. It had to be the hole that Albine had mentioned one day, the hole she said she had blocked up with brambles and stones; the brambles trailed around in scattered pieces, like bits of severed rope, the stones had been thrown aside, and the hole seemed to have been enlarged by some furious hand.

CHAPTER XVII

'Oh! I knew it!' said Albine, with a cry of utter despair. 'I begged you to take me away... Serge, I implore you, don't look!'

Serge went on looking in spite of himself, standing rooted to the ground in front of the gap. Down below, at the far end of the plain, the setting sun lit up the village of Les Artaud, draping it with gold, like a vision rising out of the dusk that already engulfed the nearby fields. The peasants' cottages could be clearly seen, scattered higgledy-piggledy along the road, with their little yards full of manure, and tiny gardens planted with vegetables. Higher up, the great cypress in the cemetery showed its sombre outline. And the red tiles of the church were like a brazier, above which the blackness of the bell looked like a face added to an unfinished sketch; while the old presbytery at the side had its doors and windows open to the evening air.

'For pity's sake,' Albine repeated, sobbing, 'don't look, Serge!... Don't forget that you promised to love me forever. Oh! will you ever love me enough, now?... Here, let me close your eyes with my hands. You know it was my hands that cured you... You can't push me away.'

But he was slowly pushing her aside. Then, while she clasped his knees, he passed his hands over his face, as if to wipe away some remnant of sleep from his eyes and his brow. This, then, was the unknown world, the foreign country of which he had never thought without an indefinable fear. Where then had he seen this country? From what dream was he waking, to feel such piercing anguish rising from his loins and growing steadily in his breast until it threatened to suffocate him? The village was astir with the return from the fields. The men were going home, with coats thrown over their shoulders, moving like weary animals; the women, standing in the doorways, called them on with a wave, while bands of children were throwing stones at the hens. Two little rascals were slipping into the cemetery, a boy and a girl, crawling on all fours alongside the little wall, to avoid being seen. Flights of sparrows were roosting beneath the tiles of the church. A blue cotton skirt had just appeared on the presbytery steps, a skirt so wide that it blocked the whole doorway.

'Oh! for pity's sake!' stammered Albine, 'he's looking, he's looking! Listen to me. A little while ago, you vowed to obey me. I beg you, turn round, look at the garden... Weren't you happy in the garden? It's the garden that gave me to you. And what happy days it has in store for us, what lasting joy, now that we know all the bliss of the shade!... Otherwise it's death that'll come in through that hole if you don't run away, if you don't carry me away. You see, it's other people, everyone, who will come between us. We were so alone, so lost to sight, so guarded by the trees!... The garden is our love. Look at the garden, I beg you on my knees.'

But Serge was shaken by a great shudder. He was remembering. The past was coming back to life. In the distance he could clearly hear the life of the village. These peasants, these women, these children, were Bambousse the mayor, coming back from the Olivettes, calculating what the next grape harvest would bring; and the Brichets, the man dragging his feet and the woman complaining bitterly of poverty; and Rosalie, getting herself embraced by big Fortuné behind a wall. And he now recognized the two kids in the cemetery, the good-for-nothing Victor and the brazen Catherine, looking for big flying grasshoppers among the tombs; they even had with them the black dog Voriau, who was helping them, hunting through the dry grass and sniffing at every crack in the old stones. Under the red tiles of the church the sparrows were squabbling before settling down for the night; the boldest among them flew back down, winging their way through the broken panes, and as he followed them with his eyes, Serge remembered the delightful clamour they made at the foot of the pulpit, and on the step of the altar platform, where there was always some bread for them. And on the threshold of the presbytery, La Teuse, in the blue cotton dress, seemed to have grown even fatter; she was turning her head, smiling at Désirée, who was returning from the farmyard laughing merrily, and followed by quite a flock. Then they both disappeared from view. At this, Serge, distraught, stretched out his arms.

'Oh, it's too late!' murmured Albine, collapsing among the broken brambles. 'You will never love me enough.'

She was sobbing. He was ardently listening, trying to capture the slightest sounds from the distance, waiting for some voice which would complete his awakening. The bell had made a little move. And slowly, through the sleepy evening air, the three strokes of the *Angelus* reached the Paradou. They were silvery whispers, a very soft and regular summons. The bell now seemed a living thing.

'Oh God!' cried Serge, now on his knees, bowled over by the little whispers of the bell.

He prostrated himself, he could feel the three strokes of the *Angelus* moving across his neck and resonating in his very heart. The voice of the bell became louder. It returned, implacable, for a few minutes which to him felt like years. It called up all his past life, his pious childhood, the joys of the seminary, his first celebrations of Mass in the scorched village of Les Artaud, where he dreamed of the solitude of the saints. It had always spoken to him in this way. He recognized even the slightest inflections of that voice of the church, which had constantly reached his ears like the voice of a grave and gentle mother. Why had he stopped hearing it? Formerly it had promised him the coming of Mary. Was it Mary who had led him away, deep into happy greenery, out of reach of the sound of the bell? He would never have forgotten, if the bell had not stopped ringing. And as he bent lower, he was alarmed by the caress of his beard on his clasped hands. He did not know he had all this hair, this silky hair that gave him an animal beauty. He twisted his beard and took his hair in both hands, seeking the bald patch of the tonsure; but his hair had grown vigorously and the tonsure was drowned in a virile flood of large curls, flowing back from his brow to the nape of his neck. His whole body, previously shaven, had the prickliness of a wild animal.

'Oh! you were right,' he said, casting a despairing glance at Albine; 'we have sinned, we deserve some terrible punishment... I was reassuring you, I didn't hear the threats that were coming to you through the branches.'

Albine tried to take him once more in her arms, murmuring:

'Get up, let's run away together... There is perhaps still time for us to love each other.'

'No, I don't have the strength now, the smallest pebble would knock me over... Listen to me, I am horrified at myself. I don't know what sort of man is in me. I have killed myself and my hands are covered in my own blood. If you took me away, you would never see anything in my eyes but tears.'

She kissed his weeping eyes. Again she went on, with passion:

'No matter! Do you love me?'

He, in his terror, could not reply. A heavy footstep on the other side of the wall was making the stones roll about. It was like the slow approach of a growl of rage. Albine had not been mistaken, someone was there, disturbing the peace of the thickets with eager breath. Then both tried to hide behind the bushes, gripped by a redoubling of shame. But already, standing at the edge of the breach, Brother Archangias was looking at them.

The Brother stood there for a moment, with clenched fists, without a word. He just looked at the couple, at Albine hiding on Serge's shoulder, with the disgust of a man who has just come upon some filth at the edge of a ditch.

'Just as I thought,' he muttered between his teeth. 'This is where he was bound to be hidden.'

He took a few steps, and shouted:

'I can see you, I know you are naked... This is an abomination. Are you an animal, to be running through the woods with this female? She has taken you quite a distance, hasn't she? She has dragged you into filth, and there you are, covered with hair like a goat... Tear off a branch and break it over her back!'

Albine, in a passionate voice, was saying quietly:

'Do you love me? Do you love me?'

Serge, with lowered head, was silent, but not yet pushing her away.

'It is fortunate that I found you,' Brother Archangias went on. 'I had discovered this hole... You have disobeyed God, you have destroyed your peace. Temptation will forever gnaw at you with its tooth of flame, and now you won't have your ignorance to help you fight it... It's this slut who tempted you, isn't it? Don't you see the serpent's tail twisting about in the locks of her hair? She has such shoulders that the very sight of them makes one vomit... Let go of her, don't touch her any more, for she is the beginning of hell... in the name of God, leave this garden!'

'Do you love me? Do you love me?' Albine was repeating.

But Serge had moved away from her, as if really burned by her bare arms, her naked shoulders.

'In the name of God! In the name of God!' the Brother shouted, in a thunderous voice.

Serge was walking, irresistibly, towards the breach. When Brother Archangias, with a brutal gesture, pulled him out of the Paradou, Albine, who had slid to the ground, her arms wildly stretched out towards her departing love, got up, her throat choked with sobs. She fled, disappearing into the trees, her untied hair flicking the trunks of the trees as she went.

BOOK THREE

CHAPTER I

AFTER the *Pater*, Abbé Mouret bowed in front of the altar, and moved to the Epistle side. Then he came down and made a sign of the cross over big Fortuné and Rosalie, kneeling side by side at the edge of the altar platform.

'*Ego conjungo vos in matrimonium in nomine Patris, et Filii et Spiritus Sancti.*'*

'*Amen*' came the response from Vincent, who was serving the Mass and, out of the corner of his eye, looking with curiosity at the face of his big brother. Fortuné and Rosalie had bent their heads, rather moved in fact, although they had nudged each other for a laugh as they knelt down. Meanwhile Vincent had gone to fetch the holy water stoup and the sprinkler. Fortuné placed the ring, a big solid silver ring, in the stoup. When the priest had blessed it, sprinkling it with the sign of the cross, he slipped it on to Rosalie's ring finger, on her hand still green from the grass stains that soap had not managed to remove.

'*In nomine Patris, et Filii, et Spiritus Sancti*,' Abbé Mouret murmured once more, giving them a final blessing.

'*Amen*,' Vincent responded.

It was early morning. The sun had not yet come in through the church's wide windows. Outside, on the branches of the rowan tree, whose foliage seemed to have pushed its way through the window-panes, the noisy awakening of the sparrows was making itself heard. La Teuse, who hadn't had time to do God's housework, was dusting the altars, stretching up on her good leg to reach the feet of the Christ bedaubed in red and ochre, rearranging the chairs as quietly as possible, bowing, crossing herself, striking her breast, and all the while not missing a single stroke of her feather duster. At the foot of the pulpit, a few steps away from the newly-weds, Mother Brichet, alone, was attending the ceremony; she was praying extravagantly; she stayed on her knees, muttering so loudly that the nave seemed full of a swarm of flies. And at the other end of the church, beside the confessional, Catherine was holding in her arms a child wrapped in a blanket; as the

child had begun to cry, she had had to turn her back to the altar, bouncing the baby up and down, and amusing it with the bell rope which was
hanging just above its nose.

'*Dominus vobiscum,*' said the priest, turning round with hands
outstretched.

'*Et cum spiritu tuo,*' Vincent responded.

Just then, three big girls came in. They were jostling with each other
to get a better view, but not daring to come in too far. They were three
friends of Rosalie's who, on their way to the fields, had rushed off, eager
to hear what the priest would have to say to the newly-weds. They had
big scissors hanging from their belts. They ended up hiding behind
the font, pinching each other, wriggling about, swinging their hips
like trollops, and stifling their laughter with clenched fists.

'Ah well!' said La Rousse quietly, a splendid girl with copper-
coloured hair and skin, 'at least we shan't have to fight our way out
through a crowd!'

'You know, old Bambousse is quite right,' muttered Lisa, a short
black-haired girl, with fiery eyes; 'when you have vines, you look after
them... Since Monsieur le Curé was so absolutely set on getting Rosalie
married, he can perfectly well do it by himself.'

The other girl, Babet, a hunchback, with bones too big for her frame,
said with a snigger:

'There's always old Mother Brichet, she's pious enough for the whole
family... can't you hear the noise she's making! She'll get paid for her
day's work. Believe me, she knows what she's doing!'

'It sounds as if she's playing the organ for them,' added La Rousse.

At this, all three burst out laughing. La Teuse, some distance away,
waved her feather duster at them. At the altar, Abbé Mouret was taking
Communion. When he went over to the side of the Epistle for Vincent
to pour the wine and water of the ablution over his thumb and forefinger, Lisa said more softly:

'It's nearly over. He'll talk to them in a minute or so.'

'So,' La Rousse remarked, 'big Fortuné will still be able to get to his
field, and Rosalie won't have lost her day's pay in the wine harvest. It's
handy getting married in the early morning... Big Fortuné looks stupid.'

'I'll say!' muttered Babet. 'He's fed up, that boy, with being on his
knees for such a long time. You can bet that hasn't happened since his
first Communion.'

But then they were distracted by the baby Catherine was trying to amuse. He wanted the bell-cord, and was reaching for it, blue with rage, and crying so hard he was choking.

'Ah! that's where the little one is,' said La Rousse.

The child was crying even more noisily, and struggling like one possessed.

'Put him down on his front, and let him suck,' Babet whispered to Catherine.

Catherine, with all the brazenness of a ten-year-old hussy, raised her head and began to laugh:

'This is no fun for me,' she said, giving the child a shake. 'Be quiet, will you, you little pig! My sister dumped him on me.'

'I'm not surprised,' said Babet, with some malice. 'She could hardly give him to Monsieur le Curé to look after!'

This time La Rousse laughed so hard she almost fell over backwards. She leant back against the wall, holding her ribs with her fists, laughing fit to burst. Lisa had thrown herself against her, finding some relief in pinching great handfuls of flesh on her back and shoulders. Babet laughed with a hunchback's laugh that came from her pursed lips with a sound that grated on the ear like a saw.

'Without that little one,' she went on, 'Monsieur le Curé would not have had to use his holy water... Old Bambousse was determined to marry Rosalie to young Laurent, from around Figuières.'

'Yes,' said La Rousse, between two gusts of laughter, 'do you know what he did, old Bambousse? He threw clods of earth at Rosalie to try to stop the child arriving at all.'

'He looks quite chubby anyway. The clods of earth did him good.'

At this, all three piled into each other in a fit of wild hilarity, when La Teuse came up, limping furiously. She had been to fetch her broom from behind the altar. The three big girls, frightened, drew back, and tried to behave themselves.

'You wretches!' stammered La Teuse. 'You even come in here with all your filthy talk!... Aren't you ashamed, you, La Rousse! Your proper place would be over there, on your knees, before the altar, like Rosalie... I'm throwing you out, d'you hear, if you so much as move!'

The coppery cheeks of La Rousse showed a faint blush, while Babet looked at her waist and sniggered.

'As for you,' La Teuse went on, turning to Catherine, 'just leave that child alone, will you? You're pinching him to make him cry. Don't say you're not!... Give him to me.'

She took him, cradled him for a moment, then laid him on a chair, where he fell asleep peacefully like a cherub. The church returned to its melancholy calm, interrupted only by the noise of the sparrows in the rowan tree. At the altar, Vincent had taken the Missal back to the right-hand side, and Abbé Mouret had just folded up the corporal and slipped it into the burse. Now he was saying the final prayers with a stern concentration that neither the cries of the child nor the laughter of the girls had been able to disturb. He seemed to hear nothing, to be totally absorbed in the prayers he was addressing to Heaven for the happiness of this couple whose union he had just blessed. That morning the sky remained grey with a heat haze that drowned out the sun. Through the broken panes there came only a reddish mist that seemed to promise a stormy day. Along the walls the luridly illustrated pictures of the stations of the Cross displayed the dark brutality of their patches of yellow, blue, and red. At the end of the nave, the dry woodwork of the gallery was creaking; and the grass on the steps outside, now grown enormously, had let in long stalks of ripe chaff, full of little brown grasshoppers, under the main door. The clock, in its wooden frame, made the rasping sound of a tubercular machine, as if to clear its throat, then dully struck the hour of half past six.

'*Ite, missa est*,' said the priest, turning to face the church.

'*Deo gratias*,' Vincent responded.

Then, after kissing the altar, Abbé Mouret turned round once more to murmur the final prayer over the bowed heads of the newly married pair:

'*Deus Abraham, Deus Isaac, et Deus Jacob* vobiscum sit...*'

His voice faded into a gentle monotone.

'There! He's going to speak to them now,' Babet whispered to her two friends.

'He's quite pale,' Lisa remarked. 'He's not a bit like Monsieur Caffin whose fat face always seemed to be laughing... My little sister Rose told me she doesn't dare tell him anything at confession.'

'Never mind,' murmured La Rousse, 'he's not a bad-looking man. His illness has aged him a bit, but it suits him. His eyes are bigger, and there are two little lines at the corner of his mouth that make him look like a man... Before his fever, he was too girlish.'

'Well, I think he has some secret sorrow,' Babet went on. 'He looks as if he's pining away. His face seems dead, but my word, his eyes gleam! You don't see it when he slowly lowers his eyelids as if to dim those eyes.'

La Teuse shook her broom at them.

'Hush,' she hissed, with such force that it was as if a gust of wind had blown into the church.

Abbé Mouret had collected himself. He began in a rather low voice:

'My dear brother, my dear sister, you are united in Jesus. The institution of marriage is the symbol of the sacred union of Jesus and his Church. It is a bond that nothing can break, and God wills it should be everlasting, so no man can put asunder those whom Heaven has joined together. In making you the bone of each other's bones, God has taught you that it is your duty to walk side by side, like a faithful couple in the paths prepared by the Almighty. And you must love each other even in the love of God. The slightest bitterness between you will be an act of disobedience to the Creator, who made you out of one single body. Therefore remain forever united in the image of the Church that Jesus wed, in giving to all of us his flesh and his blood.'

Big Fortuné and Rosalie listened, with their noses attentively uplifted.

'What's he saying?' asked Lisa, who was rather deaf.

'Goodness, he's just saying what they always say,' La Rousse replied. 'He has a glib tongue like all priests.'

Meanwhile, Abbé Mouret continued to speak, his eyes vaguely gazing over the heads of the newly-weds at a remote corner of the church. And gradually his voice softened, as he put some feeling into these words that he had learned some time ago in a manual for officiating young priests. He had slightly turned towards Rosalie, to speak to her, adding some tender words of his own when his memory failed him:

'My dear sister, be submissive to your husband, as the Church is submissive to Jesus. Remember that you must leave everything to follow him as his faithful servant. You shall abandon your father and mother, you shall attach yourself to your husband, and you shall obey him, in order to obey God himself. And your yoke shall be a yoke of love and peace. Be his rest and his joy, the sweet scent of his good works, the salvation of his hours of weakness. Let him find you, like a grace, always at his side. Let him need only to reach out his hand to meet yours. That is how you will walk together, never going astray, and finding happiness in the fulfilment of the laws of God. Oh, my dear sister, my dear daughter, your humility will bear sweet fruits; it will bring domestic virtues to your home, all the joys of the hearth, and the well-being of the God-fearing family. Have for your husband the tenderness of Rachel, the wisdom of Rebecca, the long fidelity of

Sarah.* Remember that a pure life leads to all things good. Ask God every morning for the strength to live as a woman respectful of her duties; for the punishment would be terrible, you would lose your love. Oh! to live without love, to tear your flesh from his flesh, to belong no longer to him who is half of your very self, to suffer and die far from the one you have loved! You would hold out your arms, and he would turn away from you. You would look for your joy, and you would find only shame in the depths of your heart. Listen, my daughter, it is in you, in obedience, in purity, in love, that God has placed the strength of your union.'

Just then there was a laugh at the other end of the church. The child had just woken up on the chair where La Teuse had laid him. But he wasn't being naughty now; he was just laughing to himself; he had pushed down his blanket, freeing his little pink feet, and he was waving them about in the air. And it was his little feet that were making him laugh.

Rosalie, bored by the priest's oration, looked round sharply, smiling at the child. But when she saw him jigging about on the chair, she was alarmed, and gave Catherine a terrible look.

'Oh yes, you can look at me,' Catherine muttered. 'I'm not picking him up... for him to start crying again.'

And she went underneath the gallery, to look into an ant-hole in the corner of a broken flagstone.

'Monsieur Caffin didn't have nearly as much as that to say,' said La Rousse. 'When he married La Miette he just gave her a couple of little taps on the cheek, and told her to be a good girl.'

'My dear brother,' Abbé Mouret took up again, half turned towards Fortuné, 'it's God who grants you this day a companion, for he has not wanted man to live alone. But if he has decided that she should be your servant, he requires that you be a master full of kindness and affection. You will love her because she is your own flesh, your blood, your bones. You shall protect her, because God has only given you your strong arms so that you can stretch them over her head in times of danger. Do not forget she is entrusted to you; you cannot abuse her submissiveness and weakness without committing a crime. Oh! my dear brother, what joyful pride must be yours! henceforth you will no longer live in the egoism of solitude. At all times you will have a delightful duty. Nothing is better than loving, unless it be protecting those you love. Your heart will expand for it, and your manly strength increase a hundredfold. Oh! to be a protector, to have a love to guard, to see a child give herself up entirely to you, saying "Take me, do with me what you will; I trust in your goodness." May you be damned if you should ever abandon her! It would be the most cowardly desertion that God could ever punish. As soon as she gives herself to you, she is yours forever. Carry her in your arms and never put her down on the ground, until it is safe for her. Give up everything, my dear brother...'

Abbé Mouret's voice was profoundly affected, and could only be heard now as an indistinct murmur. He had completely lowered his eyelids, his face was white, and he spoke with such painful emotion that big Fortuné himself was weeping, without knowing why.

'He hasn't recovered yet,' said Lisa. 'He's wrong to tire himself out like this... Look! Fortuné is crying!'

'Men are softer-hearted than women,' whispered Babet.

'He spoke well, just the same,' said La Rousse. 'These priests manage to find a heap of things no one would think of.'

'Hush,' cried La Teuse, who was already preparing to snuff the candles.

But Abbé Mouret was trying, with difficulty, to find his concluding remarks.

'That is why, my dear brother and my dear sister, you must live your life in the Catholic faith, which alone can assure the peace of your hearth. Your families have certainly taught you to love God, to pray every morning and evening, and to rely only on the gifts of his mercy...'

He could not finish. He turned to get the chalice on the altar and went back into the sacristy, with his head bowed, preceded by Vincent, who almost dropped the cruets and the finger-cloth, trying to see what Catherine was doing at the other end of the church.

'Oh! the heartless wretch!' said Rosalie, who left her husband standing there, to go and take her child in her arms.

The child was laughing. She kissed him and adjusted his covering, shaking her fist at Catherine.

'If he had fallen, I'd have given you such a slap!'

Big Fortuné came up, swaying his hips. The three girls had come forward, with pursed lips.

'Isn't he proud, now,' Babet whispered to the other two. 'That beggar earned old Bambousse's money in the hay behind the mill...

I used to see him every evening going off with Rosalie, crawling along beside the little wall.'

They laughed maliciously. Big Fortuné, standing in front of them, laughed even more loudly. He pinched La Rousse and Lisa said he was stupid.

He was a sturdy lad who didn't care what people thought. The priest had got on his nerves.

'Hey, Mother!' he called, in his loud voice.

But old Mother Brichet was begging at the door of the sacristy. She was standing there, all weepy and skinny, in front of La Teuse, who was slipping eggs into the pockets of her apron. Foruné had no shame. He winked and said:

'She's a canny one, that mother of mine!... Dammit, why not? if the priest wants people in his church!'

Meanwhile, Rosalie had calmed down. Before leaving, she asked Fortuné if he had asked Monsieur le Curé to come in the evening to bless their bedroom, as was customary. Then Fortuné ran to the sacristy, striding noisily across the nave as if he were crossing a field. And he came back saying that the priest would come. La Teuse, outraged at the noise these people were making, behaving as if they were out on the road, gently clapped her hands and pushed them towards the door.

'It's all over,' she said, 'go away now, go to work.'

She thought they had all gone, when she spotted Catherine, who had been joined by Vincent. They were both bending anxiously over the ant-hole. Catherine had a long straw, and was poking about in the hole so violently that a wave of frightened ants flowed over the flagstone. And Vincent was saying they must get right to the bottom to find the queen.

'Oh! you wretches!'cried La Teuse. 'What are you doing? Will you leave these creatures in peace!... That's Mademoiselle Désirée's ant-hole. She'd be ever so pleased, if she saw you!'

The children fled.

CHAPTER II

ABBÉ MOURET in his cassock, bareheaded, had returned to kneel at the foot of the altar. In the grey light coming from the windows, his tonsure made a very wide, pale patch in his hair, and the slight shiver that made him bend his neck seemed to come from the cold he must be feeling there. He was praying ardently, with hands together, so lost in supplication that he didn't hear the heavy steps of La Teuse as she went to and fro around him, not daring to interrupt him. She really seemed to suffer, seeing him like this, so crushed, and with worn-out knees. For a moment she thought he was weeping. Then she went behind the altar to keep an eye on him. Since his return, she didn't like leaving him alone in the church, having found him one evening collapsed on the ground, with his teeth clenched and his cheeks ice-cold, as if he were dead.

'Come on, Mademoiselle,' she said to Désirée, who stuck her head round the door of the sacristy. 'Here he is again, making himself ill... You know you're the only person he'll listen to.'

Désirée smiled.

'Heavens! we must have breakfast,' she whispered. 'I'm really hungry.'

And she quietly crept up to the priest. When she was very close she clasped his neck, and kissed him.

'Good morning, brother,' she said. 'Are you intending to make me die of hunger today?'

He raised a face so full of pain that she kissed him again on both cheeks; he was emerging from an agony. Then he recognized her and gently tried to push her aside, but she was holding one of his hands and would not let go. Hardly would she even let him cross himself. She led him away.

'Since I'm hungry, come on. You are hungry too.'

La Teuse had prepared the breakfast at the bottom of the little garden, beneath two big mulberry trees, whose branches spread out to create a roof of foliage. The sun, having at last conquered the stormy mists of the early morning, was warming the vegetable patches, while the mulberry tree cast a wide patch of shade over the rickety table, laid with two cups of milk and some thick slices of bread.

'You see, it's nice here,' said Désirée, delighted to be eating out in the open air.

She was already cutting enormous strips of bread, and devouring them with a splendid appetite. Then, as La Teuse was still standing there beside them, she asked:

'So, aren't you going to eat something?'

'In a while,' replied the old servant. 'My soup is warming.'

And after a brief silence, marvelling at the eager munching of that big child, she spoke again, this time to the priest:

'It's a pleasure to see her... Doesn't it make you hungry, Monsieur le Curé? You must make an effort.'

Abbé Mouret smiled, looking at his sister.

'Oh! She's really healthy,' he murmured. 'She's getting fatter every day.'

'Well, it's because I eat!' she cried. 'And you too, if you just ate properly, you'd get nice and fat... Are you ill again? You look very sad... I don't want to see all that starting again, d'you hear? I was too miserable when they took you away to be cured.'

'She's right,' said La Teuse. 'It's only common sense, Monsieur le Curé. It's no sort of existence for anyone, living like a bird on two or three crumbs of bread a day. You're not making any new blood for yourself. That's what makes you so pale... Aren't you ashamed to be staying thin as a lath when we two, who are only women, are so nice and fat. People must think we eat so much there's nothing left for you.'

And the two women, bursting with health, went on scolding him in a friendly way. His eyes were large and clear, and behind them there seemed to be an emptiness. He was still smiling.

'I'm not ill,' he said. 'I've almost finished my milk.'

He had taken two little sips, without even touching the bread.

'Animals', Désirée said thoughtfully, 'are healthier than people.'

'Well! that's a nice thing to be saying to us!' said La Teuse with a laugh.

But the dear twenty-year-old innocent had spoken with no malice.

'Of course,' she continued, 'hens don't have headaches, do they? And as for the rabbits, you can make them as fat as you like. And as for my pig, you can't say he ever looks sad.'

Then turning to her brother and looking quite excited, she said:

'I've called him Matthew, because he looks like that fat man who delivers the letters; he's grown so strong... It's not very nice of you to be always refusing to come and see him. One of these days, you will let me show him to you, won't you?'

While she was coaxing her brother, she had taken his slices of bread and was eating them with enthusiasm. She had finished one, and was just starting on the second, when La Teuse saw what she was doing:

'But that's not yours, that bread! So you're taking the food out of his mouth now!'

'It's all right,' said Abbé Mouret gently, 'I wouldn't have touched it anyway... Eat up, eat it all, my darling.'

Désirée had been quite disconcerted for a moment, looking at the bread, and trying not to burst into tears. Then she began to laugh, and finished the bread. Now she went on:

'And my cow, too, isn't sad like you... You weren't there when Uncle Pascal gave her to me, and made me promise to be good. Otherwise you would have seen how happy she was when I hugged her for the first time.'

She suddenly stopped to listen. A cock had just crowed in the farmyard, followed by an increasing uproar of flapping wings, gruntings, and raucous cries, a real panic of startled animals.

'Ah! you don't know,' she suddenly went on, clapping her hands, 'she must be in calf... I took her to the bull, nine miles away at Béage. There aren't that many bulls around, you see!... Then while she was with him, I stayed and watched.'

La Teuse shrugged her shoulders, looking at the priest with a rather displeased expression.

'It would be better, Mademoiselle, if you were to go and calm your hens down... It sounds as if all your animals are killing each other over there.'

But Désirée was determined to tell her story.

'He got on top of her, and took her between his forelegs... Some people were laughing. But there's nothing to laugh at: it's natural. Mothers have to make babies, don't they? So, do you think she'll have a baby?'

Abbé Mouret made a vague gesture. His eyelids had come down under the girl's clear gaze.

'Hey, come on, run!' cried La Teuse. 'They're eating each other alive.'

The ructions in the farmyard had become so violent that Désirée was setting off with a great rustling of skirts, when the priest called her back:

'And the milk, darling, you haven't finished the milk?'

He offered her his cup, which he had scarcely touched.

She came back, and drank the milk without a second thought, under the angry eyes of La Teuse.

Then she rushed away again, down to her farmyard, where they could hear her restoring order. She must have sat herself down in the midst of the animals; and she was humming softly, as if to lull them to sleep.

CHAPTER III

'Now my soup is too hot,' grumbled La Teuse, coming back from
the kitchen with a bowl in which a wooden spoon was standing
upright.* She stood in front of Abbé Mouret, and started to eat cautiously from the tip of the spoon. She was hoping to cheer him up,
and draw him out of the devastated silence in which he seemed to be
sunk. Since he came back from the Paradou, he kept saying he was
cured, and he never complained of anything; indeed he often smiled
with such tenderness that according to the people of Les Artaud, his
illness had redoubled his saintliness. But now and again he had crises
of silence, in which he seemed to writhe in some torture that it took
all his strength not to acknowledge; it was a mute agony that racked
him, and for hours at a time made him quite stupefied, enduring some
terrible, internal struggle whose violence could only be guessed from
the sweat of anguish on his face. At such times, La Teuse did not leave
him alone, but battered him with a flood of words until he regained
his gentle expression, that of one who had conquered the rebellion of
his blood. That morning, the old servant foresaw an attack even more
violent than the previous ones. She began to talk non-stop, while continuing to be careful with the spoon, which was burning her tongue.

'Honestly, you have to live in a land of savages to see such things.
Does anyone, in any decent village, get married by candlelight?*
That in itself shows that these Artauds are a poor lot... Now back in
Normandy, I saw weddings that created a great stir for six miles around.
There would be feasting for three days. The priest was there, the mayor
was there; indeed at the wedding of one of my cousins, the fire brigade
was there. And everyone had so much fun!... But to get the priest up
before the sun, and get married at a time when even the hens are still
roosting, there's no sense in it! In your place, Monsieur le Curé, I'd
have refused... Heavens, you haven't slept enough, and perhaps you've
caught a chill in the church. That's what's upset you. And add to that
the fact that one would prefer to marry the beasts of the field than to
marry that Rosalie and that lout of hers, and their brat who peed on
the chair... You're wrong not to tell me where you feel bad... I could
make you something hot... Eh? Monsieur le Curé, answer me.'

He answered in a weak voice that he was quite well, and only needed
a bit of fresh air. He had leaned against one of the mulberry trees,
breathing very rapidly, and letting himself sink down.

'Well, well, do just as you like,' La Teuse went on. 'Marry people when you're not really strong enough, even if it's going to make you ill. I thought it would. I said so yesterday. It's just the same now; if you listened to me, you wouldn't stay here, because the smell of the farm-yard upsets you. The stink is terrible just now. I don't know what Mademoiselle Désirée can be stirring up. But she's singing, it doesn't bother her a bit, it brings a good colour to her cheeks... Oh! I meant to tell you. You know, I did my best to stop her from staying there when the bull covered the cow. But she's like you, so stubborn! Fortunately, for her it's of no importance. It's a joy to her, her animals and their little ones. Come now, Monsieur le Curé, be sensible. Let me take you to your room. You can lie down and have a bit of a rest... No, you don't want to? Oh well! So much the worse for you, if you suffer for it! It's not right to keep pain to yourself like that, till it chokes you.'

And in her anger she swallowed a large spoonful of soup, at the risk of burning her throat. She tapped the wooden handle against the bowl, grumbling and muttering to herself:

'Was there ever such a man? He'd die first rather than say a word... Ah! Let him keep it to himself. I know enough about it; it's not that difficult to guess the rest... Oh yes, let him keep quiet. It's better that way.'

La Teuse was jealous. Dr Pascal had fought a real battle with her, to take away her patient when he had decided there was no hope for the young priest if he stayed in the presbytery. He had had to explain to her that the church bell aggravated the young man's fever, that the sacred images all over his room were haunting his brain and giving him hallucinations, and that what he needed was a total forgetting, a change of scene, so he could be reborn into the peace of a new exist-ence. And she had shaken her head, saying that never would 'the dear child' find a better nurse than she. However, she had consented in the end; she had even resigned herself to seeing him go to the Paradou, even while protesting against the doctor's choice, which seemed to her extraordinary. But she retained a real hatred of the Paradou. She felt especially hurt by the abbé's silence about the time he had spent there. She had many times manoeuvred in vain to try to make him talk about it. That morning, exasperated at seeing him so pale, and so stub-bornly insisting on suffering without a murmur, she ended up waving her spoon like a stick, and shouting:

'You'll just have to go back, Monsieur le Curé, if you were so happy

there... No doubt there's somebody there who can look after you better than I can.'

It was the first time she had dared to make any direct allusion. It
was so cruel a blow that the priest gave a little cry, and raised a grief-
stricken face. La Teuse's kindly soul was filled with regret.

'Anyway,' she said quietly, 'it's all your uncle Pascal's fault. Heavens,
I did tell him. But these scientists have their own ideas. Some of them
would have you die, just to be able to examine your body afterwards...
But it put me in such a rage that I refused to tell anyone about it. Yes,
I thought it so abominable, it's thanks to me that nobody knew where
you were. When Abbé Guyot from Saint-Eutrope, the one who
replaced you while you were away, came here on Sundays to say Mass,
I told him stories, I swore you were in Switzerland. I don't even know
where Switzerland is... Of course I don't want to cause you any pain,
but it's certainly in the Paradou that you caught your sickness. A funny
sort of cure! It would have been much better to leave you with me,
I would never have thought of trying to turn your head.'

Abbé Mouret, his brow lowered once more, did not interrupt her.
She had sat down on the ground a few steps away from him, to try to
catch his eye. She went on, in a motherly way, delighted at what
seemed his readiness to listen to her:

'You've never been willing to hear the story of Abbé Caffin. As soon
as I begin, you make me stop... Well, Abbé Caffin, in our home town
of Canteleu, had had a bit of trouble. And yet he was a saintly man,
with a character of solid gold. But you see, he was very sensitive, and
he liked delicate things. So one young lady was always prowling
around him, a miller's daughter, whose parents had sent her away to
boarding school. Briefly, what was bound to happen, happened, you
understand me, don't you? Then when it all came out, everybody was
furious with the abbé. People were looking for him to stone him to
death. He fled to Rouen and told his sad story to the archbishop. And
he got sent here. It was quite enough punishment to have to live in this
dump... Later on I had news of the girl. She married a cattle merchant.
She's very happy.'

Delighted to have been able to tell her story, La Teuse took the
priest's immobility as an encouragement. She drew nearer, and
continued:

'That good Monsieur Caffin! He wasn't stand-offish with me, he
often spoke to me about his sin. It doesn't mean he's not in Heaven,

I promise you! He can sleep in peace, just over there under the grass, for he never did anyone any harm... I really don't understand how people can blame a priest so much, when he strays from the path. It's so natural! It's not right, of course, it's a very bad thing, that must make God angry, but even so, it's better to do that than to go thieving. There's always confession, and then it's all over... Isn't that so, Monsieur le Curé, when a person truly repents, he can find salvation just the same?'

Abbé Mouret had slowly raised himself up. With a supreme effort, he had overcome his anguish. Still pale, he said in a firm voice:

'One must never sin, never, never!'

'Oh, come on,' cried the old servant, 'you really are too proud! And pride isn't a good thing, either! In your shoes, I wouldn't be quite so stiff. People talk about their troubles, and people don't cut their heart to pieces in one blow, they get used to separation gradually! It happens bit by bit... But you, on the other hand, you even avoid speaking the name of certain people. You forbid any mention of them, it's as if they were dead. Since you came back, I haven't dared give you the slightest bit of news. Well! now I'm going to speak up, and tell you what I know, because I can see all this silence is torturing your heart.'

He looked at her sternly, raising a finger to make her stop.

'Yes, yes,' she went on, 'I get news from you know where, quite often in fact, and I'm passing it on... For a start, that person is no happier than you.'

'Be quiet!' said Abbé Mouret, who even found the strength to stand up so that he could get away.

La Teuse also got up, and barred the way with her enormous figure. She was getting angry, and she shouted:

'There you go, running away again!... But you're going to listen to me. You know I'm not fond of those people over there, don't you? If I talk to you about them, it's for your sake... Some say I'm jealous. Well in fact, I'm just longing to take you there one day. As you'd be with me, you'd have no fear of doing anything bad... Do you want to do that?'

He waved her away, and with a calmer expression, said:

'I want nothing, I know nothing... We have a High Mass tomorrow. The altar must be prepared.'

Then, having started to walk away, he added with a smile:

'Don't worry yourself, my good Teuse. I am stronger than you think. I'll get better by myself.'

And he walked away, looking quite sturdy, with head held high, having conquered his emotions. His cassock made a very gentle rustling against the borders of thyme. La Teuse, who had stayed rooted to the same spot, picked up her bowl and her wooden spoon, grumbling the while. She was muttering between her teeth words that she accompanied with much hefty shrugging:

'It puts on a brave show, it thinks it's made differently from other men because it's a priest... The truth is that this one is really hard. I've known some you didn't have to cajole for such a long time. And he's capable of crushing his heart the way you crush a flea. It's his God that gives him that strength.'

She was just entering the kitchen, when she saw Abbé Mouret standing at the gate of the farmyard. Désirée had stopped him to make him weigh a capon she'd been fattening for some weeks. He kindly agreed that it was very heavy, at which the overgrown child laughed with pleasure.

'Capons are the same, they also crush the feelings of their hearts like crushing fleas,' stammered La Teuse, now quite furious. 'They have good reasons for doing that... For them there's no glory in living a good life.'*

CHAPTER IV

Abbé Mouret spent his days in the presbytery. He avoided the long walks he used to take before his illness. The scorched land of Les Artaud, and the ardent heat of this valley where only twisted vines could grow, disturbed him. Twice he had tried to go out in the morning to read his breviary along the way; but he had got no further than the village; he had gone back home, disturbed by the smells, the sun, and the wide expanse of the horizon. Only in the evening, in the cool of the approaching night, did he venture to take a few steps in front of the church on the wide path that reached down to the cemetery. In the afternoon, gripped by a need for activity that he didn't know how to satisfy, he had given himself the task of sticking panes of paper over the broken windows of the nave. That had kept him busy on a ladder for a week, very concerned to fix the panes in neatly, cutting the paper as delicately as if it were embroidery, and spreading the glue with great care to avoid smudges. La Teuse had stood at the foot of the ladder, watching over him. Désirée insisted that he shouldn't fill all the panes, so the sparrows could still get in; and to spare her tears, he did leave one or two panes unmended in each window. When these repairs were finished, he conceived the ambitious idea of beautifying the church, with no help from any mason, carpenter, or painter. He would do it all himself. He said he enjoyed this manual work, and it helped him regain his strength. Uncle Pascal, whenever he called at the presbytery, encouraged him, assuring him that hard work of this sort did more good than all the drugs in the world. Thereupon Abbé Mouret set about filling the holes in the wall with handfuls of plaster, replacing nails in the altars with much wielding of hammers, and grinding some colours to give the pulpit and the confessional a new layer of paint. It was quite an event in the locality. People talked about it for miles around. Peasants came along with their hands behind their backs, to see Monsieur le Curé at work. He, with a blue apron tied round his waist, and bruised wrists, was absorbed in this crude task which gave him an excuse for not going out. He lived his days surrounded by rubble, more tranquil, almost smiling, forgetting the outside world, the trees, the sun, and the warm breezes that disturbed him.

'Monsieur le Curé is free to do whatever he pleases, provided it doesn't cost the commune anything,' said old Bambousse with a smirk, when he came every evening to see how the work was getting on.

Abbé Mouret spent all his seminary savings on the work. His embellishments were so clumsy and naive as to raise a smile. The masonry-work soon lost its appeal for him. He contented himself with replastering all round the church to the height of a man's head. La Teuse mixed the plaster. When she spoke of repairing the presbytery too, which she still feared would fall down on their heads, he explained that he wouldn't know how to do that, it would need a builder; and this led to a terrible quarrel between the two. She yelled that it wasn't sensible so to beautify a church in which nobody slept, when right next door there were bedrooms in which they would surely some morning be found dead, crushed beneath the ceiling.

'Well,' she grumbled, 'I'll end up having my bed brought in here behind the altar, I'm so frightened at night.'

When there was no more plaster, she didn't say any more about the presbytery. Besides, the sight of Monsieur le Curé's paintwork quite delighted her. That was the special charm of all that hard work. The abbé, who had replaced missing boards all over the church, was now happily applying lovely yellow paint to the woodwork with a thick brush. The gentle to-and-fro movement of the brush had a lulling effect that almost sent him to sleep, and left him devoid of thought for hours, while he followed the thick streaks of the paint. When everything was yellow, the confessional, the pulpit, the altar platform, and even the casing of the clock, he ventured to try some marble effect to touch up the main altar. Then, getting bolder, he repainted it entirely. The main altar, now white, yellow, and blue, was quite splendid. People who hadn't attended Mass for fifty years streamed in to see it.

The paintwork was now dry. All that remained for Abbé Mouret to do was to edge the panels with a brown line. So that very afternoon, he set himself to work, wanting to get it all finished by evening, since there was High Mass on the following day, as he had reminded La Teuse. La Teuse was waiting to get the altar dressed; she had already put the candlesticks and the silver cross ready on the credenza, along with the china vases filled with artificial flowers, and the lace-trimmed cloth that was kept for special occasions. But it was so difficult to keep the brown edging neat that the work went on until nightfall. It was getting dark as he finished the last panel.

'It's going to be too beautiful,' said a rough voice emerging from the dusty grey of the twilight now filling the church.

La Teuse, who had knelt down, the better to watch the movement of the edging brush along the ruler, gave a start of fright.

'Oh! it's Brother Archangias,' she said, turning her head, 'did you come in through the sacristy then?... My heart missed a beat. I thought the voice was coming from under the flagstones.'

Abbé Mouret had gone back to work after greeting the Brother with a slight nod of the head. The Brother stood silent, with his big hands clenched in front of his cassock. Then, seeing the care the priest was taking to keep the edging lines straight, he shrugged his shoulders and repeated:

'It's going to be too beautiful.'

La Teuse, quite ecstatic, gave another start.

'Goodness!' she cried, 'I'd already forgotten you were there! You could at least cough before you speak. You have a voice that bursts out suddenly, like a voice from beyond the grave.'

She had stood up and was standing back to admire the work.

'Why too beautiful?' she went on. 'Nothing is too beautiful when it's for God... If Monsieur le Curé had had some gold, he would have used gold too, you'd see!'

Now the priest had finished, she hurriedly changed the altar cloth, taking care not to smudge the edging lines. Then she laid out symmetrically the cross, the candlesticks, and the vases. Abbé Mouret had gone to lean back against the wooden screen that separated the choir from the nave, alongside Brother Archangias. They did not exchange a word. They were looking at the silver cross which, in the gathering gloom, still had little spots of light on the feet, down the left side of the body, and on the right-hand side of the brow of the crucified Lord. When La Teuse had finished, she came towards them triumphantly.

'Well!' she said, 'it's really nice. You'll see what a crowd there'll be at Mass tomorrow! These pagans only come to visit God when they think He's rich... Now, Monsieur le Curé, we must do as much for the Virgin's altar.'

'A waste of money,' growled Brother Archangias.

But La Teuse was annoyed, and as Abbé Mouret continued to be silent, she led them both in front of the altar of the Virgin, pushing and pulling them by their cassocks.

'Just look! It clashes horribly now that the main altar looks so clean. You can't even tell whether it's ever been painted. No matter how much I wipe it over in the morning, the wood gathers dust. It's so dark, so ugly... Don't you realize what people will say, Monsieur le Curé? They'll say you don't love the Holy Virgin, that's what.'

'And so...?' demanded Brother Archangias.

La Teuse almost choked with indignation.

'And so,' she muttered, 'that would be a sin, for heaven's sake!... That altar is like one of those untended graves you find in cemeteries. If it weren't for me, spiders would be covering it with their webs, and moss would grow on it. Now and again when I can save a bunch of flowers, I give it to the Virgin... All the flowers from our garden used to be for her at one time.'

She had climbed up in front of the altar and picked up two withered bouquets that lay forgotten on the steps.

'You can see for yourself that it's just the same as in the cemetery,' she added, and threw the flowers at Abbé Mouret's feet.

He picked them up without a word. It was quite dark now. Brother Archangias bumped into the chairs and almost fell. He swore, uttering indistinct phrases in which the names of Jesus and Mary recurred very frequently. When La Teuse, who had gone to fetch a lamp, came back into the church, she simply asked the priest:

'So I can put away the pots and brushes?'

'Yes,' he replied. 'It's finished. We'll see about the rest later on.'

She walked ahead of them, taking everything away, holding her tongue for fear of saying altogether too much. And as Abbé Mouret still had the two withered bouquets in his hand, Brother Archangias shouted, as they went past the farmyard:

'Throw that stuff away!'

The abbé walked on a few steps with bowed head, then threw the flowers over the gate into the compost heap.

CHAPTER V

THE Brother, who had already eaten, stayed on while the priest had dinner, sitting astride a chair he had turned round. Ever since the priest had come back to Les Artaud, he had been installing himself like this in the presbytery almost every evening. Never before had he imposed himself so crudely. His big boots seemed to crush the floor, his voice boomed, and his fists thumped the furniture as he recounted the beatings his stick had administered to the little girls that morning, or outlined his moral code in terms as unrelenting as any stick. Then when he got bored, he suggested playing cards with La Teuse. They played 'War'* interminably, as La Teuse had never managed to learn any other game. Abbé Mouret would smile as the first few cards were slapped down furiously on the table, but would then slip into a profound reverie; and for hours on end he would forget everything, escaping, even under the watchful eyes of Brother Archangias.

That evening La Teuse was in such a mood that she talked of going to bed as soon as the table was cleared. But the Brother wanted to play cards. He tapped her several times on the shoulder, and ended up sitting her down so roughly that the chair cracked. He was already shuffling the cards. Désirée, who loathed him, had already gone off with the dessert she took upstairs with her almost every evening, to eat it in bed.

'I want red,' said La Teuse.

And the fight began. First La Teuse took a few good cards off the Brother. Then two aces fell together on the table.

'War!' cried La Teuse, with unusual vehemence.

The card she threw down was a nine, which worried her, but as the Brother only threw a seven, she gathered up the cards in triumph. At the end of half an hour, she had won nothing more than two aces, so the odds were once again even. And after nearly three-quarters of an hour, it was she who lost an ace. The comings and goings of knaves and queens and kings had all the fury of a massacre.

'This is a terrific game, isn't it!' said Brother Archangias, turning to Abbé Mouret.

But seeing him so lost in thought, so far away, and with such an unconscious smile on his face, he brutally raised his voice.

'Well, Monsieur le Curé, you're not watching us at all then? That's not very polite of you... It's for you we're playing. We're trying to cheer you up... Come on, watch the game. That will do you more good than dreaming. What were you dreaming about?'

The priest gave a shudder. He did not answer, he made a great effort to follow the game, with quivering eyelids. The game went on relentlessly. La Teuse won back her ace, then lost it again. Some evenings they fought like this over their aces for four hours, and often even went off to bed in a fury at having failed to finish the game.

'But I just remembered!' suddenly cried La Teuse, who was very much afraid she was losing, 'Monsieur le Curé was supposed to be going out this evening. He promised big Fortuné and Rosalie that he would go and bless their bedroom, according to the custom... Hurry, Monsieur le Curé! The Brother will go with you.'

Abbé Mouret was already on his feet, looking for his hat. But Brother Archangias, without letting go of his cards, expressed his annoyance:

'Oh, just leave it! Does it really need blessing, that pigsty of theirs? For whatever good they're going to do in that bedroom!... Just another custom you ought to abolish. A priest doesn't need to poke his nose into the sheets of the newly-married... Stay here. And let us finish the game. That'll be much better.'

'No,' said the priest, 'I promised. Those good people might feel hurt... You stay here, and finish the game while you wait for me.'

La Teuse was looking very anxiously at Brother Archangias.

'Ah well! Yes, I'll stay,' he cried. 'It's too silly.'

But Abbé Mouret had not even opened the door before the Brother rose to follow him, flinging his cards down angrily. He turned back and said to La Teuse:

'I was going to win... Leave the piles of cards just as they are. We'll carry on with the game tomorrow.'

'Ah, well it's all muddled up now,' replied La Teuse, who had lost no time in mixing up the cards. 'Do you really think I'm going to preserve your hand in a glass case? Besides, I might have won, I still had an ace.'

In a few strides Brother Archangias caught up with Abbé Mouret who was going down the narrow path leading to Les Artaud. The Brother had given himself the task of watching over him. He kept him under surveillance every hour of the day, accompanying him everywhere, or if he could not do it himself, having him followed by a boy from the school. He would say, with a laugh, that he was 'God's policeman'. And indeed the priest seemed like a criminal imprisoned in the black shadow of the Brother's cassock, a criminal who can't be trusted, one judged to be so weak that he would return to his sin if left out of sight for a moment. The Brother had all the harshness of a jealous old maid, the meticulous zeal of a gaoler who pushes his duties to the point of concealing any little patches of sky that might be glimpsed through the skylights. Brother Archangias was always there, ready to block out the sunlight, make sure no scent could enter, and wall up the dungeon so thoroughly that nothing from outside could ever again get in. He watched out for the slightest weakness in the abbé, recognizing any tender thoughts by the brightness of his eyes, and crushing them with a word, pitilessly, as if they were evil beasts. The abbé's moments of silence, his smiles, the paleness of his brow, the shivering of his limbs, everything was material for the Brother. Besides, he avoided ever speaking directly about the sin. His presence in itself was a reproach. The way he pronounced certain phrases gave them the sting of a whiplash. He could put into a single gesture all the filth that he cast upon sin. Like those deceived husbands who subjugate their wives with savage allusions, whose cruelty they alone understand, he never spoke of the scene in the Paradou; he was content to do no more than allude to it with a single word, to crush that rebellious flesh whenever it became necessary. He, too, had been betrayed by this priest, soiled by his divine adultery, this priest who, having broken his vows, brought back to him the distant scent of forbidden caresses, and that was enough to exasperate his continence, which was like that of a billy goat that had never satisfied its desires.

It was almost ten o'clock. The village was asleep; but at the other end of the village, near the mill, a loud noise was coming from one of the peasants' cottages which was brilliantly lit. Old Bambousse had given up one part of the house to his daughter and son-in-law, keeping the best rooms for himself. They were just having a last drink while waiting for the priest.

'They're drunk,' growled Brother Archangias. 'Do you hear their filthy goings-on?'

Abbé Mouret did not answer. It was a superb night, quite blue with a moonlight that turned the valley in the distance into a sleeping lake. And he slowed his pace, as if bathed in pleasantness by the soft lights; he even stopped at some expanses of light, with the delightful shiver one gets from the nearness of fresh water. The Brother carried on, with his long strides, scolding him and calling him on:

'Come on... It's not healthy to be running around the countryside at this time of night. You ought to be in your bed.'

But suddenly, at the entry to the village, he stopped dead in the middle of the road. He was looking up towards the high ground, where the white lines of the ruts merged into the black outlines of the little pinewoods. He uttered a growl like a dog scenting danger:

'Who's coming down from up there, at such a late hour?' he muttered.

The priest, hearing nothing and seeing nothing, was now the one who wanted to hurry on.

'Stop, stop! there he is,' Brother Archangias went on. 'He's just come round the bend. Look, the moon is lighting him up. You can see him clearly now... It's a tall man, with a stick.'

Then after a silence, he went on, his voice hoarse and choking with fury:

'It's him, it's that wretch!... I thought it was.'

When the newcomer was at the bottom of the hill, Abbé Mouret recognized Jeanbernat.

For all his eighty years, the old man hit the ground so hard with his hobnailed boots that he struck sparks from the flint in the road. He walked, straight as an oak tree, without even using his stick, which he carried over his shoulder like a gun.

'Ah! the damned scoundrel!' stuttered the Brother, now standing rooted to the spot. 'May the devil throw all the hot coals of hell beneath his feet!'

The priest, very troubled, and despairing of breaking free of his companion, turned his back to continue his journey, still hoping to avoid

Jeanbernat by hurrying to the house of Bambousse. But he had not gone five paces before the mocking voice of the old man seemed to come from directly behind him:

'Eh, priest, wait for me. Or are you afraid of me?'

And when Abbé Mouret stopped, he approached, and went on:

'Dammit! those cassocks of yours, they're not very practical, you can't run in them. Besides, it may be night, but they make you recognizable even from a distance... From the top of the hill I said to myself: "Aha! it's the little priest I see down there." Oh! my eyes are still good... So, you don't come and see us any more?'

'I've had such a lot to do,' murmured the priest, now very pale.

'Yes, all right, it's a free country. All I'm saying is just to show you I don't bear you any grudge for being a priest. We wouldn't even talk about your God, I don't mind... The little girl thinks I'm the one who's stopping you from coming back. I told her: "The priest is a fool." And that is what I think. Did I ever bother you while you were sick? I didn't even come up to see you... It's a free country.'

He spoke with a splendid indifference, pretending not even to have noticed the presence of Brother Archangias. But when the latter uttered a more threatening growl, he went on:

'Eh! priest, so you're taking your pig for a walk?'

'Just you wait, you brigand!' shouted the Brother, his fists clenched. Jeanbernat, raising his stick, pretended he had only just seen him:

'Get your paws down!' he cried. 'Ah! it's you, you Holy Joe... I should have sniffed you out by the smell of your skin. We have a score to settle, you and I. I've sworn I'll cut off your ears in your classroom. The kids that you're poisoning will really enjoy that.'

Faced with the stick, the Brother drew back, his throat crammed with insults. He spluttered, quite lost for words.

'I'll get the police on to you, you murderous scoundrel! You've spat on the church, I've seen you! You give mortal sickness to poor unfortunates just by walking past their door. At Saint-Eutrope, you caused an abortion by forcing a girl to chew a consecrated Host you had stolen. In Le Béage, you went and dug up some dead children and carried them away on your back for your abominable practices. Everybody knows about it, you wretch! You're the scandal of the region. Anyone who strangled you would go straight to Heaven.'

The old man listened, twirling his stick with a sneer. In between the insults of the other, he repeated quietly:

'Go on, go on, get it out of your system, you viper! In a while, I'll break your back for you!'

Abbé Mouret tried to intervene. But Brother Archangias pushed him away, shouting:

'You're with him, you are! Didn't he make you trample on the cross, go on, deny it!'

Then turning once more to Jeanbernat:

'Ah! you Satan, you must have had a good laugh when you got hold of a priest! May Heaven crush those who helped you in that sacrilege! What did you do at night while he was sleeping? You went and wet his tonsure with your saliva, didn't you, to make his hair grow more quickly? You blew on his chin and his cheeks to make his beard grow an inch in one night. You rubbed his whole body with evil charms, breathed the rage of a mad dog into his mouth, and made him into a rutting animal... you changed him into a beast, you Satan!'

'He's an idiot,' said Jeanbernat, putting his stick back up on his shoulder, 'and he's boring me.'

The Brother, who had grown bolder, thrust his fists out under the old man's nose.

'And your slut!' he cried. 'It was you who pushed her naked into the priest's bed!'

But he gave a scream and leaped backwards. The old man's stick, wielded with full force, had just broken on the Brother's spine. He went back further, and from a pile of pebbles at the side of the road, picked up a big piece of flint, the size of two fists, and threw it at Jeanbernat's head. It would certainly have cracked Jeanbernat's skull if he hadn't ducked in time. He ran to another pile of pebbles, sheltering behind it, and took up some stones. And from one pile of stones to the other, a terrible battle began. Pieces of flint hailed down. The moon, very bright, starkly outlined their shadows.

'Yes, you pushed her into his bed,' the Brother repeated, mad with fury. 'And you had put the figure of Christ under the mattress, so the filth would fall on him... Ha, ha! you're amazed I know all about it. You're waiting for some monster to come from that coupling. Every morning you make the thirteen signs of hell over the womb of your slut, so she will give birth to the Antichrist. You want the Antichrist, you scoundrel! Here, I hope this stone will put your eye out!'

'And I hope this one will shut your trap, Holy Joe!' replied Jeanbernat, now very calm again. 'How incredibly stupid this animal is, with his stories!... Will I have to crack your skull just to go on my way? Is it your catechism that has turned your brain?'

'The catechism? Do you want to know the catechism that's taught to the damned like you? Yes, I'll teach you to make the sign of the cross... This is for the Father, this is for the Son, and this is for the Holy Ghost... Ah! you're still standing. Just wait a bit, wait!... Amen!'

He threw a volley of little stones like grapeshot. Jeanbernat, hit on the shoulder, dropped the pebbles he was holding and calmly moved forward, while Brother Archangias was picking up two more handfuls from the heap, muttering:

'I'm going to exterminate you. It's God's will. God is in my arm!'

'Will you be quiet?' said the old man, gripping him by the neck.

Then there was a short struggle in the dust of the road that looked blue in the moonlight. The Brother, realizing he was the weaker of the two, tried to bite. The dry old limbs of Jeanbernat were like coils of rope that bound the Brother so tight he felt the knots digging into his flesh. He was silent, suffocating, trying to think of some treacherous trick. When he had him completely at his mercy, the old man went on, with a mocking laugh:

'I'm tempted to break your arm, to break that God of yours... You can see that he is not the stronger one, that God of yours. I'm the one exterminating you... Now I'm going to cut off your ears. You've tried my patience too far.'

And he calmly took out a knife from his pocket. Abbé Mouret, who had tried in vain, again and again, to come between the combatants, now intervened so forcefully that the old man finally agreed to defer that operation to another time.

'You are wrong, priest,' he murmured. 'That fellow's in need of some bloodletting. Still, since it upsets you, I'll wait. I'll be sure to meet him again somewhere or other.'

When the Brother let out a growl, he paused to shout at him:

'Don't move, or I'll cut them off right now.'

'But', said the priest, 'you're sitting on his chest. Get up so that he can breathe.'

'No, no, he'd start all his nonsense again. I won't let him go until I'm ready to leave... What I was saying then, priest, when this scoundrel interrupted us, was that you would be welcome at the Paradou. The little one is the mistress of the house, as you know. I don't cross her any more than I would my lettuces. Everything grows... Only imbeciles like this Holy Joe see any evil in it. Where did you see any evil, rascal! You invented the evil, you foul brute!'

He gave the Brother another shaking.

'Let him get up,' Abbé Mouret begged.

'In a while... The little girl has not been well for some time. I hadn't noticed anything... But she told me. So I'm going to Plassans to let your uncle Pascal know. At night it's quiet, there's nobody about... Yes, yes, the little one is not at all well.'

The priest could think of nothing to say. He was unsteady on his feet, and his head was bowed.

'She was so happy, looking after you!' the old man went on. 'As I smoked my pipe, I could hear her laughing. That was enough for me. Girls are like the hawthorn: when they flower, they flower abundantly... Anyway, you'll come if you feel like it... Perhaps that would cheer the child up... Good evening, priest.'

He had got up slowly, gripping the Brother's fists, on the watch for some dirty trick. And he went away without turning his head, with the same long, hard strides. The Brother, in silence, climbed up to the heap of stones. He waited until the old man was some distance away. Then with both hands, he started again, in his fury. But the stones just rolled in the dust of the road. Jeanbernat, not deigning to be further annoyed, just kept on going, straight as an oak, into the serenity of the night.

'That cursed wretch! Satan drives him on!' stammered Brother Archangias, throwing one last stone. 'An old man who should be crushed by the flick of a finger. He's been baked by the fires of hell. I felt his claws.'

He stamped on the scattered pebbles in impotent rage. Then suddenly he turned on Abbé Mouret.

'It's your fault,' he cried. 'You should have helped me, the two of us together would have strangled him.'

At the other end of the village, the noise in the Bambousse house had got louder. They could distinctly hear the regular thumping of glasses on the table. The priest had started to walk on, without raising his head, heading for the flood of bright light coming from the window, like the flaming of a vineyard bonfire. The Brother followed him, looking grim, his cassock covered in dust and one cheek bleeding, grazed by a stone. Then after a silence, he asked in his harsh voice:

'Will you go?'

And when Abbé Mouret did not reply, he went on:

'Take care! you're returning to sin... It was enough for that man just to pass by for your whole body to be shaken. I saw you in the moonlight, pale as a girl... Take care, do you hear? This time, God would not be forgiving. You would fall into the ultimate corruption... Ah! wretched clay that you are, it's filth that's carrying you away!'

At this the priest at last looked up. He was silently shedding big, fat tears. In a very sad and gentle tone he said:

'Why do you speak to me like that?... You are always there, you know my constant struggles. Do not doubt me, leave me the strength to conquer myself.'

These simple words, bathed in silent tears, took on, in the night, such an aspect of sublime grief that Brother Archangias himself, for all his crudeness, felt troubled. He did not add a word, shaking his cassock, and dabbing at his bleeding cheek. When they were in front of the Bambousse house, he refused to go in. He sat down a few steps away, on the overturned frame of an old cart, and waited with the patience of a faithful dog.

'Here's Monsieur le Curé!' cried all the Bambousses and Brichets sitting at the table.

And glasses were filled once more. Abbé Mouret had to accept one. There had not been any wedding breakfast. But in the evening, after dinner, they had put on the table a demijohn containing about fifty litres of wine that was to be emptied before they went to bed. There were ten of them, and already old Bambousse was able to tip the demijohn with one hand, and from it there now flowed only a thin trickle of red wine. Rosalie, very gay, was dipping the baby's chin in her glass, while big Fortuné was doing tricks, lifting chairs with his teeth. Everyone went into the bedroom. Custom required that the priest drink the wine poured for him right there: this was what was called blessing the bedroom. It brought good luck, and protected the household from quarrelling. In the time of M. Caffin, everything went on very merrily, the old priest liked to laugh; he had even gained quite a reputation for the way he drained the glass, without leaving a single drop; this was all the more important since the women of Les Artaud claimed that each drop left in the glass was one year less of love for the couple. With Abbé Mouret they joked less noisily. But he drained the glass in one draught, which seemed greatly to please old Bambousse. Mother Brichet made a face when she looked down into the glass where a little wine remained. In front of the bed, an uncle who was a local policeman was making some very risqué jokes, which made Rosalie laugh—Big Fortuné had already pushed her face down on to the edge of the mattress, by way of a caress. And when everyone had made some crude joke, they all went back to the dining room. Vincent and Catherine had stayed behind by themselves. Vincent, standing on a chair, tipping the demijohn over with both arms, was just emptying the last drops into Catherine's open mouth.

'Thank you, Monsieur le Curé,' cried Bambousse, as he saw the priest out. 'Well, they're married. You're satisfied. Ah! the wretches! If you think they're now going to say their prayers and some *Aves*... Goodnight, sleep well, Monsieur le Curé.'

Brother Archangias had slowly risen from his perch on the old cart.

'May the devil shovel hot coals between their bodies and may they die of it!' After that, he said no more. He accompanied Abbé Mouret to the presbytery and waited there for him to shut the door before leaving; he even turned round to make sure the abbé wasn't coming out again. When the priest reached his room, he threw himself fully clothed on the bed, with his hands over his ears, and his face in the pillow, so as not to hear, and not to see. He totally collapsed, fell asleep, and slept like the dead.

CHAPTER VI

THE next day was a Sunday. As the Exaltation of the Holy Cross* fell on a day of High Mass, Abbé Mouret had decided to celebrate this religious feast with special grandeur. He had developed an extraordinary devotion to the Cross; in his room, he had replaced the figure of the Immaculate Conception with a large crucifix, made of black wood, and spent long hours of adoration before it. To exalt the Cross, and keep it always before him, above all else, in a halo of glory, as the sole aim of his life, gave him the strength to suffer and struggle. He dreamed of attaching himself to it in the place of Jesus, to be crowned with thorns, have his limbs pierced, and his side riven. What sort of coward must he be, to dare to complain of an illusory wound, when his God was bleeding there before him, from his whole body, with the smile of Redemption on his lips? And paltry though it might be, he offered his own wound as a sacrifice, and finally slipped into an ecstasy, believing that blood was really streaming down from his brow, his limbs, and his breast. These were hours of comfort, in which all his impurities flowed out through his wounds. He got up again with the heroic efforts of a martyr, he longed for frightful tortures in order to endure them without a tremor of his flesh.

As soon as it was light he knelt before the crucifix. And grace fell abundantly upon him like dew. He made no effort, he had only to bend his knees to receive it upon his heart, and feel it soak through his whole body, in the sweetest, most delightful way. The day before, he had agonized without receiving any grace. It would often remain deaf to the entreaties he made as a damned soul; and then sometimes come to his aid when he did nothing more than put his hands together like a child. That morning it was a blessing, absolute trust, an impregnable faith. He forgot his anguish of the days before. He gave himself wholly to the triumphal joy of the Cross. An armour covered him to his shoulders, so impenetrable that the outside world attacked it in vain. When he came down, he walked with an air of victory and serenity. La Teuse, astonished, went to fetch Désirée so he could kiss her. Both clapped their hands, exclaiming that he had not looked so well for six months.

During the High Mass in the church, the priest completed his rediscovery of God. It was a long time since he had approached the altar with such tenderness. It was all he could do, with his mouth pressed to the altar cloth, not to burst into tears. It was a solemn High Mass. Rosalie's uncle the policeman, serving as cantor, chanted at the lectern with a deep bass voice that resounded like an organ through the crumbling vault. Vincent, in an overlarge surplice that had belonged to Abbé Caffin, was swinging an old silver censer and vastly enjoying the noise of the little chains; he was swinging it very high to get plenty of smoke, and looking over his shoulder to see if it was making anyone cough. The church was almost full. Everyone had been eager to see Monsieur le Curé's paintwork. Some of the peasant women were laughing because it smelled nice, while the men, at the back under the gallery, nodded their heads at every deep note from the cantor. The full mid-morning sun came in through the windows, filtered through the paper windowpanes, and spread upon the newly plastered walls large shimmering patches of light, in which the shadows of the women's bonnets danced about gaily like big butterflies. And the bunches of artificial flowers lying on the steps of the altar had the cheerful moisture of real flowers, freshly gathered. When the priest turned round to bless the congregation, he felt an even greater tenderness, seeing the church so clean, so full, so soaked in music, incense, and light.

After the Offertory, a whisper ran through the women. Vincent, who had looked up in curiosity, almost tipped the burning incense over the priest's cassock, and as the latter looked at him sternly, he murmured, to excuse himself:

'Monsieur le Curé's uncle has just come in.'

At the back of the church, beside one of the narrow wooden columns supporting the gallery, Abbé Mouret then saw Dr Pascal. The latter did not have his usual smiling, faintly mocking expression. Looking stern, and rather displeased, he had taken his hat off, and was following the Mass with obvious impatience. The sight of the priest at the altar, with his reverence, his measured gestures, and the perfect serenity of his face, seemed gradually to irritate him further. He could not wait for the end of the Mass. He went out and walked round his gig and his horse, tethered to one of the presbytery shutters.

'Will this fellow never be done with smothering himself in incense?' he asked La Teuse, who was just coming back from the sacristy.

'It's over now,' she replied. 'Come into the drawing room... Monsieur le Curé is changing. He knows you're here.'

'Indeed he must! unless he's blind,' muttered the doctor, following her into the cold room with its hard furniture, that she pompously called the drawing room.

He paced up and down for a few minutes. The grey and gloomy room seemed to increase his ill humour. As he walked, he kept hitting the end of his cane on the worn horsehair of the chairs, which made a sharp noise as if made of stone. Then getting tired, he stopped in front of the fireplace, where a large, garishly bedaubed Saint Joseph stood in place of a clock.

'Ah! how very sad it is!' he said, when he heard the sound of the door opening.

And going towards the abbé:

'Do you know you've made me swallow half a Mass? It's a long time since that happened to me... Anyway, I was absolutely determined to see you today. I wanted to talk to you.'

He broke off. He was looking at the priest with an expression of surprise. There was a silence.

'So you're well, are you?' he said at last, in a different tone of voice.

'Yes, I am much better,' said Abbé Mouret with a smile. 'I wasn't expecting you until Thursday. Sunday isn't your day... You have something to tell me?'

Uncle Pascal did not reply at once. He went on looking closely at the abbé, who was still soaked in the warmth of the church; he carried in his hair the smell of incense; and still had in his eyes the joy of the Cross. The uncle shook his head in the face of that triumphant peace.

'I've come from the Paradou,' he said abruptly. 'Jeanbernat came to fetch me last night... I've seen Albine. I'm worried about her. She needs very careful treatment.'

He went on studying the priest as he spoke. He saw that his eyes didn't even blink.

'Anyway, she looked after you,' he added more roughly. 'If it weren't for her, my boy, you would perhaps be in a cell in Les Tulettes,* with a straitjacket wrapped round your shoulders... Well! I've promised that you would go and see her. I'll take you with me. To say goodbye. She wants to go away.'

'I can only pray for the person you mention,' Abbé Mouret said gently.

And as the doctor began to get angry, striking the sofa hard with his stick, the priest added in a very firm voice:

'I'm a priest, I can only offer prayers.'

'Oh! of course, you're right!' cried Uncle Pascal, feeling his legs give way beneath him, and letting himself drop into an armchair. 'I am just an old idiot. Yes, I wept in my gig, while coming here, wept by myself, like a child... That's what happens when you live surrounded by books. You do some fine experiments, but you behave like a rascal... How could I ever guess that everything would turn out so badly?'

He got up, and began to walk about again, in despair:

'Yes, yes, I should have guessed. It was logical. And with you, it became abominable. You are not a man like other men... But listen, let me assure you, you were done for. Only the atmosphere she created around you could have saved you from madness. So, just understand, I don't need to tell you what sort of state you were in. It was one of my very best treatments. And yet I'm not proud of it, for now the poor girl is dying of it!'

Abbé Mouret had remained on his feet, very calm, and with a serene radiance like that of a martyr beyond the reach of the human world.

'God will be merciful to her,' he said.

'God! God!' the doctor muttered quietly, 'he would do better not to interfere in our affairs, then we'd be able to get things sorted out.'

Then raising his voice, he added:

'I had thought it all out. That's the worst of it! Oh! what a fool... You were convalescing for a month. The shade of the trees, the fresh breath of the child, all that youth around you, would get you back on your feet. And at the same time, the child would lose her wildness, you would civilize her; between the two of us we'd be making her into a marriageable young lady. It was perfect... And how was I to imagine that the old philosopher Jeanbernat would not move one inch away from his lettuces! And the fact is, neither did I move away from my laboratory... I had some work going on... And it's all my fault! I've behaved very badly!'

He was suffocating, and wanted to get outside. He cast about everywhere, looking for his hat, which in fact was on his head.

'Goodbye,' he stammered, 'I'm going now... So you refuse to come? Look, do it for me; you can see how painful this is for me. I swear she will go away afterwards. That's agreed... My gig is here. You'll be back in an hour. Come, I beg you.'

The priest made a broad gesture, one of those gestures the doctor had seen him making at the altar.

'No,' he said, 'I can't.'

Accompanying his uncle to the door, he added:

'Tell her to kneel and ask for God's help... God will hear her, just as he has heard me; he will comfort her, just as he has comforted me. There is no other salvation.'

The doctor looked him straight in the eye and shrugged his shoulders with an air of terrible finality.

'Goodbye,' he repeated. 'You are well now. You have no more need of me.'

But as he was untying his horse, Désirée, who had just heard his voice, came running up. She adored her uncle. When she was younger, he would listen for hours to her childish prattle without getting tired. Even now, he still spoiled her, took an interest in her farmyard, and would spend a whole afternoon with her among the hens and ducks, smiling at her with his keen scientist's eyes. He would call her 'my big animal', in a tone of loving admiration. He seemed to set her far above other girls. Now she threw her arms around his neck, with a surge of affection. She cried out:

'You're staying? You're having lunch with us?'

But he kissed her and refused, freeing himself from her embrace with a rather grumpy air. She laughed, and threw her arms around him once more.

'You're making a mistake,' she went on. 'I have eggs that are still warm. I was keeping an eye on the hens. They laid fourteen this morning. And we'd have eaten a chicken, that white one who keeps attacking the others. You were there on Thursday, weren't you, when he put out the eye of the big speckled one?'

The uncle was still vexed. He grew irritated at the knot in the bridle that he couldn't undo. Then she began to leap about around him, clapping her hands, and singing a flute-like song that went:

'Yes, yes, you'll stay... And we'll eat it, we'll eat it!...'

The uncle's anger was forced to give way. He raised his head, and smiled. She was so healthy, so alive, so genuine. And her gaiety was so expansive, as natural and spontaneous as the sunlight that lay on her bare skin, turning it to gold.

'My big animal!' he muttered, quite delighted.

Then taking hold of her by her wrists, while she went on leaping about, he said:

'Listen, not today. I have a poor sick girl to see. But I'll come back some other morning... I promise.'

'When? Thursday?' she went on asking. 'You know the cow is with calf. For the last two days, she hasn't looked quite right. You're a doctor, you could perhaps give her something to make her better.'

Abbé Mouret, who had stayed there quietly, could not restrain a little laugh. The doctor gaily got back into his gig, and said:

'That's it, I'll look after the cow... Come here so I can kiss you, my big animal! You smell good, you smell of health. And you're worth more than all the others. If everyone were like my big animal, the earth would be so lovely.'

He clucked his tongue at the horse, and went on talking to himself as the gig rolled down the slope:

'Yes, brute animals, there should only be animals. All would be beautiful and happy and strong. Ah! what a dream!... Things have turned out well for the girl, who's as happy as her cow. And things have turned out badly for the boy, agonizing in his cassock. A bit more blood, a few more nerves, but then what! Life just goes wrong for people... Real Rougons and real Macquarts, those two children! The tail end of the tribe, the final degeneration.'

Then, urging on his horse, he went at a trot up the hill that led to the Paradou.

CHAPTER VII

SUNDAYS were very busy days for Abbé Mouret. He had Vespers, which he usually said to empty chairs, for even Mother Brichet didn't push her devotion to the point of coming back to church in the afternoon. Then at four o'clock, Brother Archangias brought the brats from his school for Monsieur le Curé to hear them recite their catechism lesson. That recitation often lasted until quite late. When the children became too uncontrollable, La Teuse was summoned to frighten them with her broom.

That particular Sunday, towards four o'clock, Désirée found herself alone in the presbytery. As she was feeling bored, she went to gather grass for her rabbits in the cemetery, where there were always splendid poppies, which the rabbits adored. She crawled about on her knees between the tombs, and brought back apronfuls of succulent greenery which her rabbits fell upon greedily.

'Oh, what lovely plantains!' she murmured, crouching beside the tombstone of Abbé Caffin, quite delighted with her find.

There indeed, growing out of cracks in the stone, magnificent plantains were displaying their wide leaves. She had just finished emptying her apron, when she thought she heard a very odd noise. A rustling of branches and a clattering of pebbles seemed to be coming up from the gully that bordered one side of the cemetery, at the bottom of which ran the Mascle, a torrent that flowed down from the heights of the Paradou. The slope was so steep, so unmanageable, that Désirée thought it might be a lost dog or a strayed goat. She rushed forward, and as she leaned over the side, she was astonished to see a girl climbing up through the brambles with amazing agility, making use of the slightest hollows in the rock.

'I'm coming to give you a hand,' she cried. 'You could break your neck.'

Seeing herself discovered, the girl started in fright, as if she were going to go back down. But she looked up, and grew bold enough to accept the hand that was held out to her.

'Oh! I recognize you,' Désirée went on, happily, letting go of her apron to give her a hug with her childlike affection. 'You gave me some blackbirds. They're dead, poor dear things, I was so sad about that... Wait, I know your name, I've heard it. La Teuse often says it when Serge isn't there. She said I mustn't repeat it... Wait a second, I'm going to remember.'

She was trying hard to remember, and the effort made her look very serious. Then, once she found it, she enjoyed repeating over and over the music of the name.

'Albine! Albine!... It's a very sweet name... At first I thought you were a tomtit, because I had a tomtit once, and gave it a name rather like that, I don't remember exactly what.'

Albine did not smile. She was quite white, though with a flame of fever in her eyes. There were drops of blood on her hands. When she got her breath back, she said quickly:

'No, don't bother. You'll stain your handkerchief if you wipe the blood off. It's nothing, just some scratches... I didn't want to come by the road, as I would have been seen. I decided to follow the river... Is Serge here?'

Hearing that name, spoken so familiarly, and with a certain ardour, did not shock Désirée. She replied that he was over there, in the church, doing the catechism.

'We mustn't speak loudly,' she added, putting a finger on her lips. 'Serge doesn't let me speak loudly when he's doing the catechism. If we're not quiet, they'll come and scold us... We'll go into the stable, shall we? We'll be all right there, and we can talk.'

'I want to see Serge,' said Albine in all simplicity.

Désirée, the grown-up child, again lowered her voice. She cast furtive glances at the church, and whispered:

'Yes, yes... we'll play a trick on Serge. Come with me. We'll hide, we won't make any noise. Oh! this is fun!'

She had gathered up the pile of grass that had fallen from her apron. She went out of the cemetery, and with infinite precautions, went back to the presbytery, asking Albine to hide behind her, and keep down low. Just as they were running across the courtyard to hide, they saw La Teuse going through the sacristy, but she seemed not to have seen them.

'Hush! hush!' Désirée repeated delightedly when they were safely huddled in the stable. 'Now nobody will find us... Here's some straw. Stretch out on it.'

Albine had to sit on a bundle of straw.

'And Serge?' she asked, with the stubbornness of the single-minded.

'Listen, you can hear his voice... When he claps his hands, it will be finished, and the little ones will go away... Listen, he's telling them a story.'

Abbé Mouret's voice was indeed reaching them, though softened, through the door of the sacristy that La Teuse had no doubt just opened. It was like a breath of pious devotion, a murmur, in which the name of Jesus was heard three times. Albine shivered. She was just rising to her feet to run to that beloved voice, whose caress she knew so well, when the sound seemed to fly away, snuffed out by the closing of the door. Then she sat down again, and seemed to be waiting, her hands clasped together, absorbed in the one thought burning deep in her clear eyes. Désirée, stretched out at her feet, gazed at her with innocent admiration.

'Oh! You're beautiful,' she murmured. 'You're like one of the pictures Serge used to have in his bedroom. She was all white like you, and she had long curls that hung around her neck; and she showed her red heart, just there, where I can feel yours beating... but you're not listening, you're sad. Let's play a game, shall we?'

But she broke off, crying out through gritted teeth, while still restraining her voice:

'Oh, the wretched creatures! They're going to get us caught!'

She had not let go of her apronful of grass, and her animals were taking her by storm. A flock of hens had run up, clucking and calling each other, and pecking at the green stalks that were sticking out. The goat pushed its head slyly under her arm, and was munching the big leaves. Even the cow, tied to the wall, was pulling at the rope, stretching out her muzzle, and puffing out her warm breath.

'Oh, the thieves!' Désirée repeated. 'This is for the rabbits!... Will you just leave me alone! You're going to get such a slap, you are. And you, if I catch you at it again I'll twist your tail... Horrible things! they'd eat my hands if they could!'

She slapped the goat, scattered the chickens with a few kicks, and hit the cow's muzzle with the full force of her fists. But the animals shook themselves and came back, even greedier than before, jumping on her, pressing in on her, tugging at her apron. And with a wink, she whispered in Albine's ear, as if the animals had been able to understand:

'Aren't they funny, the darlings! Just wait, and you'll be able to watch them eating.'

Albine looked on with a grave expression.

'Come on, behave yourselves,' Désirée went on. 'You shall all have some. But each one in turn... Big Liza first. My! you really like your plantain, don't you!'

Big Liza was the cow. She slowly chewed a handful of succulent leaves from the tomb of Abbé Caffin. A thin trickle of saliva hung from her muzzle. Her big brown eyes were full of gluttonous contentment.

'And now it's your turn,' Désirée continued, turning to the goat. 'Oh, I know you want the poppies. And you prefer them flowering, don't you? with buds that burst under your teeth like little packets of red embers... Look, here are some really lovely ones. They come from the left-hand side of the cemetery, where the burials were last year.'

And as she talked, she held out a bunch of blood-red flowers to the goat, who munched them up. When there was nothing but stalks left in her hands, she pushed these into his teeth. Behind her, the angry hens were pecking holes in her skirts. She threw them some wild chicory and dandelions she'd gathered from around the old flagstones lined up along the wall of the church. The hens fought especially fiercely over the dandelions, and with such voracity, such a rage of wings and claws, that the other animals in the farmyard heard them. So then there was a real invasion. The big tawny rooster, Alexander, was the first to appear. He seized a dandelion, and cut it in half without eating it, then called the hens that were still outside to come along, and he stood back to let them eat. A white hen came, then a black hen, then a long line of hens who bumped into each other, jumped on each other's tails, and ended up flowing along like a pool of crazy feathers. Behind the hens came the pigeons, then the ducks and the geese, and last of all, the turkeys. Désirée stood laughing, quite drowned and lost in the midst of this living flood, repeating:

'This happens every time I bring them grass from the cemetery. They'd kill each other for it... It must have a special sort of taste.'

She was struggling, holding the last handfuls of greenery up high, to save them from the gluttonous beaks thrusting up around her, and insisting that some had to be kept for the rabbits, and she was going to get really cross, and would put them all on a diet of dry bread. But she was weakening. The geese were pulling at the strings of her apron so roughly that she nearly fell on her knees. The ducks were devouring her ankles. Two pigeons had flown up on to her head. Hens were leaping up to her shoulders. It was the ferocity of animals scenting flesh, the rich plantains, the blood-red poppies, the dandelions bursting with sap, in which lay a little of the life of the dead. She was laughing too much, she could feel she was on the point of slipping and letting go of the last handfuls, when there was a terrible grunting that spread panic all around her.

'It's you, my fatty,' she said in delight. 'Eat them up and rescue me.'

The pig came on the scene. No longer was he the little piglet, pink as a freshly painted toy, with his rump bearing a tail like a piece of string; but a big strong pig, fit for slaughter, round as a cantor's belly, and his back covered with rough bristles that oozed fat. His belly was amber-coloured from sleeping on the dungheap. With his snout thrust forward, he rolled along and hurled himself among the animals, which allowed Désirée to escape and run to give the rabbits the few bits of greenery she had so valiantly defended. When she got back, peace had been restored. The geese were gently lolling their necks, stupid and satisfied; the ducks and turkeys were moving off along the walls, with the careful lumbering movements of unsteady animals; the hens were quietly cackling, pecking at invisible seed in the hard ground of the stable, while the pig, the goat, and the big cow were blinking their eyes as if slowly falling asleep. Outside, a thundery rain was beginning to fall.

'Oh well! here comes a shower,' said Désirée, who sat herself down on the straw again, with a shiver. 'You had better stay there, my darlings, if you don't want to get soaked.'

She turned to Albine to add:

'Don't they look silly! They only wake up to fall upon their food, these creatures!'

Albine had remained silent. The laughter of this splendid girl, struggling in the midst of those voracious necks and those greedy beaks that tickled her, kissed her, and seemed to want to eat her very flesh, had made Albine even whiter than before. So much joy, so much health, so much life, made her despair. She gripped her feverish arms, and pressed the emptiness to her bosom, drained by desertion.

'And Serge?' she asked, in her firm and stubborn voice.

'Hush!' said Désirée, 'I just heard his voice, he hasn't finished yet... We certainly made plenty of noise just now. La Teuse must be deaf this evening... Let's just stay quiet now. It's nice to listen to the rain falling.'

The rain came in through the open door, hitting the ground in large drops. Some chickens, nervous after venturing out, had retreated to the back of the stable. All the animals were taking refuge there, around the skirts of the two girls, except for three ducks who had gone off happily for a walk in the rain. The coolness of the water streaming down outside seemed to push the torrid fumes of the farmyard back inside. It was very warm in the straw. Désirée pulled over two big bales, stretched out on them as if they were pillows, and sank into them. She was very comfortable, enjoying it with her whole body.

'That's nice, so nice,' she murmured. 'Lie down like me. I just sink into it, I'm supported all over, and the straw tickles my neck... and when you rub it, the tickle runs along your whole body, as if you had mice hiding under your dress.'

She rubbed herself, and laughed, giving little slaps to right and left as if defending herself against the mice. Then she stayed with her head down, and knees in the air, and carried on:

'Do you roll in the straw, when you're at home? There's nothing I like better... Sometimes I tickle myself under my feet. That's quite fun too... Tell me, do you tickle yourself?'

But the big rooster who had been gravely approaching, seeing her stretched out, jumped on to her breast.

'Will you get away, Alexander!' she cried. 'Isn't he stupid, this creature! I can't lie down without him jumping on me like that... You're gripping me too hard, you're hurting me with your claws, d'you hear!... I'm quite willing to let you stay, but only if you're good, and you won't peck at my hair, all right?'

And she didn't bother about him any more. The rooster stayed firmly on her bodice, seeming at times to look at her under her chin, with burning eyes. The other animals gathered around her skirts. After rolling about a bit more, she had finally fallen into a sort of daze, in a comfortable position, with her limbs stretched out and her head thrown back. She went on:

'Oh! it's too nice, it makes me feel tired straight away. Straw makes you sleepy, doesn't it?... Serge doesn't like that. Perhaps you don't, either. So, what do you like, then?... Tell me, so I'll know.'

She was slowly dozing off. For a moment, she kept her eyes wide open, as if searching for some pleasure she did not know. Then she lowered her eyelids with a peaceful sigh, as if fully satisfied. She seemed to be sleeping, when, after a few minutes, she opened her eyes again and said:

'The cow is going to have a calf... That's nice too. That will be more fun than anything.'

And she slipped into a deep sleep. The animals had ended up climbing all over her. She was covered by a living flood of feathers. Hens seemed to be brooding on her feet. Geese laid the down of their necks upon her thighs. On the left, the rooster was keeping her side warm, while the goat, on the right, stretched out his bearded head right up to her armpit. And more or less everywhere there were pigeons perching, on her open hands, in the dent of her waist, and behind her drooping shoulders. And she was all pink as she slept, caressed by the cow's stronger breath, and smothered by the weight of the rooster, who had moved down below her breast, with flapping wings and crest blazing, his tawny belly burning her through her skirts with a caress of flame.

The rain outside was now much lighter. A patch of sunshine, escaping from the corner of a cloud, spattered the mist of flying raindrops with gold. Albine, keeping quite still, looked at Désirée sleeping, this handsome girl who satisfied her flesh by rolling in the straw. She wished she could be exhausted and swooning like that, lulled to sleep with pleasure, just through a few bits of straw tickling her neck. She envied those strong arms, that firm breast, that totally physical life in the fertile warmth of a herd of farmyard animals, that purely animal blossoming that made the plump child a tranquil sister of the big brown-and-white cow. She dreamed of being loved by a tawny rooster, and herself loving naturally, the way the trees grow, without shame, opening each of her veins to the spurts of sap. It was the earth that satisfied Désirée, when she lay down on her back. Meanwhile, the rain had completely stopped. The three cats of the household were walking along one after the other beside the wall in the yard, with infinite precautions to avoid getting wet. They poked their heads into the stable and came straight to the sleeping girl, purring, and lay down beside her, with their paws on a bit of her skin. Moumou, the big black cat, huddled up against one of her cheeks, and began gently licking her chin.

'And Serge?' Albine asked, mechanically.

What was the obstacle? Who was preventing her from satisfying herself in the same way, happy in the midst of nature? Why could she not love, why could she not be loved, out in the sun, freely, as the trees grow? She did not know, she felt herself to be abandoned forever, bruised forever. And she felt a wild obstinacy, a need to recapture her love in her arms, to hide it and enjoy it again. Then she stood up. The door of the sacristy had just been reopened; a slight clapping of hands was heard, followed by the noise of a band of children clattering over the flagstones with their wooden shoes; the catechism was over. She quietly left the stable, where she had been waiting for an hour in the warm steamy air of the farmyard. As she slipped along the corridor of the sacristy, she saw the back of La Teuse, who returned to her kitchen without turning her head. And, certain she had not been seen, she pushed the door, keeping her hand on it so that it would not make a noise. She was in the church.

CHAPTER VIII

AT first she could see nobody. Outside it was raining again, with a fine, persistent drizzle. She went behind the main altar and then on to the pulpit. In the middle of the nave were the benches disarranged by the catechism children. The pendulum of the clock was beating dully in the emptiness. Then she went down and knocked on the woodwork of the confessional that she could see at the other end. But as she was passing the chapel of the Dead, she found Abbé Mouret prostrated at the feet of the big, bleeding Christ. He did not move. He must have thought that La Teuse was rearranging the benches behind him. Albine laid a hand on his shoulder.

'Serge,' she said, 'I've come to get you.'

The priest looked up with a start; he was very pale. He remained on his knees, and crossed himself, while his lips went on mumbling his prayer.

'I waited,' she went on. 'Every morning, every evening, I looked to see if you were coming. I counted the days, then I stopped counting. It's been weeks... Then when I realized you weren't going to come, I came myself. I told myself: "I'll take him away." Give me your hands, and let's go.'

She held out her hands, as if to help him get up. He crossed himself again. He went on praying as he looked at her. He had calmed that first tremor of his flesh. In the grace which had flooded into him since that morning, like some celestial bath, he found superhuman strength.

'This is not the right place for you,' he said gravely. 'Leave now... You are only making your suffering worse.'

'I'm not suffering any more,' she went on with a smile. 'I'm better now. I'm well again, now I can see you... Listen, I pretended to be more ill than I really was, so that they'd send for you. I can admit it now. It's like that promise I made, to go away, to leave this part of the world, once I'd found you again, you can't have imagined I would have kept it. Oh well! I would have carried you away on my shoulders rather than that... The others don't know, but you know perfectly well that I can't now live anywhere except in your arms.'

She became happy again, drawing near him with the easy caresses of a child, not seeing his cold and rigid attitude. Growing impatient, she clapped her hands joyfully, crying:

'Come on, make your mind up, Serge! You're making us waste time! There's no need for so much thinking about it. I'm just taking you away, that's all! It's quite simple... If you don't want to be seen, we'll go away along the Mascle. It's not an easy route, but I did it by myself, and with two of us, we can help each other. You know the way, don't you? We cross the cemetery and go down to the edge of the torrent, then we only have to follow it until we reach the garden. And there, after all, we're quite at home! There's nobody there, nobody, just bushes and lovely round stones. The riverbed is almost dry. As I came, I thought: "When he's with me, in a little while, we'll walk along quietly, in a warm embrace." Come on, hurry up. I'm waiting for you, Serge.'

The priest seemed no longer to be hearing her. He had returned to his prayers, asking Heaven for the courage of the saints. Before engaging in the supreme battle, he was arming himself with the flaming swords of faith. For a moment he feared he might weaken. He had needed the heroism of a martyr to keep his knees firmly on the flagstones while Albine's every word called out to him: his heart went out to her, all his blood rose up to throw him into her arms, with an irresistible longing to kiss her hair. With the very scent of her breath, she had in a single second awakened and passed over to him the memories of their love, the vast garden, the walks beneath the trees, the joy of their union. But grace bathed him with its most abundant dew; it was only the torture of a moment, it drained the blood from his veins and nothing human was left in him. He was now no more than a thing that belonged to God.

Albine had to touch his shoulder again. She was worried, and gradually becoming irritated.

'Why don't you answer? You can't refuse, you are going to follow me... Just think it would kill me if you refused. But no, that's just not possible. Remember. We were together, and we were never going to be parted. A score of times you gave yourself to me. You told me to take you, all of you, to take your limbs, your breath, and your life... I didn't dream that, did I? There is no part of your body that you didn't give me, not one hair of your head that is not mine. You have a birthmark on your left shoulder. I have kissed it, it belongs to me. Your hands are mine, I have held them in mine for days. And your face, your lips, your eyes, your brow, all of that is mine, I have had them all at my bidding, for my love. Do you hear, Serge?'

She stood majestically before him, stretching out her arms. In a louder voice she repeated:

'Do you hear, Serge? You belong to me.'

Then, slowly, Abbé Mouret stood up. Leaning against the altar, he said:

'No, you are wrong, I belong to God.'

He was full of serenity. His bare face was like that of a stone saint whose entrails are free of any troubling warmth. His cassock fell in straight folds like a black shroud, revealing not the slightest hint of a body. Albine shrank back at the sight of this sombre ghost of her love. No longer could she see that abundant beard, that abundant hair. Now, in the middle of the shorn hair she could see a pallid patch, the tonsure, which disturbed her like some strange disease, some malignant wound that had developed there to devour the memory of the days of happiness. She could not recognize his hands, once so warm and caressing, nor could she see his supple neck, once resonant with laughter, nor his agile feet that had galloped along, carrying her through all the greenery. Was this really the boy with the strong muscles, whose open collar showed the hair of his chest, whose skin was radiant with sun, his loins vibrant with life, and in whose embrace she had lived a whole season? Now he seemed no longer made of flesh, his hair had shamefully fallen off, and all his virility was dried up in that woman's garment that left him devoid of sex.

'Oh!' she murmured, 'you're frightening me... Did you think me dead, so you're in mourning? Take off that black thing, put a shirt on. You'll roll up your sleeves, and we'll go fishing for crayfish again... Your arms were as fair as mine.'

She had laid her hand on his cassock as if intending to tear the fabric. He pushed her away with a gesture, without touching her. He gazed at her, strengthening himself against temptation, never taking his eyes off her. She seemed to have grown up. No longer was she the wild girl collecting bunches of wild flowers, casting her gypsy laughter to the winds, nor the lover in white skirts, bending her slim waist, and walking slowly and fondly between the hedges. Now a peachlike down adorned her lips, there was a freedom of movement in her hips, her bosom had blossomed like a ripe flower. She had become a woman, with her long, oval face seeming to express her fertility. Life lay dormant in her broadened frame. On her cheeks, and on her very skin, lay the adorable ripeness of her body. And the priest, wrapped in the passionate scent of the mature woman, felt a bitter joy in facing the caress of her red lips, the laughter of her eyes, the appeal of her bosom, the intoxication that flowed from her at her slightest movement. He pushed his courage so far as to seek out the places on her body that he had once madly kissed, the corners of her eyes, the corners of her lips, her narrow temples, soft as satin, her amber neck, silky as velvet.

Never, not even in Albine's arms, had he felt the happiness he now experienced in this voluntary martyrdom, as he boldly faced the passion he was refusing. Then he feared he might yield to some new temptation of the flesh. He lowered his eyes, and said softly:

'I cannot listen to you here. Let's go outside, if you really wish to increase the pain for both of us... Our presence in this place is a scandal. We are in God's house.'

'God? Who's that?' cried Albine, returning once more to the great child of nature she had been. 'I don't know him, your God, and I don't want to know him if he's stealing you away from me, who have never done him any harm. My uncle Jeanbernat is quite right then to say that your God is an invention of wickedness, just a way of frightening people, and making them weep... You're lying, you don't love me any more, your God doesn't exist.'

'You are in his house,' Abbé Mouret repeated insistently. 'You are blaspheming. With one breath he could reduce you to dust.'

She gave a proud and scornful laugh. She raised her arms, she was challenging Heaven.

'So,' she said, 'you prefer your God to me! You think he is stronger than me! You imagine he will love you more than I do... Well, you're just a child. Leave this nonsense. We'll go back to the garden together, and love each other, and we'll be happy and free. That will be life.'

This time she had managed to clasp him by the waist and was pulling him away.

But he freed himself, his body quivering from her embrace, and went and leant against the altar, forgetting himself so far as to address her as *tu*, as he had done before: 'Go away,' he stammered. 'If you still love me, go away. Oh! Lord, forgive her, forgive me, for soiling your house. If I were to go through the door behind her, I might perhaps follow her. Here, in your house, I am strong. Allow me to stay here to defend you.'

Albine was silent for a moment. Then in a calmer tone, she said:

'Very well, let's stay here... I want to speak to you. You cannot be wicked. You cannot let me leave without you... No, don't defend yourself. I shan't take hold of you again since that hurts you. You see, I'm very calm. We are going to talk quietly, like the times when we lost our way and didn't even try to find our way again so that we could go on talking.'

She was smiling, and then went on:

'I don't really know. Uncle Jeanbernat would not allow me to come to church. He would say: "Silly girl, since you have a garden, what would you be doing in a hovel of that sort?..." I grew up very happy. I looked into nests, but never touched the eggs. I didn't even pick flowers in case I made the plants bleed. And you know I never caught an insect and tormented it. So why would God be angry with me?'

'You have to know him, pray to him, and give him the homage that is his due, every hour of the day.'

'That would be enough, would it?' she continued. 'Then you'd forgive me, and love me again?... Well, I want whatever you want. Tell me about God. I'll believe in him, I'll worship him. Every single word of yours will be a truth that I shall hear on my knees. Have I ever had any other thoughts than yours?... Once more we'll go on our long walks, you will teach me, you will make of me whatever you will. Oh! Just say yes, I beg you!'

Abbé Mouret pointed to his cassock.

'I cannot,' he said simply; 'I am a priest.'

'Priest!' she repeated, no longer smiling. 'Yes, Uncle says priests have no wife, no sister, no mother. That's true, then... But why did you come? You took me as your sister and your wife. Were you just lying?'

He raised his face to her, pale, and showing beads of anguished sweat.

'I have sinned,' he murmured.

'As for me,' she went on, 'when I saw how free you were, I thought you weren't a priest any more. I thought that was over and done with, and you'd always be there, for me and with me... And now what do you expect me to do, if you take away my whole life?'

'The same thing that I do,' he replied: 'get on your knees, die on your knees, don't get up until God has forgiven you.'

'So you're a coward, then?' she said, full of anger again, with her lips curled in scorn.

He staggered, but kept silent. A dreadful suffering gripped his throat, but he remained strong, overcoming his pain. He held his head up straight, with even the hint of a smile at the corner of his trembling lips. Albine held him for a moment in a fixed stare. Then, with renewed passion, she cried:

'Come on, answer me, accuse me, tell me it was I who came and tempted you.* That will be the last straw. Go on, I'll allow you to excuse yourself. You can even beat me. I'd rather feel your blows than your corpse-like stiffness. Do you now have no blood in your veins? Don't you hear me calling you a coward? Yes, you are a coward, you should not have loved me, since you cannot be a man... Is it your black robe that's holding you back? Tear it off. When you're naked, perhaps you'll remember.'

The priest slowly repeated the same words:

'I have sinned, I have no excuse. I am doing penance for my sin, without hoping for forgiveness. If I tore off my robe, I'd be tearing off my body, for I have given myself to God, my whole self, my soul and my bones... I am a priest.'

'And I? What am I?' came Albine's final cry.

He did not bow his head.

'May your sufferings be counted against me as so many crimes! May I be eternally punished for the way I must now abandon you! That will be just... All unworthy as I am, I pray for you every night.'

She shrugged her shoulders with utter discouragement. Her anger had abated. She was filled with something like pity.

'You're mad,' she said quietly. 'Keep your prayers. It's you I want... You will never understand. I had so much to tell you! And there you are, just making me angry with your stories of the other world... Look, let's both be sensible. Let's wait until we've calmed down. We'll talk again... It's simply not possible for me just to go away like that. I can't leave you here. It's because you're here that you're like a dead person, with skin so cold I don't dare touch you... Let's not talk any more now... Let's wait.'

She stopped talking, and moved a few steps away. She was examining the little church. The rain was still pattering down the windows like grey ash. A cold rain-soaked light made the walls look wet. No sound came from outside save the monotonous rumble of the rain. The sparrows must have hidden away under the roof tiles, the rowan tree stretched out vague branches, drowned in a watery mist. The clock struck five, each stroke seeming torn, one after the other, from its cracked, wheezy chest; then the silence deepened, became more mute, more blind, more despairing. The new paintwork, scarcely dry, made the main altar and the woodwork look clean but gloomy, like a convent chapel that never sees the sun. The whole nave was filled with a terrible agony, splashed with the blood flowing from the limbs of the big Christ; and along the walls, the fourteen stations of the Cross displayed their atrocious drama, bedaubed with yellow and red, exuding horror. Life itself was agonizing here, in this shudder of death, in these altars like tombs, in all the bare starkness of a funeral vault. Everything spoke of slaughter, night, terror, extinction, and nothingness. A last whiff of incense hung in the air, like the last loving breath of some dead woman, lying jealously suffocated under the flagstones.

'Ah!' said Albine at last, 'how lovely it was in the sunshine, do you remember? One morning, just to the left of the flower garden, we were walking beside a hedge of tall rose bushes. I remember the colour of the grass: it was almost blue, with a shimmer of green. When we got to the end of the hedge, we turned and walked back, the sunshine there had so sweet a scent. And that was our whole walk that morning, twenty steps forward and twenty steps back, a place of such happiness you did not want to leave. Honeybees were buzzing, and a blue tit stayed with us, flitting from branch to branch; all around us troupes of creatures went off on their own errands. You were murmuring "How good life is!" Life was the grass, the trees, the streams, the sky, the sunlight in which we stood, blond beings with hair of gold.'

She seemed to dream for a moment, then went on:

'Life was the Paradou. How big it seemed to us! We never were able to find the end of it. All that greenery seemed to roll away to the horizon with no bounds, with a sound like the sea. And so much blue above our heads! We could grow, fly, and run like the clouds, without meeting any more obstacle than they do. The very air was ours.'

She paused, and gestured at the crumbling walls of the church.

'And here, you're in a grave. If you stretched out your arms, you'd graze your hands on stone. The vaulted roof hides the sky and robs you of sunlight. It's so small that your limbs grow stiff, as if you were buried alive.'

'No,' said the priest, 'the church is as big as the world. It can hold God in his entirety.'

With another wave of her hand, she pointed to the crucifixes, the dying Christs, the agonies of the Passion.

'And you live with death all around you. The grass and the trees, the streams, the sun and the sky, everything lies dying around you...'

'No, everything is reborn, everything is purified, everything returns to the source of all light.'

He had stood up, his eyes ablaze. He left the altar, invincible now, burning with such faith that he no longer feared the dangers of temptation. He took Albine's hand, speaking to her in the familiar *tu* form, as if she were his sister, and led her over to the distressing pictures of the stations of the Cross.

'Look,' he said, 'this is what my God suffered... here Jesus is being beaten with rods. As you see, his shoulders are bare, the flesh is torn, and blood is flowing down his back... Jesus is crowned with thorns. Red tears stream from his pierced brow. A big cut has opened up his temple... Jesus is mocked by the soldiers. His executioners have thrown a strip of purple cloth around his shoulders to mock him, and they spit on his face, they strike him, they use a stick to press the crown of thorns deeper into his brow...'

Albine turned away to avoid seeing the crudely coloured pictures on which scars of red paint cut across the ochre of Jesus's body. The purple cloak round his neck looked like a shred of his torn skin.

'Why all this suffering and dying?' was her answer. 'O Serge! if you would just remember!... You told me, that day, that you were tired. And I knew you were lying, because it was a cool day and we had not been walking more than a quarter of an hour. But you wanted to sit down so you could take me in your arms. At the end of the orchard, as you know, there was a cherry tree growing on the edge of a stream, and you could not walk past it without needing to kiss my hands, with little kisses that went up along my shoulders to my lips. The cherry season was over, so you were eating my lips instead... The fading of flowers made us cry. One day, you found a little warbler dead in the grass, and you turned quite pale, and clasped me to your breast, as if to forbid the earth ever to take me.'

The priest led her over to the other stations.

'Be quiet,' he said, 'look some more, listen some more. You must prostrate yourself in grief and pity... Jesus collapses under the weight of the Cross. The climb to Calvary is very hard. He has fallen on his knees. He does not even wipe the sweat off his face, but gets up again, and goes on walking... again Jesus collapses under the weight of the Cross. At every step, he staggers. This time he has fallen on his side, fallen so hard that for a moment he is left breathless. His torn hands have let the Cross slip. His suffering feet leave bloody footprints behind him. He is crushed by an appalling weariness, for he carries on his shoulders the sins of the whole world.'

Albine had looked at Jesus, in a blue skirt, stretched out beneath the disproportionately huge cross, with the blackness of its colour running over and staining the gold of his halo. Then gazing vaguely into the distance, she murmured:

'Oh! the paths of the grasslands!... So you have no more memory, Serge? You no longer know the lanes of fine grass that go across the meadows, surrounded by great lakes of greenery?... On the afternoon I'm telling you about, we had set out just for an hour. But we kept going onward, so that when the stars appeared, we were still walking. It was so soft, that endless carpet, smooth as silk! Our feet never touched a stone. It was like a green sea, whose mossy waters cradled us. And we knew very well where they were taking us, those tender paths that led nowhere. They were taking us to our love, to the joy of living with our arms around each other, to the certainty of a whole day of happiness... We returned home with no tiredness. You were lighter than when we set out, because you had given me your caresses, and I had not been able to return them all.'

Abbé Mouret, his hands trembling in anguish, pointed to the last of the images. He stammered out:

'And Jesus is nailed to the Cross. Hammer blows drive the nails into his open hands. One nail is enough for the feet, where the bones snap. He, while his flesh quivers in pain, smiles, raising his eyes to Heaven... Jesus is between the two thieves.* The weight of his body horribly stretches his wounds. A sweat of blood streams down from his brow and his limbs. The two thieves insult him, passers-by jeer at him, the soldiers share out his clothes. And darkness descends, the sun is hidden... Jesus dies on the Cross. He gives a great cry, and renders up his spirit. O terrible death! The Temple veil* was ripped in two from top to bottom, the earth shook, rocks split apart, and graves opened...'

He had fallen on to his knees, his voice choked by sobs and his eyes on the three crosses of Calvary, on which writhed the pallid bodies of the crucified, their bodies made hideously skeletal in the crude drawing. Albine placed herself in front of the images so that he should no longer see them.

'One evening,' she said, 'during a long twilight, I had put my head on your lap... It was in the forest, at the end of that long avenue of chestnut trees through which the setting sun threaded its last rays. Oh! what an affectionate farewell! The sun lingered at our feet with a kind and friendly smile, bidding us "au revoir". The sky was slowly growing paler. I told you with a laugh that it was taking off its blue robe, and putting on its black robe with the gold flowers on it, to go out for the evening. You were waiting for the shade, eager to be alone, without the sun bothering us. And it wasn't night that came, it was a gentle quietness, a veiled tenderness, a little nest of mystery, like one of those very dark paths one enters just to hide for a moment, knowing that at the other end one will find again the joy of full daylight. That evening the twilight in its pale serenity carried the promise of a splendid morning to come... So, seeing that the day was not disappearing fast enough for you, I pretended to fall asleep. I can tell you now that I was not asleep while you kissed my eyes. I enjoyed those kisses. I had to make an effort to keep from laughing. My breathing was regular and you drank in my breath. Then, when it was dark, it was like being slowly lulled to sleep. For the trees, you see, were no more asleep than I was... That night, you remember, the flowers had a stronger scent.'

As he remained on his knees, his face flooded with tears, she gripped his wrists, and pulled him up, then said with passion:

'Oh! if you only knew, you would tell me to carry you off, you would bind your arms round my neck so I couldn't go away without you... Yesterday, I decided to see the garden again. It's even bigger, more profound, and more unfathomable than ever. I found new scents in it, scents so exquisite they made me cry. In the avenues, I met showers of sunshine that drenched me with a shivering of desire. The roses spoke to me of you. The bullfinches were astonished at seeing me alone. The whole garden was sighing... Oh! come, never have the grasses unrolled such soft beds. I have marked with a flower the secret place to which

I want to take you. It's deep in the shrubbery, an open patch of greenery as wide as a large bed. From there you can hear the garden living,
with its trees, its streams, and its sky. The breathing of the earth itself
will lull us to sleep... Oh! come, and we shall love each other in the
love of everything around us.'

But he pushed her away. He had come back in front of the chapel
of the Dead, facing the big Christ of painted cardboard, the size of
a ten-year-old child, in a death agony represented with horrible ver-
acity. The nails really looked like iron, and the wounds gaped ever
wider, hideously torn.

'Jesus who died for us,' he cried, 'tell her of our nothingness! Tell
her that we are dust, filth, and damnation! Ah wait! let me cover my
head with a hair shirt, and lay my head at your feet, and let me stay there,
unmoving, until death comes to rot me... The earth will no longer exist.
The sun will be extinguished. I shall no longer see, no longer feel, no
longer hear. Nothing in this wretched world will come to distract my
soul from worshipping you.'

He was growing more and more excited. He walked towards Albine,
his hands in the air.

'You're right, this is a place of death, death is what I want, death
that delivers and saves us from all corruption... Do you hear? I deny
life, I refuse it, I spit upon it. Your flowers stink, your sun blinds people, your grass makes lepers of those who lie in it, your garden is a char-
nel house in which the corpses of all things lie rotting. The earth exudes
abomination. You lie when you speak of love and light and a life of
happiness in your palace of greenery. Where you live there is only
darkness. Your trees distil a poison that turns men into beasts; your
thickets are black with the venom of vipers; your rivers bear pestilence
in their blue waters. If I stripped your nature of its skirt of sunshine and
its belt of leaves, you would see it hideous as a harpy devoured by
vices, with ribs like a skeleton... And even if you spoke the truth, if
your hands were full of delights, if you were to carry me off on a bed
of roses to offer me the dream of paradise, I would defend myself with
even greater desperation against your embrace. Between us, there is
a war, centuries-old and implacable. You see, the church is indeed
small, it is poor, it is ugly, it has a confessional and a pulpit of pine,
a plaster font, and altars made of four planks that I repainted myself.
What does that matter! It is bigger than your garden, this valley, and
the whole earth. It's a powerful fortress that nothing will overthrow.

In vain will it be assailed by winds and sun, by forests and seas, and by every living thing; it will remain standing, not even shaken. Yes, let the bushes grow, let them batter the walls with their thorny arms, and let swarms of insects rise through the cracks in the ground to come and gnaw at the walls; the church, no matter how ruined, will never be carried away in that overflowing of life! It is impregnable death... And do you know what is going to happen one day? The little church will become so enormous, and cast such a shadow that all of nature will die. Ah! death, the death of everything, with the heavens gaping to receive our souls above the abominable ruins of the world!'

He was shouting now; and pushing Albine roughly towards the door. She, very pale, was moving back, step by step. When he fell silent, she said gravely, in a strangled voice:

'So this is the end, and you're driving me away?... And yet I am your wife. You made me what I am. After allowing that to happen, God cannot punish us to that extent.'

She was on the threshold. Then she added:

'Listen, every day when the sun goes down, I'll go to the end of the garden, to the place where the wall has crumbled... I'll be waiting for you.'

And she went away. The door of the sacristy closed with a muffled sigh.

CHAPTER IX

THE church was silent. But the rain, falling more heavily now and beating on the roof, echoed through the nave like an organ. In the sudden calm, the priest's anger subsided; he felt a wave of tenderness. And it was with a face streaming with tears, and shoulders heaving with sobs, that he went back and threw himself on his knees before the big Christ. An expression of ardent gratitude burst from his lips.

'Oh! thank you, my God, for the help you have so kindly given me. Without your grace, I would have listened to the voice of my flesh, and returned to the wretchedness of my sin. Your grace girded my loins like a warrior's shield; your grace was my armour, my courage, the inner support which held me up with no weakening. O my God, you were within me; it was you who spoke in me, for I no longer felt the cowardice of my fleshly being, I felt strong enough to cut all the bonds of my heart. And here is my heart, my bleeding heart; it now belongs to no one, it is yours. For you I have torn it away from the world. But do not think, my God, that I draw any pride from this victory. I know I am nothing without you. I cast myself down at your feet in my humility.'

He sank down, half sitting on the altar step, no longer able to find words, but letting his breath escape like incense from between his half-open lips. The plenitude of grace bathed him in an inexpressible ecstasy. He turned in on himself, seeking Jesus in the depths of his being, in the sanctuary of love that he was constantly making ready, in order to receive him worthily. And Jesus was present, he could tell he was there, by the extraordinary sweetness that flooded through him. He then began, with Jesus, one of those inner conversations during which he felt carried away from the earth, talking mouth to mouth with his God. He stammered out the verse from the Song of Songs:* 'My beloved is mine, and I am his: he feedeth among the lilies. Until the day break, and the shadows flee away.' He pondered on the words from *The Imitation of Christ*:* 'It is a great art to know how to hold converse with Jesus, and to know how to keep Jesus is wisdom indeed.' Then there was an adorable familiarity. Jesus came down and talked with him for hours about his needs, his joys, and his hopes. These confidences had all the tenderness of two friends meeting again after a separation, and sitting together on the bank of some solitary river; for Jesus, at these times of divine freedom, deigned to be his friend, his best, most faithful friend, who could never betray him, and who, in return for some affection, offered all the treasures of eternal life. This time especially, the priest meant to keep him a long time. He was still listening to him, in the silence of all living creatures, when six o'clock struck in the quiet church.

This was a confession of his whole being, a free exchange without the cumbersome intervention of the tongue, a natural effusion of the heart, flying out even before thought itself. Abbé Mouret told Jesus everything, as to a God who had entered into the intimacy of his feelings, and could be told everything. He confessed that he still loved Albine; he was amazed that he had been able to ill-treat her and drive her away without a complete revolt of his very entrails; it astonished him; and he smiled serenely, as if looking upon some act of miraculous fortitude accomplished by another. And Jesus replied that it should not astonish him, for the greatest saints were often unknowingly instruments in the hands of God. Then the abbé expressed a doubt: had he not been less worthy, having taken refuge at the foot of the altar and even in the Passion of his Lord? Was he not, after all, of but feeble courage, since he did not dare to fight alone? But Jesus was tolerant; he explained that the weakness of mankind is the constant concern of God, he especially loved suffering souls, whom he would visit, and sit with, like one going to the bedside of a sick friend. Was it a damnation to love Albine? No, if that love went beyond the flesh, and if it added a hope to the desire for another life. But how should he love her? Without saying a word, without taking one step towards her, but letting that pure affection rise up like a sweet scent pleasing to Heaven? Then Jesus gave a little laugh, full of kindness, drawing nearer and encouraging his confessions, so the priest gradually grew bold enough to describe in detail the beauty of Albine. She had the fair hair of the angels. She was all white, with large, gentle eyes, like the haloed saints. Jesus was silent, but still laughing. And how tall she had grown! She was like a queen now, with her rounded figure and her splendid shoulders. Oh! to hold her round her waist, if only for a second, and feel those shoulders falling back beneath his embrace! The laughter of Jesus grew faint and died away, like the light of a star disappearing on the horizon. Abbé Mouret was talking to himself now. Really, he had been too hard on her. Why did he drive Albine away without a single tender word, when love was permitted by Heaven?

'I love her, I love her!' he cried aloud, in a desperate voice that echoed through the church.

He could still see her there. She stretched out her arms to him, she was desirable enough to make him break every one of his vows. And he threw himself upon her breast, with no respect for the church; he seized hold of her limbs, and possessed her under a hail of kisses. It was before her that he knelt, imploring her for mercy, begging forgiveness for his brutality. He explained that at times there was a voice in him that was not his. Would he ever have ill-treated her? It was only that alien voice that had spoken to her. It could not be he, he who would not have touched a hair of her head without trembling. And he had driven her away, the church really was empty! Where should he run to find her again, to bring her back, and dry her tears with his caresses? The rain was falling harder now. The roads were lakes of mud. He imagined her battered by the rain, stumbling along beside the ditches, with her skirts soaked and sticking to her skin. No, no, it was not he, it was that other, that jealous voice, that had been cruel enough to want the death of his love.

'O Jesus!' he cried, more desperately still, 'be kind, give her back to me.'

But Jesus wasn't there any more... Then Abbé Mouret, awakening with a start, turned dreadfully pale. He understood. He had not been able to keep Jesus with him. He was losing his friend, leaving himself with no defence against evil. Instead of the inner light that had illuminated his whole being, and in which he had received his God, he now found nothing within him but darkness, a noxious vapour that irritated his flesh. Jesus, in leaving, had taken away his grace. He, who since that morning had been so strong with Heaven's help, now suddenly felt wretched, abandoned, with the weakness of an infant. And what an atrocious fall, what colossal bitterness! To have fought heroically, to have remained invincible and implacable when temptation was there, present and living, with her rounded figure, her splendid shoulders, her scent of womanly passion; then to succumb so shamefully, panting with abominable desire, when the temptation was no longer there, having left behind her only the rustling of a skirt, and a fragrance floating up from a blonde neck! Now, with nothing more than memories, she came back all-powerful, invading the whole church.

'Jesus! Jesus!' the priest cried out one last time, 'come back, come back into me, speak to me again!'

Jesus remained deaf to his cry. For a moment, Abbé Mouret implored Heaven, his arms raised in desperate supplication. His shoulders seemed to be breaking with the extraordinary force of his appeals. But soon his hands fell down in discouragement. In Heaven there was one of those hopeless silences sometimes experienced by the devout. Then he sat down again on the altar step, his face ashen, pressing his sides with his elbows as if to master his fleshly being. He was trying to shrink away from the bite of temptation.

'My God! you are abandoning me,'* he murmured. 'Your will be done.'

And he spoke not another word, breathing heavily like a hunted animal paralysed by fear of cruel teeth. Ever since his sin, he had become the plaything of grace, subject to its caprices. It would refuse even his most ardent appeals, then arrive, delightful and unexpected, just when he thought he would not receive it for years. The first few times he had been angry, speaking like a betrayed lover, demanding the immediate return of that great comforter, whose kiss made him so strong. Then, after useless fits of anger, he had understood that humility was less damaging to him, was indeed the only thing that could help him to bear his abandonment. So for hours, even days, he humbled himself, expecting a relief that never came. In vain did he put himself totally in the hands of God, abasing himself before Him, and endlessly repeating the most effective prayers: he could no longer feel the presence of God; his body, escaping from restraint, rose up in desire; his prayers, stumbling on his lips, ended in a filthy mumbling. It was a slow agony of temptation, in which the weapons of faith fell, one by one, from his faltering hands, and he became merely an inert thing in the clutches of his passions, observing with horror his own ignominy, without finding the courage even to lift a little finger to drive away sin. Such was his life now. He knew all the ways in which sin could attack. Not a day went by without his being tested. Sin took on a thousand different guises, crept in through his eyes and ears, rounded on him and gripped him by the throat, jumped treacherously on to his shoulders, or tortured him in his very bones. His sin was always with him; the nakedness of Albine, dazzling as a sun, lit up the greenery of the Paradou. He saw her constantly, save when grace kindly closed his eyelids with its cool caress. And he hid his suffering like a shameful disease. He shut himself away in those bleak silences that no one could make him break, filling the presbytery with his martyrdom, and exasperating La Teuse who, behind his back, shook her fist at Heaven.

This time he was alone, he could suffer his agony without any shame. Sin had felled him with such a blow that he did not have the strength to get up from the altar step, on which he had fallen. He stayed there, panting noisily, burning with anguish, and finding not a tear. And he thought of the serenity of his former life. Oh, what peace, what calm confidence he had in his first days at Les Artaud! Salvation then seemed a beautiful path. At that time he would laugh when people spoke of temptation. He lived surrounded by wickedness, without recognizing it, without fearing it, certain that for him it would be powerless. He was a perfect priest, so ignorant before God, able to be led along by the hand of God like a small child. Now all that childlike innocence was gone. God visited him each morning and straight away tested him. Temptation had now become his very life on earth. Age and sin had carried him into an eternal combat. Was it then that God now loved him more? The great saints had left shreds of their flesh upon the thorns of the Via Dolorosa.* He tried to find some comfort in this belief. At each tearing of his flesh, each cracking of his bones, he promised himself extraordinary rewards. Heaven could never punish him enough. He went so far as to despise his former serenity, that easy fervour which had him kneeling in girlish delight, without even feeling the bruising of his knees on the ground. He put his mind to finding pleasure in the depth of suffering, to lie on it, and sleep on it. But while he went on blessing God, his teeth chattered with ever greater horror, and the voice of his rebellious blood screamed that all of that was a lie, and that the only desirable joy was to lie in the arms of Albine, beside the flowering hedges of the Paradou.

Meanwhile, he had abandoned Mary for Jesus, sacrificing his heart in order to conquer his body, striving to put virility into his faith. Mary troubled him too much with her narrow bands of hair, her outstretched hands, and womanly smile. He could not kneel before her without lowering his eyes for fear of seeing the hem of her skirts. He also accused her of making herself too kind to him in former times; she had kept him so long in the folds of her skirt that he had let himself slide from her arms into the arms of a human creature, without even noticing that he was transferring his affections. And he remembered the brutalities of Brother Archangias, his refusal to worship Mary, and the suspicious gaze with which he seemed to look at her. He despaired of ever reaching that degree of roughness; he simply neglected her, hid her pictures, and deserted her altar. But she remained deep in his heart, like an unacknowledged love, always present. With a sacrilege that filled him with horror, sin had made use of her to tempt him. When he still called upon her at moments of irresistible tenderness, it was Albine who appeared in the white veil, with the blue sash tied round her waist, and the gold roses on her bare feet. All the different images of the Virgin—the Virgin with the golden royal cloak, the Virgin with the crown of stars, the Virgin visited by the angel of the Annunciation, the peaceful Virgin standing between a lily and a distaff—all brought back to him the memory of Albine, her smiling eyes, her delicate mouth, or the soft curve of her cheeks. His sin had killed the virginity of Mary. So, with a supreme effort, he drove womanhood out of religion, taking refuge in Jesus, whose gentleness also disturbed him sometimes. He needed a jealous God, an implacable God, the God of the Bible, surrounded by thunder, showing himself only to punish the terrified world. There were no more saints, no more angels, no more mother of God; there was only God, God the omnipotent master, who demanded every breath for himself. He felt the hand of God crushing his back, holding him at his mercy in space and time, like a guilty atom. To be nothing, to be damned, to long for hell, to struggle in vain against the monsters of temptation, that was good. From Jesus he would take only the cross. He had that same obsession with the cross that has worn away so many lips upon the crucifix. He took the cross, and he followed Jesus. He made it heavier, made it crushing, and had no greater joy than to collapse beneath it, and carry it when he was on his knees, his back broken. He saw in the cross the strength of the soul, the joy of the spirit, the supreme achievement of virtue, the perfection of sanctity. In the cross there was everything, and everything led to dying upon it. Suffering, dying, these words resounded constantly in his ears, like the peak of human wisdom. And when he had attached himself to the cross, he had the boundless consolation of the love of God. It was no longer Mary that he loved with filial tenderness and the passion of a lover. He loved for the sake of loving, in the absoluteness of love. He loved God more than himself, more than all else, in a splendour of light. He was like a torch that consumes itself in light. Death, when he wished for it, was in his eyes only a great surge of love.

What, then, had he failed to do, to be subjected to such severe trials? He wiped away with his hand the sweat that flowed from his brow; and reflected that only that morning he had examined his conscience without finding any serious offence. Was he not leading a life of austerity and mortifications? Did he not love God solely and blindly? Oh, how he would have blessed him, if he had at last granted him peace, judging him sufficiently punished for his sin. But perhaps that sin could never be expiated. And in spite of himself, his thoughts returned to Albine, to the Paradou, and to his burning memories. At first, he tried to find excuses for himself. One evening, he had fallen on the tiled floor of his room, struck down by a brain fever. For three weeks he had been taken over by this physical crisis. His raging blood had washed his veins even to the ends of his limbs, and roared through him with a noise like a torrent unleashed; his body, from the tip of his head to the soles of his feet, had been scoured, renewed, and battered by such a great labour of illness that often, in his delirium, he had thought he could hear the hammers of workers nailing his limbs back together. Then one morning, he had awakened as a new man. It was like a second birth, freed from everything that twenty-five years of life had gradually deposited in him. His devotions as a child, his education at the seminary, his innocent faith as a young priest, everything had gone, submerged, swept away, leaving an empty space. Surely only hell could have thus prepared him for sin, disarming him, making his body a bed of softness into which sin could enter and sleep. And he, in his ignorance, had abandoned himself to the slow slide towards sin. When he opened his eyes in the Paradou, he had felt bathed in a new childhood, with no memory of the past, no trace of the priesthood. His organs had played a sweet game, delighted and surprised at starting life anew, as if they did not know what life was, and thought it the greatest possible joy to find out. Oh! such a delightful apprenticeship, such charming encounters, such adorable discoveries! That Paradou was a huge happiness. In placing him there, hell knew very well he would be defenceless. Never, during his first youth, had he tasted such pleasure in growing up. That first youth, if he recalled it now, seemed to him to be entirely dark, an unlovely time, pallid and sickly, spent without any sunshine. So how he had greeted the sun, how he had marvelled at the first tree he saw, the first flower, the tiniest insect perceived, the smallest pebble picked up! The very stones had enchanted him. The horizon was an amazing miracle. With a bright morning shining in his eyes, the scent of jasmine in his nostrils, the song of a lark in his ears, his senses had aroused emotions so strong that his limbs gave way beneath him. He had taken pleasure in slowly learning about the slightest quiverings of life. And that morning when Albine came into being at his side, among the roses! He still laughed with ecstasy at that memory. She rose like a star that was necessary to the sun itself. She lit up everything, explained everything. She completed him. Then he began to go over again their walks to the four corners of the Paradou. He remembered the little hairs that fluttered on her neck when she ran in front of him. She smelled good, and as her warm skirts swung as she walked, their rustling was like a caress. When she took him in her bare arms, supple as snakes, he quite expected to see her, slender as she was, curl up on his body and fall asleep pressed to his skin. It was she who led the way. She had taken him along a winding path on which they lingered, not wanting to arrive too soon. She had given him a passion for the earth. He learned to love her by seeing how the plants love each other; it was a love groping its way along for some time, but whose great joy they had one evening discovered, under the giant tree in the sap-filled shade. There, they had reached the end of their journey. Albine, lying down with her head lolling back among her loosened hair, held out her arms to him. He took her in his embrace. Oh! to take her, possess her, once more to feel her body tremble with fecundity, to create life, to be God!

The priest suddenly uttered a low groan. He stood up as if bitten by invisible teeth; then he fell back once more. It was temptation that had bitten him. Into what filth, then, were his memories wandering? Did he not know that Satan knows every trick, and can slip his serpent's head right into the soul, even during times of self-examination? No, no, no excuses! Illness did not justify sin. It was up to him to be on his guard, and find God again at the end of his fever. But he, on the contrary, had taken pleasure in wallowing in his flesh. What proof this provided of his abominable appetites! He could not even confess his sin without sliding, in spite of himself, into the need to commit it again, at least in thought. Would he never be able to silence his inner foulness! He dreamed of emptying his skull to avoid more thinking, of opening his veins so that his guilty blood would no longer torment him. For a moment he remained with his face in his hands, shivering and hiding every slightest bit of his skin, as if the beasts that seemed to prowl around him had made his hair stand on end with their hot breath.

But he still went on thinking, and the blood went on beating in his heart. His eyes, though he held them closed with his fists, still saw, traced in fire upon the darkness, the supple outline of Albine's body. Her bare breast was as blinding as the sun. With every effort he made to press his fists against his eyes, she became more luminous, standing out more clearly, as she arched her body backwards, holding out her arms invitingly in a way that drew an agonized groan from the priest. So was God now totally abandoning him, and was there no refuge left for him? And in spite of all the efforts of his will, the sin would start all over again, its every detail etched with frightening clarity. He could see once more the tiny bits of grass on the hem of Albine's skirts; he saw again, caught in her hair, a little thistle flower on which he remembered pricking his lips. Even the scents and the slightly acrid sweetness of the crushed stems came back to him, even the distant sounds that he seemed still to be hearing, the repeated cry of a bird, a great silence, then a sigh moving through the trees. Why did Heaven not strike him down at once with a thunderbolt? He would have suffered less. He was enjoying his abomination with all the sensual pleasure of the damned. He shook with rage as he listened to the wicked words he had pronounced at Albine's feet. They echoed loudly now, accusing him before God. He had acknowledged the woman as his sovereign. He had given himself to her as her slave, kissing her feet and longing to be the water she drank, the bread she ate. Now he understood why he could no longer master himself. God had abandoned him to the woman. But he would fight her, he would break her bones to make her let go of him. It was she who was the slave, the impure flesh, to whom the Church should not have granted a soul. Then he hardened himself, and brandished his fists at Albine. And his fists opened, and flowed over her bare shoulders with a soft caress, while his mouth, full of insults, was pressed to her hair, stammering out words of adoration.

Abbé Mouret opened his eyes. The burning vision of Albine disappeared. It was a sudden, unhoped-for moment of relief, and he was able to weep. Slow tears cooled his cheeks, while he took long breaths, not yet daring to move for fear of being caught again by the neck. He could still hear a wild growling behind his back. Then it was so sweet to be suffering less intensely that he allowed himself to enjoy this moment of relief. Outside, the rain had stopped. The sun was setting in a vast red glow that seemed to paint the windows with curtains of pink satin. The church now was warm and alive, with this last breath of the sun. The priest confusedly thanked God for the respite he had allowed him. One wide ray of light, like a golden mist, went across the nave and lit up the far end of the church, the clock, the pulpit, the main altar. Was this, perhaps, grace coming back to him on this path of light coming down from Heaven? He looked intently at the atoms toing and froing with amazing speed along the ray of light, like a host of busy messengers endlessly bearing news of the sun to the earth. A thousand lighted candles would not have filled the church with such splendour. Behind the main altar hung curtains of gold, and over the whole church flowed streams of golden jewels, candlesticks blossoming into sheaves of bright light, censers burning with glowing gems, sacred vessels gradually enlarged and gleaming like comets; and everywhere there was a shower of luminous flowers falling over fluttering lace, and pools, bouquets, and garlands of roses, whose hearts, as they opened, let fall stars. Never had he even wished for such riches for his poor church. He smiled, dreaming of fixing all this magnificence where it was, and arranging it as he pleased. He would have liked to see the cloth-of-gold curtains hanging higher up; the sacred vessels seemed to be scattered rather carelessly; he picked up the flowers that had fallen, tying the bouquets together again, and giving the garlands a gentle curve. But how marvellous it was to see all this splendour spread out before him! He became the pontiff of a church of gold. Bishops, princes, women with royal cloaks, crowds of believers, their heads bowed in the dust, came to see the church, camped in the valley, waiting at the door for weeks before being able to enter. People kissed his feet, because his feet too were gold, and they performed miracles. The gold went up to his knees. A golden heart beat in his golden breast, with a musical sound so clear that the crowds outside could hear it. Then an immense organ filled him with delight. He was an idol. The ray of sunshine climbed still higher, the main altar was aflame, the priest began to believe it was really grace returning to him, since he felt such inner joy. The wild growling behind him became a gentle coaxing. On his neck he now felt only a velvet paw, as if some cat were caressing him.

And he continued his reverie. Never had things appeared to him with such total clarity. Everything now seemed easy, so strong did he feel. Since Albine was waiting for him, he would go and join her. That was only natural. In the morning he had married big Fortuné and Rosalie. The Church did not forbid marriage. He could see them again, smiling at each other, nudging each other, even as his hands were blessing them. Then in the evening he had been shown their bed. Every one of the words he had spoken to them now burst loudly upon his ears. He had told Fortuné that God was sending him a companion, because he did not want man to live alone. He had told Rosalie that she must bind herself to her husband, never leave him, and be his faithful servant. But he had said all those things also for himself and Albine. Was she not also his companion, his faithful servant, the one sent to him by God so that his virility should not wither away in solitude? Besides they were already bound together. He remained surprised that he had not understood that immediately, and not gone away with her, as duty demanded he should. But it was decided now, he would rejoin her on the morrow. He could be with her in half an hour. He would go through the village and take the hill path; it was much shorter that way. He could do everything, he was the master, no one could say anything. If people looked at him, he would make a gesture that would make

them bow their heads. Then he would live with Albine. He would call
her his wife. They would be very happy. The gold climbed yet higher,
and streamed between his fingers. He was once more in a bath of gold.
The sacred vessels he carried off for use in his household, which would
be very grand, and people would be paid with bits of chalice that he
fairly easily twisted off with his fingers. He hung over his marriage
bed the curtains of cloth of gold from the altar. For jewels, he gave his
wife the gold hearts, the gold chaplets, and the gold crosses hanging
round the neck of the Virgin and the saints. The church itself, if he
added one more floor, could serve as their palace. God would have no
objections, since loving was allowed. Anyway, what did God matter!
Wasn't it now he himself who was God, with his feet of gold that the
crowd came and kissed, his feet that worked miracles?

Abbé Mouret stood up and made that sweeping gesture Jeanbernat
had made, that gesture of denial, that took in the whole horizon.

'There is nothing, nothing, nothing,' he said. 'God does not exist.'

A great shudder seemed to run through the church. The priest,
alarmed and once again deathly pale, was listening. Who had been
speaking? Who had blasphemed? Suddenly the velvety caress whose
softness he had felt on his neck had become ferocious; claws were
tearing at his neck, he was bleeding once again. But he remained standing, fighting against this attack. He threw insults at the triumphant
sin that sniggered around his temples, on which all the hammers of
evil were again starting to beat. Did he not know sin's trickeries? Didn't
he know that it often plays this game of approaching with gentle paws,
only then to dig them in like knives into the bones of its victims? And
his rage redoubled at the thought that he had been caught in the trap
again, like a child. So he would always be knocked to the ground, with
sin squatting victoriously upon his breast! And now indeed he was
denying God. That was the fatal downward slope. Fornication killed
faith. Then dogma began to crumble. One doubt from the flesh, pleading its filthy cause, was sufficient to sweep away all of Heaven. Divine
law became an irritation, the mysteries were risible; in one corner of
toppled religion, man lay down and discussed his sacrilege, until he
had dug a hole for himself to sleep off his filth. Then came new temp-
tations: gold, power, an unfettered life, an irresistible need for sexual
pleasure, which brought everything back to total debauchery, wallowing on a bed of wealth and pride! And God was robbed. The sacred
monstrances were broken, and hung on the impurity of a woman. Well!

he was damned. Nothing held him back now, sin could speak aloud in him. It was good not to struggle any more. The monsters which had prowled behind his neck, now fought in his entrails. He swelled his loins to feel their teeth more sharply. He abandoned himself to them with a terrible joy. A movement of rebellion made him shake his fists at the church. No, he no longer believed in the divinity of Jesus, he no longer believed in the Holy Trinity, he believed only in himself, in his muscles, in the appetites of his organs. He wanted to live. He felt the need to be a man. Oh! to run in the open air, to be strong, to have no jealous master, to kill his enemies with stones, and throw passing girls over his shoulder and carry them off! He would come back to life from the tomb where cruel hands had buried him. He would awaken his virility, which could only be sleeping. And let him just die of shame if he found his virility dead! And let God be cursed, if he had drawn him away from other creatures by touching him with his finger, just to keep him for his sole service!

The priest stood there, hallucinating. He thought that at this new blasphemy the church was collapsing. The pool of sunlight that had drowned the main altar had gradually lengthened, lighting up the walls with a fiery redness. Little flames of light still arose and licked the ceiling, only to die in a bloody glow like burning coals. The church suddenly became totally dark. It seemed as if the fire of this setting sun had just burst the roof, split the walls, and everywhere made gaping breaches open to attacks from outside. The whole dark carcase of the building shook, in expectation of some terrible assault. And night very quickly deepened.

Then from very far away, the priest heard a murmur rising from the valley of Les Artaud. He had previously had no understanding of the ardent language of these sun-scorched lands, in which the only movements were the twisting of knotty vine-stocks, gaunt almond trees, or old olive trees, stretching awkwardly on their infirm limbs. He had moved through all that passion in the serenity of his ignorance. But today, with his new fleshly knowledge, he could grasp even the slightest sighs of leaves swooning in the sun. At first, on the far horizon, it was the hills, still warm from the farewell of the setting sun, that shuddered and seemed to shake with the muffled tramping of an army on the march. Then the scattered rocks, the stones on the roads, and all the pebbles in the valley, they too rose up, rolling and clattering as if jerked forward by the need to move. And after them, the stretches of red earth, the few fields hard won by the pick, all began to flow and growl, like rivers bursting their banks, carrying, in the waves of their blood, conceptions and new seeds, bursting new roots, and the copulation of plants. And soon everything was moving: vine stocks crawled about like huge insects; thin stalks of wheat and dried-up grasses formed battalions, armed with tall lances; trees shook off their leaves as they ran, and stretched their limbs like wrestlers preparing for combat; the fallen leaves were on the march, the very dust on the roads was marching. It was a multitude, recruiting new forces with every step, a whole nation in rut, its breathing getting nearer, a tempest of life whose breath was like a furnace, carrying everything before it in a whirlwind of colossal birth pangs. Suddenly the attack began. From the far horizon, the whole countryside rushed upon the church: hills and stones, earth and trees. Under the first shock, the church cracked. The walls split, tiles flew off the roof. But the big Christ, though shaken, did not fall.

There was a brief respite. Outside, even more furious voices could be heard. Now the priest could make out human voices. It was the village, the Artauds, that handful of bastards growing out of the rock with the obstinacy of brambles, who were now breathing out a wind that carried with it a huge swarming of beings. The Artauds fornicated on the ground, planting from one relative to another a forest of men, whose trunks consumed all the space around them. They were climbing right up to the church, they broke down the door with one shove, it looked as if they would clog the nave with the invading branches of their race. Behind them, in the tangles of undergrowth, came the animals, bulls trying to break through the walls with their horns, herds of donkeys and goats, and flocks of sheep, beating against the ruined church like living waves, whole colonies of woodlice and crickets attacking the foundations, reducing them to rubble with their saw-like teeth. And on the other side, there was still Désirée's farmyard, its dungheap giving off clouds of asphyxiating stench; Alexander, the big rooster, sounded the charge with his bugle, the hens loosened the stones with their beaks, the rabbits burrowed away even under the altars to undermine and spoil them; the pig, so fat he could hardly move, grunted, waiting for the sacred ornaments to be no more than a handful of warm ash on which he could warm his belly. A frightening noise arose, a second charge was mounted. The village, the animals, this whole tide of overflowing life for an instant swallowed up the church under a frenzy of bodies that made the rafters give way. In the midst of this turmoil, females dropped from their entrails a constant stream of new fighters. This time, a section of the church wall was knocked down; the ceiling started to give way, the wooden frames of the windows were torn away, and the smoky air of twilight, growing ever darker, came in through the dreadful, yawning gaps. On the cross, the big Christ held on only by the nail on his left hand.

The crumbling of the section of wall was greeted by a clamour. But the church was still standing in spite of its wounds. It held on stubbornly, savagely, silent and dark, just clinging on to the slightest stones of its foundations. It seemed that this ruin needed nothing more to stay upright than one slim pillar, which by a miracle of balance held up the broken roof. Then Abbé Mouret saw the hardy plants of the plateau getting to work, those terrible plants, hardened in the dryness of the rocks, knotted as snakes, their wood hard and bulging with muscles. The rust-coloured lichens gnawed at the flaking plaster like an inflamed leprosy. Then thyme thrust its roots down between the bricks like iron wedges. Lavender slid long, clawed fingers under all the loose bits of masonry and tugged, pulling them out with a long, continuous effort. Juniper trees, rosemary, and thorny holly bushes climbed up higher, pushing irresistibly. Even the grasses, those grasses whose dried stalks came in under the church door, stiffened themselves into spears of steel, smashing down the door, and advancing into the nave, where they uprooted the flagstones with their strong pincers. This was a victorious uprising, Revolutionary Nature was putting up the barricades with overthrown altars, demolishing the church which for centuries had overshadowed it. The other combatants allowed the grasses, the thyme, the lavender and lichen to get on with it, this gnawing by the little plants being more destructive than the hammer blows of the big ones; it was their crumbling away of the base that would finally bring down the whole building. Then suddenly, it was the end. The rowan tree, whose high branches had already made their way in through the broken windows under the vaulted roof, made a violent entrance in a tremendous thrust of greenery. It planted itself in the middle of the nave. From there, it grew extravagantly, its trunk became colossal to the point of making the church burst apart, like an overstretched belt. The branches stretched out on all sides with huge knots, each one of which tore off a piece of wall or a fragment of roofing, and they went on multiplying, each branch dividing into further branches, and a new tree growing from each knot, with such a fury of growth that the wreckage of the church, riddled with holes, just exploded, scattering something like fine ash to the four corners of the heavens. Now the giant tree was touching the stars. Its forest of branches was a forest of limbs, of arms and legs, torsos and bellies, all dripping with sap; women's hair hung in the air, and men's heads spurted out of the bark with a chuckle like newborn buds; at the top, pairs of lovers, swooning on the edge of their nests, filled the air with the music of their pleasure and the smell of their fertility. One last blast of the hurricane that had fallen upon the church blew away the dust, the shattered pulpit and confessional, the lacerated holy pictures, the melted sacred vessels, and all the rubble, at which the flock of sparrows that formerly lived under the roof, was avidly pecking. The big Christ, torn off the cross, stayed hanging for a moment, caught in the hair of one of the women's heads floating in the air, then was carried off, whirled about, then lost from sight, to fall at last with a resounding crash in the depths of the black darkness. The tree of life had just burst the heavens. And it was now higher than the stars.

Abbé Mouret applauded furiously, like a damned soul, at this vision. The church was defeated. God no longer had a home. God would not bother him any more. He could go to Albine, for she had triumphed. And how he laughed at himself, his asserting, just an hour before, that the church would swallow up the earth in its shadow! The earth had avenged itself by swallowing the church. The mad laugh he gave pulled him with a jerk out of his hallucination. Stupefied, he gazed at the nave slowly sinking into the dusk; patches of sky, studded with stars, showed through the windows. And he stretched out his arms, to feel the walls, when the voice of Désirée called him from the passage of the sacristy:

'Serge! are you there?... Answer me! I've been looking for you for half an hour!'

She came in. She was carrying a lamp. Then the priest saw that the church was still standing. He simply could not understand, and fell into a state of dreadful doubt, between the invincible church, springing up again out of its ashes, and all-powerful Albine, who could shake God himself with just one breath.

CHAPTER X

Désirée came towards him, with her noisy cheerfulness.

'There you are! there you are!' she cried. 'Are you playing hide-and-seek? I've called you at least ten times, at the top of my voice... I thought you must have gone out.'

She looked inquisitively into the dark corners. She even went rather stealthily over to the confessional, as if she half expected to come upon someone hidden there. She came back, disappointed, and went on:

'You're on your own, then? Perhaps you were asleep? What can you find to do all by yourself, when it's so dark?... Let's go, come on, we're ready to eat.'

He, meanwhile, was running his feverish hands over his brow, to wipe away the thoughts that everyone would surely read upon it. He tried, mechanically, to do up the buttons on his cassock which seemed to be open and torn, in a shameful disorder. Then he followed his sister with a stern face and no quiver of emotion, stiffened by his priestly will to hide the agonies of the flesh in the dignity of the priesthood. Désirée did not even see that he was troubled. She simply said, as they entered the dining room:

'I've had a good sleep. But you've been talking too much, and you look quite pale.'

In the evening, after dinner, Brother Archangias came to play a game of 'War' with La Teuse. He was immensely jolly that evening. When he was jolly, he would punch La Teuse in the ribs, and she would respond by hitting him back as hard as she could. That made them both laugh, a laughter that shook the ceiling. Then he would invent all sorts of extraordinary pranks: he would lay plates flat on the table, and break them with his nose, he would bet he could crack the dining room door with his bottom, or he'd throw all the tobacco in his pouch into the old servant's coffee, or bring in a handful of little pebbles and drop them down the front of her dress, pushing them in with his hand, right down to her belt. These outbursts of jollity would arise out of nothing in particular, in the midst of his usual, surly bad temper; and quite often, something that made no one else laugh would give him a real fit of noisy, wild laughter, and he would stamp his feet and spin round like a top, holding his belly.

'So you don't want to tell me why you are so merry?' asked La Teuse.

He did not answer. He was sitting astride a chair on which he was galloping round the table.

'Yes, yes, go on being an ass,' she went on. 'Heavens! how silly you are! If the good Lord can see you now, he must be pleased with you!'

The Brother had just fallen over backwards, with his spine on the floor and his legs in the air. Without getting up, he said gravely:

'He can see me, and he is pleased with me. It's he who wants me to be merry... When he is kind enough to allow me some amusement he rings a bell in my body. Then I roll about laughing. And that makes all paradise laugh.'

He walked himself over to the wall on his back; then, raising himself on his shoulders, he drummed on the wall with his heels, as high as he could reach. His cassock fell away and uncovered his black trousers, mended at the knees with patches of green material. Then he went on:

'Monsieur le Curé, look how high I can reach. I bet you can't do that... Come on, laugh a bit. It's better to drag oneself around on one's back than to want the skin of a slut for your mattress. You know what I mean. You can be an animal for a moment, scratch yourself, and be rid of your vermin. It's soothing. I, when I scratch myself, I imagine I'm God's dog, and that's what makes me say that all paradise looks out of the windows laughing, just to see me... You too can laugh, Monsieur le Curé. This is for the saints, and for you. Look, a somersault for Saint Joseph, and here's another for Saint John, yet another for Saint Michael, one for Saint Mark, and one for Saint Matthew...'

And he went on, running through a long list of saints, somersaulting around the room. Abbé Mouret, who had remained silent, with his wrists on the edge of the table, had finally smiled. The jollities of Brother Archangias usually worried him. Then, as the Brother came within reach of La Teuse, she gave him a kick.

'Well, then,' she said, 'are we going to play cards or not?'

Brother Archangias answered only with grunts. He had got down on all fours. He went straight at La Teuse. As soon as he reached her, he thrust his head under her skirts, and bit her right knee.

'Will you just leave me alone!' she cried. 'Are you thinking filthy thoughts now?'

'I!' stammered the Brother, so amused by the idea that he stayed where he was, unable to stand up again. 'Oh, look! I'm choking, just through having tasted your knee. It's too salty, your knee... I bite women, then I spit them out, you see.'

He was using the familiar *tu* form to her, and he spat on her skirt. When he had managed to get himself upright again, he puffed for a moment, and rubbed his sides. Great gales of jollity were still shaking his belly, like a wineskin being shaken empty. At last, in a serious voice, he said:

'Let's play... If I laugh, that's my business. You don't need to know why, La Teuse.'

And the game began. It was ferocious. The Brother punched the cards down on the table. When he cried 'War!' the windows rattled. It was La Teuse who was winning. She had had three aces for a long time, and was watching for the fourth with gleaming eyes. Meanwhile Brother Archangias began to indulge in further pranks. He lifted the table, at the risk of breaking the lamp; he cheated shamelessly, defending himself with outrageous lies which, he added, were just for a joke. Suddenly he began to sing Vespers, in a deep voice, like the cantor at the lectern. And he did not stop, roaring on lugubriously, emphasizing the end of each verse by tapping his cards against the palm of his left hand. When his jollity was at its height, and he couldn't find anything more to express it, he would sing the Vespers like this for hours. La Teuse, who knew him well, leant over, in the middle of the bellowing that was filling her dining room, to shout at him:

'Stop this noise, it's unbearable!... You are altogether too jolly this evening.'

Then he started on the *Compline*.* Abbé Mouret had gone to sit by the window. He seemed neither to see nor hear what was going on around him. During dinner, he had eaten in his usual way; he had even managed to answer Désirée's endless questions. Now he had given up, his strength exhausted; he was drifting, broken and crushed in the furious conflict going on relentlessly within him. He lacked even the courage to rise from his chair and go up to his room. Then he began to worry that if he turned his face towards the lamp, the tears he could no longer hold back would be seen. He leant his brow against the window, and looked at the darkness outside, gradually getting sleepy, and sliding into a nightmarish torpor.

Brother Archangias, still intoning the psalms, winked and gave a nod towards the sleeping priest.

'What is it?' asked La Teuse. The Brother repeated his meaningful wink and nod.

'You'll end up putting your neck out of joint!' said the servant. 'Try speaking and I'll understand you... Look, a king. Good! I'll take your queen.'

He laid down his cards for a moment, leaned over the table, and whispered right in her face:

'That trollop's been here.'

'I know,' she replied. 'I saw her going into the farmyard with Mademoiselle Désirée.'

He gave her a terrible look, and brandished his fists:

'You saw her and you let her in! You should have called me, and we'd have hanged her by her feet from a nail in your kitchen.'

But this made her angry, though she kept her voice low to avoid waking up Abbé Mouret.

'Oh, fine!' she stammered, 'you're a nice one! Just you try to go hanging someone in my kitchen!... Of course I saw her. And I even looked the other way when I saw her going to join Monsieur le Curé in the church, after catechism. They were free to do whatever they wanted. Is that my business? Didn't I need to get my beans cooking?... Personally, I loathe her, that girl. But when she represents the health of Monsieur le Curé... she can come whenever she likes, at any hour of the day or night. I'd lock them up together, if that's what they want.'

'If you did that, La Teuse,' said the Brother, with icy fury, 'I'd strangle you.'

She began to laugh, she too using the *tu* form as he had done.

'Don't say such stupid things, you silly boy! You know perfectly well that women are as forbidden to you as the *Pater* is to a donkey. Just try to strangle me one day, and you'll see what I'll do. Now, just behave yourself, and let's finish the game. Look, here's another king.'

He, holding the card he had picked up, went on growling:

'She must have come by some path known only to the devil to have escaped me today, for I keep watch every day up there in the Paradou. If I catch them together once more, I'll introduce that trollop to a cane of dogwood that I cut specially for her... Now I'll keep guard on the church as well.'

He played, and lost a knave to La Teuse, then threw himself back in his chair, shaken once more by huge peals of laughter. He did not seem able to be seriously angry that evening. He muttered:

'No matter, if she did see him, she still fell flat on her face... I'll tell you about it anyway, La Teuse. You know it was raining. I was standing at the school door when I saw her coming down from the church. She was walking along with a straight back, in that proud way she has, in spite of the shower. And then, when she reached the road, she hit the ground full length, the ground must have been so slippery. Oh, how I laughed! how I laughed! I clapped my hands... When she got up again, she had blood on one of her wrists. That gave me enough joy to last a week. I can't even think of her lying on the ground without feeling some ticklings in my throat and my belly that make me burst with pleasure.'

Puffing out his cheeks, and paying full attention now to the game, he sang the *De Profundis*.* Then he started it again. The game ended with this lament, some parts of which he sang particularly loudly, as if to enjoy them more. He had lost the game, but he did not seem at all put out by that. When La Teuse had shown him out, after waking up Abbé Mouret, he could be heard, as he disappeared into the blackness of the night, repeating the last verse of the psalm: *Et ipse redimet Israël ex omnibus iniquitatibus ejus** with quite extraordinary jubilation.

CHAPTER XI

ABBÉ MOURET slept like a log. When he opened his eyes, rather later than usual, he found his face and hands bathed in tears; he had wept all night long in his sleep. He did not say Mass that morning. In spite of his long rest, his tiredness of the previous evening was such that he stayed in his room until midday, sitting on a chair at the foot of his bed. The torpor, which he was experiencing more and more frequently, took away even his sense of suffering. He now felt only a great emptiness, as if relieved of a burden, amputated and annihilated. Reading his breviary required a supreme effort; the Latin of the verses seemed to him a barbarous language, whose words he now could not even spell out. Then, throwing the book on the bed, he spent hours looking at the countryside through the open window, without the strength to go and lean on the sill. In the distance he could see the white wall of the Paradou, a thin, pale line, running along the crest of the high ground, between the dark patches of the little pinewoods. On the left, behind one of those woods, was the breach in the wall; he could not see it but knew it was there; he remembered even the smallest bits of bramble scattered among the stones. Even the day before, he would not have dared to gaze in this way at that challenging horizon. But now he could with impunity let himself pick out again the broken thread of the wall behind the patches of greenery, like the edging of a skirt caught on the bushes. This did not even provoke a faster beating of his heart. As though contemptuous of the thinness of his blood, temptation had abandoned his cowardly flesh. It had left him incapable of struggle, deprived of grace as he was, no longer even feeling the passion of sin, and ready, in his torpor, to accept everything he had rejected so furiously the day before.

For a moment he caught himself speaking aloud. Since the breach in the wall was still there, he would go back to Albine at sunset. He felt a slight annoyance at this decision. But he could not see what else he could do. She was waiting for him, she was his wife. When he tried to recall her face, he could see only a very pale and distant image. He was also worried about how they would live together. It would be difficult for them to stay in the region; they would have to go away, without anyone knowing; and even then, once they were hidden away somewhere, they would need a lot of money to live happily. He tried, a score of times, to fix on a plan for getting away, and arranging their existence as happy lovers. He tried in vain. Now he was no longer mad with desire, the practical side of the situation appalled him, bringing him, with his feeble hands, face to face with a complicated task he could not begin to comprehend. Where would they get horses for their escape? If they went off on foot, wouldn't they be arrested as vagrants? Besides, would he be capable of doing a job, of finding some occupation or other to earn the wherewithal to support his wife? These were things he had never been taught. He knew nothing of life: casting through his memory, all he could find were fragments of prayer, details of ceremonial ritual, and some pages of Bouvier's *Instruction in Theology*, which he had learned by heart at the seminary. Even trivial details bothered him a great deal. He wondered whether he would dare to take his wife's arm out in the street. He would certainly have no idea how to walk with a woman on his arm. He would look so awkward that people would turn and stare. They would guess he was a priest, and then insult Albine. In vain would he try to wash away his priesthood. He would always have its sad pallor, and carry with him the smell of incense. And if some day he had children? That unexpected thought made him shudder. He felt a strange repugnance. He thought that he would not love them. However, there were two of them, a boy and a girl. He pushed them away from his knees, distressed when he felt their hands on his clothes, and not enjoying bouncing them up and down, as other fathers did. He could not get used to this flesh of his flesh, which always seemed to him to exude his own male impurity. The little girl especially troubled him with her big eyes, in which womanly tenderness was already visible. But no, he would not have children, he would avoid the horror he felt at the idea of seeing his own limbs growing again, and living again eternally. Then he found the hope of being impotent very soothing. All his virility had no doubt disappeared during his long adolescence. That decided him. That very evening, he would run away with Albine.

However, when evening came, Abbé Mouret felt too weary. He put off his departure to the next day. On the next day, he found another pretext: he could not leave his sister like that, on her own with La Teuse; he would leave a letter, asking for her to be taken to Uncle Pascal. For three days he promised himself he would write that letter; the sheet of paper, the pen and ink were ready on the table in his bedroom. And on the third day he went off without writing the letter. He had suddenly taken his hat and set off for the Paradou, out of stupidity, just obsessed and resigning himself to it, going there as if for some chore he could find no way of avoiding. The image of Albine had grown even fainter; he could not see her any more, he was acting in obedience to old resolves, now dead for him, but whose impetus still persisted in the great silence of his being.

Outside, he made no attempt to hide. He stopped at the end of the village to chat for a moment with Rosalie; she told him that her child was having convulsions, yet she still laughed out of the corner of her mouth in her usual way. Then he plunged on through the rocks, and walked straight to the breach. Out of habit, he had brought his breviary. As it was a long way, he grew bored and, opening the book, read the appointed prayers. When he tucked it back under his arm, he had forgotten the Paradou. He still went on walking ahead, thinking about a new chasuble he wanted to buy to replace the cloth-of-gold chasuble, which was really falling to pieces; he had been hiding twenty-sou coins for some time, and he worked out that in seven months he would have enough money. He was just reaching the high ground, when the sound of a peasant singing in the distance reminded him of a canticle he had learned long ago at the seminary. He tried to recall the first lines of the canticle, but found he could not. It annoyed him that his memory was so poor. Then when he finally managed to remember them, it gave him delightful pleasure to sing, under his breath, the words that came back to him, one by one. It was a homage to Mary. He smiled, as if some fresh breath from his youth had just blown on to his face. How happy he had been at that time. Of course, he could still be happy; he had not really grown up, he still desired the same kind of happiness, a serene peace, a little chapel with a spot marked out for his knees, a life of solitude, enlivened by lovely, childish fancies. He had gradually raised his voice, and was singing the canticle with flute-like tones, when he saw the breach suddenly before him.

For a moment he seemed surprised. Then, no longer smiling, he simply murmured:

'Albine must be waiting for me. The sun is already beginning to set.'

But as he climbed up to push aside the stones so he could get through, he was disturbed by a fearful snore. He had to go back down; he had almost put his foot flat on the face of Brother Archangias, who lay sprawled on the ground, fast asleep. Sleep no doubt had overtaken him while he was guarding the entrance to the Paradou. He was blocking the way, having fallen full length, with his legs and arms spread out in a shameful posture. His right hand, thrown back behind his head, had not let go of the dogwood cane that he still seemed to be brandishing like a flaming sword.

Abbé Mouret gazed at him for a moment. He envied that sleep, like that of a saint rolling in the dust. He tried to drive away the flies, but the flies stubbornly returned, sticking to the mauve lips of the Brother, who did not even feel them. Then the abbé stepped over that large figure and entered the Paradou.

CHAPTER XII

A FEW steps beyond the wall, Albine was sitting on a carpet of grass. She rose to her feet when she saw Serge.

'You're here!' she cried, trembling from head to foot.

'Yes,' he said calmly, 'I have come.'

She threw her arms around his neck. But she did not kiss him. She had felt the cold pearls of his collar-flap* on her bare arm. She observed him closely, anxious already, and went on:

'What's the matter? You didn't kiss me on the cheeks as you did before, you know, when your lips sang to me... No matter, if you're sick, I shall cure you again. Now you're here, we shall begin our happiness again. No more sadness... You see, I'm smiling. You must smile, Serge.'

As his face remained unsmiling:

'Of course, I too have been very unhappy. I'm still quite pale, aren't I? I've been living there, on the grass where you found me, for a week. I only wanted one thing, and that was to see you coming in through that gap in the wall. I got up at every sound, and rushed to meet you. And it wasn't you, it was just leaves blowing in the wind... But I knew you would come. I would have waited for years.'

Then she asked:

'Do you still love me?'

'Yes,' he replied, 'I still love you.'

They stood there, facing each other rather uncomfortably. A heavy silence fell between them. Serge, undisturbed, made no attempt to break it. Albine twice opened her mouth but closed it again, surprised at the things that were rising to her lips. She could now find only words of bitterness. She felt tears welling up in her eyes. What was she feeling then, how could she not be happy at the return of her love?

'Listen,' she said at last, 'we must not stay here... we are being chilled by that breach in the wall... Let's go home. Give me your hand.'

And they plunged into the Paradou. Autumn was coming and the trees looked sad, their yellow heads dropping their leaves one by one. A bed of dead foliage, thoroughly wet, already lay on the paths, on which each footstep sounded like a stifled sigh. At the end of the lawns, a haze hung in the air, casting a cloak of mourning over the faraway blue in the distance. And the whole garden was silent, breathing out only melancholy breaths that went by like shudders. Serge was shivering in the avenue of tall trees that they had entered. He said in a low voice:

'How cold it is here!'

'You are cold,' Albine murmured sadly. 'My hand no longer warms you. Shall I wrap a piece of my dress around you?... Come on, we're going to find all our old tenderness again.'

She led him to the flower garden. The arbour of roses was still fragrant, but the last flowers had a bitter scent, and the leaves, now

grown much too large, lay on the earth like a stagnant pool. But Serge
showed such reluctance about entering these thickets that they stayed
on the edge, seeking only from a distance the paths they had taken in
the spring. She could remember each little bit of the way: she pointed
out the grotto where the marble woman lay sleeping, the hanging tresses
of the honeysuckle and clematis, the fields of violets, the fountain that
seemed to spit out red carnations, the big flight of steps covered with
a stream of wild wallflowers, the ruined colonnade in the centre of
which lilies were building a white home. It was there that they had
both been born in the sunshine. And she recounted all the tiniest details
of that first journey, how they had walked, and how the air smelled
different in the shade. He, meanwhile, seemed to be listening, but
then he would ask a question that showed he had not understood. The
slight shivering which made him so pale simply did not stop.

She led him to the orchard, which they could not even get near.
The river had swollen, and Serge no longer thought of taking Albine
up on his back, and carrying her across with three great leaps. And
yet, just over there, the apple trees and pear trees were still loaded with
fruit; and the vine, with fewer leaves now, was bent beneath the weight
of its blond clusters, in which each grape still bore the russet mark of
the sun. How they had frolicked about in the appetizing shade of
those venerable trees! They were just children then. Albine still smiled
at the shameless way she had shown her legs whenever a branch broke.
Did he at least remember the plums they had eaten? Serge replied
only with a shake of his head. He seemed tired already. The orchard
with its green depths, its confusion of mossy stems like broken-down,
ruined scaffolding, disturbed him, put him in mind of some dark, damp
place, full of nettles and snakes.

She led him to the meadows. There, he had to take a few steps in
the grass. It rose up to his shoulders now. It seemed to him like a mass
of thin arms trying to bind his limbs and roll him along and drown
him in that endless green sea. He begged Albine to go no further. She
was walking ahead and did not stop; then, seeing he was ill, she stood
at his side, growing sadder and sadder, and ended up shivering just
like him. However, she went on talking. With a broad wave of her hand
she pointed to the streams, the lines of willows, the patches of grass
stretching away to the horizon. All of that had formerly been theirs.
Over there, between those three willows, beside that stream, they had
played at being lovers. At that time, they would have liked the grass to

be above their heads so they could get quite lost in its moving stream, and be even more alone, far from everything, like larks roaming in the depths of a cornfield. So why then was he trembling today, when he merely felt the tip of his foot dip into the grass and disappear?

She led him to the forest. Serge found the trees even more frightening. He did not recognize them in all the solemnity of their dark trunks. Here, more than anywhere else, the past seemed dead, among these tall, stern trees, through which light descended freely. The first rains had erased their footprints from the sandy path, and the winds were carrying off whatever remained of them on the lowest branches of the bushes. But Albine, her throat choked with sadness, protested only with her eyes. She searched out on the sand the slightest traces of their walks. At every bush the old warmth that they had left there as they brushed against it came back into her face. And with pleading eyes she still sought to reawaken Serge's memories. Along this path they had walked in silence, both very moved, but not daring to say they loved each other. In this glade they had stayed very late one evening, just looking at the stars that rained down on them like drops of warmth. Further on, beneath this oak, they had exchanged their first kiss. The oak still kept the sweet scent of that kiss; even the mosses were still talking about it. It was a lie to say the forest had become dumb and empty. And Serge turned away his head to avoid meeting Albine's eyes that wearied him.

She led him to the big rocks. Perhaps there he would stop shivering with that air of frailty that made her despair. Only the big rocks, at this hour of the day, were still hot with the fiery red glow of the sunset. They still kept their tragic passion, their burning beds of pebbles on which fleshy plants rolled about in monstrous couplings. And without a word, without even turning her head, Albine dragged Serge up the steep climb, wanting to take him higher, ever higher, above the springs, until they were both once again in the sun. They would rediscover the cedar, beneath which they had felt the anguish of their first desires. They would lie down on the ground, on the ardent flagstones, and wait for the rutting earth to overcome them. But soon Serge's feet began to stumble badly. He could no longer walk. First he fell over on to his knees. Albine, with the mightiest effort, pulled him back up and bore him along for an instant. Then he fell again, and lay defeated in the middle of the path. There, below, the immensity of the Paradou stretched before him.

'You lied,' cried Albine, 'you do not love me any more.'

And she wept, standing at his side, realizing she could not take him any higher. She was weeping for their dying love. He lay there, crushed.

'The garden is dead, and I'm still cold,' he murmured.

But she took hold of his head and with a wave, showed him the Paradou.

'But just look!... Ah, it's your eyes that are dead, and your ears, your limbs, your whole body. You have walked past all our joys without seeing, hearing, or feeling them. And all you've done is stumble along, then fall down here with weariness and boredom... You do not love me any more.'

He protested, quietly and calmly. Then she had a first moment of violence.

'Be quiet! Could the garden ever die! It will sleep this winter, and wake up again in May, bringing back to us all that we have confided to it of our love; our kisses will bloom again in the flower garden; our vows will grow up again with the grass and the trees... If you could only see it, if you could hear it, it feels more deeply, and is more sweetly, more poignantly loving in this season of autumn, when it is falling asleep in its fruitfulness... You do not love me any more, you cannot understand.'

Looking up at her, he begged her not to be angry. His face was pinched and pale with a childlike fear. A raised voice made him shudder. He finally persuaded her to rest for a moment beside him in the middle of the path. They would talk quietly and sort things out between them. And the two, with the Paradou in front of them, without even holding each other by their fingertips, talked of their love.

'I love you, I do love you,' he said in a steady voice. 'If I didn't love you, I would not have come... It's true that I am weary. I don't know why. I had thought that here I would find once more that lovely warmth, of which the mere memory was a caress. And I'm cold, and the garden seems pitch dark; I see in it nothing of what I left here. But it's not my fault. I am struggling to be like you, I would like to make you happy.'

'You do not love me any more,' Albine again repeated.

'Yes, I do love you. I suffered a great deal the other day, after sending you away... Oh! I loved you with such passion, you know, I would have crushed you in my embrace, if you had come back and thrown yourself into my arms. Never have I desired you so furiously. For hours, I had your living presence still before me, tormenting me with your supple fingers. When I closed my eyes, you lit up like a sun, and enveloped me in your flames... So I just trampled over every obstacle, and came to you.'

He was silent for a while, looking thoughtful, then he went on:

'And now, my arms seem broken. If I wanted to clasp you to my breast, I wouldn't be able to hold you, I'd let you fall... Wait for this shuddering to leave me. You will give me your hands, I shall kiss them again. Be kind, don't look at me with those angry eyes. Help me to get my heart back.'

He showed such real sadness, and such evident desire to get back to their former life of tenderness that Albine was touched. For a moment she became very gentle. She questioned him with real concern.

'Where does it hurt? What is wrong with you?'

'I don't know. It seems as if all the blood of my veins is draining away... A little while ago, on my way here, I felt as if someone had thrown a cloak of ice over my shoulders, a cloak that turned my whole body to stone, from head to foot... I have felt that cloak on my shoulders before... I don't remember when.'

But she interrupted him with a friendly smile.

'You are a child, you'll have caught a chill, that's all... Listen, I at least don't frighten you, do I? In the winter, we won't stay hidden in this garden like two savages. We'll go wherever you like, to some big city. We shall love each other in the outside world just as peacefully as among the trees. And you'll see that I'm not just a good-for-nothing capable only of bird's-nesting and walking for hours without getting tired... When I was little, I wore embroidered petticoats, and patterned stockings, and lace and frills. Perhaps nobody told you that?'

He wasn't listening, he suddenly cried:

'Ah! I remember!'

And when she asked him about it, he refused to answer.

He had just recalled the sensation of the seminary chapel falling about his shoulders. That was the icy cloak that had turned his whole body to stone. Then he was irresistibly carried back into his priestly past. The vague memories that had occurred to him along the way from Les Artaud to the Paradou grew stronger, and imposed themselves with sovereign authority. While Albine continued to talk of the happy life they would live together, he was hearing the ringing of the bell for the elevation of the Host, and seeing the censers tracing fiery crosses in the air above the heads of great crowds of people on their knees.

'Ah well,' she said, 'for you, I shall put on my embroidered petticoats again... I want you to be happy. We shall look for things that will
distract you. You will love me more perhaps, when you see me looking
beautiful, and dressed like a lady. I shall no longer have my comb stuck
sideways in my hair, with hair hanging down my neck. I'll stop rolling
up my sleeves to the elbows. I'll fasten my dress so it no longer reveals
my shoulders. And I still know how to curtsey, I know how to walk with
poise, and with little movements of my chin. You'll see, I shall be
a pretty woman on your arm, in the street.'

'Did you ever go into any churches when you were little?' he asked,
quietly, as if he were continuing aloud the train of thought that prevented him from hearing her. 'I could never go past a church without
going in. As soon as the door closed silently behind me, I felt as if
I were in paradise itself, with angels' voices whispering sweet stories
in my ear, and the breath of the saints caressing my whole body... Yes,
I would have liked to live there, forever, lost in all that blessedness.'

She looked at him fixedly, while a little flame sprang up in the tenderness of her eyes. She went on, still submissive:

'I shall be whatever you may fancy. I used to play music once; I was
an accomplished young woman, brought up to have all the graces...
I'll go back to school, I'll take up music again. If you want to hear me
play some piece you love, you'll only have to tell me, and I'll study it
for months, then play it for you one evening in our house, in a cosy
room with all the curtains drawn. And you will reward me with just
one kiss... Won't you? a kiss on the lips, which will bring all your love
back to you. You'll take hold of me and you'll be able to crush me in
your arms.'

'Yes, yes,' he muttered, still responding only to his own thoughts,
'my great pleasures at first were lighting the candles, preparing the
cruets, carrying the Missal with my hands clasped. Later, I experienced the slow approach of God, and I thought I'd die of love...
I don't have any other memories. I know nothing. When I raise my
hand, it's to give a blessing. When I offer my lips, it's to kiss the altar.
If I look for my heart, I can't find it any more: I offered it to God and
he has taken it.'

Albine became very pale, her eyes aflame. She went on in a tremulous voice:

'And I want my daughter to be always with me. If you wish, you can
send the boy to boarding school. I shall keep the dear little blondie

right beside me. I myself will teach her to read. Oh! I'll remember enough, and I'll take on tutors, if I've forgotten things... We'll live with our little family all around us. You will be happy, won't you? Answer me, tell me that you'll be warm again, that you'll smile, that you'll have no regrets?'

'I have often thought about the stone saints, deep in their little alcoves, sprayed with incense for centuries,' he said, very quietly. 'In the end they must be soaked right through with incense... And I am just like one of those saints. I have incense in the innermost parts of my organs. It's that embalming that gives me my serenity, the tranquil death of my flesh, the peace I enjoy through not living... Ah! may nothing disturb me from my immobility! I shall remain cold and rigid, with the endless smile on my lips of stone, incapable of descending to the world of men. That is my only desire.'

She stood up, angry and threatening. She shook him and shouted:

'What are you saying? Are you just dreaming aloud?... Am I not your wife? Didn't you come here to be my husband?'

He drew back, trembling more than ever.

'No, leave me alone, I'm frightened,' he stammered.

Then he uttered that ultimate cry:

'I cannot! I cannot!'

Then, for a moment, she remained silent, facing this unhappy man who lay shivering at her feet. A flame seemed to light up her face. She had opened her arms, as if to take him and press him to her breast in an angry surge of desire. But she seemed to think again; she simply took his hand, and pulled him to his feet.

'Come!' she said.

And she led him to the giant tree, to the place where she had given herself to him, and he had possessed her. It was the same happy shade, the same trunk that breathed like a human breast, the same branches that spread out wide, like protecting arms. The tree was still good, robust, powerful, and fertile. As on the day of their nuptials, a boudoir-like languor, the gleam of a summer night fading away on the bare shoulder of a woman in love, and indistinct mumblings of love, falling suddenly into a great, silent, spasm, still lingered in the glade, bathed in a soft green light. And, in the distance, the Paradou, in spite of the first chills of autumn, found once more its ardent whisperings. It became once more complicit. From the flower garden, the orchard, the grass-lands, the forest, the big rocks, and from the vastness of the sky, came once again the sound of voluptuous laughter, and a wind that seemed to sow in its path a dust of fertility. Never, even on the warmest spring evenings, did the garden have such profound tenderness as on these last beautiful days when the plants were going to sleep and saying farewell. Through the now less dense foliage, the scent of ripe seeds was bearing the intoxication of desire.

'Do you hear? Do you hear?' Albine whispered in the ear of Serge whom she had let fall on to the grass at the foot of the tree.

Serge was weeping.

'You see, the Paradou isn't dead. It's begging us to love each other. It still wants our marriage... Oh, remember! take me in your arms. Let us belong to each other!'

Serge went on weeping.

She said no more. She gripped him herself in a wild embrace. She pressed her lips upon this corpse, to bring it back to life. And Serge still had nothing but tears.

After a long silence, Albine spoke. She was standing up, contemptuous and resolute.

'Go away!' she said quietly.

Serge stood up with an effort. He picked up his breviary, which had rolled into the grass. He went away.

'Go away!' Albine repeated, raising her voice and following him, driving him before her.

And she pushed him on from bush to bush, led him back to the gap in the wall among the solemn trees. And since Serge hesitated there, with bowed head, she shouted very loudly:

'Go away! Go away!'

Then, slowly, she returned to the Paradou without looking back. Night was falling, and the garden was now only a great coffin of darkness.

CHAPTER XIII

BROTHER ARCHANGIAS, awake now, and standing over the gap in the wall, was hitting the stones with his stick, and swearing dreadfully.

'May the devil break their thighs! May he nail them rump to rump like dogs! May he drag them by their feet, with their noses in their filth.'

But when he saw Albine driving the priest away, he stood there in surprise for a moment. Then he hit out even harder, and was shaken by a tremendous fit of laughter.

'Goodbye, slut! Good riddance! Go back and fornicate with the wolves!... Ah, a saint is not enough for you. You want a far stronger body! Oak trees are what you want! Would you like my stick? Here, make love with this! That's the stout chap who'll satisfy you!'

And with all his might, he threw his stick after Albine into the dusk. Then, seeing Abbé Mouret, he growled:

'I knew you were in there. The stones were disturbed... Listen, Monsieur le Curé, your sin has made me your superior. God tells you through my mouth that hell has not torments terrible enough for priests who are sunk in the sins of the flesh. If he ever forgives you, it will be too kind of him, and discredit his justice.'

Walking slowly, the two went back down towards Les Artaud. The priest had not opened his mouth. He had gradually raised his head, and was no longer trembling. When he saw in the distance, against the mauve of the sky, the black outline of the Lone Tree, and the red patch of the tiles on the church roof, he gave a weak smile. In his clear eyes a great serenity was dawning.

Meanwhile the Brother, from time to time, was kicking the stones. Then he turned, and demanded of his companion:

'Is it all over, this time?... I myself, when I was your age, was possessed; a demon gnawed at my loins. And then he got bored and went away. I don't have loins any more. I live in peace... Oh! I knew you would come. I've been watching out for you for three weeks now. I could see into the garden through the hole in the wall. I would have liked to cut down the trees. Often I threw stones. When I broke one of the branches, I was happy... So, tell me, is it so extraordinary then, what you enjoy in there?'

He had stopped Abbé Mouret in the middle of the road, looking at him with his eyes gleaming with a terrible jealousy. The half-glimpsed delights of the Paradou tormented him. He had been there for weeks, on the threshold, scenting damnable delights far off. But when the abbé remained silent, he began to walk again, sneering, and growling lewd remarks. Then, more loudly:

'You see, when a priest does what you've done, the scandal hits every other priest... I myself felt I was no longer chaste, just through walking beside you. You were poisoning our sex... Now you are behaving reasonably again. Well, you have no need to make confession. I know what has happened to you. Heaven has broken you, as it has broken others before you. So much the better! So much the better!'

He was triumphant, he clapped his hands. The abbé, lost in reverie, was not listening. His smile had widened. And when the Brother left him at the door of the presbytery, he walked round and went into the church. It was all grey inside, just as it was on that dreadful, rainy evening when he had been so severely shaken by temptation. But it remained poor and reverent, with no streams of gold, no gasps of anguish rising from the countryside. It kept a solemn silence. It seemed filled with just one single breath of mercy.

Kneeling before the big Christ of painted cardboard, weeping tears that he allowed to pour down his cheeks like tears of joy, the priest murmured:

'O my God! It is not true that you are pitiless! I feel it, you have already forgiven me. I feel it through your grace, which for hours has been descending on me once more, drop by drop, slowly and surely bringing me salvation... O my God! It was when I was abandoning you that you protected me most thoroughly! You hid from me, the better to deliver me from evil. You let my flesh move forward, to batter me against its impotence... and now, O my God! I see that you had forever marked me with your seal, that awesome seal, full of delights, that sets a man apart from other men, and whose imprint is so ineradicable that it reappears sooner or later even upon guilty limbs! You have broken me in sin and in temptation. You have devastated me with your flames. You have willed that there be nothing left in me but ruins, so that you could descend upon me safely. I am an empty house in which you can dwell... Blessed be your name, forever!'

He prostrated himself, and stammered on into the dust. The Church was victorious; it stood upright, over the head of the priest, with its altars, its confessional, its pulpit and crucifixes and sacred images. The world had ceased to exist. Temptation had been extinguished like a fire no longer needed for the purification of this flesh. He was now in a state of superhuman peace. He uttered this ultimate cry:

'Beyond life, beyond all creatures, beyond all things, I am yours, yours alone, O my God! for ever and ever!'

CHAPTER XIV

Aᴛ that same time, Albine was still wandering about in the Paradou, with the dumb agony of a wounded animal. She was no longer weeping. Her face was white, with one deep furrow on her brow. Why was she suffering such a death? What sin had she committed that the garden no longer kept the promises it had made her since she was a child? And she went on questioning herself, just walking onward, without seeing the paths which were gradually filling with darkness. But she had always obeyed the trees. She could not remember ever having broken a flower. She had remained the beloved girl of the green plants, had listened to them submissively, trusting herself to them, full of faith in the happiness they intended for her. When, on the last day, the Paradou had cried out to her telling her to lie down beneath the giant tree, she had so lain down, and had opened her arms, repeating the lesson the grass had whispered to her. So, if she could find nothing with which to reproach herself, it must be that the garden was betraying and torturing her, simply for the pleasure of seeing her suffer.

She stopped and looked around. The great dark masses of foliage maintained a reflective silence; it seemed black walls were being built in the paths, which were becoming dead ends of darkness; the stretches of grass in the distance were lulling to sleep the winds that brushed over them. And she held out her hands in desperation, and uttered a cry of protest. It just couldn't end like that! But her voice was stifled beneath the silent trees. Three times she begged the Paradou to give an answer, but no explanation came down from the high branches, and not a single leaf took pity on her. Then, when she started wandering again, she felt as if she were walking into the fatality of winter. Now that she had stopped questioning the earth, like a rebellious creature, she could hear a low voice coursing along the ground, it was the plants, saying farewell, and wishing each other a happy death. Having drunk up the sun for a whole season, having lived always among flowers, and breathed out constant fragrance, and then leave at the first torment, with the hope of growing again somewhere else, was that not a life well filled, a life that would be spoiled by living any longer? Ah! how lovely it must be to be dead, with an endless night before one, to think about that brief day lived, and fix forever its fleeting joys!

Albine stopped again, but made no more protest, surrounded by the great, contemplative silence of the Paradou. She thought she understood now. The garden was doubtless arranging death for her, as a supreme pleasure. It was towards death that it had been leading her with such tenderness. After love, there was nothing else but death. And never had the garden loved her more; she had shown ingratitude in her accusations; she was still its most beloved daughter. The silent leaves, the paths blocked by darkness, the lawns on which the winds fell asleep, all remained quiet, only to invite her to the joys of a long silence. They wanted her with them, in the restfulness of the cold; they longed to bear her away, wrapped in their dry leaves, her eyes frozen like the water of the springs, her limbs stiffened like bare branches, her blood sleeping the sleep of all sap. She would live their existence to the very end, to their death. Perhaps they had already decided that next year she would be a rose tree in the flower garden, a pale willow in the grasslands, or a young birch tree in the forest. It was the great law of life: she was going to die.

Then, one last time, she resumed her journey through the garden in search of death. What sweet-scented plant had need of her hair to heighten the fragrance of its leaves? What flower requested the gift of her satin skin, the pure whiteness of her arms, the tender pink of her breast? To what ailing tree was she to offer her young blood? She would have liked to be useful to the grasses that grew alongside the paths, to kill herself there, so that from her would spring new, splendid, lush verdure, full of birds in May and ardently caressed by the sun. But the Paradou still remained silent for a long time, not yet ready to confide in what last kiss it would carry her away. She needed to go back everywhere, and repeat the pilgrimage of her former walks. It was now almost completely dark, and it seemed as if she were gradually entering into the earth. She climbed up to the big rocks, interrogating them, asking them whether it was upon their stony beds that she was to breathe her last breath. She went through the forest, always waiting, with a desire that slowed her passage, for some oak to collapse and bury her in the majesty of its fall. She went along the rivers in the grasslands, leaning over at almost every step, looking deep into the water to see if a couch had been prepared for her among the water lilies. Nowhere did death call out to her, or offer her its cooling hands. And yet she was not mistaken. It was the Paradou that would teach her how to die, just as it had taught her to love. She began again to beat back the shrubbery, even more hungrily now than when she was seeking love. And suddenly, as she reached the flower garden, she discovered death, in the fragrance of the evening. She ran forward, with a laugh of deep pleasure. She was to die with the flowers.

First she ran to the arbour of roses. There, by the last glimmer of twilight, she searched through the thickets, and picked all the roses that were drooping at the approach of winter. She picked them off the ground, without bothering about the thorns; she picked them in front of her, with her two hands; and picked them from above her head, standing on tiptoe and pulling the branches down. She was driven by such haste that she broke some branches, she who had such respect for the slightest blades of grass. Soon she had armfuls of roses, such a burden of roses that she staggered beneath it. Then after stripping the arbour, she went back to the lodge, carrying even the fallen petals; and when she had let her load of roses slide on to the floor of the bedroom with the blue ceiling, she went back down to the flower garden.

Now she looked for violets. She made enormous bouquets of them that she clasped, one by one, to her bosom. Then she picked carnations, cutting everything down to the buds, and tying up gigantic sheaves of white carnations like bowls of milk, and giant sheaves of red carnations like bowls of blood. Then she picked stocks, mirabilis,* heliotropes, and lilies; she gathered handfuls of the last flowering stalks of stocks, pitilessly crumpling their satin ruffs; she devastated the beds of mirabilis, barely open in the evening air; she scythed the field of heliotropes, gathering her harvest of flowers into a heap; she put bundles of lilies under her arms, like bundles of reeds. When she was fully loaded again, she went back to the lodge and threw down the violets, carnations, stocks, mirabilis, heliotropes, and lilies, alongside the roses. And without stopping to get her breath back, she went down again.

This time she went to the gloomy corner which was rather like the graveyard of the flower garden. An especially warm autumn had created there a second growth of spring flowers. She fell most eagerly upon beds of tuberoses and hyacinths, kneeling in the grass, and harvesting them with the meticulous care of a miser. The tuberoses seemed to her to be precious flowers, which would, drop by drop, distil gold and riches, amazing wealth. The hyacinths, all pearly with their flowering seeds, were like necklaces whose every pearl would offer her joys unknown to mankind. And although she was disappearing under the armful of hyacinths and tuberoses she had cut, she still went on to ravage a field of poppies, and even managed to raze to the ground a field of marigolds. On top of the tuberoses, on top of the hyacinths, were

heaped marigolds and poppies. She ran back to unload herself in the
room with the blue ceiling, making sure the wind did not rob her of
a single pistil. Then she went back down.

What was she going to pick now? She had harvested the whole of
the flower garden. When she stood on tiptoe, she could see only the
dead garden in the grey shade, which no longer held the tender eyes
of its roses, the red laughter of its carnations, or the perfumed hair of
its heliotropes. But she couldn't go back up with empty arms. So she
fell upon the grasses, the green plants; she crawled along, breast to
the ground, seeking, in an ultimate, passionate embrace, to carry off
the earth itself. It was a harvest of scented plants, filling her skirt with
citronella, mint, and verbena. She came upon a border of balsam, and
left not one leaf. She even took two big fennel plants, that she threw
over her shoulder like trees. If she had been able, she would have
dragged away behind her, between her clenched teeth, the whole green
floor of the garden. Then, at the doorway of the lodge, she turned for
one last look at the Paradou. It was totally dark, night had now completely fallen and thrown a black cloak over all of it. And she went up,
never to come down again.

The large bedroom was soon adorned. She had placed a lighted lamp
on the side table. She sorted out the flowers heaped in the middle
of the floor, and made big bunches that she distributed around the
room. First, behind the lamp on the side table she placed the lilies,
like tall strips of lace that softened the light with white purity. Then she
carried handfuls of carnations and stocks on to the old sofa, whose
coloured upholstery was already scattered with red bouquets that had
faded a hundred years ago; the upholstery disappeared, the sofa now
spread against the wall a bed of stocks, dotted with carnations. She
then arranged the four armchairs in front of the alcove; the first one
she filled with marigolds, the second with poppies, the third with mirabilis, and the fourth with heliotropes; the armchairs, now submerged,
showed only the ends of their arms, and looked like mileposts made of
flowers. Finally she turned her attention to the bed. She rolled a little
table over to the head of the bed, and on it she set a huge stack of violets. And she covered the bed with large armfuls of all the hyacinths
and tuberoses that she had brought; it was so thick a layer that it overflowed, on the top, in the front, at the foot, and over the sides, with
streams of blossoms trailing to the floor. The bed was simply a vast
explosion of flowers. But the roses still remained. She threw them about

randomly all over the room; she did not even look to see where they fell; the side table, the sofa, the armchairs, all had some roses; one corner of the bed was flooded with roses. For a few minutes, it rained roses, in big clumps, a shower of heavy flowers like a stormy downpour, making pools of flowers in the indentations of the floor. But the heap she had brought did not seem to be any smaller, so she ended up plaiting them into garlands that she hung on the walls. The plaster cupids, misbehaving over the alcove, had garlands of roses round their necks, on their arms, and around their waists; their bare bellies and bare bottoms were all dressed in roses. The blue ceiling, the oval panels framed by bows of flesh-coloured ribbon, the erotic pictures eroded by time, found themselves draped in a mantle of roses, in festoons of roses. The large room was fully decorated. Now she could die there.

She stood and looked around for a moment. She was thinking, wondering whether death was there. And she gathered up the scented plants, the citronella, mint, verbena, balsam, and fennel; then she twisted and folded them, making them into thick wads which she used to block up the slightest gaps and holes in the door and the windows. Then she drew the curtains of roughly sewn white calico. And silently, without a sigh, she lay down on the bed, on the great flowering mass of hyacinths and tuberoses.

This was a final rapture. With her eyes wide open, she smiled at the room. How she had loved in this room! And how happily she was dying there! Nothing impure came to her now from the plaster cupids, nothing disturbing came down from the paintings, with their display of women's limbs. There was nothing now beneath the blue ceiling save the suffocating perfume of the flowers. And it seemed as if that perfume were no other than the odour of a bygone love that still warmed the air of the alcove, an odour intensified a hundredfold, so strong now that it was asphyxiating. Perhaps it was the breath of that lady who died there a hundred years before. She, in her turn, was being ravished in that breath. Keeping entirely still, with her hands folded on her breast, she continued to smile, listening to the perfumes that whispered inside her throbbing head. They played a strange music of scents that slowly, and very gently, put her to sleep. First there was a gay, childish prelude; her hands that had twisted the scented green plants, gave off the harsh smell of the crushed grasses, and told of her girlish escapades in the wildness of the Paradou. Then the sound of a flute was heard, little musk-scented notes that dropped like beads from the heap of violets on the bedside table; and this flute, embroidering its melody around the tranquil breath and steady accompaniment of the lilies on the side table, was singing of the first delights of their love, the first confession of love, the first kiss in the forest. But she was suffocating more now, passion came with the sudden burst of the peppery scent of the carnations, whose brassy voice for a moment overpowered all the others. She thought she was going to die in the sickly strains of the marigolds and poppies that reminded her of the torments of her desires. Then suddenly, all became calm and she breathed more freely, she was slipping into a greater sweetness, lulled by a descending scale from the stocks that slowed down and sank away into the lovely song of the heliotropes, whose vanilla-scented breaths announced the coming of the wedding. The mirabilis, here and there, piped up a discreet trill. Then there was a silence. The roses, languidly, made their entrance. Voices flowed down from the ceiling, a distant choir. It was a large ensemble that she heard at first with a slight shiver. The choir grew larger, and soon it was all vibrant with marvellous sonorities that exploded all around her. This was the wedding, the fanfares of the roses announced the awesome moment. She, with her hands pressed more and more firmly against her heart, swooning and dying, was gasping. She opened her mouth, seeking the kiss which would extinguish her, when the hyacinths and tuberoses gave off their fumes and wrapped her in a last sigh, a sigh so deep it drowned the choir of roses. Albine had died in the ultimate gasp of the flowers.

CHAPTER XV

NEXT day, just before three o'clock, La Teuse and Brother Archangias were talking on the steps of the presbytery when they saw Dr Pascal's gig dashing through the village at a gallop. The whip was lashing out violently from the lowered hood of the gig.

'Where is he racing to, like that?' muttered the old servant. 'He's going to break his neck.'

The gig had reached the bottom of the slope on which the church was built. Suddenly the horse reared and stopped and the doctor's head, quite white and dishevelled, stretched out from under the hood.

'Is Serge here?' he shouted in a furious voice.

La Teuse had come forward to the edge of the slope.

'Monsieur le Curé is in his room,' she replied. 'He must be reading his breviary... Do you want to speak to him? Do you want me to call him?'

Uncle Pascal, looking thoroughly shattered, made a terrible gesture with his right hand, which held the whip. Then, leaning out so far that he risked falling out, he went on:

'Ah! he's reading his breviary!... No, don't call him, I'd strangle him, and there's no point... I only want to tell him that Albine is dead! Dead, do you hear? Tell him from me that she's dead!'

And he disappeared, giving his horse such a lash of the whip that the horse almost bolted. But twenty paces further on, he stopped again, stretching his head out again, and shouting even more loudly:

'And also tell him from me that she was pregnant! He'll be pleased to hear that.'

The gig resumed its wild race. With alarming jolts, it climbed the rocky hill road that led to the Paradou. La Teuse stood where she was, dumbfounded. Brother Archangias sniggered, looking at her with eyes gleaming with savage delight. She gave him such a push she almost sent him headlong down the steps.

'Go away,' she stammered out, angry now, and venting her anger on him. 'I shall end up hating you!... How can anyone rejoice in someone's death? I never liked the girl. But when someone dies at her age, it's not funny... Go away, do you hear! And stop laughing like that, or I'll throw my scissors in your face!'

It was not until about one o'clock that a peasant, who'd come to Plassans to sell his vegetables, had told the doctor about the death of Albine, adding that Jeanbernat was asking for him. The doctor now felt a little better after his shouts as he passed by the church. He had gone slightly out of his way to allow himself that satisfaction. He reproached himself for this death, as if it were a crime in which he had taken part. The whole of the way he had not stopped heaping insults on himself and having to wipe his eyes just to be able to guide his horse, driving the gig over great heaps of stones, as if secretly hoping to turn the gig over and break his bones. When he entered the lane that ran along the interminable wall of the park, he felt a sudden flicker of hope. Perhaps Albine had only fainted away. The peasant had told him that she had suffocated herself with flowers. Ah! if he arrived in time, perhaps he could save her! And he whipped his horse ferociously, as if he were whipping himself.

It was a really beautiful day. As in the lovely days of May, the lodge was bathed in sunshine. But the ivy, which went right up to the roof, now had leaves tinged with russet, and the honeybees were no longer buzzing around the wallflowers that had sprung up between the stones. He quickly tethered his horse and pushed open the gate of the little garden. There was the usual total silence in which Jeanbernat smoked his pipe. But the old man was not there, sitting on the bench in front of his lettuces.

'Jeanbernat!' the doctor called out.

No one answered. Then, going into the hall, he saw something he had never seen before. At the end of the corridor, at the bottom of the staircase, was a door open on to the Paradou; the huge garden, in the pale sunlight, was rolling its yellow leaves about, displaying its autumnal melancholy. He went through that door and took a few steps on the damp grass.

'Ah! it's you, Doctor!' said the calm voice of Jeanbernat.

The old man was vigorously digging a hole at the foot of a mulberry tree. He had straightened his tall figure when he heard footsteps. Then he had gone back to work, taking out an enormous clod of rich earth with each effort.

'What are you doing there?' asked Dr Pascal.

Jeanbernat straightened up again, and wiped the sweat off his brow with the sleeve of his coat.

'I'm digging a hole,' he replied simply. 'She always loved the garden. She'll be able to sleep in comfort there.'

The doctor was choked with emotion. He stood for a moment on the edge of the grave, quite unable to speak, watching Jeanbernat vigorously wielding his spade.

'Where is she?' he said at last.

'Up there, in her room. I've left her on the bed. I want you to listen to her heart before I put her in here... I listened myself, and heard nothing.'

The doctor went upstairs. The room had not been touched, only a window had been opened. The flowers, faded, and suffocated in their own perfume, now gave off only the feeble odour of their dead flesh. At the far end of the alcove, however, there lingered an asphyxiating warmth, which seemed to flow into the room, and then escape in wisps of vapour. Albine, very white, with her hands folded on her breast, was sleeping with a smile on her face, on her couch of hyacinths and tuberoses. And she was well content, she was truly dead.* Standing in front of the bed, the doctor gazed at her for a long time, with that fixed stare scientists have when attempting resurrections, but he decided not even to disturb her folded hands; he kissed her on the brow, where her maternity had already marked her with a slight shadow. Down below in the garden, Jeanbernat's spade was still delving with heavy and regular strokes.

But after a quarter of an hour, the old man went up. He had finished his task. He found the doctor sitting in front of the bed, so lost in thought that he seemed not to be aware of the big tears rolling down his cheeks, one after another. The two men exchanged but one glance. Then after a silence:

'You see, I was right,' Jeanbernat slowly remarked, making once more his sweeping gesture, 'there is nothing, nothing, nothing... All that stuff, it's just a farce.'

He was still standing, gathering up the roses that had fallen off the bed, and throwing them one by one on to Albine's skirts.

'Flowers now, they only live for a day,' he went on, 'while prickly old weeds like me wear out the stones they grow on... Now goodnight, I might as well peg out. My last bit of sunshine has been blown away. It's all a farce.'

And he too sat down. He wasn't weeping, he had the rigid despair of an automaton with broken machinery. Mechanically he stretched out his hand and took up a book from the little table covered with violets. It was one of the books from the attic, a battered volume of Holbach* that he'd been reading since the morning, while he watched over Albine's body. As the doctor, overwhelmed with grief, was still silent, he began to turn the pages again. But then he suddenly had an idea.

'If you were to help me,' he said to the doctor, 'we could bury her with all the flowers.'

Uncle Pascal gave a shudder. Then he explained that keeping bodies like that was not allowed.

'What do you mean—not allowed!' the old man cried. 'Well, I shall allow it! Doesn't she belong to me? Do you think I'm going to let her be taken away from me by the priests? Just let them try, if they want to be shot at.'

He was standing now, and brandishing his book in a fearsome way. The doctor took hold of his hands, and pressed them into his own, begging him to calm down. He talked for a long time, saying all the things that rose to his lips; he blamed himself, let fall scraps of confession, and referred, in a muddled way, to those who had killed Albine.

'Listen,' he said at last, 'she is no longer yours; you have to give her up to them.'

Jeanbernat shook his head, and made a gesture of refusal. But he was shaken. In the end he said:

'Very well. Let them take her, and may she break their arms! I'd like her to leap out of their earth to make them all die of fright... Besides, I have something to attend to over there. I'll go tomorrow... Goodbye, Doctor. The hole will serve for me.'

And when the doctor had gone, he sat down again at the bedside of the dead girl, and gravely began to read once more.

CHAPTER XVI

THAT morning there was a great commotion in the farmyard of the presbytery. The butcher from Les Artaud had just killed Matthew the pig, in the shed. Désirée, enormously excited, had held Matthew's feet while he was being bled, kissing him on his back all the while, so that he would not feel the knife so much, and explaining that he really had to be killed now that he was so fat. No one could cut off the head of a goose with one stroke of the hatchet like Désirée, or cut a hen's throat with a pair of scissors. Her love of the animals very cheerfully accepted such massacre. It was necessary, she would say; it made room for the little ones growing up. And she was in very good spirits.

'Mademoiselle,' La Teuse kept scolding her every minute, 'you're going to make yourself ill. There's no sense in getting yourself into such a state just because we're killing a pig. You're as red as if you'd been dancing all night.'

But Désirée was clapping her hands, whirling around and keeping busy. La Teuse, on the other hand, felt as if her legs were giving way beneath her. She had been trundling her huge bulk to and fro from the kitchen to the farmyard since six o'clock that morning. She still had to make the black pudding. She had beaten the blood herself, two large bowls of it, all pink in the sun. And she would never get finished, because Mademoiselle kept on calling her for one silly thing after another. It must be said that at the very moment when the butcher was bleeding Matthew, Désirée had had quite a shock when she went into the stable. Liza, the cow, was giving birth there. Then, seized with an amazing joy, she had finally lost her head.

'One goes away, and another arrives,' she cried, jumping up and down and twirling around. 'But come, La Teuse, come and see!'

It was eleven o'clock. From time to time a sound of chanting came from the church. A confused murmuring of grieving voices could be heard, in the midst of which some fragments of Latin phrases, loudly declaimed, would suddenly be heard.

'Come on!' Désirée repeated for the twentieth time.

'I have to go and ring the bell,' said the old servant, 'I'll never get finished... What do you want now, Mademoiselle?'

But she did not wait for the reply. She hurled herself into the middle of a flock of hens who were greedily drinking the blood in the bowls. Furious, she kicked them away. Then she covered the bowls and said:

'Listen! Instead of bothering me all the time, you should keep an eye on these wretched creatures... If you just let them do what they like, you'll have no black pudding, understand?'

Désirée laughed. If the hens drank a bit of blood, what was the harm? It would make them fat. Then she wanted to take La Teuse to see the cow, but the old servant refused.

'I must go and ring the bell... The funeral's about to come out. You can hear.'

At that moment, the voices swelled in the church, then lingered on a mournful note. The sound of footsteps could clearly be heard.

'No, look,' Désirée insisted, pushing La Teuse towards the stable. 'Tell me what I need to do.'

The cow, stretched out on the straw, turned her head and gazed at them with her big eyes. And Désirée thought she needed something. Perhaps one could do something to make her suffer less. La Teuse shrugged her shoulders. Didn't animals always know how to fend for themselves? It was best not to bother her, that's all. La Teuse was at last making her way to the sacristy, when, as she passed the shed, she cried out once more:

'Oh! just look, just look!' she cried, brandishing her clenched fist. 'Oh! the wicked creature!'

In the shed, Matthew, waiting to be singed,* was stretched out flat on his back, with his feet in the air. The gash made by the knife, still fresh, had drops of blood oozing out of it. And a little white hen, with a very delicate air, was pecking up, one by one, the drops of blood.

'My word! she's having a feast,' was all Désirée said.

She leaned over, and patted the pig's bloated belly, adding:

'Aha! my old fatty, you stole their food often enough, so now you can let them have a bit of your neck.'

La Teuse quickly took off her apron and used it to cover Matthew's neck. Then she hurried away and disappeared into the church. The main door had just set its rusty hinges squealing and a burst of chanting broke on the air, into the calm sunlight. And suddenly the bell began to toll with regular strokes. Désirée, who had remained kneeling in front of the pig, still patting his belly, raised her head and listened, still smiling. Then seeing she was alone, she glanced furtively around and slipped into the stable, closing the door after her. She was going to help the cow.

The little gate of the cemetery, that had been opened wide to make room for the body to come through, was now hanging, almost torn off its hinges, against the wall. In the empty field, the sun was sleeping on the dry grasses. The procession entered, chanting the last verse of the *Miserere*. Then there was a silence.

'*Requiem aeternam dona ei, Domine,*' went on the grave voice of Abbé Mouret.

'*Et lux perpetua luceat ei,*'* added Brother Archangias in his bellowing cantor's voice.

At the head of the procession came Vincent, in his surplice, carrying the cross, a big brass cross which had lost half its silvering, and which he carried very high, using both hands. Then came Abbé Mouret, pale in his black cassock, his head held high, chanting, with no trembling of his lips, his eyes gazing into the distance ahead. The lighted candle he carried brought scarcely any drop of warmth to the bright daylight. And two paces away, almost touching him, came the coffin of Albine, borne by four peasants on a sort of stretcher, painted black. The coffin, barely covered by a black cloth that was too short, revealed at the foot the new pine of the planks, with the steel heads of the nails sparkling on it. In the middle of the black cloth, flowers were scattered, handfuls of white roses, and hyacinths and tuberoses, gathered from the very bed of the dead girl.

'Be careful!' shouted Brother Archangias at the peasants, as they tilted the stretcher a bit to get it through, without catching on the gate. 'You'll drop the whole thing on the ground!'

And he steadied the coffin with his huge hand. As there was no other cleric, he was carrying the vessel of holy water, and he was also standing in for the cantor, the rural policeman, who had not been able to come.

'Come on in, you others,' said Brother Archangias, turning round.

It was another little procession, Rosalie's baby having died the previous day, after a fit of convulsions. The father, the mother, old Mother Brichet, Catherine and two big girls, La Rousse and Lisa, were there. The last two were carrying the baby's coffin, one at each end.

Suddenly the voices were hushed. Then there was a silence. The bell was still tolling, unhurriedly, with a desolate sound. The procession went across the whole cemetery in the direction of the corner between the church and the farmyard wall. Swarms of grasshoppers rose in the air, and lizards rushed back to their holes. Heat still hung quite heavily over this patch of lush grass. The slight noise made by the stalks crushed under the trampling feet of the procession began to sound like the murmur of stifled sighs.

'Stop here,' said the Brother, barring the way to the two girls carrying the baby's coffin. 'Wait your turn, we don't need you underfoot.'

The two girls put the baby on the ground. Rosalie, Fortuné, and old Mother Brichet stopped in the middle of the cemetery, while Catherine just quietly followed Brother Archangias. Albine's grave had been dug to the left of the tomb of Abbé Caffin, whose white tombstone seemed, in the sunshine, to be strewn with flecks of silver. The gaping hole, freshly dug that morning, lay open among thick clumps of grass; the stalks of tall plants, half uprooted, leaned over the edge; at the bottom, one flower had fallen, splashing the black of the earth with its red petals. When Abbé Mouret came forward, the soft earth gave under his feet, and he had to step back to avoid falling into the grave.

'*Ego sum*,'* he intoned, in a resonant voice that could be heard above the mournful tones of the bell.

And during the antiphon, everyone instinctively cast sidelong glances into the depths of the still empty hole. Vincent, who had planted the cross at the foot of the grave, facing the priest, was amusing himself by pushing little trickles of earth into the grave with his shoe, and watching them fall; and that made Catherine laugh, as she leaned over, behind him, to see. The peasants had laid the bier on the grass. They were stretching their arms, while Brother Archangias prepared the sprinkler for the holy water.

'Here, Voriau!' shouted Fortuné.

The big black dog, who had gone over to sniff at the bier, came back reluctantly.

'What did you bring the dog for?' cried Rosalie.

'Honestly, he just followed us,' said Lisa, chuckling quietly.

Everyone was talking in subdued tones around the coffin of the little one. The mother and father seemed at times to forget about it, then fell silent when they noticed it again, lying between them at their feet.

'Old Bambousse refused to come then, did he?' asked La Rousse.

Old Mother Brichet raised her eyes heavenwards.

'He was threatening to break everything yesterday, when the little one died,' she whispered. 'No, he's not a good man, I say it in front of you, Rosalie. Didn't he come close to strangling me, yelling that he'd been robbed, and he'd have given one of his cornfields to have the little one die three days before the wedding.'

'We weren't to know,' said Fortuné with a sly look.

'What's it matter if the old chap gets mad?' added Rosalie. 'We're married anyway, now.'

They smiled at each other over the little bier, with shining eyes. Lisa and La Rousse nudged each other. Everyone became very serious again. Fortuné had picked up a clod of earth to chase away Voriau, who was now prowling around among the old tombstones.

'Ah! it looks as if they're nearly finished,' Rosalie whispered very quietly.

Abbé Mouret was just finishing the *De Profundis*. Then he slowly went up to the coffin, drew himself up, and gazed at it for a moment, without a quiver of his eyelids. He seemed taller, and on his face was a serenity that transfigured him. Then he stooped and picked up a handful of earth that he scattered over the bier in the shape of a cross. Then he recited, in a voice so clear that not a syllable was lost:

'*Revertitur in terram suam unde erat, et spiritus redit ad Deum qui dedit illum.*'*

A shiver ran through those who were present. Lisa, looking thoughtful, said with a troubled air:

'It's not much fun really, is it, when you think it'll be your turn one day?'

Brother Archangias had passed the sprinkler to the priest, who shook it several times above the body and said in a low voice:

'*Requiescat in pace.*'*

'*Amen,*' Vincent and Brother Archangias responded together, the one voice so high, and the other so deep, that Catherine had to clap her fist to her mouth not to burst out laughing.

'No, no, it's not much fun,' Lisa went on, 'and there's absolutely no one attending this burial. If we weren't here, the cemetery would be empty.'

'They say she killed herself,' said old Mother Brichet.

'Yes, I know,' La Rousse chipped in. 'The Brother didn't want her to be buried with Christian folk. But Monsieur le Curé replied that eternity was for everyone. I was there... Never mind, but all the same, the Philosopher could have come.'

But Rosalie shushed them, and whispered:

'Oh! look, there he is now, the Philosopher!'

Indeed, Jeanbernat was entering the cemetery. He walked straight over to the group around the grave. He walked with his usual lithe step, still so supple that he made no noise. When he reached them, he stood directly behind Brother Archangias, upon whose neck he seemed to gaze fondly for a moment. Then, just as Abbé Mouret finished the prayers, he calmly took out a knife from his pocket, opened it out, and in a single movement, cut off the Brother's right ear.*

No one had time to intervene. The Brother uttered a shriek.

'The left one will keep for another time,' said Jeanbernat peaceably, tossing the ear to the ground.

And then he left. Everyone was so stupefied that no one even went after him. Brother Archangias had fallen on the pile of fresh earth from the grave. He had made a wad of his handkerchief and pressed it to his wound. One of the four bearers tried to carry him off, to take him home. But he waved him away. He stayed there, savagely waiting, determined to see Albine go down into the hole.

'At last, it's our turn,' said Rosalie with a faint sigh.

However, Abbé Mouret still lingered by the grave, watching the bearers tying ropes around the coffin to slide it gently into the grave. The bell was still tolling, but La Teuse seemed to be tiring, for the strokes were less regular, as if irritated by the length of the ceremony. It was hotter now in the sun, and the shadow of the Lone Tree moved slowly over the grass dotted with mounds for the tombs. When Abbé Mouret at last had to move back, to get out of the way, his eyes lit on the marble tomb of Abbé Caffin, that priest who had loved, and who lay there so peaceful beneath the wild flowers.

Then suddenly, as the coffin was going down, supported by the ropes, with their knots creaking, a frightful noise arose from the farmyard behind the wall. The goat was bleating. The ducks, the geese, and the turkeys were all clicking their beaks and flapping their wings. The hens were clucking as if they had all just laid an egg. The tawny rooster Alexander was uttering his clarion call, and you could even hear the rabbits leaping about and shaking the planks of their hutches. And over and above all the lively din of this little nation of animals, a huge laugh rang out. There was a rustling of skirts. Then Désirée, with her hair on end, and arms bare up to the elbows, her face flushed with triumph, appeared, her hands holding on to the coping on top of the wall. She must have been standing on a heap of dung.

'Serge! Serge!' she called.

At that moment Albine's coffin had just reached the bottom of the hole. The ropes had just been pulled away. One of the peasants threw down a first handful of earth.

'Serge! Serge!' she cried more loudly still, clapping her hands, 'the cow has had a calf!'

EXPLANATORY NOTES

Quotations from the Bible are from the King James Authorized Version.

3 *soap-making*: it was at that time customary for households to make their own washing soap in tablet or else in liquid form, as is the case here.

tripoli: a kind of earth, burnt by volcanic action, used rather like sandstone for polishing metal.

4 *chasubles . . . prescribed*: the Church prescribes specific colours for vestments for various celebrations and liturgical seasons.

lamb . . . rays: Henri Mitterand (vol. i of the Pléiade edition) explains that Zola took these details from the description of a chasuble in the catalogue of S. Beer, a contemporary maker of church ornaments in Paris.

5 *maniple . . . cord . . . alb . . . amice*: the maniple is a band of material in the same colour as the chasuble, worn on the left arm of the priest during the Mass; the cord is worn on the priest's back in memory of the bonds of Jesus during the Passion; the alb is a long white robe worn over the cassock while celebrating Mass; the amice is a small piece of fine material with a cross at its centre, worn around the neck of the celebrant.

purificator . . . paten . . . pall: the purificator is a small white linen cloth used for wiping the chalice after each communicant; the paten, a small rounded vessel for receiving the Host; and the pall a stiffened square of white linen, often embroidered with a cross, used as a protective covering for the materials of the Eucharist.

the corporal . . . burse: the corporal is a small white cloth on which the chalice and paten are placed for the celebration of Mass; the burse is the case in which the corporal is carried to and from the altar.

6 *manuterge*: a small white towel for drying the priest's fingers after the ritual washing.

7 *tabernacle*: the vessel containing the Blessed Sacrament in the Catholic Church; formerly placed on the altar where Mass is served, in more recent times, it is placed on a separate altar.

'Introibo . . . Dei' 'Ad . . . meam': 'I will go in to the altar of God' and 'To God who giveth joy to my youth'.

'Dominus vobiscum' 'Et cum spiritu tuo' . . . 'Oremus': 'The Lord be with you', 'And with thy spirit' . . . 'Let us pray'.

8 *'Deo gratias'*: 'Thanks be to God.'

9 *'Orate fratres'*: 'Pray, brothers.'

10 *Canon of the Mass*: the Anaphora, the most solemn part of the Mass, during the consecration of the bread and wine as the body and blood of Christ,

known until Vatican II (1962–5) as the Canon of the Mass, now more generally known as the Eucharistic Prayer.

11 *'Hoc . . . meum'*: 'This is my body.'

    'Hic . . . calix': 'This is verily the chalice.'

    'Per omnia saecula saeculorum': 'For ever and ever' (literally 'for all centuries of centuries').

    Pater: an abbreviation of *Paternoster* (Our Father), the Lord's Prayer.

    Agnus Dei: Lamb of God.

    Communion in both kinds: Communion with both bread (the body) and wine (the blood). The officiating priest must take Communion in both kinds, while the laity may take Communion in one species alone, the whole Christ—both body and blood—being present in either one.

13 *'Ite, missa est'*: the dismissal at the end of the Mass; literally, 'Go, the Mass is done'. The English version is 'The Mass is ended, go in peace'.

    'Benedicat . . . Sanctus': 'The Blessing of Almighty God, the Father and Son and Holy Spirit'.

19 *drama*: that drama, involving the death of Serge's parents, Marthe and François Mouret, is related by Zola in *The Conquest of Plassans*.

    elder brother: Octave Mouret, who features in *The Conquest of Plassans*, *The Ladies' Paradise* (*Au Bonheur des Dames*), and *Pot-Luck* (*Pot Bouille*).

20 *kingdom of Heaven*: a reference to 'Blessed are the poor in spirit for theirs is the kingdom of Heaven', one of the Beatitudes of the Sermon on the Mount, Matthew 5:1–12. The word *esprit* in French means both 'mind' and 'spirit'.

    Imitation: *The Imitation of Christ*, a Catholic devotional book, second in importance only to the Bible. A spiritual handbook, stressing humility and self-denial, in Latin (*De Imitatione Christi*) in the early fifteenth century. Its authorship is generally ascribed to Thomas à Kempis.

21 *Christian Brothers*: Brothers of the Christian Schools (Frères des Écoles Chrétiennes), also known as Lasalliens, a religious institute founded in France in 1694 by Jean-Baptiste de La Salle, and formally recognized by the French government in 1808. The Brothers, vowed to chastity, poverty, and obedience, were devoted especially to the education of the working-class poor.

23 *Gomorrah*: one of the cities of the plain destroyed by God with fire and brimstone as a punishment for wickedness (Genesis 19: 24–5).

25 *rabat*: a sort of collar-flap, a piece of material, sometimes edged with pearl, at the neck of the cassock.

32 *Pascal Rougon*: second son of Pierre and Félicité Rougon; brother of Eugène, Aristide, Sidonie, and Marthe Mouret (née Rougon), Serge's mother.

33 *your aunt Félicité, your uncle Rougon*: in fact Serge's grandparents.

    chart: Pascal's 'chart' of the family is a reflection of Zola's own map of the

Rougon-Macquart family, with details of the individual members. Pascal's files reappear in the final volume, *Doctor Pascal* (*Le Docteur Pascal*).

46 *Cybele*: goddess of Nature and fertility, also known as Kybele and Rhea, mother of the gods in Greek mythology.

Puget: Pierre Puget (1620–94), French painter, architect, and sculptor best known for his baroque sculpture, especially the works created for the gardens of Versailles. He lived most of his life in the Midi, in Aix (Zola's 'Plassans'), in Toulon, and in Marseilles, where he was born and where he died.

56 *Ignorantine*: the Christian Brothers were sometimes called *ignorantins* on account of their lack of academic qualifications.

63 *La Rousse*: 'Rousse' (red) because she's a redhead.

69 *'Woman . . . thee?'*: the words of Jesus to his mother at the marriage of Cana. See John 2:1–5.

religious pictures: cheap cards bearing prayers and pictures of saints were very popular.

71 *Saint John saw her*: after the Crucifixion, St John the Apostle and Evangelist took Mary into his care as the last legacy of Jesus (John 19:25–7). St John is generally held to be the author of the Book of Revelation, in which appears a vision of a pregnant woman, clothed with the sun, with the moon under her feet, and on her head a crown of twelve stars (Revelation 12:1); this is taken to refer not only to the Church but also indirectly to Mary the mother of Jesus.

David: David, the King of Israel. I have not been able to trace the quotation from the Psalms, which is cited by St Louis de Montfort in *True Devotion to Mary: With Preparation for Total Consecration*.

72 *Ave . . . Domina*: the various hymns invoked here and below are 'Hail, Star of the Sea', 'Hail Queen', 'Queen of Heaven', and 'O Glorious Lady'.

Bonaventure: a Franciscan monk of the thirteenth century, follower of St Augustine. His Psalter is largely concerned with the Virgin Mary's intercessional role with her Son. His theology tried to combine faith and reason.

scapular: the devotional scapular, often adorned with sacred images, is a garment of piety, worn mainly but not exclusively by Roman Catholics. It goes over the shoulders and hangs down over the wearer's chest and back. Scapulars devoted to the Blessed Virgin are especially favoured.

chain: a small chain (*chaînette*) worn around the neck, symbolizing a mystic union.

73 *fourteen joys*: in medieval devotional literature there were originally five 'joys of the Virgin', then seven: the Annunciation, the Nativity, the Adoration of the Magi, the Resurrection, the ascent of Christ into Heaven, Pentecost, and the Coronation of Mary in Heaven. There are, however, fourteen 'stations of Joy' marking fourteen points at which Jesus demonstrated his Resurrection to his followers.

73 *mystery*: twenty mysteries are associated with the Rosary, divided into four parts, the Joyful, the Luminous, the Sorrowful, and the Glorious. The first decade relates to the Joyful Mysteries, including the Annunciation; the Luminous includes the baptism of Christ and the institution of the Eucharist; the Calvary is in the Sorrowful, and the Coronation of Mary Queen of Heaven is the last of the Glorious.

five happy mysteries: the Annunciation, the Visitation, the Nativity, the Presentation of Jesus to the Temple, and Jesus preaching in the Temple at the age of 12.

Elizabeth: Elizabeth, the sterile wife of Zacharias; an angel appeared to Zacharias and promised him a child. The child would become John the Baptist (Luke 1:41–5).

Simeon: a devout old man in Jerusalem, who had been told by the Holy Spirit that he would not die before he had seen the Lord's Christ. On holding the child Jesus in his arms in the Temple, Simeon recognized the promise had been kept (Luke 2:25).

five sorrowful mysteries: the Agony in the Garden, the Flagellation, the Crowning with the Crown of Thorns, the Carrying of the Cross, and Death on the Cross.

garden . . . Olives: the garden of Gethsemane where the Apostles fell asleep while Jesus prayed.

74 *Calvary*: throughout this whole passage Zola shows Serge Mouret imagining Mary as inwardly partaking of all the suffering of her Son.

Sacred Heart of Mary: the term 'Sacred Heart' is normally applied only to the Sacred Heart of Jesus.

pierced by a sword: an echo of Simeon's prophecy to Mary: 'Yea, a sword shall pierce through thy own soul also' (Luke 2:35).

75 *Magnificat*: the canticle of Mary in the Liturgy: 'My soul doth magnify the Lord' (from Luke 1:46–55).

76 *Mystic Rose*: this and other metaphors in this passage are mostly derived from the Litany of the Blessed Virgin in Catholic liturgy.

77 *shepherds*: in September 1846 some children and two shepherds claimed to have seen the Virgin Mary on a mountain near La Salette; the shrine of Our Lady of Salette became in consequence a place of pilgrimage.

80 *Saint Ignatius*: St Ignatius Loyola (1491–1556), founder of the Society of Jesus; his teachings are much preoccupied with suffering and endurance to get closer to God.

'What use . . . soul?': an echo of the question posed in the Bible: 'For what shall it profit a man, if he shall gain the whole world, and lose his own soul?' Mark 8:36.

Aquinas: thirteenth-century Dominican friar, influential theologian, author of the celebrated *Summa Theologica*.

83 *Office . . . seminarists*: the 'Little Office of Our Lady' also known as 'Hours

of the Virgin' is a simplified liturgical devotion to the Blessed Virgin Mary. It is a cycle of psalms, hymns, and readings from the Scriptures. The 'Little Hours' are fixed daytime hours of prayer.

crozier . . . mitre: ceremonial accoutrements of bishops.

84 *Rohrbacher*: René François Rohrbacher (1789–1856), ecclesiastical historian, author of the monumental *Universal History of the Catholic Church* (1842–9).

Gousset: Thomas Marie Joseph Gousset (1792–1866), cardinal and theologian.

Bouvier: Jean-Baptiste Bouvier (1783–1854), bishop of Le Mans and theologian.

Bellarmin, Liguori, Suarez: all Jesuit theologians; the Italians Bellarmin (1542–1621) and A. M. de Liguori (1696–1787), and the Spaniard F. Suarez (1548–1617).

85 *Carmelite*: member of the order of the Brothers of the Blessed Virgin Mary of Mount Carmel. This was a contemplative religious order, also known as the White Friars, founded in the twelfth century.

dalmatics: wide-sleeved ecclesiastical vestments marked with two stripes, worn by deacons and bishops on special occasions.

Host: the wafer of sacramental bread used in the ritual of the Mass; a large wafer would be perhaps 2 inches in diameter.

86 *'Accedite'*: 'Come hither'; the Bishop calls the ordinands to him for the priestly ordination.

alb tied at his waist: the alb (see note to p. 5) was fastened at the waist with a type of belt called a 'cincture'.

'Accipe . . . sunt': 'Receive the Holy Spirit: those whose sins you absolve are absolved, and those whose sins you do not absolve remain in sin.'

88 *De . . . confessariorum*: 'Concerning Sexual Matters for the Use of Confessors'.

89 *Cybele*: see note to p. 46.

92 *mystic rose bush*: the rose figures considerably in religious writing, as a symbol of God's love, paradise, martyrdom, or Christ himself as the flower (rose) sprung from the 'bush' of the Virgin Mary. The mystic rose (*rosa mystica*) became a privileged symbol of the Holy Virgin in Catholic liturgy.

98 *tu*: 'you' in French has two forms: *tu* (thou) and *vous*: Serge and Albine now use the intimate *tu* form rather than *vous* and will continue to do so.

108 *four streams*: Zola is echoing here the four rivers of paradise: 'And a river went out of Eden to water the garden; and from thence it was parted and became into four heads' (Genesis 2:10).

127 *spikemoss . . . nemophila . . . saponaria*: spikemoss is *sélaginoïdes* in Zola's text. Selaginella exists in various forms; the one closest to Zola's description here would seem to be spikemoss. The variety of nemophila referred to here is probably *Nemophila insignis*, known popularly as 'Baby Blue

Eyes'. Saponaria is also known as soapwort; the variety that bears yellow
flowers is *Saponaria bellidifolia* or Alpine soapwort.

127 *fraxinellas . . . valerian . . . hound's tongue*: fraxinellas, also known as Burning Bush, or White Dittany. Valerian: Zola uses the name 'Centranthus',
'Centranthus-ruber Albus' is the white form of red valerian. Hound's
tongue: [cynoglosses] *Cynoglossum officinale*, also known as Chinese
forget-me-not.

schizanthus . . . butterfly flowers: the genus *Schizanthus* is itself also known
as butterfly flower or poor man's orchid.

128 *viscaria . . . linanthus . . . lagurus grass*: viscaria, known popularly as 'Sticky
catchfly' because of the stickiness of its stem. Linanthus: probably *Leptosiphon
grandiflorus*, commonly known as large-flower linanthus, a member of the
phlox family. Lagurus grass has the popular name 'Bunny tails'.

129 *daturas*: a showy, poisonous plant also known as 'trumpet flower'.

140 *May trees*: trees (usually tall trees) planted on the first of May in a traditional
ceremony celebrating spring and rebirth.

155 *Babel*: the huge Tower of Babel, described in Genesis 11:1.

162 *Shulamite*: the Shulamite is the name given to the beautiful bride in the
Song of Solomon 4:3, whose 'lips are like a thread of scarlet'.

191 *'Ego . . . Sancti'*: 'I unite you in wedlock in the name of the Father and of
the Son and of the Holy Ghost. Amen.'

194 *Abraham . . . Isaac . . . Jacob*: the three, whose stories are told in the Old
Testament, are known in Judaism as the Patriarchs, or Founding Fathers:
Abraham is the father of Isaac and Isaac is the father of Jacob.

196 *Rachel . . . Rebecca . . . Sarah*: beautiful wives who feature in three biblical
love stories, and the virtues traditionally associated with them. All three
bore children in accordance with God's plan: Rachel, wife of Jacob and
mother of Joseph (Genesis 29); Rebecca, wife of Isaac and mother of Jacob
(Genesis 24); Sarah, wife of Abraham and mother of Isaac (Genesis 18).

202 *wooden . . . upright*: thus demonstrating that the soup was of a proper thick-
ness for a rustic soup.

candlelight: that is, so early in the morning that candles have to be lit.

206 *'Capons . . . life'*: capons are cockerels or roosters that have been castrated
and are fattened to improve the quality of their meat.

210 *'War'*: in the French text, they are playing a game called 'À la bataille' ('To
battle!'), a name appropriate to the context. This can be translated as the
English game of 'beggar-my-neighbour', but as that game closely resem-
bles another English game called 'War', I have used 'War' to keep closer to
the original.

219 *Exaltation of the Holy Cross*: usually celebrated on 14 September in the
Church calendar, this feast celebrates the Cross as the instrument of sal-
vation, and commemorates both the discovery of the True Cross by
St Helena in 320 and the dedication in 335 of the basilica and shrine built by

Constantine on the site of the Crucifixion. The church of the Holy Sepulchre now stands on the site.

222 *Les Tulettes*: a lunatic asylum in which Adelaïde Fouque ('Tante Dide'), Serge's grandmother, and founding mother of the Rougon-Macquart family, was interned, as was Serge's father, François Mouret (*The Conquest of Plassans*).

237 *tempted you*: this makes a wonderfully ironic comment both on Brother Archangias's earlier comments on Albine as the diabolical seductress, and on the Bible story in which Eve is indeed seen as the temptress.

240 *the two thieves*: the two thieves crucified at the same time as Jesus.

The Temple veil: the veil covering the Ark of the Covenant. This whole passage very closely follows the account given in Mark 15.

244 *Song of Songs*: the Song of Solomon 2:16, 17.

The Imitation of Christ: see note to p. 20. The words quoted here come from chapter 33.

246 '*My God . . . abandoning me*': Serge here echoes the words of Jesus on the cross: 'My God, my God, why hast thou forsaken me?' (Mark 15:34).

248 *Via Dolorosa*: the 'Way of Sorrow', the route that Jesus took on the way to Calvary.

261 *Compline*: the last church service of the day, consisting largely of psalms, hymn, lesson, the *Kyrie Eleison*, and benediction.

263 *De Profundis*: the first line of Psalm 130: 'Out of the depths have I cried unto thee, O Lord.' Penitential psalm used in liturgical prayers for the dead.

Et . . . ejus: also from Psalm 130: 'And He shall redeem Israel from all its iniquities.'

267 *collar-flap*: see note to p. 25, 'rabat'.

279 *mirabilis*: the Royal Horticultural Society lists twenty-two varieties of plants of the genus *Mirabilis*: this is perhaps the bushy *Mirabilis jalapa*, also known as 'four-o'clock flower' or *Mirabilis jalapa* 'Red Glow', also known as 'marvel of Peru'.

285 *truly dead*: this flower-laden death inspired a painting by the British late Pre-Raphaelite painter John Collier (1850–1934). Exhibited in 1895 at the Royal Academy of Arts in London under the title *The Death of Albine*, the painting was thought lost, surviving only as the engraving reproduced in *The Graphic* in August 1895, of which an example may be viewed in the British Museum. However, the painting has recently been discovered in the archives of the Museum of Glasgow, through the Glasgow Museum Resource Centre, and can be accessed online at www.artandperfume. blogspot.co.uk.

Holbach: probably the work *Éléments de la morale universelle, ou Catéchisme de la nature* (*Elements of Universal Morality or Catechism of Nature*) by Paul

Henri Thiry Baron d'Holbach, written in 1765, published in Paris by de Bure in 1770. Vizetelly comments in his translation: 'Doubtless Holbach's now forgotten *Catechism of Nature*, into which M. Zola himself may well have peeped whilst writing this story.' Baron d'Holbach is known mainly for his atheistic and materialist philosophical works; his *Catechism of Nature* offers a striking alternative to the catechism of the Church.

287 *singed*: in France the killed pig is singed to remove hair and soften skin; in England the dead pig is scalded.

288 *Miserere . . . ei*: the three Latin chants, part of the Requiem Mass, are *Miserere*, a setting of Psalm 51 '*Miserere mei, Deus*' (Have mercy on me, O God); '*Requiem . . . Domine*' ('Grant him/her eternal peace O Lord'); and '*Et lux . . . ei*' ('And let perpetual light shine upon him/her').

289 '*Ego sum*': 'I am', the beginning of 'I am the resurrection, and the life: he that believeth in me, though he be dead, yet shall he live', the words of Jesus, in John 11:25, used in the Requiem Mass.

290 '*Revertitur . . . illum*': 'It returns to the earth whence it came, and returns the spirit to God who gave it.' Adapted for the burial service from Ecclesiastes 12:7: 'Then shall the dust return to the earth as it was: and the spirit shall return to God who gave it.'

'*Requiescat . . . pace*': 'Rest in peace.'

291 *cut off the Brother's right ear*: this echoes the cutting off of the ear of the high priest's servant, after Jesus's betrayal. The deed is attributed to Simon Peter by Luke, but in the other gospels simply to one of Jesus's companions. In the Gospel of St Luke, Jesus is said to have healed the ear (Luke 22:50, 51). Jeanbernat could be seen as punishing the servant of the Church which condemned Albine.

MORE ABOUT **OXFORD WORLD'S CLASSICS**

American Literature

British and Irish Literature

Children's Literature

Classics and Ancient Literature

Colonial Literature

Eastern Literature

European Literature

Gothic Literature

History

Medieval Literature

Oxford English Drama

Philosophy

Poetry

Politics

Religion

The Oxford Shakespeare

A complete list of Oxford World's Classics, including Authors in Context, Oxford English Drama, and the Oxford Shakespeare, is available in the UK from the Marketing Services Department, Oxford University Press, Great Clarendon Street, Oxford OX2 6DP, or visit the website at www.oup.com/uk/worldsclassics.

In the USA, visit www.oup.com/us/owc for a complete title list.

Oxford World's Classics are available from all good bookshops. In case of difficulty, customers in the UK should contact Oxford University Press Bookshop, 116 High Street, Oxford OX1 4BR.

ÉMILE ZOLA

L'Assommoir
The Belly of Paris
La Bête humaine
The Conquest of Plassans
The Fortune of the Rougons
Germinal
The Kill
The Ladies' Paradise
The Masterpiece
Money
Nana
Pot Luck
Thérèse Raquin

	Eirik the Red and Other Icelandic Sagas
	The Kalevala
	The Poetic Edda
LUDOVICO ARIOSTO	**Orlando Furioso**
GIOVANNI BOCCACCIO	**The Decameron**
GEORG BÜCHNER	**Danton's Death, Leonce and Lena, and Woyzeck**
LUIS VAZ DE CAMÕES	**The Lusiads**
C. P. CAVAFY	**The Collected Poems**
MIGUEL DE CERVANTES	**Don Quixote**
	Exemplary Stories
CARLO COLLODI	**The Adventures of Pinocchio**
DANTE ALIGHIERI	**The Divine Comedy**
	Vita Nuova
J. W. VON GOETHE	**Elective Affinities**
	Erotic Poems
	Faust: Part One and Part Two
	The Sorrows of Young Werther
JACOB and WILHELM GRIMM	**Selected Tales**
E. T. A. HOFFMANN	**The Golden Pot and Other Tales**
HENRIK IBSEN	**An Enemy of the People, The Wild Duck, Rosmersholm**
	Four Major Plays
	Peer Gynt
FRANZ KAFKA	**The Castle**
	A Hunger Artist and Other Stories
	The Man who Disappeared (America)
	The Metamorphosis and Other Stories
	The Trial
LEONARDO DA VINCI	**Selections from the Notebooks**
LOPE DE VEGA	**Three Major Plays**

	Late Victorian Gothic Tales
	Literature and Science in the
	Nineteenth Century
JANE AUSTEN	**Emma**
	Mansfield Park
	Persuasion
	Pride and Prejudice
	Selected Letters
	Sense and Sensibility
MRS BEETON	**Book of Household Management**
MARY ELIZABETH BRADDON	**Lady Audley's Secret**
ANNE BRONTË	**The Tenant of Wildfell Hall**
CHARLOTTE BRONTË	**Jane Eyre**
	Shirley
	Villette
EMILY BRONTË	**Wuthering Heights**
ROBERT BROWNING	**The Major Works**
JOHN CLARE	**The Major Works**
SAMUEL TAYLOR COLERIDGE	**The Major Works**
WILKIE COLLINS	**The Moonstone**
	No Name
	The Woman in White
CHARLES DARWIN	**The Origin of Species**
THOMAS DE QUINCEY	**The Confessions of an English**
	Opium-Eater
	On Murder
CHARLES DICKENS	**The Adventures of Oliver Twist**
	Barnaby Rudge
	Bleak House
	David Copperfield
	Great Expectations
	Nicholas Nickleby